STAY WITH ME

Following the death of her parents in the Tay Bridge disaster, Lena Carnforth expects to inherit at least half of her father's thriving shipping and merchant business but, though leaving her comfortably off, her father bequeaths the business to his stepson, James. When Lena meets attractive shipping rival Peter Hustwick it seems the answer to her prayers. She now has the opportunity to help build up Peter's business and undermine James's firm, which she regards as rightly hers, but when disaster strikes Lena is devastated to realise just how carried away she's become with her desire for success...

STAY WITH ME

STAY WITH ME

by

Jessica Blair

Magna Large Print Books
Long Preston, North Yorkshire,
BD23 4ND, England.

British Library Cataloguing in Publication Data.

Blair, Jessica
    Stay with me.

    A catalogue record of this book is
    available from the British Library

    ISBN   978-0-7505-3189-4

First published in Great Britain in 2009 by Piatkus Books

Copyright © 2009 by Jessica Blair

Cover illustration © Angelo Rinaldi by arrangement with
Artist Partners

The moral right of the author has been asserted

Published in Large Print 2010 by arrangement with
Piatkus Books, an imprint of Little, Brown Book Group

Magna Large Print is an imprint of Library Magna Books Ltd.

Printed and bound in Great Britain by
T.J. (International) Ltd., Cornwall, PL28 8RW

For Jill

whose bright light guided me
through dark waters

Acknowledgements

I thank my four children for their continued support and encouragement in my writing life. Without them the enjoyment would not be as complete. They are always interested in the development of my latest novel. In this one Judith played an active part, vetting the work as it progressed; Geraldine read the work in its entirety and made suggestions for clarity; Anne and Duncan were ever ready to enquire the progress I was making and thereby spurred me to get on.

I must thank Kate Strachan, Assistant Archivist National Meteorological Archive and Hazel Clement of the Met Office for information about the weather conditions in 1879.

I also must thank all the staff at my publisher Piatkus for their help and support, particularly throughout the period of becoming an imprint of Little, Brown.

All my Jessica Blair books have been expertly and sympathetically edited by Lynn Curtis, this one no less so. Thank you, Lynn.

Chapter One

From her home, high on Whitby's West Cliff, twenty-three-year-old Pauline Carnforth gazed across the River Esk to the older part of the town where red roofs stepped their way up the cliff towards the ancient church and ruined abbey. Her hazel eyes, wide and alert, did not linger on that aspect for more than a moment but sparkled anew when her gaze passed to the view upstream which, for her, was the best in her home town on the Yorkshire coast. A swing bridge spanned the river; beyond, masts and rigging of all manner of vessels resting at the quays trellised the clear sky. It was Christmas Eve 1879. The bustle on the quays was winding down but in two days the ships and quays would be swarming with people again: merchants having a word with their captains, clerks hurrying with manifests, stevedores being harangued to forget their hangovers and prepare their ships to sail to distant shores. Sailors would curse their superiors under their breath and labourers would groan under the heavy crates and bales they heaved on board.

Pauline brushed a stray strand of dark brown hair back into place, sighing, and wishing, not for the first time, that she had been born a boy, able to sail to the farther reaches of the ocean, to see the magical worlds that lay beyond the horizon and do all the things a girl was not allowed to by this strait-laced society. Not that she was dissatisfied with her lot; she counted herself lucky to have a broad-minded, loving mother, an understanding father, and to want for nothing, knowing she enjoyed her privileged position because of his hard work and astute mind.

John Carnforth had inherited his father's yawl at the age of twenty, when the older man had been lost at sea while herring fishing. John was already steeped in the same trade, but saw it as a means primarily of furthering his ambitions to become a ship-owner whose vessels would trade with every part of the world. In this ambition he had been equalled by his good friend Albert Nash who had matched him with a similar enterprise.

They had become rivals, but the rivalry was friendly with each man prepared to help the other. The two powerful mercantile firms prospered alongside each other in Whitby and the respective families became close.

Even though it had become customary for them to spend Christmas Eve together, alternating as hosts, they followed the recognised custom of sending out invitations three weeks before. This year Jennie Carnforth had sent the invitations and had received replies within twenty-four hours as etiquette demanded.

Pauline recognised the sound of her mother's footsteps; she did not turn round but curled her long fingers around her mother's when she came and stood beside her.

'You love that view, don't you, Lena?' commented Jennie in the gentle Scottish lilt she had

14

never lost in the twenty-four years she had lived in Yorkshire.

'I do, Mama. It's one I will never forget. You'll be looking forward to leaving it and going to Dundee, I expect?'

'Of course. Being with my family at Hogmanay is always special.'

'You still miss them then?'

'Yes, but I bless the day your father, following the fleet south, decided to put into Dundee to celebrate his birthday. It was love at first sight for us both, and I was lucky to find a man willing to take on a widow with a son. James was but two at the time.'

'And you were prepared to leave your home and come to Whitby?'

'I would have followed John anywhere, and with my family's blessing, too. I've never regretted it. Your father understands that I miss them some-times, though, and has insisted every year that we spend New Year in Dundee.' A faraway lilt had come to Jennie's voice and her eyes seemed to be focused on something beyond the view from the window. A moment passed; she started. 'I think we had better stop chatting,' she announced light-heartedly, 'and get ourselves ready. It won't be long before the Nashes are here.' They both turned away from the window and headed for the door. 'What are you going to wear, Lena?' she asked her daughter.

'I thought my new green dress, if that doesn't clash with yours?'

'It won't. I'll wear my light blue.'

They parted on the landing, each going to her

15

own room. Lena turned the highly polished brass knob and pushed open the heavy oak door to hers.

'Ah, miss, there you are!' The maid looked up from a pile of clothes she was folding. 'I'm sorting your underclothes for your visit to Scotland. Will you see if...?'

Lena dismissed the rest of the query with a wave of her hand. 'You know what I'll want, Sarah.'

'Yes, miss.' The girl was pleased to be trusted with the choice. 'Which dresses, miss?'

Lena crossed the room to a large hanging cupboard. She flung open the double doors and, without hesitation, said, 'That, that and that.'

'They're all day dresses, miss. You'll need an evening dress.'

'The red one then. I'll wear the green this evening. Now help me get ready for our guests.'

'Yes, miss.' Sarah's eyes brightened. She had loved the bustle and excitement of party days ever since she had come here, six years ago as a fifteen-year-old, to work for the Carnforth family. Soon afterwards she became Miss Pauline's personal maid as well as helping with more general duties in the house.

An hour later, her toilette completed, powder and scent applied, the green dress fitted and smoothed into place, Lena viewed herself in the cheval glass positioned to take full advantage of the light from the room's tall sash window. She gave a little nod of satisfaction, pleased with the choice she'd made when she had consulted her dressmaker two months ago. The dress fitted

16

closely to the waist, emphasising her bust and hips. The high-necked bodice of Valenciennes lace gave way to green silk that flared out in a series of ruffles below the small bustle. Green bows circled the elbows from which the sleeves came tight to the wrist. A small circular *calotte* decorated with tiny ribbons of silk and lace nestled on her head, complementing her dark brown hair that had been swept up from the nape of the neck.

'Oh, you do look lovely, miss!' Sarah's eyes were wide with admiration but she blushed crimson then, realising she was out of place in making such a personal observation to her mistress.

Lena smiled generously and put her maid at ease, 'Thank you, Sarah.' She gave one more glance at herself in the cheval glass and left the room.

As she started for the top of the stairs she heard a door open behind her, and turned to see James coming out of his room. He raised his eyebrows in admiration.

'You look extremely well, Lena. A new dress? It suits you.'

She smiled as she acknowledged the compliment. It pleased her that her brother always commented on her appearance.

'Wait until you see the red one I bought at the same time!'

'Saving that for Dundee?'

She nodded. 'Yes.'

He held out his arm so that he could escort her down the stairs.

'It will have to be something to better that one,'

he said. 'It gives you a real aura of elegance. I'm sure Alistair will approve.'

She caught the teasing twinkle in James's eyes and countered with, 'And no doubt you are out to impress Olivia.' Her brother cut a fine figure, at just over six foot tall, his dark hair, almost black, and rugged features that combined with a gentle manner to make him a very presentable young man. His dark eyes were usually alert with interest and whoever came under their gaze felt drawn to him. Tonight the black cutaway coat, grey single-breasted waistcoat and matching grey trousers he wore were tailored to perfection, to reveal his slim athletic figure.

He gave a little chuckle. 'Father would be pleased if we both married a Nash.'

Lena's answering laughter confirmed this. It was indeed likely that such matches would please John Carnforth.

Their mother and father were already in the drawing-room, enjoying a glass of Madeira. When Lena came in John rose to his feet and his eyes dwelt admiringly on his daughter. 'You look very fine,' he commented.

Lena smiled and inclined her head in thanks.

'And you too, James,' he added quickly, careful always to treat them equally and never give his step-son the impression that he was any less valued.

Jennie had always been grateful for her husband's attitude towards her son. Once James had reached the age to understand, she had explained his true parentage but without question he regarded John as his true father.

He came to his mother now, holding out his hand for her to take while she stood up. 'Let us look at your dress and see our two lovely ladies side by side,' he suggested.

Jennie, flattered that he should be interested, took his hand. This was her son all over, a natural charmer.

'That dress is just right for you, Mama,' Lena approved, her eyes drifting over the pale blue silk bodice and skirt with matching peplum. Tight sleeves fell from the covered shoulders where a lace neck-line mirrored the trim around the cuffs and dust ruffle.

Jennie flicked her skirt with her fingers and did a small twirl before standing alongside Lena, both of them flattered by the attention the men were giving them.

'Now, Madeira for you both,' said John, crossing to the decanters and wine glasses set on a table on the opposite side of the room from the ornate fireplace. Once he had served them he resumed his chair and fished in his waistcoat pocket for his half-hunter. He glanced at the time and returned the watch to his pocket. 'Another half-hour,' he commented, and relaxed in his chair as if gathering himself for the lively evening to come.

James glanced at his sister and winked, then spoke to his father. 'Still wearing the same waistcoat, Father?'

John looked sharply at him. 'I'll have you know this is new.'

'Then why didn't you get one like mine?'

'Black's more befitting.'

'Oh, Papa, you'd look so handsome in light-coloured trousers and waistcoat,' put in Lena, playing along with her brother. 'Wouldn't he, Mama?'

Jennie saw the twinkle in her daughter's eyes. 'I'm sure he would,' she agreed.

'Now don't you start, Jennie,' countered her husband.

'You should adopt the modern trends,' James argued.

'Older men still wear black.'

'Oh. So if you consider you are old, where does that put me?' His wife assumed a hurt expression while trying to suppress the twitching of her lips.

'Now, Jennie, I wasn't implying that you—' John stopped talking when he realised that he had risen to their bait once again. It happened every time his choice of clothes was mentioned. He held up his arms in surrender. 'All right, I've fallen for it again, but you still won't get me to change.'

'You're too conservative, Papa,' said Lena. 'I'll bet Uncle Albert has been more forward-looking.'

John gave a grunt of contempt. 'What? He's more staid than I am.'

'Well, maybe,' James granted.

John missed the knowing look that passed between James and Lena and on to their mother.

The tap of a maid's footsteps across the hall, heading for the front door, heralded the arrival of their guests. They were all quickly out of their chairs and into the hall to greet their friends who were being shepherded into the house. Two other maids, ready to take the new arrivals' outdoor clothes, swiftly appeared.

'Georgina!' Jennie hurried forward to greet her dear friend. They had been close ever since John had first brought his bride to Whitby, and Jennie had never forgotten the way her friend had helped her settle in to what was to her a strange land. They embraced, and all around them warm greetings were being exchanged.

The handshake between John and Albert marked a friendship that had endured since their schooldays. It had survived the trials and tribulations of herring fishing and the move to greater things, their trading across the world bringing wealth not only to themselves but benefiting the economy of their home town too. The Carnforth and Nash families were highly regarded in Whitby because of it.

While Jennie and John were welcoming their good friends, their sons, with merriment in their eyes, were talking in the low easy way that only comes with long acquaintance. As different as they were in what they wanted from life, James planning to follow his father and Alistair to become a doctor, their friendship was still close.

As they turned to Pauline and Olivia, who were also busy exchanging greetings, James caught Alistair's dark blue eyes alight admiringly on Pauline before his own exchanged a glance with Olivia. She inclined her head in acknowledgement and felt the nervous quiver inside that she always did when James greeted her this way.

'Isn't Pauline's dress beautiful?' commented

Olivia with genuine appreciation.

'Yours equals it,' replied Lena. It was plainer than hers, without so much lace, but its simple unfussy lines suited Olivia, as did the yellow silk faille trimmed with pale blue. 'Don't you think so, James?' she added, knowing Olivia hung on every word her brother uttered.

'Of course! You both have impeccable taste. Exchange dresses and both of you would look perfect frights.'

'Not very diplomatic,' commented Alistair. 'But true.'

The maids had collected the outdoor clothes and were away with them to the closet near the front door. The two families, chattering amongst themselves, went into the drawing-room. As everyone found chairs, John and James started serving Madeira.

'We told you, Father,' said James.

'What's that?' asked John, knowing full well what his son was getting at but hoping he would not draw attention to it.

'Uncle Albert has adopted the new trend.'

John's lips tightened as his family joshed him. Laughingly, Jennie explained what had transpired shortly before their friends arrived.

'You've let me down, Albert,' reprimanded John.

'Sorry, but don't you think I look smart? Time you shed some of that black.'

John made no comment but looked accusingly at his family. 'I think you had prior knowledge of this change.'

'Who? Us?' said James in mock innocence.

'Or else you schemed with Uncle Albert,' replied his father, suspicion in his eyes. He glanced at his friend who shrugged as if to say, I am innocent.

The light-hearted tone of the evening was set. It continued in such a mood, conversation flowing easily but at times becoming *tête-à-tête*. When it was announced that dinner was served, John escorted Georgina; Albert, Jennie; James, Olivia; and Alistair, Pauline to the dining-room. While they followed the etiquette appropriate to their station in life, they had known each other long enough to dispense with some of the more formal rules and make this a relaxed occasion. The meal brought praise for Jennie who had chosen a menu that catered for all tastes, and equal praise for the accomplishment of her cook. Afterwards light-hearted chatter flowed, especially among the young ones, and everyone enjoyed songs round the piano, gracefully accompanied by Lena.

'We've done well, Albert,' commented John quietly but with great satisfaction, his glance taking in their wives, deeply engrossed in chatter that was meant only for women's ears. His gaze moved to their offspring, laughing together over a game of cards. 'And those four couldn't do better than to pair up,' he added, inclining his head in the direction of the group.

'Aye, I agree. It would give me great satisfaction to see our families united and our firms continuing to thrive in friendly rivalry. Sadly for that scheme, Alistair has his heart set on being a successful doctor and, though he understands the business to some extent, has little interest in taking over from me. But I've always believed, let your children do what they want and they will succeed. Let parents advise only if advice is wanted.'

'You're an understanding man, Albert. I'm sure you are seeing the results of that in the way Alistair is making such a success of his chosen departure. As far as my firm is concerned, I'm pleased James has always shown a great interest in it, though his father and grandfather were not men of the sea. He has applied himself well and is proving very capable.'

When Christmas Eve had nearly slipped away, John recharged all their glasses and in the first seconds of the new day he raised his own: 'A Merry Christmas to you all.'

Greetings were exchanged, with kisses and laughter all round, then Jennie called, 'To the servants,' and led the way through the house to the servants' quarters where they were gathered around the table in the centre of their dining hall. Jennie knew that such gestures, along with careful consideration of their terms of employment, kept her servants loyal and happy.

After greetings had been exchanged below stairs, the two families settled down again in the drawing-room for another hour before Georgina finally made a move to leave.

As they donned their outdoor clothes for the short walk home she took Jennie's hands in hers. 'This has been a wonderful evening, and I'm only sorry that Albert and I won't be coming with you to Scotland. I felt I should stay and be near my niece when her baby is born, as her only relative.'

'I'm sorry too,' replied Jennie. 'I do hope all goes well for her.'

'Thank you. And thank you too for including Olivia and Alistair in your visit north.'

'It wouldn't be the same without taking some of you; it has become such a tradition.'

'There is no need for them to stay here, and I know they are looking forward to it as usual.'

John finally announced, 'If we don't see you tomorrow, we'll pick Olivia and Alistair up at ten-thirty on Boxing Day.'

'Where's Lena?' said Alistair as goodbyes were being made.

She appeared from the closet beside the front door. 'Right behind you,' she said, laughter on her lips as she brought out a sprig of mistletoe from behind her back and held it over her head. Alistair was not going to miss this opportunity. He kissed her full on her lips as lively comments flowed from the others.

'Do you want it, Olivia?' cried Lena, tossing the sprig to her friend.

Her eyes were bright as she caught it and held it over her head to receive the kiss she wanted from James. She looked round. 'It's yours, Mama!' She tossed it in the air.

Georgina held it and a moment later felt Albert's lips on hers, but before she could pass it to John he'd taken it from her, turned to his wife, held it over her head and kissed her. 'For my favourite Scottish lass!' he said proudly.

Jennie's eyes were bright. 'And may we exchange many more of those in the Christmases to come.'

Their friends were departed; their children gone to their own rooms. John closed the bedroom door and came over to Jennie who was sitting in front of her dressing-table, combing her hair. He stood behind her and held the sprig of mistletoes over her head again, leaning down to kiss her neck. She stayed still for a few moments, enjoying the touch of his lips, and then slowly stood up and embraced him.

'Now enjoy Hogmanay in Dundee,' he whispered.

'I will if you are there,' she replied quietly as she slid her arms round his neck and looked deep into his eyes. 'I love you, John Carnforth. Thank you for coming into my life and staying there.'

Chapter Two

John surveyed the clear sky with a sailor's experienced eye as he and his family walked on the West Cliff during the early-afternoon of Christmas Day. The morning had been devoted to their final packing for their journey to Dundee and now they enjoyed relaxing in each other's company.

'Should be fine for our ride to York tomorrow,' he commented.

'And hopefully for the rest of our journey,' added Jennie.

At ten-thirty the following day, at precisely the

26

time John had stated, the coach he had hired from the White Horse hostelry in Church Street pulled up outside their residence in New Buildings on the West Cliff. Amidst all the bustle and excitement their luggage was carefully stored on top of the coach.

'Have you wrapped up well against this fog?' Jennie asked her daughter as she came downstairs.

'Yes, Mama,' replied Lena in a jocular tone, displaying her grey coat with its three layers of shoulder capes. Embellished with large buttons down the front, it flared slightly from the waist to the top of her black shoes. The comfortable sleeves had deep cuffs. She wore dark blue gloves to complement her close-fitting bonnet.

'There's a breeze, Mama,' called James, coming out of the drawing-room, pulling on a pair of leather gloves. 'It'll blow the fog away.'

'Maybe,' she returned doubtfully. 'But it's cold, and could be colder still across the moors.'

'You're looking quite elegant, brother,' commented Lena. 'Trying to impress our cousins or the Scottish lasses?' She hesitated a moment and then added teasingly, 'Oh, maybe the new coat's to attract Olivia's attention?'

'It doesn't matter whose, so long as you like it,' he said.

'Very smart.' She admired the tight black frock-coat as he strutted around the hall. 'And it goes well with those grey-striped trousers.'

'Come along, come along!' The urgency in John's tone as he came through the front door put an end to all exchanges of compliments.

27

Servants bustled around, seeing to the family's final needs and plying Jennie and Pauline with rugs as they settled in the coach. A few moments later the coachman sent the horses forward and in a matter of minutes they were outside the Nashes' house. More luggage was stowed; greetings between the two families soon giving way to goodbyes.

'Sorry not to be coming! Have a safe journey,' called Albert and Georgina as the coach rumbled away and gained momentum.

The coachman urged the two horses on the climb out of Whitby but once they had reached the moorland heights he allowed them to settle into an easier pace. Similarly the excitement inside the coach at the start of the 'adventure' quietened somewhat, though conversation still flowed easily. John showed concern for everyone's comfort by occasionally asking them if they were warm enough, especially when they experienced dampness from the persistent fog on the heights. Once they started to negotiate the long incline towards the market town of Pickering they began to leave the mist behind. Though it was still cold and they did not see blue sky as they had done yesterday, they were thankful at least that it was not freezing. They stopped at the White Swan for warming drinks and then made quicker progress across the flat country to York.

Silence descended on the coach as it eventually pulled up outside the Royal Station Hotel.

'This looks magnificent,' commented Jennie, her eyes wide with wonder as she surveyed the impressive architecture.

'Should be,' observed John. 'It was only built last year. The station is just behind so is very handy for tomorrow. I want you all to enjoy this evening.'

His requests, made previously by letter, were all fulfilled and his generous tips on arrival ensured they were well looked after by the staff, who were also very helpful the next day when the visitors left for Edinburgh where they were to stay the night.

The journey north remained uneventful. Although it was familiar to them from previous years they always found it interesting, looking out for new landmarks while recognising those that were more enduring.

Reaching Waverley Station in Edinburgh, they quickly transferred to the Royal British Hotel. Once again John saw to their well-being and, after the evening meal, when they were all seated in the lounge, he reached into his pocket.

'These are for your onward journey to Dundee in the morning,' he announced as he handed four tickets to James. 'I'm sorry your mother and I will not be travelling with you but I had an invitation to meet Charles McVee with whom I have a trading venture. He suggested we might meet when he learned I would be in Edinburgh. It will give us the opportunity to clear up some final points and then seal the deal to our mutual satisfaction.'

'Would you like me to stay, Father?' offered James.

'Not at all, but thank you for the thought! I know you are very familiar with what is in hand

and the progress we have made, but there is nothing to keep you here. Your cousins have organised a special party for you young ones tomorrow, starting in the afternoon, so you be on that train in the morning. Your mother and I will catch the four-fifteen from Edinburgh and will join you later.'

They spent a pleasant evening together and, when they rose to go to bed, Alistair and Olivia made a special point of thanking Mr and Mrs Carnforth for their kindness and hospitality.

'Think nothing of it,' replied John. 'It is a pleasure having you both with us and I am sure you will have an enjoyable day tomorrow. You'll know almost everyone there from previous years.'

The following morning Jennie and John saw them off at the station. Jennie lingered long, watching the train until it had completely disappeared.

'Come along, love,' said John quietly, taking her arm.

'Will they be all right?' she asked, a catch in her voice.

'Of course.' He gave a little laugh at her concern. 'They are young men and women, no longer children. And they have each other.'

'But...'

'There are no buts about it,' he said. 'Now fasten up that coat, the wind is getting a bit snarly.' He reached out and gently fastened her thick coat at the neck. He held his finger at the last button after he'd fastened it and looked tenderly into her eyes. 'Don't worry, love, nothing's going to happen to them.' Oblivious to the other people on the station platform, he kissed her gently on the lips. 'Now, let us enjoy the rest of our day.'

'There they are!' Lena was the first to spot her cousins among the people meeting the train from Edinburgh at Dundee station. Her smile broad with pleasure, she waved and then glanced at her brother. They had always got on well with their cousins, Avril, Fiona and Robbie, and knew they would spend a joyful New Year together. Not wanting her friend to be left out of the intimacy of the occasion, she held out her hand. Olivia, appreciating the meaning behind the gesture, took it gratefully.

Olivia and Alistair had first come north ten years ago with their father and mother to experience a Scottish New Year with Jennie's brother's family, and an immediate rapport had arisen between the MacBrides and the Nashes, with the result that the invitation to come for Hogmanay had been extended to the Nashes every year since.

At fifty, Martin MacBride, a leading General Practitioner in Dundee, had a formidable reputation for getting things done to better the welfare of his city's people. He would be at home, waiting to extend a warm Scottish welcome to the two families from England, and especially to his sister Jennie whom he knew would be arriving later in the day.

'Come on!' James said brightly as he slapped Alistair on the shoulder and matched the pace set by Lena and Olivia.

The words that passed between them all were

31

as warm and full of excitement as the hugs and kisses that were exchanged.

'The carriage is waiting,' announced Avril, the eldest girl, taking charge, and then she added with a teasing note in her voice, 'It will be a bit of a crush but I don't think any of us will mind that.'

'I'm not having Fiona sitting on my knee,' protested Robbie, the youngest.

'I can think of better knees to sit on,' she countered.

'I'll sit on it,' offered Lena.

'So I'll have Avril,' called Alistair, 'and James can have Fiona.'

'What about me?' cried Olivia with mock hurt.

'You're the lucky one,' teased James. 'You'll have a space all to yourself.'

The mood for their New Year celebrations was set.

Once they were settled and the coachman had set the horse away, Avril announced that all was ready for the party, which was to begin in the late-afternoon, and then asked, 'Aunt Jennie and Uncle John will definitely be coming today?'

'Oh, yes,' answered Lena. 'Papa is sorry they aren't with us but this meeting was a chance he could not afford to miss. He said they would be on the train leaving Edinburgh at four-fifteen.'

'Good.' Enthusiasm rose in Avril's voice as she added, 'We're going to have a splendid New Year.' And everyone voiced their agreement with a cheer.

Uncle Martin and Aunt Mary gave the four travellers from Whitby a warm welcome and, once they had settled in, Martin took Alistair into his study.

'Sit down, young man, and tell me – are you happy in your studies with Doctor Jollif?'

'Oh, yes, sir. He is most generous in imparting his knowledge and often allows me to sit in during his consultations and examinations.'

'That is good. And you are still happy in your choice of profession?'

'Yes. I wouldn't want to pursue any other career. I would like to do for the people of Whitby what you have done, and are doing, in Dundee.'

Martin smiled and gave a dismissive wave of his hand, trying to play down the compliment, but nevertheless felt proud that this young man wanted to be like him. 'I'm flattered, sir. And your father still has not raised any serious objections to your doctoring?'

'No, sir. As you know, when I first announced that I wanted to be a doctor he told me he'd always hoped I would follow in his footsteps. But he quickly assured me, and still does, that I am free to pursue whatever course I wish.'

'A very understanding man.' Martin nodded his approval. 'Others would have been more than annoyed that an only son did not follow his father into a thriving business. I wonder what he will do with it when he decides to retire?'

Alistair's reply was never uttered for at that moment there was a knock on the door and Mary walked in. Both men immediately rose to their feet.

'Now, Martin, you should not be keeping this young man from enjoying himself. Our New

Year's celebrations are starting. I told you, all medical talk is forbidden unless you have an urgent call – which, please God, you won't.'

'But, Mary…'

'Don't "but Mary" me. What we agreed, and you approved, stands.' She drew herself up, her eyes sharp, deterring any objections he might try to raise. The formidable medical man of Dundee was putty in her hands. She knew it and loved him for it, as well as revelling in his devotion. 'Off with you, Alistair.' She shooed him from the room, then turned to her husband with eyes now softened with admiration. She came over to him and kissed him. 'Enjoy yourself with your family and friends. Let Dundee look after itself.'

Martin liked being among the younger generation and his lively wit and humour endeared him to them all. They knew he would discreetly absent himself from their celebrations when the time was right. They, in their turn, were respectful and appreciative of all the effort he and his wife had gone to today.

The main room had been cleared of furniture and was given over to dancing. Tables in the dining-room had been arranged and set to accommodate twenty-seven young people and the four more mature adults who would dine with them when John and Jennie arrived from Edinburgh. Two drawing-rooms were available for relaxation and conversation, and the parlour would soon ring to a singsong around the piano. The young guests started arriving at five o'clock and soon there was a buzz of excitement and enjoyment as the party got underway. No one noticed the wind rising outside.

'Was your meeting with Mr McVee satisfactory?' asked Jennie when her husband came back into their hotel room.

'Very. It should lead to a profitable transaction. It has certainly been worthwhile, waiting until that later train.'

'Good. Then I'm pleased.'

'I ordered some tea to be served in the lounge as I came up. We have time. Are you ready?'

'Just get my coat.' She went to the wardrobe, took out her outdoor coat and draped it over her arm.

At that moment there was a knock on the door and in answer to John's 'Come in' a page-boy appeared.

'Your luggage, sir?'

'There you are.' He indicated the two suitcases.

They followed the page-boy from the room. While they went to the lounge to enjoy their cup of tea, he installed their luggage in the cab that was waiting to take them round to the station. Twenty minutes later they were on their way. The horse was skittish but the cabby's skill kept it under control.

'I don't like that wind,' shuddered Jennie, disturbed by the howling sound as the wind chased along the street and around the buildings, whisking smoke from chimneys and sending paper scudding along the pavements.

John and Jennie lost no time in getting to their carriage, relieved to be out of the Edinburgh gale.

Jennie gave a sigh of relief as she sank back on the seat. 'I'll be glad when we get to Mary and Martin's.'

Scottish fervour swept everyone into a party spirit which Avril set on course with an opening sing-song. The small orchestra played, the dancing began, and once into its swing kept going. The floor was never empty. Chatter and laughter resounded throughout the house. The deteriorating weather outside was never given a thought until James approached Dr MacBride.

'Sir, my parents...?'

The doctor's raised hand halted his question. 'All taken care of, my boy. I am about to depart for the station myself.'

'Would you like me to accompany you, sir?'

'Wouldna dream of it. You must stay and continue to enjoy the party. I will see to your mother and father. No need at all for you to face the inclement weather. We'll soon be joining you.'

As the train, shaking from the force of the gale, rattled towards the bridge over the Tay, Jennie grasped her husband's arm and looked at him in naked alarm. 'We shouldn't be jolting around like this. I don't like it at all.'

He patted her hand reassuringly. 'Nothing's going to happen, my love,' he replied confidently. 'It's only the wind. Ignore it.'

'That's easier said than done.' Her grip tightened when the wooden sides of the coach groaned in protest at a fresh onslaught.

'We're safe enough,' he comforted her. 'These

trains are strong, built to withstand anything.'

'I hope so. Oh, I wish we were there!'

'We soon will be. And then we can enjoy the feast I'm sure Mary will have prepared for us.' John tried to sound reassuring, having just glanced out of the window and distinguished, in the fading light, the waters of the Tay heaving towards the iron bridge ahead of them.

'The horse is very restless, sir,' said Dr Mac-Bride's coachman. 'Doesnae like this wind. I'm afeared to take him out the neet, sir.'

'Then I shall walk, Angus,' replied Martin.

'I'll accompany you, sir. Tae help with the luggage. We can mebbe borrow a trolley.'

'Good man! We'll bring only what is necessary. The rest can wait at the station until tomorrow when you pick it up with the carriage.'

'Very good, sir.'

Buttoning their coats tightly and cramming their hats more securely on their heads, the two men set off. They matched each other stride for stride as they leaned into the fierce wind.

The train rocked.

'John!'

'It's all right, my dear.'

The whirling air shrieked between the buildings. Martin's lips tightened. This was no time to be out, but needs must. He had to see to the welfare of his sister and brother-in-law, could not let them fend for themselves in this. His steps faltered then. A splintering crash on the pave-

37

ment a short way ahead brought both men to a sharp halt.

'My God, sir! That could have killed us,' gasped Angus, staring with alarm at the slate that lay shattered at their feet.

'Aye, and there might be more,' returned Martin. 'Quick, man, cross the road!'

They ran, eager to be clear from the danger.

The train rumbled on, clinging precariously to the tracks.

The band struck up the next tune. Joyous laughter rang around the room as couples chose their partners.

The wind ripped at the waters of the Tay, tossing them into a maelstrom of foam-topped waves, the whiteness emphasising the yawning depths below.

Forwards, backwards, swirl around. Pretty dresses sent waves of colour undulating round the room.

John fished his watch from his waistcoat pocket. 'Soon be at the bridge.' Jennie did not respond except to grip her husband's hand tighter. The carriage shook. He felt her tremble.

The windows rattled. Lena cast an anxious glance at them and then at the clock on the mantelpiece. Six-fifteen. 'They'll soon be here,' said James, knowing she was thinking of their parents.

A sudden crack, the sound of tearing of timber ... a huge branch, torn from a tree as if it was a matchstick, crashed into the road a few paces ahead of the two hurrying men. They leaped clear of it,

'Not far,' yelled Martin. 'We'll be safer in the station.'

They reached it with relief and found some other people too had braved the raw night to meet the Edinburgh train.

A violin string, caught accidentally by the musician's bow, sent a screeching sound around the drawing-room.

The wind howled through the station like a demented banshee, wanting to awe and intimidate with its display of power.

'Enjoying yourself, James?' Olivia asked as his hand took hers for the waltz.

'Now that I'm with the best dancer in the room,' came the flattering reply.

'You exaggerate.' Olivia blushed but thrilled with pride at his compliment.

'Not long now,' said John reassuringly, close to his wife's ear, hoping to calm the tension he could feel when she huddled closer to him.

The train rumbled on to the bridge. He glanced out of the window and took comfort from the sight of those solid black girders.

Mary eased a curtain back a little and looked out

into the darkness. Nothing to see. The window frame rattled. She hoped her husband was all right, and was thankful he was not alone. She glanced back into the room, pleased that the young folk still seemed oblivious to the ferocious storm outside.

Lena slipped as she whirled in to the dance with Alistair. Always sure on her feet, she had never done so before and was thankful now that he was there to support her. As he grasped her more tightly her face came close to his and she felt his lips touch hers, driving away any fear.

The train lurched. Another jerk as if something had impeded its progress. It lurched again. Rocked. Tilted.

'John!' screamed Jennie as she tumbled against him, her eyes widening with fear. They were both thrown sideways.

'John!'

He grasped her. Pulled her close. He heard timber tear, metal screech. The carriage toppled. They were falling, falling. He held her tight. 'I love you, Jennie, always have, and always will ... wherever we are.'

His lips met hers and they stayed locked together as they fell, fell, fell, and icy waters rushed in to claim them.

Chapter Three

Martin was uneasy. He reckoned the train should have arrived twenty minutes ago. He sought out a railway official who was already being pressed for news by other people.

'Have you any word of the train?' he asked, his features creased with concern.

'None, sir! I'm sure everything is in order, though, or we would have heard. This storm's bad. Could have caused a delay for any number of reasons.'

Martin knew how true that was. After all, he himself had witnessed trees uprooted and masonry torn down. Something could easily have caused a blockage on the line.

'We are awaiting news from the south side of the river. I'll let you all know as soon as we hear.'

As the minutes passed unease mounted among the crowd at the station. Enquiries became more agitated, voices demanding news, urging something be done to ascertain it.

'What's that?' The query came from near the station entrance.

'No!'

'Did you hear that?'

'The bridge has collapsed!'

'It can't have!'

'Who told you?'

'Came from someone outside.'

41

'How do they know?'

'It's a rumour! Must be. The bridge is strong, not long built.'

'Stand anything.'

'Shouldn't spread alarm ... we've relations on that train.'

Calls and comments were flowing fast. No one knew what to believe.

Harassed officials tried to quell the rumours, calling for everyone to keep calm, but then a fresh wave of anxiety swept through them when, a few minutes after seven, communication was lost between the signals cabins to either side of the bridge. Public demand for something to be done ran high. Pressure mounted on the railway officials. Disturbed by this latest setback and the lack of any concrete news, they decided an investigation should be made.

Martin did not like feeling so helpless. He was used to being in charge of situations, but here there was nothing he could do but wait. He saw some railwaymen huddle together in what appeared to be serious discussion, clearly agitated, shaking their heads and nodding violently. Then he saw one man, ignoring what appeared to be protests from the others, leave the group and stride off down the track towards the bridge.

Other people saw him go and soon speculation was running rife amongst the crowd. What exactly was Mr Roberts, superintendent of the locomotive department, doing?

Roberts disappeared into the gloom, hoping he would soon be able to confound the spreading rumours.

With every step he took, the wind seemed to grow in ferocity. It was as if it was bent on preventing him finding out what had happened, even to the extent of hurling him into the murky depths of the Tay to stop him doing so. His determination to discover the truth quelled the fear rising in him as he inched his way forward, until finally he had to crawl on hands and knees.

'Mama, Papa should have been back with Aunt Jennie and Uncle John by now,' Avril said to her mother who had hidden her own concern about the delay thus far.

'I know, my love.' Though worry plagued her mind, Mary tried to sound reassuring.

'Everyone's getting hungry.'

'If they aren't here in five minutes, we'll make a start. Something must have held them up. I'm sure they won't mind.'

Mr Roberts hunched his shoulders against the wind and gripped the rails even harder as he crawled along. If the train had had to stop on the bridge, as seemed likely by its non-appearance, he should be able to see it, even in the dark, but there was nothing. He advanced slowly. A few more yards ... then he stopped and stared with horror at the scene before him: the entire centre-section of the bridge, where girders had formed a tunnel-like structure, had disappeared and all that remained were its supporting piers, rising finger-like from the river.

Terror gripped him, forcing disbelief from his mind, as he tried to grasp the only conclusion to be drawn from that missing section. Despair filled him. There was nothing left for him to do but to return with the devastating news: the train from Edinburgh and all its passengers must now lie deep on the muddy bed of the Tay.

With a heavy heart, he inched his way round and returned to the north side, wondering how on earth he could break such tragic news. By the time he'd reached solid ground he knew there was nothing for it but come straight out with the truth.

The crowd surged towards him when he reached the station. The questions they flung at him in their eagerness for news faltered as they sensed he had nothing good to tell them.

'The centre portion of the bridge has gone.' The words seemed to stick in Roberts's throat.

The disbelief that ran through the crowd was palpable.

'What – collapsed?'

'Can't be!'

'It was built to withstand anything...'

'What about the train?'

The putting of that question silenced all others. Everyone strained to hear the reply.

'I couldnae see it. There wasn't a sign of it on the south side. And if it's no' there,' his voice faltered, 'then I believe it now lies at the bottom of the river.'

The shock of this announcement sent minds reeling. For one moment there was a heavy silence broken only by the mocking cries of the wind. Then pandemonium broke out, with cries of disbelief and howls of agony as folk struggled

44

to take in what this tragedy meant to them. Then shouts of vilification were hurled at all those concerned with the building of the bridge. Some railway officials tried to calm the situation while others struggled to decide what to do next.

The news brought a cold dread to Martin's heart. He stood still for a moment, oblivious to what was happening around him. He felt drained of all energy, his legs leaden, his throat constricted. He wanted to cry out to heaven for allowing his dear sister to be taken when she had so much to live for, but felt a touch on his arm and stayed silent.

'Sir,' said Angus tentatively.

Martin started.

'I think we should go home, sir.'

He nodded.

'I'm sorry for your loss, sir.' Angus's voice was husky with emotion and tears streamed down his lined cheeks.

Martin nodded. 'Thank you. You're right. There is nothing we can do here.' His sigh was one of despair. He had faced many things in his lifetime, taking heartbreaking news to so many families, but never anything to compare with this. He would bring home devastation to his beloved niece and nephew.

Mary had got the meal underway. Even though she was enjoying the laughter and conversation that eddied around the table, she had been half listening for the front door opening. Then the sound she wanted: they must be back! She hurried into the hall.

Her smile vanished when she saw that her husband was alone, and his face... 'What is it, Martin?'

He bit his lip but could not hold back the tears that flowed then. She was by his side in a moment, taking into her arms a man from whom all strength had gone. She held him tight and gently patted his shoulder. She let him cry for a few moments before asking. 'What is it, my dear?'

He still clung to her, wanting to grasp at any comfort he could. 'The bridge collapsed.' His words came in a whisper. 'The train went down with it.'

A shudder ran through Mary. 'Oh, no!' She clutched at her husband. She needed to be strong for herself, but even more for him. She had lost a dear sister-in-law, but he had lost the sister to whom he was devoted. And James and Pauline had lost their mother and father... The laughter and gaiety coming from the dining-room pierced her heart.

'I must tell...' Martin's voice faltered as he eased himself away from her.

She gripped his arms to stop him. Looking up into his face and reading the anguish there, she said, quietly but firmly, 'No, Martin, I'll do it.'

She held him for a moment longer, then released her hold and walked to the dining-room door. She paused, automatically smoothed her dress, took three paces into the room and stopped.

All eyes turned towards her, expecting to see the new arrivals follow. The chatter subsided into an uneasy silence as everyone sensed that something momentous had happened. Where were Mr and Mrs Carnforth? Why had such a serious aura entered the room with Mrs MacBride?

Mary gripped her hands together in front of her. 'James, Lena,' she said quietly, but with authority, and turned back into the hall.

Lena felt a chill sweep over her. She glanced anxiously at her brother and saw a troubled expression cloud his face. They both rose from their chairs and left a room that had fallen into an uneasy hush.

'What is it, Aunt?' asked James tentatively as the door closed behind them.

'Where are Mama and Papa?' queried Lena, her voice strained.

'I'm afraid I have some bad news for you. There has been a tragic accident. The bridge collapsed and took the train with it.' Mary regretted she had to be so blunt but could find no other way of imparting this devastating news.

There was a moment of absolute silence filled with disbelief, and then a low moan came from Lena. 'No!' She looked at James and saw he had gone deadly white, his face expressionless, as if the impact of the words had not reached him yet.

Mary stepped forward and took Lena into her arms. Tears were streaming down their faces. Lena was racked by heaving sobs of utter despair. Though Mary too felt utterly distraught she knew she had to be strong for her niece. Martin had lost a very dear sister and could not disguise his distress as he opened his arms to James. Male protocol fell away; the men embraced each other and did not stifle their tears.

Mary finally eased Lena from her but still held

her hand as she said, 'I must tell the others.' She glanced at the two men and they came to support Lena. 'Take her to the drawing-room,' she said.

Mary dabbed the tears from her eyes, rubbed her cheeks and drew herself up. She knew she must not weaken. Strength would be needed in the days to come. She should show it now. She opened the door to the dining-room. A charged silence met her. Questioning eyes were on her as she went to stand at the head of the table.

'It was terrible news I had to tell Pauline and James,' she explained. 'The railway bridge has collapsed and taken the Edinburgh train with it. There can be no survivors.'

Shock and incredulity filled the room. Everyone stared in disbelief at her until Avril broke the silence.

'But, Mama, the bridge...' Not knowing what she was going to say she let her voice trail away.

This was the signal for Mary to take charge. 'It would be best if you all leave. Avril, Fiona, Robbie, see your friends out and then come to the drawing-room. Alistair, Olivia, you go there now, see if you can be of any assistance.'

Everyone did their best to help. Olivia, wanting and needing to be with James, was in a turmoil of emotion, trying to come to terms with the realisation that she would never again see the two people she'd regarded as her second mother and father. The shock made Alistair long to be with Lena; she would need him, and he wanted to be needed in such a crisis. His face was deathly white as he took his sister's hand and they hurried from the room, while the three young MacBrides ushered the rest of the guests from the dining-room, promising to pass on their expressions of sympathy.

Olivia and Alistair were unable to speak when they first entered the drawing-room but both James and Lena knew from their expressions and embraces that they, too, were suffering at this dreadful news.

When Mary came into the room she brought with her a sense of calm for which everyone was thankful. 'There is much to be thought about but we will wait for the children to join us,' she announced.

Her husband came to her. 'I think maybe we could all do with a glass of wine.'

'A good idea,' she agreed, knowing that giving people something to do, even if it was only holding a glass, could help ease the moment.

Martin went to the decanter and James and Robbie joined him. Alistair started to move too but Lena's grip on his hand tightened. He squeezed her hand reassuringly. She mustered a wan smile of thanks. His heart cried out to her; he wanted to kiss away the dampness in her eyes.

Once everyone was seated, Mary said, 'We have to decide what to do now. The four of you,' she glanced across to her nephew and niece and their friends from Whitby, 'can stay as long as you wish.' She glanced toward her husband for his approval.

'Quite right, my dear,' replied Martin, reading the signs that she was relieving him of taking charge. 'Alistair, how will that sit with Dr Jollif?'

'Sir, I'm sure he will understand, I will write to

49

him tomorrow, explaining the situation.' He glanced at Lena. 'I'll stay as long as I can be of help.'

'Thank you, Alistair.' She pressed his hand again.

'What about you, James?' Mary asked.

'There is the business to run so I can't be away too long. But as you know, Ralph Bell is a competent manager, well trained by ... father. I'll write to him. He needn't take any major decisions. That will be up to me now.'

The firmness behind his final words registered on Lena's mind, but her thoughts were in too much of an upheaval for her to comment on it.

'I hope Lena and I can return together, and I'm sure we would welcome the support and strength of Alistair and Olivia upon our homecoming.'

'Whatever you wish, James,' said Olivia, receiving a nod of agreement from her brother.

'Then it is settled,' Mary said with relief. Her eyes turned to her own children. 'You must do all you can to help your cousins through the trying days ahead.'

They were all sincere in their offers to do whatever they could.

She decided it was best to keep everyone's minds occupied, so said, 'Now, we must think about clothes. You men are easily dealt with – dark suits.'

'I have my dark jacket and frockcoat but I'll need some black trousers and a black cravat,' said James.

'That applies to me too,' said Alistair.

'Nae problem,' Dr MacBride assured them.

'You will need mourning dresses, Lena. If you are to follow etiquette, which I think you should, that will mean black crêpe for six months, then you can change to silk for three months followed by half-mourning when you can wear greys or mauves. We have a Family Mourning Warehouse in Dundee so I suggest we pay a visit tomorrow.'

'What about me and Fiona?' asked Avril.

'Three to six months in black silk, nothing ornate, the only adornment a piece of jet. Olivia is no relation so is not bound by the same etiquette.'

'I would like to do the same as your daughters, ma'am,' she replied.

Mary nodded her approval. 'And I will follow the apparel expected of a sister though I am no blood relation.'

'That is very kind of you,' said Martin, a lump in his throat. He straightened his shoulders and took a grip on his feelings. 'James, Pauline, it is understandable that you will want to return to Whitby. You have your friends and there is the business to run. You are old enough, and competent enough, to make your own decisions, but I want you to understand that your aunt and I will be ready with our advice and support, should you require them.'

'That is most kind of you, Uncle. And you, Aunt,' said James. 'I know I speak for Lena also in expressing my thanks.'

'You have nothing to thank us for,' said Martin with a dismissive gesture. 'Stay until you feel ready to face Whitby again.'

51

Gloom hung over Dundee. Few people saw any reason to celebrate the coming of the New Year. Enquiries were started. Rumours about the cause of the collapse circulated, and fingers were pointed. But none of this helped to ease the gloom in the MacBride household.

James and Lena could not yet grasp the reality of the situation, their minds too numbed by tragedy. It was difficult for them to accept what had happened. They still expected their parents, so full of good health and energy, to walk in at any moment. Their uncle, aunt and cousins tried to ease the situation for them, though they too were hard hit by the disaster. Life could never be the same for any of them and each of them knew they would have to find their own way forward. Her best course came to Pauline four days into the New Year.

Dr MacBride had been called out to an emergency, telling Mary not to wait lunch for him as he did not know what time he would be back. The rest of the family had finished their luncheon when Lena caught everyone unawares by saying in a firm voice, 'Aunt, will you take me to the river?'

There was a moment of stunned silence.

'Yes,' replied Mary quietly, 'but do you think that's wise?'

'That river is my mother and father's grave. If they had been buried in a churchyard I would have visited them, so I must go to the river instead.' She glanced at James, saw agreement in his eyes, and knew he had been thinking the same but had held back the suggestion for fear of

52

upsetting her.

Mary recognised that she should not raise any further objection; this was something Lena had to do. 'Of course I'll take you. Angus can drive us there.'

Alistair and Olivia accompanied them but, not wanting to intrude on family grief, stood to one side and paid their own respects to the two people they'd held in high esteem.

Lena stood between her brother and aunt, staring into the waters of the Tay. They had wrapped up well against the chill in the air, but it was a different kind of chill that gripped Lena then. It came from within her and there was little she could do to combat it as she gazed at the water, bereft today of the power it had held while it pounded the bridge. Her parents lay lifeless beneath its quiet flow. She would never see them again. Silent tears trickled down her cheeks.

James fought his tears, as he knew his father would have wanted him to. He needed to be strong for his sister and for what faced them when they returned to Whitby. And that had to be soon. His hand sought Lena's and each found solace in the other's touch.

Mary saw the gesture and knew they would cope together with what lay ahead. She was not surprised when, on the journey back to the house, James told her, 'I think we ought to return to Whitby soon. There will be much to see to there and it is our home.'

Chapter Four

Martin and Mary insisted on accompanying them to Edinburgh, where they stayed overnight. With everyone holding their feelings in check, the parting at Waverley Station was nevertheless a tearful one, with Martin extracting promises from Pauline and James to get in touch if the necessity arose.

Conversation as far as York was desultory, with Alistair and Olivia uncertain whether to try to distract their friends or leave them to their thoughts.

James and Olivia were contemplating the future in different ways. James was trying to work out how his father would want him to develop the business, but dismissed that thought by reminding himself his ideas would naturally differ from John's and he was now in charge. Lena saw little consolation ahead for her. In the year's mourning she faced, there would be little social contact. Sympathisers would call and leave their cards unseen; close friends would linger a while but soon be gone, leaving her to her own thoughts in the big empty house with all its memories. Why hadn't she been born a boy? Men had it so much easier at these times; they could escape into their work.

Alistair took charge in York. He booked rooms for the night, considerately choosing a different hotel from that they had used when heading north. The coach he had hired to take them to Whitby the next day arrived on time. Once the coachman saw they were comfortably seated he set the horses on their way.

The night's rest had lightened spirits a little but, as the descent from the moors towards the coast started, the sombre feeling that permeated the coach was replicated in the grey clouds overhanging the town.

When they neared New Buildings, Alistair asked, 'Would you like us to come in with you?'

James glanced at Lena, thoughtfully leaving the decision to her.

'It is kind of you, Alistair, but I would rather the two of us faced our homecoming alone.'

'Are you sure?' queried Olivia quickly.

'Certain.' Lena gave her a wan smile. 'You have both been pillars of strength and we are grateful to you for staying with us, but this is something James and I must face together.'

Alistair and Olivia respected their wishes and made their goodbyes. James left the coachman to see to their luggage and took Lena's arm supportively as they walked up the garden path towards the elegant house. Lena bit her lip and forced herself to hold back the threatening tears. This was certainly not the homecoming she had envisaged when leaving the house on Boxing Day.

As they neared the front door it opened and Mrs Campion the housekeeper stepped out. She was neatness itself in her slim-fitting grey dress, calm and practical, respected by all. Once the travelling arrangements had been made, Dr

MacBride had written to her informing her of the date and time of James and Pauline's arrival. The commiserations she offered them now were heartfelt. She promised to do everything she could to assist Lena, whom now she regarded as mistress of the house.

Lena was comforted to see her kind, familiar face. Mrs Campion had come to them as housekeeper when she was but twenty-five, after entering service in Scarborough at fifteen. Highly competent and with a sharp mind, she had mastered all the duties and skills of a housekeeper by the time she was twenty.

Once James had expressed thanks on behalf of himself and Lena, and the housekeeper had dismissed the rest of the staff, she made her own condolences with considerable feeling, expressing what wonderful employers Mr and Mrs Carnforth had been to her, and saying she hoped she would be able to continue in the service of the two persons she had watched grow up over the last ten years.

Two hours later, seeking to occupy Lena's mind, the housekeeper was talking with her in the drawing-room when a maid announced Miss Nash was calling.

'Show her in,' said Lena.

'I'll leave you, miss,' said Mrs Campion, rising from her chair. 'We can continue this tomorrow.'

'Thank you,' replied Lena. 'You have been most kind.'

'It is a pleasure to be of service, miss, though I wish it was not in such tragic circumstances.'

The door opened then and the maid announced,

'Miss Olivia Nash.'

Olivia hurried in, but some of her concern vanished when she saw Lena's demeanour.

'I'm glad you came,' she said accepting her friend's kiss on the cheek and then indicating a chair to her.

'I had to know how you are or I wouldn't have slept tonight,' Olivia told her.

'Then rest easy, dear friend,' replied Lena. 'It may sound strange, but I feel more at ease now that I am home. There is still so much of Mama and Papa here, I am finding it a great comfort.'

Olivia looked a little surprised. 'I would have thought it would have made things harder?'

'That was my expectation while I was in Dundee, but now I am home, even in this short time, I don't find it so. I received heartfelt sympathy in Dundee, but it was in danger of becoming overpowering. I am better here, where I can be peaceful.'

'I am glad you see things this way. I'm sure your mother and father would approve.'

'I must thank you too for all you did there.'

'My dear Lena, I hope I will always be around to help if ever you need me.'

'And I for you, Olivia.' She leaned forward and pressed her friend's hand. As Lena straightened up she said, 'Now tell me, what happened at Robin Hood's Bay? Did your cousin have her baby?'

Olivia raised her eyebrows a little. 'No. Mother and Father are still there. Been a slight miscalculation, if you ask me. Father rides to Whitby every other day to the office. He left a note at home yesterday, saying he had received Alistair's letter telling him what had happened and explaining when we would be back. He hopes to see you and James when he is in Whitby tomorrow. At the end of his note he said Mother sends her love to you both.'

Pleased to see Lena looking settled, Olivia left after half an hour.

The following day, on his way to the office across the river, James was stopped on numerous occasions by people who wished to express their sympathy at what had happened. Lesser acquaintances expressed their feelings by touching their forehead or by a respectful inclination of the head. John Carnforth had been a much admired man in Whitby. That walk made James realise he had something to live up to, and stiffened his determination to do so.

'Good day, Ben, Jude,' he acknowledged the firm's two middle-aged clerks when he looked into the outer office.

'Good day, Mr Ja— er, sir,' they spluttered, uncertain as to how they should address him now. They had seen him grow up from a boy who loved to be around Whitby's quays and ships and he had been called Master James then until promoted in their estimation to Mr James. Now he would be Mr Carnforth since there was only one remaining.

James smiled to himself at their confusion. 'Is Ralph in?' he asked.

'Yes, sir,' they both chorused.

He went down the corridor to the next room

which served as the manager's office. Like the one he would be occupying, it had a view across the roadway to the quays and the river, beyond which could be seen the shipbuilding yards. Carnforth's offices were at the hub of Whitby's activities, only a short distance away from Nash's thriving concern.

'Ralph!' James greeted the manager brightly as he entered the room.

'James!' He sprang to his feet and the two young men exchanged firm handshakes. Ralph was pleased that the relationship they had built up as youngsters, Ralph being only two years older than James, did not appear to have been affected by the fact that James would now own the firm – or at least that was what he expected. He lost no time in extending his commiserations and sympathy, and added, 'This has been a terrible tragedy and a great shock to you. Take your time coming back. Everything is in hand here. You can see...'

James held up his hand to stop him. 'No, Ralph, I'm taking no more time away. I'll be better off being involved. I know you are capable of carrying on but there are certain things...'

'I fully understand,' his friend interrupted, 'and I think it's the best approach. I know your father would approve of such an attitude too. So let me bring you up to date with what has happened while you were away.'

'Good man, Ralph! I couldn't have a better person by my side. Stay with me – you won't regret it.'

Ralph made no comment but opened a ledger

and started to explain their current financial situation.

Half an hour later, James leaned back in his chair. 'The accounts show us to be well set up. I think we are well placed to make some shrewd investments in specialist cargoes.'

Ralph nodded. 'We'll cast around. You might pick up some more hints about possible new markets now that you will be mixing with other owners and merchants.'

'My ears will be ever attuned,' said James, smiling.

A knock on the door stopped any further conversation between them. Ben came in.

'This has just been delivered for you, sir.' He handed over an envelope to James.

'Is the messenger waiting for an answer?'

'He is, sir.'

James tore the paper open. He glanced quickly at it and, looking up, said to Ben, 'Tell him that will suit me.'

'Very good, sir.'

When the door closed Ralph gave a little chuckle. 'Sir! You've been promoted. Are you expecting that from me?'

James grinned. 'If I said yes, you'd up and leave.'

'True.'

'We understand each other.' James assumed a serious expression then and his eyes never left Ralph's. 'We'll consult as Father and you did, but the final decision will now be mine, as it was his.'

Ralph's face conveyed no emotion as he said, 'Of course,' and started to rise. 'The *Mary Jane* is due to sail within the hour. I'm going to make a final check with Captain Muldoon.'

'Then I'll come too,' said James, getting to his feet. But he got no further. At that moment there was another knock on the door and Ben reappeared.

'Mr Nash to see you, sir.'

'Show him in, Ben.' James glanced at Ralph. 'Carry on.'

He acknowledged Mr Nash as he left.

'James, my dear boy, what can I say?' Albert's rugged features were drawn with concern. He clasped James's hand firmly. 'To say that I'm sorry is barely adequate. What a terrible tragedy! An awful time for you. How are you and Pauline managing?'

'As well as you'd expect after such a tremendous shock, but we received staunch support from our relations in Dundee, and of course Alistair and Olivia were towers of strength.'

'I'm glad to hear it.' Albert took the chair indicated by James. 'Now,' he went on as he sat down, 'if there is anything Mrs Nash or I can do for you or for Pauline, please don't hesitate to ask. Your father and I were lifelong friends and our two families have always been close. Always will be, I hope'

The words rolled off his tongue. James realised he was speaking so fast to avoid breaking down in front of the younger man.

'It's kind of you to be concerned for our welfare, sir, and rest assured, neither I nor Lena will hesitate to come to you if necessary.'

'Good, good,' Albert sighed and asked tentatively, 'The business...? I expect you will be taking over?'

'I don't know. The Will has not yet been read. As a matter of fact, I have just received a note from Mr Witherspoon, asking if he may visit tomorrow.'

Albert nodded. 'I'm sure you will inherit and be in sole charge. Your father thought you highly competent and said you contributed much to the firm, so I'm sure he will have entrusted the business to you. Besides, what else could he do, you being the only male in the family?'

'We shall know tomorrow.'

They talked for another hour. Albert seemed in no rush to leave, but then took his watch from his waistcoat pocket. 'Oh, my goodness!' he gasped. 'How time flies without us realising it.' He sprang to his feet. 'I'm late for an appointment with a merchant from Hull.' He gave a little grunt of disgust with himself. 'I'll be behind all day now. It's a devil ... once behind and you never seem to make it up. *And* I promised Mrs Nash I'd be back in Robin Hood's Bay by three.' He started for the door where he paused to shake hands with James. 'I won't be able to visit Pauline now. Very remiss of me. Please apologise and tell her I'll call next time I'm in Whitby.'

'I will, sir. I'm sure she'll understand.'

As he walked home James experienced a sense of satisfaction: he would be in charge now and would run the firm his father had built up to the best of his ability; in fact he would expand it as a memorial to his parents, his mother and the stepfather who had viewed him as his own. Then he was touched by doubt. His father's Will still had not been read ... maybe the firm would not be his. After all, he was only John Carnforth's step-son. What if...? No, that thought was too ridiculous. Who else could he have left it to? Apart from Ralph, who else knew as much about the business as he did? Lena? Well, she had always shown an interest in it, and he knew Father had always encouraged her do so even though he'd never involved her in the actual day-to-day running of things. No, he couldn't have left it to her ... surely not? After all, she was a woman and it was unthinkable for them to become involved in a man's world. But even with this thought came an extra nagging doubt; it was only an unwritten law. He knew of two cases in Hull, in fact, where women had taken over when their husbands had died.

Reaching home, he found Lena in the drawing-room reading.

'How have you been?' he asked solicitously.

'I'm settling back in, James. Don't worry about me. Oh, I will mourn and miss Mama and Papa, but life has to go on and I know they would not want me to withdraw into myself, mope and moan about the cruelty of life.

'I've seen Olivia and Alistair. His was a quick visit as he was on his way to see some patients. There have been the expected sympathisers calling, too, but I coped with them. Mind you, I'll be pleased when all that is over and I can get out of these.' She indicated her mourning clothes. 'Even though I say it so soon after getting into them, I know Mama would sympathise and agree. She would want me to get on with my life.'

'I expect she would,' replied James, surprised at his sister's observation but deciding that if this was her attitude, he would go along with it. It would be for the best and would enable her to come to terms all the sooner with the devastating loss they had just suffered. 'I'm glad to find you so reconciled to your new condition. I hope it won't be a setback to have to sit through the reading of the Will tomorrow? I received a note from old Mr Witherspoon, Father's solicitor. He would like to come here tomorrow morning at ten to read the Will. I sent word back that it would be acceptable. I hope you agree?'

Lena nodded. 'Yes, I do. How were things at the office?'

'Ralph had looked after everything, but of course he couldn't make any major decisions.'

'Have there been any to make?'

'No. It has been a quiet time, though the growth of the Empire generally suggests there may well be chances for expansion for the more far-sighted.'

She nodded. 'Father did mention that possibility to me two months ago.'

James started. 'He never said anything of it to me.' The sudden harshness in his voice with was not lost on Lena.

She was quick to come to her father's defence. 'It was just a casual remark he made one day when I visited the office. I don't know where you were – possibly at the *Wanderer*. She had just docked with a cargo from the West Indies. Her arrival may have prompted him to suggest there were further opportunities to be had in that direction.'

James felt a pang of jealousy that Lena had been taken into their father's confidence and that this possible development had not been mentioned to him personally. He tried to persuade himself that it had been merely an oversight on Father's part or that such an advance was not an immediate proposition. Nevertheless, it did raise a query in his mind – had John left any provision in his Will to involve Lena in the future running of the firm?

Similar thoughts entertained her mind as she settled into bed for the night. Lena admitted to herself that she had experienced a touch of delight to discover that her father had confided something in her and not in James. Did this signify she would be permitted, by a clause in his Will, to have a say in the future management of the family firm? She felt secretly sure that it would be so. After all, her father had always encouraged her interest in the business and how it was run. Tomorrow would reveal all.

Walter Witherspoon arrived at precisely ten o'clock. The maid who answered the door had been instructed about his arrival. After taking his hat and coat she escorted him to the drawing-room where Lena and James were awaiting him.

The solicitor was nervous and it showed in the way his narrow shoulders, set on a thin frame, seemed to stoop more, giving him a hunched appearance and the impression that he was peering at whomever he addressed. In spite of forty years spent in the profession he had entered at the age of twenty-five, he had never grown easy about reading Wills to bereaved relations, for he had never mastered the art of expressing commiserations and sympathy.

'Mr Witherspoon.' A friendly tone in his voice, James rose from his chair and extended a hand in welcome.

The solicitor felt his own bony hand crushed in its firm grip. He gulped a little but managed to splutter, 'Mr James ... er ... Mr Carnforth. I'm sorry for your loss.' He turned quickly to Lena who sat in a chair, hands primly placed together on her lap. 'Miss Carnforth, my commis – er ... commiserations.' He bowed to her. 'A terrible loss.'

Lena inclined her head. 'Indeed, Mr Witherspoon.' Then she added quickly, to relieve his nervous embarrassment, 'You'll take some chocolate?'

'Very kind, Miss Carnforth. Very kind indeed.'

She glanced at her brother who was already on his way to the bell-pull beside the fireplace, to send the prearranged signal to the servants' quarters for chocolate to be served, with the result that two maids appeared with the necessary items almost before the solicitor was seated in the chair James had placed for him.

When the cup of chocolate was put beside him and the maids had left the room, Mr Witherspoon cleared his throat.

'It is a simple Will. Would you like me to read it in its entirety or would you prefer me to summarise it and leave a copy for you to peruse at your leisure?' he asked, his eyes darting from one to the other of them.

'Summary?' queried James, glancing at his sister.

'If that is satisfactory?' she agreed, addressing the solicitor.

He nodded, relieved that this meeting need not be prolonged. 'Very well.' He took a drink of chocolate as if to draw strength from it. 'Your father made this Will two years ago. Obviously your mother was provided for in the case of his death, but under the present circumstances those provisions no longer apply and so the whole of your father's estate is directed as per the other clauses in the will.

'There are bequests to members of your staff, according to their rank and length of service. You will be able to read these for yourself, but I assure you while your father has been generous they are amply taken care of by the return from his investments. To you, Miss Carnforth, he has left this house and all its contents, with a request that you give your brother a home here until such time as he marries. He has also made you a very generous regular allowance, which again is financed by his investments. I must say, your father was very shrewd in where he placed his money. I have consulted with Mr Chapman at the bank and he assures me that the investments are sound. However, if the bank deems it wise to cash them, the capital will come to you, Miss Carnforth, and in the case of the servants the capital linked to them will be divided proportionately, according to the terms of the Will.

'Now we come to the business. The first item here concerns your manager and two clerks. They are each given a lump sum, to do with as they wish. That money will be taken directly from the business. The rest, and all other assets connected with it, go to Mr James.'

Lena gave a little gasp but stifled it quickly. Though her mind whirled at this news and she sensed the delight in James, she forced herself to concentrate on what Mr Witherspoon was saying.

'However, Mr James, your father has made certain provisos. He wants to see the name of the firm, "John Carnforth and Children", as he set it up many years ago, remain the same so that Miss Carnforth still feels she is connected to the business. He says in the Will that he hopes you,' his eyes fixed on James, 'will continue to expand the firm. With this in mind, he has set up various funds, the details of which are in the hands of the bank – Mr Chapman will enlighten you.'

The solicitor paused, cleared his throat and then said, 'I have covered the main items but there is one other clause I think I had better mention verbally. Your father expresses the hope that Miss Carnforth should continue to show an interest in the firm, as she has done all her life. He does stress, however, that it must be without interference, though she is entitled to look at the accounts because a small proportion of the profit from the business goes into the investments that provide for and increase her income as the years pass. These provisions for Miss Carnforth continue in force even if she marries. You can read the details in the copies of the Will I will leave with you. Another will be deposited in my office and a copy will go to the bank.' He tapped the table in front of him as if to indicate that was the end of the matter.

There was a moment's silence and then James, looking at his sister, asked, 'Have you any questions?'

She shook her head, unable to speak as the disappointment about the business churned in her mind.

'Nor have I, Mr Witherspoon,' said James, drawing the matter to a close. 'Thank you for coming and for offering us the explanation so clearly.' He rose from his chair.

The solicitor did likewise. Relieved that this was over, he made a hasty goodbye to Lena and followed James from the room.

With the closing of the door Lena felt as if part of life had been closed to her. It seemed as if her father had ignored all the interest she had shown in the firm. Surely he had realised that she wanted to participate in it; to be involved in its day-to-day running? She realised he had never given her any responsibility within the firm to date, but she had hoped that would come. She slapped her thigh in frustration. Why hadn't she spoken to him about it, asked to be trusted in this way? Had she misjudged her own father? Was he like others who thought that the worlds of the ship-owner and merchant were the exclusive domain of men, barred to women? He had never voiced that opinion so she had thought he held more liberal views. Now she chided herself for her own shortsightedness. Her lips tightened. There was nothing she could do about it – oh she could show an interest as her father had indicated, but that was all; she could go no further. Why had he laid down such rules? After all, she was his blood child while James was not, and yet *he* was the one who was going to get what she most desired. Lena stamped her foot. Why hadn't she been born a boy?

The door opened then and her brother came into the room. 'Well, Father has left you comfortably off,' he commented as he went to pour a glass of Madeira.

A retort sprang to Lena's lips then but, as hurt as her feelings were, she held the words back. She did not want to alienate her brother or show dissatisfaction at their father's Will. She would abide by it. There were other ways to enter the world where her heart lay, even though she was a woman. Oh, why had Alistair become a doctor? Why hadn't he been interested in his father's business, then she could have...

Chapter Five

James stepped into the building in Grape Lane occupied by the long-established banking firm of Simpson, Chapman & Co. Friendly and local, it had handled Carnforth affairs from the moment John Carnforth's father first sought capital to finance the boat, on which he'd established himself as an exceptional herring fisher, until his tragic death at sea. John then took over and went on to expand into the company that was now in James's hands, as a consequence of a second tragic death.

He was thankful to be inside; it had been a cold walk from New Buildings and he had felt the sting of the wind blowing in from the sea as he crossed the bridge to the east side of the river before turning into Grape Lane.

'Good day, sir.' With a smile the young clerk slipped from his high stool when James walked into the outer office. 'You are expected, sir, please follow me.'

James followed him down the corridor to a door on the right. The clerk knocked and hesitated a moment, his head inclined as if listening. He gave a tiny nod of satisfaction, opened the door and announced, 'Mr Carnforth, sir.'

James strode into the room to see a man in his late-fifties rising from his chair behind a sturdy oak desk.

'Mr Carnforth.'

'Mr Chapman.'

Their handshake was firm.

'Let me take your coat.'

James slipped out of his redingote and handed it, along with his hat and cane, to Mr Chapman who placed them on a coat stand near the door.

'Do sit down.' He indicated a chair to James. 'Thank you for your note of yesterday,' he added as he returned to his seat.

'Thank you for seeing me so soon. I hope it has not upset any of your prior arrangements?'

'Nothing that couldn't be rescheduled. Because you indicated it was a business matter regarding your father's firm, I realised it was something you would like to deal with as soon as possible.'

James was conscious of coming under scrutiny from a pair of shrewd eyes. Chapman held himself firmly upright yet betrayed a benevolent demeanour, emphasised by his open, friendly face.

'That is true, Mr Chapman. I mean no dis-respect at this time, but as you will no doubt appreciate a business cannot afford to stand still.'

'Indeed.' He acknowledged James's point genially.

'I had better say at the outset that my father's firm has been left in its entirety to me. No other person is involved. If you require confirmation then Mr Witherspoon is sending you a copy of the Will.'

'Proof, Mr Carnforth? Your word, like your father's, is good enough for me. I hope that you will continue to bank with us?'

'I see no reason to change the arrangement.'

'Anticipating that you would wish to know the financial standing of the firm, I have prepared the relevant documents.' He tapped the two piles of papers on his desk.

'All those, Mr Chapman?'

The banker smiled. 'There are more but these are the ones to which we may have to refer, depending on how deeply you want to go into the situation now.'

'Mr Chapman, I am sure you can apprise me of the financial situation with a summary of the current state of affairs.'

'Indeed I can. That is probably the best way to proceed. If you want more detail, we have it all here.'

'That sounds splendid.'

Chapman nodded. 'Good. Then let us do this in a civilised manner over a glass of Madeira.' He rose from his chair as he was speaking and went to a cabinet where he poured them two glasses. He gave one to James, raised the other and said, 'To a successful relationship.'

James acknowledged this with a smile.

Once he was seated again Mr Chapman came straight to the point. 'Your father was a very shrewd businessman. After inheriting his father's ship, he continued in the herring trade then widened his horizon by trading with the Continent and eventually beyond. But you know all this. I seek only to remind you how your inheritance came about. Your father has left three working ships, the *Mary Jane, Wanderer* and *Suzanna*. I always split the profits he made from them into five bank accounts which, according to the documents drawn up, signed by him and witnessed by me, must always be kept separate and be supplemented proportionately in the way he laid down, from the profits made by each ship and any subsequent ship added to the fleet.'

James was surprised; he had never had any inkling that his father had organised the firm in such a way, but he kept a closed countenance and waited for Mr Chapman to answer his question. 'These five accounts?'

The banker sipped his wine, his eyes intent on

James. 'One is to cover the everyday running of the firm. A second for future investments that are deemed beneficial to its advancement.'

'Does that include buying more ships?'

'No. Your father saw that expansion and success depended on the size of the fleet. He therefore instituted a third fund for this purpose plus necessary repairs. Of the two further funds – one is to buy goods that become available over and above the everyday regular purchases, which are the bedrock of the firm.'

'And the final one?' James prompted as Chapman reached for his glass.

'That is a contingency fund, available to help any of the others should it become necessary.'

A puzzled frown furrowed James's brow. 'I don't see the necessity for separating the funds. My father was running the firm and now I will be running it. Surely we could...'

Mr Chapman smiled and held up his hand to halt him. 'That is how it must appear to you, and in fact did to your father when he first made these arrangements on my advice. But the separate funds make sure the available capital can't be diverted to the advantage of one particular section, which might undermine the others and so threaten the solvency of the entire firm. These conditions now apply to you.'

'But surely neither he nor I would seek to undermine our own business? There was no need to set up such a complicated system.'

'I beg to differ. And, in time, your father wrote in certain further safeguards that applied to himself and to anyone who followed him in running the business. The use of these funds and the movement of money from them, with the exception of the day-to-day expenses of the firm, have to be agreed by myself and Mr Witherspoon.'

James stared at him in amazement. His mind cried out against such an arrangement but his tongue remained silent. He knew it would be useless to protest. He had no doubt that these conditions were all laid down in black and white and duly witnessed.

'Let me reassure you that neither Mr Witherspoon nor I interfere in the running of the firm. We merely supervise the placement of the profits, see that each fund is managed properly and advise in any major investments you wish to make.' James nodded. 'I hope you won't see this as a father doubting a son's ability – that never entered John's head. After all, he would have been expecting to run the firm himself for many years to come. No, he instituted these conditions so that he himself was supervised – purely as a precautionary measure, so that his family would not suffer from his possible mismanagement or poor investment.'

James nodded again. 'I can see the wisdom in that but it will take me a little while to come to terms with the restrictions placed upon me.'

'Don't consider them restrictions, Mr Carnforth. Your father never meant them as such. They are merely precautions he saw as necessary to keep the firm on a sound basis.'

'Then supposing I was to say I wish to add a ship to the fleet?'

Mr Chapman smiled. 'Ah, I see, an enterprising young man. I would call a meeting of the three of us, and the figures would be studied in the light of your proposal: the size of the ship, what its purpose was, who would build it and so on, plus of course the funds available.'

'And are there sufficient funds available now?'

'Come to me with more details and we shall see.'

'Make the meeting for a week today at this time then.'

'It shall be done.'

James started to rise but Mr Chapman stopped him. 'There is something else I should tell you now.' He paused, seeing that he had James's full attention. 'Your father, wisely, made two more provisions. Nothing to do with the running of the firm as such, but within it there are two accounts, one in your name and one in your sister's. These two funds are financed from investments made in your names – the capital cannot be touched, but the interest is divided equally between you and your sister, to do what you will with.'

James had much to think about when he left Mr Chapman's office. It had been his intention to take up certain matters relating to future developments with Ralph, but now he would have to rethink his approach. He strolled along the quay, crossed the bridge, walked along St Anne's Staith and Pier Road deep in thought, barely aware of people acknowledging him. It was only when he reached the West Pier and passed beyond the protective cliff that the icy blast reminded him it was still only February. He stared across the restless sea. His future lay there; he would use it to accomplish his dreams in memory of his father.

James nodded with satisfaction, turned and walked back at a brisk pace. Lena would be anxious to know what Mr Chapman had said.

She listened intently while they drank some chocolate together.

'Father certainly gave a lot of thought to setting up the business,' she commented.

'At first I thought it was too restrictive, but in fact it isn't.'

'Precautionary and sensible,' agreed Lena. 'I know you are ambitious, James, that is only natural in a young man of your calibre, but do proceed with care. It would be so easy to get carried away and wreck what Father built. I only wish...'

He guessed what was in her mind from the note of regret in her voice. There was no provision for her to be involved in the business, she was only entitled to know what was going on. But from her childhood Lena had always wanted to be in the forefront of anything that was happening.

'Lena,' he said, cutting her words off sharply, 'I know what I want to do and I'll do it. Rest assured, whatever I do will benefit the firm and, indirectly, you.' Before she could comment he went on quickly. 'The first thing I'm going to do is expand our trading capacity by building another ship. I have already arranged a meeting with Chapman and Witherspoon to discuss the financial aspect. Chapman assured me there is sufficient money available, but how much I spend will depend on the type of vessel I commission. They are there to see I don't overspend. You need have no worries on that score.'

'I hope not,' replied Lena a little coldly. 'Why move so quickly?'

'Why not?' rapped James. He jumped to his feet and paced towards the window. 'It sounds as though you are objecting,' he flung over his shoulder. He swung round then, eyes narrowed. 'Let me remind you, Father explicitly stated you are not to be directly involved in the business; you are only to be kept informed.'

Lena had no doubt he would remind her of that point again should she venture to express any suggestion or criticism. She was not entitled to offer advice.

He saw he had touched a sore spot. 'Lena, please don't let us fall out about this. Let us follow Father's wishes. And, let me say, I have decided to call the new vessel the *John Carnforth*.'

His suggestion placated her and her tone softened. 'Father would have liked that.'

'I want to get started on it right away, to occupy my mind.'

Lena felt a stab of jealousy at that. It was different for James; he could escape into another world, and the period of mourning would not drag for him as it would for her with so little to do. Oh, she would still receive close friends but even their visits would not carry the gaiety she had been used to. That would only return at the end of the recognised mourning period, as would her attendance at social engagements. How she longed for time to race by! How she wished she were involved in the business and her mind full of exciting prospects ahead.

'Miss Olivia Nash,' the maid announced.

Olivia hurried into the room and Lena placed her book on the small table beside her as she rose from the armchair she had positioned near the window, to better catch the light of a dull April afternoon.

The two friends exchanged greetings and, when the maid had taken Olivia's cloak and bonnet, she stood back and viewed her friend critically. 'You're still looking peaky.' She sat down opposite Lena. 'You're beginning to worry me.'

Lena gave a wan smile. 'I am beginning to tire of my own company. As the weeks have passed callers have tailed away, but you're a faithful friend, Olivia, and I'm grateful for your support.'

'I am only too pleased to help, and hope I lighten the days for you a little.'

'Of course you do. Besides, I wouldn't hear any gossip if it wasn't for you.'

'Father should have visited you more often when he came into Whitby.'

'He has a business to run,' Lena pointed out. 'It was good of him to call when he could.'

'Well, I bring you news. Mother and Father arrived home from Robin Hood's Bay late yesterday.'

'Is all still well there?'

'Yes. The baby's recovered and my cousin is up and about again after her illness following the birth.'

'I'm so pleased.'

'Mother sent her love and will visit you to-morrow. I've warned her not to overtax you. You know how she loves to fuss. What you want is something more than reading to occupy your mind. Do you ever play the piano?'

'I've never felt like it. It would remind me of what we were doing on the night of the...' Her voice faltered. 'And it doesn't seem right, after what happened.'

Olivia nodded sympathetically. 'It will pass, I'm sure of it, and you'll enjoy playing again. What about the household duties? Can't you...'

'Mrs Campion's so efficient,' Lena interrupted, 'that I really have no need to get involved. Oh, she is kind enough to consult me, but there is no reason why I should alter anything.'

'Doesn't Alistair visit you?'

'Yes, but his doctoring gets in the way, and when he does call it's more often than not only briefly, because he has to be off to a patient.'

Olivia pulled a sympathetic face. 'That's him, absorbed in his calling. I think he was smitten when we visited your uncle and aunt in Scotland the first time, and the desire to help people has never left him.'

'Very noble of him,' commented Lena with a touch of sarcasm. 'I wish he'd followed his father.'

'If he had, he might still be just as absorbed in his work,' Olivia defended her brother.

'Maybe, but at least it would have been interesting, unlike his doctoring. The subject is so unpleasant.' Lena pulled a face to show her disgust. 'And I can't understand half of what he talks about.'

'I'm sure he talks about other things?'

'But he always brings them round to illness and treatments.'

'I think you are still suffering after what happened in Scotland. You should fix your mind on brighter things.'

'Getting out of these sombre clothes would do it,' snapped Lena.

'Time will soon pass.'

'I hope it will move more quickly then, so I can get some colour back into my life.'

'You shouldn't wish time away.'

'Fiddlesticks!'

Seeing her friend growing more irritable, Olivia changed the subject, hoping it would help. 'What about James? Talk to him about the business.'

Lena gave a grunt of contempt. 'I don't see a lot of him. We breakfast and then he's off – and more often than not I don't see him again until our evening meal, and even then he might be off again. It's the business and the building of this new ship. He's got so involved he doesn't seem to have time for anything else, even talking to me. And he's supposed to keep me informed about what is going on.'

'Point that out to him then.'

'I've tried to but he always fobs me off with some excuse. "I haven't time." "Tell you later." "I have an appointment with Mr Chapman." It's as if he doesn't want me to know.'

'I'm sure that's not it,' Olivia sprang to James's defence. 'He's merely very busy and wants to

81

make a success of expanding the firm.'

'Well, beware, Olivia, of a man who gets so involved in his work that he hasn't any time left to spend with you.'

'Oh, come, Lena, I think you exaggerate. You'll see things in a different light when...'

'I hope so!' she cut in roughly.

'I think you must have had a word with Alistair,' said Lena to her friend three weeks later. 'He's been a more frequent visitor of late and tries hard to keep away from the subject of doctoring although, being wrapped up in it and wanting to do good in Whitby, he finds it hard.'

'Well, at least it's a step in the right direction.'

'What about you and James?'

Olivia gave a wan smile. 'He's attentive when he calls at the house, which isn't as often as I would like, but I think like you he finds the mourning period somewhat restrictive.'

'At least he has more freedom and can escape to his work.'

'Have you got him talking about that yet?'

Lena gave a shake of her head as she pulled a regretful face. 'I still don't see much of him. Don't forget what I told you, Olivia.'

Lena was reminded of it herself eight weeks later when Alistair paid her a visit one afternoon. After their exchange of greetings, Lena said, 'You'll take tea with me?'

He held up his hand in a gesture of refusal. 'No. I haven't time today. And it may be some time again before I can visit you as often as I have been doing lately.'

Her face clouded over with disappointment. 'Why?'

'There are signs of an epidemic in two of the yards off Church Street. They are both over-crowded and conditions are particularly bad there. I've got to try to stem any spread of the disease, not only by treating the sick but by trying to improve living conditions.'

'Isn't such improvement the business of the town?' Lena protested impatiently.

'Yes, but unless I cajole and insist on bringing the cases to public notice, nothing is done. I've got to be involved and that will take up a lot of my time, as will my attentions to the sick, to try to prevent this illness from spreading. I'll call again as soon as I can but I can't give a definite date at the moment. I hope the trouble will soon be resolved. I'm sorry, Lena, but that is the situation. If only you weren't in mourning, you could work alongside me.'

He hurried away, leaving her with his last sentence haunting her, as it was to do for weeks to come.

Work alongside me? Among the sick, poverty-stricken and depraved! Was this how Alistair saw their life together if they married? That 'if' became a very big one as the days passed and she had time to reflect that life with him would always be lived surrounded by illness. Could she stand that? Could she stay beside him, helping him as he expected? Did she really have the devotion to him to overcome such hardship and vicissitude?

Lena was pleased that Alistair was happy in his work. She knew it took a strong character to engage in a profession that not only took him to the homes of the well-off but into scenes of poverty and dire living conditions. She admired his desire to improve such conditions and his devotion to the health of Whitby's populace, but wondered if he would ever succeed in his aims; so much more was needed than one man's medical expertise. Was he storming a brick wall? She began to wonder if she could face life with a man who would expect her to be of like mind and to help him blindly.

If only his interest lay in his father's business then she could have become involved in a trade in which she was already interested, and would willingly have faced life beside him, come what may. She began to wonder if she had ever been in love with Alistair or had merely believed she was because everyone else in their social circle expected them to marry. Had that expectation in others rubbed off on them so that they thought they were in love without any strong basis?

Questions mounted day after day and, restricted as she was in her outlets, Lena's mind became more and more troubled.

'Lena!' Alarm rose in Olivia's voice as she crossed the room to greet her friend who was sitting listlessly near the window. The light falling across her face accentuated her pallid drawn features. 'I've been away a fortnight, and look at you! Hasn't Alistair been to see you? Hasn't Mrs Campion called anyone in?'

Sensing more questions to come, Lena held up her hand to stem them. 'I'm all right, Olivia.'

'All right? You don't look it! You need medical attention and I'll see you get it. Alistair will get my tongue round him too!'

'Olivia, please. You know he was called away ten days ago to Staithes. Four fishing vessels were wrecked. Terrible injuries. He's called on me whenever he's managed to get to Whitby, but the visits were brief as he was so tired.'

'Shouldn't have been too tired to notice *you*. And what about Mrs Campion? She should have got someone else in to see you if Alistair couldn't.'

'Olivia, I forbade her. Please don't upset her. She has been looking after me very well and I am improving.'

Olivia's lips tightened. 'Very well,' she replied, 'but I'll have Alistair round here as soon as I see him.'

She was true to her word and two days later he walked in, full of concern. 'Lena, I'm so sorry. Olivia told me... I should have noticed...'

'Alistair, don't reproach yourself. You were needed at Staithes. It's been hard on you.'

'But I should have seen you were not well. Now, let me put things right.'

'I'm improving, Mrs Campion will tell you that.'

'That may well be but I'm going to check you.' When Lena started to protest he held up his hand to stop her and exerted his authority in no uncertain terms. 'You are not well. You are not the Lena I know, and I insist you tell me everything so I can judge what is best for you. I will not stand for any further protests. You are

85

important to me, Lena.' He took her hand, and if she was not mistaken it was more than a doctor's touch when his fingers felt for her pulse.

When he was finished, Alistair nodded. 'You are healthy enough but you are run down. I think it is late shock at what happened in Scotland, and the fact that you have missed being among people in the way that you are used to. I will give you something to take and I want you to eat plenty of nourishing food, but most of all I want you to stop worrying about what happened and dismiss any other concerns you may have. Try to occupy your mind with pleasant things. I'll get Olivia to visit you every day. It was unfortunate that she was away when you were not well. I'll try and visit you daily myself. Certainly I'll be here tomorrow.'

An hour after Alistair had left, James rushed in and was on his knees in front of Lena almost before she'd realised he was there.

'Lena! Alistair's just paid me a visit. Why didn't you tell me? I didn't notice.' The concern in his voice was matched by the look in his eyes as he took her hands in his.

She smiled. 'You never were observant unless it was of ships, and what was happening on the Whitby quays and in the shipyards, and who was trading what with whom.'

'I'm sorry.'

'Don't be. I'm all right. Alistair has given me things to take.'

'Well, if there is anything else you need, tell me.'

'I will. And you can sit down now and tell me

exactly how the business is progressing and how the *John Carnforth* is shaping.' She held up her hands to stem any protest. 'I promise not to question your decisions or make any suggestions.'

'There'll be no need for any when you hear what I have to say.' James pulled a chair near to her and sat down. By the time he had finished he knew he had done Lena good; there was a new light in her eyes and he realised her heart lay with the ships and the quays and the world they brought near. Part of him wanted to offer her a position in the firm, but he knew that would not work. There was no room for two principals. He realised his father had known this, too, and had wisely worded his Will so it could not happen, while providing financially for Lena's future.

His sister's eyes followed him as he left the room. How she envied James the world in which he moved.

Chapter Six

'Here!' Ben tossed a coin in the air, sending five urchins scrambling for it. A cheeky, dirt-smattered face emerged triumphant from the mêlée with a yell of, 'Mine!'

Ben laughed. 'Away to lookout. The *Suzanna*'s due!' The boy started off. 'Hi, come back here!' The youngster pulled up sharp and turned enquiring eyes to him. 'Mind you tell no one but me. Knock on the office window and I'll come out.'

87

The lad nodded and scampered off.

An hour later the rap on the window sent Ben hurrying outside.

'*Suzanna* beating in fast, sir.'

He tossed another coin, which the urchin grabbed with dexterity then yelled his thanks and raced away.

Ben bustled into the building and stepped briskly to Mr Carnforth's office.

'The *Suzanna*'s been sighted, sir,' he announced, elated at being the first with the news.

James sprang from his chair and hurried to the door. In the passage he paused to tell Ralph, who was beside him in a moment. Both men hurried out into the balmy August morning, observing the activity of a busy port, bringing wealth to ship-owners and merchants and putting money in the pockets of stevedores and labourers.

'West Pier?' called Ralph.

'East!' replied James. 'Won't have to wait for the bridge closing.'

They hurried along Church Street into Henrietta Street beneath the towering East Cliff, negotiated the steep incline on to the stone pier itself, and strode out to the lighthouse from where they were afforded a view of the *Suzanna*, beating in towards the safety of the river.

James felt a rush of pride as he watched her skillfully handled by Captain Merryweather, an experienced sailor of many years' standing whose first voyage as a ten-year-old had been on James's grandfather's herring boat.

'She looks well,' commented James.

'Aye, she does that,' said Ralph. He was no

sailor but he loved ships and had always been around them, and knew he would be ever grateful to John Carnforth for giving him a job, one in which hard work and the use of his sharp brain had enabled him to reach the post of manager. He saw his future as bright alongside the present owner with his ambitions to expand. Maybe the *Suzanna* was bringing home the fruits of the first suggestion he had made to James.

They watched the ship slip through the gap between the piers with the minimum of fuss. In the calmness of the river she was taken in tow by boats ready for that purpose. As she was taken upstream and beyond the swing bridge to an east-side quay, James and Ralph hurried back the way they had come. As soon as the gangway was run out they went on board where a ruddy-faced Captain Merryweather greeted them with a broad smile, a firm handshake and an excited glint in his eyes.

'Welcome home, Captain,' James greeted him enthusiastically.

'Good to see you back, Captain.' Ralph, eager to hear the skipper's news, searched his face for any indication.

'My cabin, good sirs,' said Merryweather and turned towards the stern. Within a few moments he was ushering them into his quarters. A bottle and three glasses stood ready on the table. Without a word he quickly filled the glasses and handed one to each of them saying, 'Try that, gentlemen.'

They savoured the wine and looked at Merryweather with questioning eyes as they both murmured their approval then added, 'Excellent.' 'The best Madeira I have tasted.'

'Good! Good! I'm glad you approve.' The captain was filled with pride. His expression showed delight at their comments. 'I've a hold full of it.'

'What?' both men gasped. They exchanged glances that were a mixture of disbelief, exuberance and astonishment.

'It worked!' There was laughter in Ralph's face as he spoke to James.

'Your idea – genius!' James grasped his hand and shook it vigorously. He turned back to the Captain. 'You've done well, getting this cargo.'

Captain Merryweather's face shone with pleasure. 'The idea of giving your captains responsibility for the return cargo, which the firm will trade, naturally ensures we look for the best. It is far more interesting than merely picking up something someone back here has ordered.'

'And you earn yourselves a better bonus,' said James. 'Well done! Did you make any enquiries about what I suggested?' He glanced at Ralph, who looked at him questioningly. 'I didn't say anything about this before sailing because I didn't want to steal your thunder if the idea hadn't worked. Well, Captain?'

'The firm from whom I bought the Madeira is an import and export business. Yes, they will take any wool we can ship from here, starting next year.'

James let out a whoop of delight. 'Well done, Captain, well done!' He raised his glass. 'To the future!' Draining it, he addressed his manager once more. 'Attend to things here, Ralph. I'll see you tomorrow.'

He disembarked from the ship and hurried on his way among the crowds on the quay and streaming both ways across the bridge. James lost no time in reaching New Buildings.

'Home at this time and looking very pleased with yourself?' commented Lena when he strode into the drawing-room.

'I am,' he grinned, flinging himself into a chair opposite his sister. He went on to tell her what had happened and concluded, 'This was my first trading venture completely on my own initiative. Everything before had been set in motion by Father.'

'Congratulations,' she said. 'He would have been proud of you.' Though she hoped she'd kept it out of her expression, she could not deny the touch of jealousy she felt then.

'I thought you would be pleased to hear it. How have you been feeling of late?'

'I'm much better, thank you.'

'You are losing that wan colour and your eyes are brighter. It must be due to Alistair's more frequent visits.'

Lena smiled. 'Maybe. Thank goodness there have been no more epidemics.'

'I hear he did well to curtail the last one. Dr Jollif speaks highly of him and his devotion to his calling. Well, I must be off. I want to tell Olivia the good news.'

Within a few minutes his arrival there was being announced by the maid to Mrs Nash and Olivia, who were busy with their patchwork in the sewing-room.

91

'Show him into the drawing-room.' When the maid had gone, Mrs Nash eyed her daughter with a twinkle in her eye. 'I'm sure it's only you he wants to see, Olivia. Off you go – don't keep a young man waiting.'

Olivia blushed but sprang from her chair and was gone in a flash, wondering what brought him here at this time of day. He had been a fairly regular visitor of late but she longed for the day when he would be out of mourning and able to escort her to social functions and private gatherings in the town. She slowed when she reached the hall, smoothed her dress, patted her hair and then made her entry.

'James!' she exclaimed. 'What a pleasant surprise. What brings you here at this time of day?'

The door clicked shut behind her. He strode across the room. The bright excitement in his eyes startled her. He swept her into his arms and hugged her.

'James! What is it?' she cried.

He released her. 'Sit down here,' he said, leading her to a sofa. He sat down beside her, still holding her hand. Olivia's heart was racing. What was coming?

'I've completed my first transaction completely on my own ... well, the idea came from Ralph but had to be authorised by me. I made some amendments – and it worked!' He went on to tell her what it was all about. 'From now on everything will be the way *I've* planned it.' Excitement rose in his voice. 'And the new ship, *my* idea, will play its part. It's all so exciting!'

'I'm very glad for you, James.' Olivia expressed

enthusiasm although inwardly she was chiding herself for thinking he had been going to announce something else. 'Have you told Lena?'

'Yes.'

'Good. I'm sure the news will help her to a full recovery. You know she's very interested in the firm. Keep that interest going, James. She wishes she was more involved.'

'You are must solicitous, Olivia, but I can't involve her any more than by keeping her informed,' he said in a cool voice, and she decided not to interfere further.

'Lena, I think it would be wise if you had a few walks in the fresh air, say along the West Cliff, before the autumn days turn more chilly. Your illness ... I call it so though I believe there was nothing medically wrong with you ... was caused by the tragedy and it has taken a long time to right itself. You must never let dark thoughts into your mind again. You must resist any movement in that direction, especially when you are on your own. If ever you feel bound to consider them, talk to me. I am always here to help.'

'Thank you, Alistair. Considerate and wise as always. You are going to be a wonderful doctor.'

'I hope so. I will call for you at two tomorrow and we'll take the first stroll. I must be away now – several visits to make.' He rose from his chair. 'I now throw off my role as your medical adviser,' he said, and bent to kiss her on the lips. Lena's hand clasped his arm and he allowed the kiss to linger. 'I must go,' he said reluctantly. 'Take care. You are very precious to me.' He kissed her quickly again and turned away.

Lena watched him go. His step was firm, resolute; one which she knew would instil confidence in a patient, as would his manner and gentle voice. She admired much about him but still regretted his lack of affinity with the sea and the life of a merchant venturer. She had seen the excitement with which that could charge a man, watching James walk from this very room.

Alistair's kiss and his words 'You are very precious to me,' took her attention then. Was a proposal near? Probably when her period of mourning was over, and that was only eight weeks away. Lena's mind spun. What, then, should her answer be? She and James had grown up with Alistair and Olivia, been their constant companions. She had shared her first kiss with Alistair. She smiled at the thought of that hasty peck when she was twelve, out of sight of the picnicking families, when they had veered away from James and Olivia in a game of tag. Alistair had been her good companion and friend always. They had shared much and, though unspoken, had both taken it for granted that they would spend their lives together. But when he had begun his medical training, she'd realised that was not the life she had envisaged sharing and that a certain spark in her feelings for him had disappeared. She knew no one else would realise it, not even Alistair for his love for her would blind him. She would soon be faced with a decision that would affect not only her life but that of others. So many people expected them to marry; it was probably why no other men had ever ventured close to her. When the moment came, should she do the expected? It would be far easier that way, after all. She bit her lip in frustration. A doctor's wife? She visualised herself taking tea with the ladies of Whitby, discussing raising funds for the poor, helping at charity events and keeping up appearances as befitted her position. And Alistair had already hinted at her helping in his ministering to the poor and badly housed people of the town. Lena shuddered. Her mind turned instead to the excitement surrounding the activities of the bustling port; the life she had been near to all her years, and one she had visualised continuing with Alistair ... until the day he had told her of his decision to become a doctor and the different dreams he held.

Lena sprang out of her chair and crossed to the window and its view across Whitby. She stamped her foot with impatience. 'Oh, Alistair, why didn't you follow your father? You could have taken over a business that could have meant so much to us, and in which I could have helped you!' she cried aloud. 'What am I to say to you now?'

There was a new spring in Alistair's step as he walked away from the Carnforths' residence. Lena was well on the way to a full recovery. He sensed she had almost thrown off the ill effects of losing her mother and father so tragically. He knew there could always be scars but hoped he would be able to erase them completely when her mourning period was over and then they could build a life together.

He had been close to proposing to her but had held back, deeming it inappropriate to do so while the period of mourning, as demanded by society, still hung over her. Time would pass. He could easily wait another two months in his certainty that the girl he had loved since schooldays would then become his wife. The thought brought a smile of joy to his face. To spend the rest of his life with Lena would be wondrous, and to have her by his side as a doctor's wife, able to devote her time to helping his endeavours to make Whitby a healthier and better place to live, would be the pinnacle of his dreams.

He knew she and James had always been closer to the mercantile life of Whitby than he and Olivia had. They had never been as adventurous as their friends, and Alistair realised he and his sister had probably inherited their gentler approach to life from their mother, whereas Lena and James seemed to have inherited a taste for risk-taking from Jennie and John. Be that as it may, he did not see it as a disadvantage in a doctor's wife. In fact, he thought it could be quite an asset, for Lena would surely have less abhorrence for what she might have to face than any other gently raised girl.

'Is work on your new ship progressing well?' asked Olivia as she and James left New Buildings one bright Sunday afternoon a week later.

'Very well,' he replied, a new light coming into his eyes at the mention of it. 'She should be ready early next year. Would you like to go and see her now?'

'I'd rather stroll on the West Cliff.'

He hid his disappointment and said, 'As you wish.' If he had put the question to Lena, he knew she would have jumped at the chance. The thought of his sister prompted him to say, 'I'm pleased Lena is looking so much better, thanks to Alistair, and of course to you.'

'It's all due to Alistair. He has watched over her recovery carefully.'

'That's as may be, but I think your frequent visits have also helped enormously – and from what Lena has told me, she believes you were instrumental in getting him to visit more frequently, as her doctor.'

Olivia gave a little shrug of her shoulders. 'He was getting so wrapped up in Whitby's welfare, he was failing to see Lena was not well and needed his advice.'

'We will always be grateful to you. You are a good friend to us both, but...' James stopped and, with his hand on her arm, turned her to him. 'Olivia, you are more than a friend to me.'

Her heart beat faster as James pulled her to him and kissed her gently on the lips. 'I'm in love with you. I think I always have been, ever since we were children.'

She smiled, looking deep into his eyes. 'I know I have been with you. You were always my hero. I loved to see you climbing around on the ships, and imagined you sailing into port and rescuing me from pirates.' She chuckled at the recollection. 'And now look at you, a handsome figure who still has that aura of adventure around him. A successful merchant with his own ships.'

'And one of my very own, not one I have inherited, to be launched next March. Maybe on that day I'll have something special to say to you.'

Her heart skipped a beat. 'What is that?' she asked breathlessly.

'Ah, you'll have to wait until then.'

The next day Lena sensed Olivia had something exciting to tell her. 'Out with it,' she prompted before her friend could sit down.

'James told me that the day the *John Carnforth* is launched, he will have a special announcement to make.'

'Did he say what?' asked Lena, matching Olivia's enthusiasm with her own.

She shook her head. 'No, but I think it might concern our future.'

'Olivia!' Lena hugged her friend. 'Are you thinking what I am thinking?'

'I think so – yes. But don't say anything, will you?'

'My lips are sealed.'

Lena knew the time for some decision-making of her own was imminent.

James kept his sister's enquiries satisfied, and she was careful not to criticise or suggest too much or become overly opinionated when he expounded some of his ideas. He was always forthcoming about the building of the *John Carnforth* and she was pleased he was pressing for completion to be made by the date in March he had set. The anniversary of the Tay tragedy would be past then and mourning clothes be cast aside. Lena would take a full part in the excitement of launching day.

Lena laid down her knife and fork at the breakfast table and said 'James.'

'Oh, from your tone of voice this is serious,' he remarked.

'It is,' she replied, but her lips twitched in amusement. 'I don't suppose we have any thought of paying our usual visit to Dundee this year?'

'It is the last thing I would want to do. I expect you feel the same?'

'I do. I could not bear it, so I'm thankful indeed that you have no thought of going. But I have been wondering about Aunt Mary and Uncle Martin and our cousins ... I wonder how they will feel.'

'I think the memories will be hardest for them then, with the usual Scottish celebrations going on around them – as I'm sure they will, with the town trying to forget what happened a year ago.'

'So should we ask them to come here for New Year, do you think? Not to make a special occasion of it but rather to give them a chance to escape the celebrations in Dundee.'

'Lena, that is a splendid idea. Will you write to them?'

'I will do it today.'

A week later a reply came from their aunt, expressing grateful thanks for their concern and consideration and accepting the invitation, adding that the MacBride family would arrive two days after Christmas.

'We had better inform Mr and Mrs Nash and Alistair and Olivia that the MacBrides are coming,' said James on hearing this news.

'I'll arrange for them to come to us for a quiet meal at New Year,' said Lena.

When she announced the arrangements to Mrs Campion, the housekeeper was delighted; with all the preparations and the visit itself, the minds of her young master and mistress would be constantly diverted from dwelling too much on the tragedy of a year ago. She promised she would see Lena was involved in all the decisions concerning the arrangements for the visit.

The following day Lena called on the Nashes and made her invitation.

'That is most kind of you, Pauline,' said Mrs Nash, accepting the offer. 'It will be very agreeable to see Dr and Mrs MacBride again. I am pleased they will be away from Dundee, too. Now, about Christmas ... you and James must come to us on all three days.'

'That is extremely kind of you, but we could not impose on you all that time.'

Georgina Nash brushed her comment aside. 'It will be our pleasure. We cannot leave you on your own at Christmas. Isn't that so, Olivia?' She turned to her daughter to reinforce her invitation.

'Of course you must come,' said Olivia emphatically. 'I will look forward to having you both, and I know Alistair feels the same.'

'There you are, my dear,' added Georgina. 'You cannot say no.'

Lena felt a lump rise in her throat. 'You are very kind. Thank you.'

Later that same day Alistair called on Lena. 'This is splendid news I hear,' he said after he had made his greetings. 'You are both going to be with us for three days at Christmas. I look forward to it.'

'So do I.' She smiled. 'And then to the MacBrides coming.'

'Good. I know there will be some sadness for you, but we'll all make it as pleasant a time as possible.'

Lena looked at him thoughtfully then. 'Just one thing, Alistair – you and Uncle Martin are *not* to talk doctoring. I'll warn him too when he arrives.'

Alistair smiled indulgently. 'Do you think you can stop him?'

'Oh, yes. I'll ban him from smoking cigars in my house if he mentions one word about sickness or disease!'

Alistair laughed. 'This will be good to see. I'll make sure I'm on hand when he throws an apoplectic fit!'

Two weeks into November James made a suggestion over breakfast. 'Lena,' he said, looking up from his bacon and egg, 'I am going to Hull next week and will be away four nights. Why not come with me? It will be a gentle easing back into society for you. No one in Hull will know you are still in mourning, so for those four days you could escape the weeds you are wearing. I know you have been longing to shed them.'

Lena met his gaze for a moment in disbelief, but when she saw the reassurance in his eyes she squealed with delight, sprang from her chair and rushed round the table to hug him.

'You're the most considerate of brothers!' she cried. 'Yes, yes, I'll come!'

'Very well.' He laughed at her exuberance. 'I'll send word and book rooms at the Cross Keys in the Market Place.'

'What is the purpose of the visit?' she asked as she resumed her seat.

'William Hustwick and Son is seeking a ship to transport timber from the Baltic as soon as it is ice-free next year.'

'About the time you launch the *John Carnforth?*'

'Yes. They have only one ship themselves and there is more timber than she can handle. I think it will be ideal for me to use the *John Carnforth* that way for her first voyage.'

'But wouldn't that mean she'd be sailing from Hull and manned by a Hull crew instead of Whitby men? I think Papa would have wanted her first crew to be from her home port.'

'A valid comment, dear sister,' replied James amiably. 'You have kept your mind sharp with your interest in the firm's affairs over the last few months. Father would be pleased by that.' Then he added as a gentle reminder, 'Though, of course, all decisions about the *John Carnforth* are mine to make.'

'The firm will always be important to me. After all, I was brought up with it.'

'I'm glad to hear that. Well, you can play your part in this visit to Hull. I intend to get this con-tract because I can see it leading to more trade with and through the Hustwicks, and maybe even to greater things.'

Lena interrupted him with a shrewd, 'And you want me to be charming when, as I suspect, you entertain Mr Hustwick and his son. I presume a son does indeed exist?'

'Oh, yes, he does. I made it my business to find out. The son is an only child – Peter. Same age as me. His mother died two years ago. His father was much older and so the son has become more involved in the firm lately, although he seems to lack much drive or ambition, being content to let things proceed as they are, bringing in steady returns but nothing spectacular.'

'Give me some idea of what this timber deal is about so that I can appear to be more than just a charming accessory?'

James explained what was involved and Lena's pertinent questions led him to comment, 'It's a good job Alistair has no interest in his father's firm. If he had, you and he would make formidable rivals, albeit friendly ones.'

Lena did not comment but said, 'I shall have to plan what to wear. Maybe I'd better buy something in Hull, and then the maids can't talk about what I have packed.'

'Good idea,' James approved.

The succeeding days were full of excitement for Lena. The outside world beckoned once again. A trip to Hull, then Christmas, New Year and the launch of the *John Carnforth!*

With a bitter chill in the wind, James was solicitous for his sister's comfort and warmth in the coach when they left for Hull. They made a stop in Scarborough to take luncheon, and on arrival at the Cross Keys in Hull were pleased to see a crackling fire in the lounge and in their respective rooms. After James had checked on his coachman's accommodation and was satisfied that the horse and vehicle were in good hands, he informed Lena that they would dine at six, and tomorrow morning would go shopping for her new dresses so that she could look her best when they entertained William Hustwick and his son Peter to dinner at six-thirty.

Lena spent a thoroughly enjoyable time choosing three dresses. She felt as if she had been let out of a cage. James was pleased to see the bright, sparkling Lena of old emerge from her cocoon of mourning, and felt that their mother and father would be smiling down with approval too.

He was in the hotel lounge at six, relaxed and awaiting the arrival of his guests. At quarter-past a page-boy appeared in the open doorway followed by two men. The boy spoke quietly to them while indicating the gentleman they were to meet. Seeing them approaching, James sprang to his feet. 'Mr Hustwick'?' he enquired with a broad smile.

'Aye,' replied the older man whose rotund figure indicated a liking for good food and drink. He stuck out a broad hand which held James's in a tight grip. 'And no doubt tha's James Carn-forth?'

'The very same, sir.'

William Hustwick snorted as he eyed James. 'Hmm ... thought you'd be much older. I want no dealings with young whippersnappers. I only deal with the top man.'

'I assure you, sir, I am the owner of Carnforth's. It came into my hands somewhat prematurely when my father was killed in the Tay Bridge disaster.'

'Aye, well, I'm sorry for your loss.' Feeling uncomfortable with this line of discussion, Hustwick added quickly, 'This is my son Peter. He's involved in my firm.'

James detected that Peter was embarrassed by his father's curt attitude towards him but quickly put him at his ease with a firm handshake and expressions of pleasure at their meeting. 'Shall we sit down, gentlemen? And can I order you something to drink?'

William lowered his bulk into an easy chair but Peter chose an upright one while James indicated to a waiter that they required service.

'A tankard of ale, thank you kindly,' said William.

'Make that two,' James informed the waiter, and then cast a questioning look at Peter.

'A glass of Madeira, please.'

James ordered two and then offered an explanation. 'One is for my sister Pauline who will be joining us in a few minutes.'

Mr Hustwick smiled. 'When you informed me you would be accompanied by your sister, I thought, Ah, Mr Carnforth is thinking he can soften us up with her feminine charm!'

James threw up his hands in mock horror. 'Nothing was further from my mind! My sister is just coming out of mourning and I thought this a

105

good opportunity for her to emerge into society once again.'

'Very thoughtful of you.'

The line of conversation was broken by the arrival of the drinks and was never taken up again because, as the waiter left, Pauline made her entrance.

James stifled the gasp that came to his lips. Lena looked so elegant and held herself with a poise that demanded attention. She made a slight pause in the doorway, knowing that it would concentrate everyone's attention on her. She smiled as she approached them, the only sound in the whole room the faintest rustle from her silk dress. The bodice was cut tight across the breast and emphasised her slim waist. Jet buttons adorned the front from a high collar fastened at the neck. The skirt, embroidered with a delicate leaf motif and edged with matching lace, flared slightly to the toes of her shoes.

'Gentlemen,' she said, smiling at them all although it was the younger Hustwick who commanded her attention.

William meanwhile had pushed himself to his feet. 'Miss Carnforth,' he greeted her. 'It is my pleasure to meet you.' He gave her a small bow.

'And mine to meet you, Mr Hustwick. I am sure we will spend a pleasant evening together.' She turned to Peter who, wide-eyed, had also sprung from his chair. When his father had told him Mr Carnforth would be accompanied by his sister, he had expected to have to make conversation with a plain female of indeterminate age. Instead he was facing this beautiful young

106

woman who exuded self-assurance. He felt embarrassed by his own thoughts.

'Mr Hustwick.' Lena picked up her glass of Madeira, raised it and said, 'To an enjoyable evening. Leading, I hope, to a business association of advantage to both our firms.'

The men picked up their drinks and raised them in answer to her toast. As they sat down Lena felt sure she had made a good impression on Peter Hustwick. If anyone had asked, she would have had to admit that he seemed likeable enough, if a bit subdued in the overbearing presence of his father. Judging from her first impressions of Mr Hustwick, even before they moved to the dining-room, she concluded he kept his son firmly under his thumb and that Peter had little autonomy in the running of the business, but at least he was involved in trading. He was handsome, too, and Lena concluded must have inherited his good looks from his mother. Maybe that was where he had gained his retiring personality too, but that was something that could be overcome, with determination, if he was so minded. Lena sensed his gaze upon her. The intensity of his blue eyes was only for her. This man was interested in her in a way she had never felt before, and yet she suspected he was not forthcoming enough to express it. He needed to be drawn out but whoever tried that would have to demolish the protective barrier cast around him. Was she up to the challenge?

As he escorted her into the dining-room she felt desire flash between them. Hers? His? On both sides? The moment was soon gone. They were

107

shown to their table and presented with menus. Little passed between any of them as they made their choices and James ordered the wine. When they were settled, Mr Hustwick cleared his throat and looked directly at James.

'Mr Carnforth, I suggest we don't spoil the evening by talking business. The excellent food and wine they serve here may addle our minds and we could both make decisions we would regret in the morning. I think we would be better discussing such matters tomorrow afternoon in my office. That will give us time to recover from what I know is going to be a splendid repast. I also suggest, on Peter's behalf because I know he won't, that he shows your charming sister something of Hull.'

Lena glanced at Peter then and saw his lips tighten with annoyance. Whether it was because he didn't want to escort her or because his father had taken charge and detailed him without any consideration for his son's feelings, she didn't know. She suspected it was the latter, or at least she hoped so.

'Very well, Mr Hustwick. If that is what you prefer,' said James.

'Indeed it is, young man. I always say, Never mix business with pleasure. And with such a charming young woman gracing us with her presence, how can we spoil that pleasure by talking business? You and I will deal with business affairs tomorrow.'

The evening settled down and was pleasant enough for Lena in spite of Mr Hustwick dominating the conversation as the wine loosened his tongue, not that he was objectionable but he obviously liked being the centre of attention. She was aware that Peter was embarrassed by this but he did nothing to try to change matters. It was not until they were leaving the dining-room that he managed to have a word with her on her own.

'I must apologise for my father monopolising the conversation.'

'Think nothing of it,' replied Lena. 'In fact, I found much of what he said fascinating. I know he kept away from the specifics he and James will discuss tomorrow, but he did reveal much about general trading conditions and prospects in Hull.'

Peter gave a small smile as if to say, I know you are being polite, but his actual words turned to themselves. 'If you don't wish to see Hull with me, I do understand. Father really shouldn't try to direct my whole life.'

Lena's smile matched the sincerity of her words. 'But I look forward to tomorrow.'

Later, as she lay in bed with her thoughts dwelling on the prospects ahead, she began to wonder if her attraction to Peter was formed by sympathy for him or if her interest ran deeper? How could it though? She hardly knew him.

As she turned over to make herself more comfortable she realised that Alistair had not entered her thoughts at all until this moment. She had been swept back into the world to which she had been born, and it had been a heady experience. Excitement coursed through her veins. Was it possible that she could persuade her brother to allow her greater participation in the firm? He could not deny that she had done well tonight. Would he allow her to contribute further, or did he wish her nothing more than the role of doctor's wife? One for which she had seriously begun to question her suitability.

Chapter Seven

As she came gracefully down the stairs, Lena was aware of Peter Hustwick's admiring gaze on her. Glad to have thrown off her mourning clothes, she had revelled in taking particular care of her appearance today. The silken sheen of her blue-lavender grosgrain dress shimmered in the light. It hugged her breasts and came tight to the waist before flaring, with only the tiniest of bustles, to meet the tips of her shoes. A small black bonnet, tied under her chin with a bold ribbon of yellow, allowed her hair to frame her face. Over her left arm she carried a fawn-coloured cape. She made each step sway provocatively while her eyes took in her effect on the man who awaited her.

She thought Peter looked every inch elegant in his fitted knee-length frockcoat. Its grey collar and six buttons were matched by his necktie, suede gloves and the top hat he carried in his left hand. His grey-striped trousers brushed the top of his highly polished black shoes. In his right hand he held a silver-topped cane.

Lena saw pleasure in his smile as he stepped towards her, dexterously switched his cane to his left hand and helped her from the bottom step.

'Miss Carnforth, may I say how radiant you look?' He gave her a small bow but his eyes never left hers.

Lena inclined her head in acceptance of his compliment. 'Thank you, Mr Hustwick, you are most kind.' They started towards the door. 'Now, what have you planned for today?'

'I am pleased to see that you have brought a cape. First I'm going to take you along the north bank of the Humber upstream from Hull; there are some fine prospects across the river to Lincolnshire. Then I have a surprise before we go on to dine at a hostelry where I know we'll be well looked after. This afternoon I'll show you something of our town then return you to your hotel before collecting you and your brother to dine with my father this evening.'

'It sounds as if you have planned this day carefully?'

'For such a charming young lady, of course.'

As they stepped out of the door Lena saw a chaise with its hood drawn up, attended by two urchins who spoke soothingly to the black mare standing between the shafts.

'Your carriage awaits you,' said Peter.

Lena swung her cape around her shoulders. Peter led her to the chaise and helped her on to the seat. He turned, tossed a coin to each of the boys and instructed them to hold the horse steady. He then climbed in beside Lena and laid a rug across her lap.

'Thank you,' she acknowledged the attention.

Peter called to the boys who unhitched the

mare from the rail. He took up the reins, flicked them and sent the horse forward. He guided her with unerring accuracy until the animal relaxed once they had moved into open country from which there were wide views across the Humber.

'You drive well, Mr Hustwick,' Lena commented.

Peter smiled. 'Thank you for the compliment. Father deemed it necessary so that I could drive him about, chiefly when matters of business demand it.'

'Does he not use the chaise for pleasure?'

Peter laughed dryly. 'That is hardly Father's sort of pleasure.'

'So what is?'

'His club, good food, good wine and the gaming tables. What he gets up to beyond that, I do not know.'

Lena surmised what that might mean but knew it would not be lady-like to pursue the subject further and asked instead, 'And you, what are your pleasures?'

'The countryside. I like using the chaise to explore and enjoy the banks of the Humber beyond our country residence.'

'You have another house out here?'

'Yes.' He tightened his lips and scowled. 'There, I've let it out. That was to be my surprise.' The exasperation in his voice was directed at himself.

'It will still be a surprise to me, Mr Hustwick.'

He smiled. 'You are too kind. Please forgive my bad manners.'

'No offence taken. So which is your principal residence?'

112

'Mother loved the country. So did Father until she died. Then it seemed he could not settle here so he moved into our town house. I live out here most of the time.'

'And go into Hull most days?'

'Yes, though sometimes I wonder if it is worth it. Father rules the business. He gives me little scope but to follow his ways.' Peter paused slightly, as if he was making a quick review of his life. 'I suppose I am fortunate enough. We are comfortably off.'

'You have no further ambition then?'

He shrugged his shoulders. 'As regards the business, why take on any more worry?'

'But surely there is more to you than that?'

'Outside of the firm, I enjoy myself in my own ways.'

'And what might they be?'

'I fence.'

'Any good?'

'Well, I like to think so. The main thing is, I enjoy it.'

'Then you must be good, because if you didn't enjoy it you wouldn't do it.'

'Ah, a thoughtful head on pretty shoulders. Now what about you, Miss Carnforth?'

'I don't think you have finished, Mr Hustwick.'

'There's not much more to tell. I ride. I like sailing on the Humber.'

'You have a boat?'

'An old coble I found derelict. I had a local joiner make her as good as new, and got two friends interested in sailing her. We have a landing just down from the house.'

'You had previous experience of sailing then?'

Peter laughed. 'None! Neither had my friends, but they knew a family of three fishermen who had sailed cobles all their lives and got them to show us how to handle the boat.'

'So you fish?'

Peter laughed even louder. 'Good heavens, no! We just sail her for pleasure. This coble's a three-man boat but two of us can handle her for what we want. We'll take you sometime, if you are interested?' The invitation was out before he realised it and so he added quickly, 'Oh, but that is hardly lady-like. I'm sorry, I...'

'Don't be, Mr Hustwick. I would love to take up your invitation some time.'

'You would?' Peter's eyes had lit up with delight and surprise.

'There's no reason why not. Oh, some people may frown, but they're old fuddy-duddies. I think women should have more choice in their lives and not be bound by conventions which really originate from you men wanting things all your own way.'

'Oh, you are quite the radical I see, Miss Carnforth.'

'I think we females should stick up for our rights and believe we could contribute much to your man's world.'

'Did your father bring you up to think like this?'

'I don't think he would have disapproved of what I have said. He did encourage me to show an interest in his business.'

'So you help your brother?'

'No, I am precluded from doing so by my father's Will, though it does stipulate that I am to be kept informed of its workings and progress. So, Mr Hustwick, I hope you will show me the commercial area of Hull this afternoon?'

'If that is your wish, I certainly will.'

'I look forward to it.'

Throughout this conversation the horse had been plodding steadily along. Now Peter pulled it to a halt on a flat expanse of turf beside the rutted path.

'I like the view from here,' he said, indicating the Lincolnshire scene beyond the water.

The sharpness of the air brought clarity to the view, while the sun and white clouds sent shadows chasing across the landscape and a changing light glinting on the water.

Lena looked at her companion, saw he was entranced and knew she should not disturb his absorption. She was most intrigued by the light in his eyes. Did they see far horizons, the haunts of adventure, or were these the eyes merely of a contented dreamer? But even as she wondered that, she felt a strange sensation of being drawn into his world. She did not resist but allowed her gaze to float back across the river. Time drifted away.

'Enchanting.' The whispered word startled her. She came to as if out of sleep and saw Peter's eyes, filled with admiration, fixed upon her.

Lena blushed and started. 'Yes, it is, Mr Hustwick,' she spluttered, staring at the view again to evade his attention.

'Look in a mirror and recall that word, Miss

115

Carnforth.' He flicked the reins and sent the horse on its way.

She did not reply as embarrassment and pleasure mingled with thoughts of what the future might hold. She stiffened then and dismissed such considerations. She had only met this man yesterday; she did not know him, and yet...

'Here we are.' Peter was turning the chaise between open iron gates, hanging from huge stone pillars, on to a grass swath cut through a small wood dense enough to hide what lay ahead. Silence descended. Only the gentle breeze sighed a song of welcome to the Hustwick Estate.

They emerged from the wood and Lena saw the broad path of grass, rutted by carriage wheels, sweep towards an unpretentious two-storey brick-built house, not grand, but big enough for its proportions to be impressive even from this aspect which she judged to be the back, for beyond it she could see the river. Whoever had built it had thoughtfully orientated the façade towards the water. A manicured lawn surrounded the house, and as they took the driveway to the front she saw the well-tended grass continued to roll expansively down to the river.

'What a beautiful position,' commented Lena. 'Did your parents choose the site?'

'No. My maternal grandparents did. They made their money sheep farming in Lincolnshire, built this place, never really settled here and moved back to Lincolnshire when I was four, giving this estate to my mother.'

'So you were brought up here.'

'Yes.' Peter drew the horse to a halt. As he

stepped to the ground a groom who must have seen them approaching hurried round the end of the house.

'Good day, sir.' He glanced at Lena and touched his forehead. 'Miss.'

He held the horse steady as Peter helped Lena from the chaise.

'A couple of hours, Tom.'

'Yes, sir.'

'Should I tell Mrs Nevill you are here, sir?'

'You can do that, but I suspect she'll have seen us from a back window,' Peter replied with a knowing twinkle in his eyes.

'I expect she will, sir,' replied Tom, with an answering smile.

'Mrs Nevill?' queried Lena as Tom led the horse away.

'Our cook-housekeeper. She looks after the place with the help of three upper maids and a kitchen maid. She is a wonder, was devoted to my mother. Tom is our only groom. The grounds and estate, which are not big by standards around here, are looked after by three men and a boy who live nearby.'

As he was speaking Lena had been casting her eyes over the front of the house. Its proportions were simple with two sash windows set to each side of a charming front door with a fanlight above, all emphasised by a small classical portico with a triangular architrave. Though it was not exceptionally wide, Lena realised from her observations as they approached the house that it was two rooms deep, and with an extension, no doubt housing the kitchen, dairy and scullery at ground

117

level on the east side, would be spacious inside. An opinion that was confirmed when Peter showed her round.

'Good day, sir,' a pleasant voice greeted him.

'Ah, Mrs Nevill,' said Peter.

Lena swung round to see a person of medium height in a plain black dress, with only an ivory brooch for decoration, approaching them from a door she had left slightly ajar at the back of the square entrance hall.

'Mrs Nevill, this is Miss Carnforth from Whitby. She is accompanying her brother who is negotiating some business here with my father.'

'A pleasure, miss. Welcome to Raby Hall.'

'Thank you, Mrs Nevill. I am delighted to be here and to meet you.' Lena knew she had just been assessed by a long-serving member of the household who was clearly wondering about her relationship with the young man she had long regarded as her charge.

'Chocolate, sir?'

'Thank you, Mrs Nevill.'

'Will you take it in the drawing-room?'

He nodded.

'Can I take your cloak, miss?'

'Thank you.' Lena slipped it from her shoulders and removed her bonnet.

As Mrs Nevill left the hall, Peter escorted Lena into the drawing-room.

She found herself in a pleasant, light, airy room, with just the right amount of furniture to keep its spacious proportions. Three of the walls were hung with paintings. A highly polished mahogany sideboard took pride of place while the only other furniture consisted of two arm-chairs and a sofa, all covered in a delicate chintz that matched the curtains and complemented the painted wallpaper.

'I suspect Mrs Nevill has kept the touches your mother brought to this room,' commented Lena.

'Indeed she has, and it is the same throughout the house.'

'Maybe that is why your father spends more time in your town house.'

'Maybe. Mother's death hit him hard and changed him, but he has continued in his own way.'

This was not a topic either of them wanted to pursue and they both felt relief when Lena diverted the subject with a question. 'Why is the house called Raby Hall?'

'Raby was the name of my mother's family.'

The maids arrived then with the chocolate.

They spent the rest of the morning pleasantly. Peter gave her a tour of the house, which Lena found charming in every aspect. When they had donned their outdoor clothes again they strolled down to the river where he pointed out the boatshed, positioned unobtrusively, where he kept the coble.

'I hope one day you'll accept my offer to take you sailing, Miss Carnforth,' he reminded her as they turned away from the water.

'I will keep it in mind, Mr Hustwick,' she replied, feeling thrilled at the possibility of venturing out on the water – something Alistair would never have suggested. She pulled her thoughts up sharp. She should not be making such comparisons.

Nevertheless when they reached the chaise, which Tom had brought to the front of the house, she glanced back wistfully in the direction of the Humber.

Peter drove to a nearby hostelry where he was known and immediately shown to a cosy private room where, bearing in mind that they were dining in Hull that evening, they chose a light luncheon.

'This has been most pleasant, Mr Hustwick. I hope you will now show me some of the mercantile elements of Hull,' Lena prompted him.

'Your wish is my command, Miss Carnforth.'

He set a brisk pace but after half a mile slowed and looked at her with apologetic concern. 'I'm sorry, Miss Carnforth, I should have considered your comfort and kept to a more leisurely pace.'

Lena threw her head back and let laughter fill the air. 'Mr Hustwick, don't apologise, it was delightful. I'd like more and more.'

'Then you shall have it, Miss Carnforth. As I said, your wish is my command.' He put the horse into a gallop, threw his hat down beside him and let his laughter join hers. Lena was swept away by his carefree attitude, flung her own bonnet down and let the cool wind sweep through her hair. Their eyes met, each revelling in the joy of sharing these exhilarating moments.

The beat of the horse's hooves reminded Lena that she was seeing a different person now from the one she had met the evening before. Here, Peter was free from his father's scrutiny. Was this the real Peter Hustwick or was it only a momentary illusion? Would he ever free himself from his father's dead hand? When the time came, could he make his own mark on the firm, create his own thriving concern?

Then she cast aside these thoughts to enjoy the ride. Peter Hustwick's future was no concern of hers.

After another two miles, with the outskirts of Hull in sight, he slowed the horse to a walking pace. He looked at her and smiled. 'Enjoy that?'

'Wonderful. It sent life coursing through me.'

'I suppose we had better behave with a little more decorum in Hull. Who knows who might see us?'

Lena picked up her bonnet, grinned and looked at him coyly as she said, 'Then I will be prim and proper.'

He chuckled and watched her adjust her hair and tie her bonnet. 'Now for your tour of Hull, or at least the parts that are suitable for you to see.'

'I hope that includes the business section and the dock area?'

'Indeed! Well, most of it. There are parts I would not take a lady.'

'You sound as though you know them,' she said, with a twinkle in her eyes. In a short space of time this man was beginning to intrigue her.

He chuckled. 'Not intimately, only by reputation.'

'I think it is the same in every port. I hear about them in Whitby too. I imagine you have seen many changes in Hull.'

'Most certainly. The old town developed where the River Hull flows into the Humber, an excellent position for a port. It was small, cramped, enclosed by stone walls, and it was not until these were knocked down that real expansion took place. Three main docks were built; more and more people moved in from the country seeking work. Houses were built in a similar pattern to those in the old town to accommodate these people, while the better-off built houses befitting their status in new areas within the town or else moved into the countryside.'

'Or did both, as your father has done?'

'Thank goodness he did! It provides me with an escape.'

From him or from Hull? The question sprang to Lena's mind but before she could voice it she realised she would be overstepping the boundaries of decorum. After all, she should not probe into family matters. She should not invade Peter's privacy.

'Do you not like the work of a merchant and ship-owner?'

'I like it well enough but I'm content with the way things are. It brings us a more than comfortable living, so why change things? Why risk undermining what we have? There's always a chance that new enterprises could go wrong.'

'But your father...?'

'He runs the business and will have his way. It's easier to go along with him than try to oppose him. All I can do is to keep an eye on what is happening and make sure our established contacts remain steady.'

'Not easy for you.'

'It isn't, but so far I have managed to tread the right line and hope my father does nothing to the detriment of the business overall. But enough of my worries, you are here for a pleasant time.'

They had reached the first houses and Lena, knowing it was wisest not to probe any further into Peter's private life, contented herself with gaining knowledge of the busy port.

Pointing out interesting buildings on the way, he drove her to Nelson Street where he drew the horse to a halt beside the wide pavement. 'Shall we take a stroll?'

'That would be pleasant,' Lena agreed, and accepted his hand to help her alight from the chaise.

'Yonder is the Victoria Pier. See, the ferry is coming in from New Holland on the Lincolnshire side of the Humber.'

They watched it dock amidst hustle and bustle, then strolled past the cab-stand where carriages for hire awaited passengers disembarking from the ferry, the coachmen hoping to be hired in preference to the horse-drawn tram that was also waiting nearby.

'I'll make a circular tour of the docks before returning you to your hotel,' Peter said as he helped her back on to the chaise.

'The hub of Hull's trade.'

'True, but they need the nearby offices where all the transactions are carried out otherwise business would die and the docks be useless.' He drove along Wellington Street across the lockpit between the Humber Dock and the dock basin then turned into Railway Street from which Lena could see several trading vessels at the quays in the Humber Dock.

'You'll see this dock is linked to the next one, Prince's Dock, which in turn is linked to Queen's Dock, so vessels can sail through the docks from the Humber to the River Hull,' Peter explained.

'And trade can flow more readily,' commented Lena.

'Most certainly, Miss Carnforth. The men who built it had an eye to the trade that could be attracted to Hull, with its easy access to the Humber and closeness to the Continent.'

Lena stored this away in her mind, realising Hull's future potential was greater than that of Whitby.

All three docks and the River Hull buzzed with activity. Ships were being laden with goods for all parts of the world while others were being relieved of their cargoes. From the end of Humber Dock Street, she saw horse-drawn vehicles being loaded with barrels.

'Those rullies look to have a consignment of sugar being stacked on them,' Peter pointed out.

'Rullies?' she asked.

'Yes, that's what the flat wagons on the railway lines are called.'

The lines passed close to covered open-sided sheds lining the quay where stevedores were rolling barrels to other waiting rullies.

Lena became fascinated by the scene of activity as labourers strained under the heavy goods they were moving. The air was filled with shouts as overseers urged them on, and owners and merchants sought the latest information on the trade they were pursuing.

She had no doubt that such trading went on

behind the closed doors of many of the buildings they passed, while the warehouses were stacked with the goods they were trying to buy and sell. She had been, and still was, fascinated by the quays and trade that made Whitby such an important port, but here the facilities she saw presaged a much greater opportunity to move ahead in the mercantile world. Lena realised her father would have been fascinated and wished he could have been by her side now to see it all. She felt an urge to do something about it, for his sake.

As he drove along Prince's Dock Street, Peter pointed out St John's Church, the Wilberforce Monument, the Dock Offices and Monument Bridge that spanned the lockpit between Prince's Dock and Queen's Dock, the longest of the three docks. Vessels with captains eager to be about their business, for time meant money, manoeuvred in all of them. From their vantage point Peter indicated the warehouses lining the sides of the River Hull, and these convinced Lena even more of the potential of this thriving port.

'Holy Trinity Church,' he informed her when she admired its architecture. 'The largest parish church in area in England. The statue in the middle of the road is King William III, known around here as King Billy.' So his tour went on, informative but never boring, angled to keep her interest, not that he needed to work hard at that because she found she wanted to know as much about Hull and its commercial life as possible.

Finally Peter drew the chaise to a halt outside her hotel. 'Here we are, Miss Carnforth.'

Lena turned to him with a smile. 'Mr Hustwick,

I am so grateful to you for such an enjoyable day.'

'It has been my privilege, Miss Carnforth. It has truly been a delight to escort you and show you so many aspects of Hull. I look forward to the evening ahead.'

'So do I, Mr Hustwick.'

'I will call for you and your brother at six.'

'We are not dining here then?' asked Lena, with a hint of surprise crossing her face.

'Oh, no, Father has arranged for us to meet him at his rather exclusive club.'

'And what might that be?'

Peter smiled. 'Ah, you must wait and see.' He jumped down from the chaise and came to help her to the ground.

'Now I'll be playing a guessing game with myself until you reveal our destination.'

He led her into the hotel where Lena thanked him again.

'Until later.' He bowed and was gone.

Many thoughts raced through her mind as she went upstairs to her room without calling on James. Whitby, Hull, Alistair, Peter ... so much potential, so many possibilities. Were new horizons beckoning her? Should she allow them to do so and find herself in a world she longed for, or should she resist and join a world of tea and lace overlaid with illness and poverty?

Chapter Eight

James, examining his cravat in the mirror, adjusted it to his liking, straightened up and grabbed his jacket. He was sure he had heard Lena's door close. He strode briskly along the corridor, tapped lightly on her door and, on hearing her call, entered the room.

'How did you get on with Peter?' he asked, going to the chair near the window.

The urgency in his tone betrayed that his interest lay in what she might have learned about the Hustwick business rather than in what sort of a day she had passed.

'We had a very pleasant time. He took me along the banks of the Humber to their country house...'

'Oh, they have a country house too?' James interrupted, surprised.

'Yes. Not grand but big enough – in a beautiful setting with the grounds running down to the Humber. Then we had luncheon at a favourite place of Peter's before returning to Hull where he showed me round the town.' Lena sat down on the stool in front of the dressing-table.

'And?' prompted James when she stopped talking.

'He showed me the three docks. There is great potential in trading from Hull. If you seal a deal with Mr Hustwick, it could give you a valuable foothold in this port.'

'Interesting to hear you say that,' mused James. 'Mr Hustwick hinted that, if the timber deal is handled to his satisfaction, there is every possibility he will hire our vessels frequently.'

'Good,' replied Lena. She could tell he was being guarded in what he told her. 'You got on well with Mr Hustwick then?'

'Oh, yes, I played him like a fish without its being obvious. He is not too interested in expansion but content to keep the firm running as it is, showing a profit that keeps him comfortably off.'

'I gathered the same from Peter.'

'Doesn't he have any ambitions of his own?'

'I think his father's attitude has rather brushed off on him. He's charming, considerate and...'

'Handsome?' prompted James as Lena let her voice trail away.

'Oh, yes, certainly,' she replied without giving away anything about her own feelings. 'He has little say in the running of the firm but I believe he knows more about it than he lets on. However, he won't go against his father's wishes.'

'But some day the firm will be his. I wonder what he will do then?'

Lena shrugged her shoulders. 'I don't know. He didn't say.'

'Not even a hint?'

'No. Now off with you! I want to get changed.'

James stood up and headed for the door but stopped halfway across the room. 'Lena, I'm going to invite them both to the launching. After all they have an interest as the *John Carnforth* will be carrying their timber. So back up my suggestion if necessary.'

'If they accept, as I have no doubt they will, I can regard the offer made to me by Peter as a return for your invitation.'

James looked curious. 'What's this?'

'Peter and two friends renovated an old coble and use it for pleasure to sail on the Humber. He suggested I might like to sail with him.' Lena left a slight pause then said, 'Not very lady-like, I know.'

'Whenever did you miss the opportunity to cock a snook at convention?' Her brother grinned. 'Why not accept? It could help cement our trading relationship with the Hustwicks.'

'You think I should?'

'Why not? There's no harm in it,' James called over his shoulder, and was gone.

Lena sat for moment, smiling at her own thoughts. Harm? No harm at all unless…

She drove the thought away, but then the vision of a handsome considerate man, who would one day inherit a mercantile company with great potential, came back to mind. She sat still for a few minutes, her thoughts moving in flights of fancy until one sobering one halted them in their tracks. Alistair!

'Thank you, Olivia, for coming with me to see Old Peg Peart. I know she appreciated your presence when I examined her,' Alistair said as they made their way out of Harpooner's Yard into Church Street.

'I read your notes saying that the case was hopeless.'

'I'm afraid it is, but I saw no sense in telling her that.'

'Has she no family? No one to look after her during her last days?'

'No. Maggie Morton next-door looks in, but she has her hands full with six kids in a house no bigger than Peg's.'

'What?' Olivia gasped.

'And those houses are better than many in the town. How folk exist in them, I don't know. I wish I could do more to persuade the authorities that conditions on the east side need bettering – fast. Peg has been lucky in a way, she's had a long life, but there are many hereabouts who won't live half her years.'

Olivia heard the distress in his voice and placed her hand on his arm. 'You can only do so much. I admired the way you were with Peg, she quickly trusted you.'

Alistair gave a little smile. 'I think it was the soup you brought her.'

'I'll bring her some more tomorrow, if you think it helps.'

'I'm sure it will comfort her.'

'Alistair, I'll do what I can to help, you only have to ask.'

He blessed his good fortune in having such an understanding and generous sister. 'I could not presume on your time.'

'You can. Well, until...' Olivia left her statement hang in the air but Alistair saw a light in her eyes that prompted him to grab her arm and propel her out of the throng of people near the bridge. He searched her face for an answer to the query that had instantly risen in his mind.

'James? Has he...?'

Her laugh rang out 'No, not yet, but he certainly hinted.'

'What do you mean?'

'There might soon be more to celebrate than the launching of the *John Carnforth!*'

'And you believe he meant a betrothal?'

'Well, how else would you interpret it?'

'Just like you.' Alistair's eyes shone with delight. 'I can think of no better match for you.'

'Unless it be you and Lena?'

He laughed. 'That's a nice way of putting it.'

'Then ask her.'

'I can't while she's in mourning. Then I would like her to ease her way back into society before we move on. Besides, I don't want to take away any of the excitement for you and James.'

'You are a very considerate man.' Olivia glanced around. 'I think we had better move on. People are looking at us, standing here in earnest conversation.' They resumed their walk. 'Oh, Alistair, not a word. James hasn't proposed yet.'

He put a finger to his lips and said, 'Sealed.'

Lena cast aside her thoughts of Alistair to concentrate on choosing a dress for the evening. After taking particular care over it and finding herself doing the same with her toilette, she wondered why and for whom? To make an impression on Mr Hustwick, for James's sake? To lighten what could degenerate into a dour, uneasy male-centred evening? Or was it to impress Peter who she now believed had more to him than had appeared on first meeting?

Satisfied with her appearance when she surveyed herself in the mirror, Lena picked up her cloak and was about to make for the door when there was a knock upon it. Opening it, she found James outside, top hat in hand.

'Are you ready?' he asked.

Lena spun around to show herself off. 'What do you think?' she asked with a smile.

'Perfect,' he said. 'You'll be the talk of everyone.'

'It's good to get out of those drab mourning clothes,' she said as she linked arms with him, wanting his assistance down the stairs.

'Then why go back to them?'

Surprised by his attitude, she stopped and looked him in the eye. 'You think it will be all right if I don't?'

'Why not? The end of the recognised mourning period is not five weeks away.'

'But what about folk in Whitby?'

'Do you really care at this stage?'

'No,' Lena replied lightly. 'Not at all.'

'Then that is settled.'

They fell into step and kept their pace steady as they went downstairs. Lena squeezed his arm in appreciation of his support of an end to her mourning. James read not only thanks but also sensed the joy in her whole bearing and aura. Lena would impress tonight and he was pleased about that; it would help in his dealings with Mr Hustwick, and who knew what might come of them?

With the pall of conventional mourning gone

from her mind, Lena felt she could give her full attention to Peter and what the future might hold. Tonight could bring her a greater insight into the Hustwick family and their mercantile business.

She knew they had caught the eye of several people in the hall but was disappointed not to find Peter among them. Barely had the thought entered her mind when, as if on cue, the door opened and he walked in, his step brisk as if he were trying to make up time. He caught sight of them both and stopped. His eyes fixed on Lena and did not move until she and James reached the bottom step. That final movement seemed to break the spell and brought him forward to greet them.

'Sorry not to have been waiting for you,' he apologised. 'I was held up.'

'Think nothing of it, Mr Hustwick.' James spoke for them both.

Peter bowed to Lena. 'May I say how exquisite you look, Miss Carnforth?'

She inclined her head in acknowledgement of his observation. 'Thank you, Mr Hustwick.'

'Now, the carriage awaits you. May I help you with your cloak, Miss Carnforth? There is a nip in the air.' Peter took the garment from her and slipped it on to her shoulders.

'Thank you.' Both men watched Lena's nimble fingers fasten the clasp. Satisfied, she looked at them both with a smile and said, 'Ready.'

Peter escorted them to the carriage where a coachman sat waiting. When the three of them were seated comfortably, Peter called to him,

'You know where, Giles?'

'Indeed I do. Your father's club, sir.' He flicked the reins and the carriage rumbled forward, only gaining greater momentum when Giles deemed it wise to do so.

Lena felt very happy to be sitting between two young gentlemen. One was her staunch ally whose consideration and brotherly love she found uplifting, giving her confidence to face whatever the future held; the other was handsome if practically unknown to her, yet he held an attraction she found enticing even though he had observed the utmost decorum. He was also heir to the sort of mercantile company of which she had always hoped to be a part. Amidst the chatter she wondered about her future, seeing two such differing lives ahead. Did she really have a choice between them? Had a new world opened to her through this unexpected visit to Hull or would her time here show her that her destiny truly lay in Whitby?

To distract her mind from these disturbing thoughts, she put a question to Peter. 'Mr Hustwick, I think you said you are also a member of this club we are going to?'

'Yes, but I don't use it as frequently as my father, even though Stockley House is in the centre of town. It is very useful for entertaining clients, though.'

'Like now?' said James, amusement in his voice.

'You could say that, but this occasion is graced by a beautiful young lady.'

'And no such person has graced previous visits?' asked Lena.

Peter laughed. 'You are fishing, Miss Carnforth. Well, I'll be truthful, yes, I have brought young ladies here, generally friends of the family.'

'That sounds as though none of them was special to you?'

'Though I'll bet it was not for want of trying by some of them,' commented James jocularly.

'I suppose so, but there's been no one with whom I could have spent the rest of my life. Maybe it is my fault. Maybe I'm too particular about finding the right person. But what about you, Mr Carnforth? Does someone hold your future in her hand?'

'Yes,' put in Lena quickly before her brother could answer. 'Olivia Nash. And I think my brother will be proposing before too long.'

'Then let me be the first to congratulate you, Mr Carnforth.'

'Thank you, but I have not put the question yet. I have known Olivia since childhood.'

'And has she a brother?' asked Peter.

'She has. Alistair,' put in James. 'He's been sweet on my sister since schooldays.'

Peter knew it would not be right to follow up on that information now. Maybe he could glean more about the relationship later. 'They are from Whitby too?' he asked.

'Yes,' Lena answered.

'Then I expect he is in the same trade as your brother.'

'He could be, he is an only son and his father has a thriving business, but Alistair showed no interest in it.'

'So what does he do?'

'He's a doctor.'

Before any more information could be imparted the carriage began to slow. 'We must be there,' said Peter.

When the vehicle came to a halt he was quickly out to help Lena to the ground. As he did so he whispered close to her ear, 'Did I detect a certain dislike of the profession this Alistair is following?'

Lena was startled. She had not realised her attitude could be read so easily. A sharp retort sprang to her lips, but at that moment James was out of the coach and beside them so she held back. It would have to wait until later.

'Welcome to Stockley House.' Peter's soft voice cut through her seething thoughts.

'It certainly has an imposing exterior,' commented James, eyeing the two-storey building with a critical gaze. The front had four large bays separated by ornamental columns adorned with hanging lanterns, their lights reflecting in the tall sash windows.

They entered through an imposing oak door and were immediately attended by two footmen who greeted them and took their outdoor coats.

'Mr Hustwick, your father told us to direct you to the lounge. He'll be there.' The footman indicated double doors to the right.

Lena glanced around admiringly at the large hall, sparsely but elegantly furnished, from which a wide staircase with a delicate iron banister swept to the upper floor in a graceful curve. They entered the lounge and her admiration mounted when she saw the ornate Palladian-style plaster ceiling. Heavy patterned curtains covered the windows, exuding an atmosphere of warmth in spite of the size of the room.

William Hustwick, who had placed himself conveniently to be able to see the door, pushed himself up from his chair and came towards them. 'Miss Carnforth, a delight to have you here.' He bowed and took her proffered hand.

'Thank you, Mr Hustwick. And may I also thank you for your hospitality?'

He waved away her thanks as if embarrassed then turned and greeted James. 'Good to see you again, my boy. A profitable day for us both, I hope.'

'I see no reason why it shouldn't be, sir.'

Hustwick gave a brief satisfied nod. 'Wine, Peter, wine,' he blustered. 'Sit down, my dear.' He indicated a chair to Lena. As he escorted her to it, he said, 'Then an old man can get the weight off his feet.'

'Mr Hustwick, you are far from old,' Lena said with a smile. She looked up at him as she sat down. 'I'm sure you have many years in you yet.'

He puffed and blustered, flattered by the praise. 'The medicine man ... that's what I call him ... keeps telling me not to eat and drink so much, but what the...'

'If you enjoy them, why not?' Lena knew she was saying the right thing and had it confirmed when William agreed.

'You sound like a young lady after my own heart. There's precious little else. Well, pleasant female company and my business, but beyond that...' He glanced at James who was taking a seat alongside. 'What do you think, Mr Carnforth?'

137

'If you have what you want, why not? You must have worked hard all your life.' He glanced at his sister. 'Mr Hustwick told me he built his business from nothing, has got where he wants and is encouraging Peter to keep it that way.'

'You wouldn't want your son to expand your trade then?' asked Lena.

'Why give himself all that worry? The firm is built on a solid foundation, and to carry on as we are won't jeopardise that. Expansion would need more investment and could well undermine the foundations.'

'I suppose there is something in what you say,' she agreed.

Peter had ordered wine from a waiter. On his way to rejoin his own group, he had paused to have a word with two friends whom Lena saw casting glances in her direction.

When their wine came, Mr Hustwick raised his glass and glanced at James and Lena. 'It is a pleasure to have met you both. To the future!'

'The future,' they said in unison.

Lena wondered where life would take her, but wasn't that up to her? Such speculation was quickly dismissed as she was brought back into the conversation.

Lena was struck by the elegance of the dining-room which outshone that of the lounge. Pristine white linen tablecloths covered the twenty round tables spaced so that the conversations at one did not intrude on others. Silver cutlery shone beside shimmering glasses.

The waiters were ever attentive throughout the meal. The food was superb, every course cooked and presented to perfection.

'You are lucky to have such a place as this so near,' commented James towards the end of the meal, during which their conversation had touched on many topics.

'Indeed we are,' agreed Mr Hustwick. 'Two enterprising young men built on their experiences after working in London. I would say they have taken all the good points of London restaurants and tea-houses and brought them here after seeing a lively market among Hull's growing business class. This is a town with a great future and those two young men realised it.'

'I cannot offer you a place as sumptuous as this,' said James, 'when I make you an invitation as I am about to do, but we will do our best to wine and dine you well. My new ship the *John Carnforth* will be launched in March next year as you know. This is the ship that will transport your timber on her maiden voyage. I hope you and Peter will attend the launching ceremony and be our guests for four days.'

'That is very civil of you, Mr Carnforth,' commented William, blowing out his cheeks with satisfaction as he leaned back in his chair. 'What say you, Peter?'

Lena, who had caught a quick glance from him as her brother made the invitation, already knew what Peter's answer would be.

'Very civil indeed. It's rather exciting, too, knowing the ship's first cargo will be ours.' He picked up his glass and said, 'To a successful launching, maiden voyage, and a happy association between our two firms.'

Arrangements were made for the visit and the evening settled into conviviality until William leaned forward, an action that seemed to emphasise his bulk. 'I think, Peter, it is time to introduce our friends to the other delight of Stockley House.' The knowing glance he shot his son was not lost on Lena whose sharp eyes took in Peter's reaction, which she felt sure was tinged momentarily by annoyance. His father did not wait for an answer but was already pushing himself to his feet.

'After such a meal, what other pleasure could there be?' asked James.

'Follow me and you shall see.' William started for the door a little unsteadily. Peter stepped quickly beside him but his support was not necessary; William straightened and moved on with a determined step. He led the way across the hall and started up the stairs, James beside him. Two steps behind, Peter offered Lena his arm which she gratefully took.

'I'm sorry about this,' he whispered, his brow creasing into a frown.

Curious, she asked, 'What is there to be sorry about?'

'It depends how you look at it.'

'You make it sound even more intriguing.' He gave a slight shrug of his shoulders. 'I gather you don't approve?' she added.

'It might spoil your evening and I would not want that.'

'Then, for your sake, I'll see that it doesn't.' She squeezed his arm to reassure him.

When they reached the top of the stairs, Lena

stopped to look back in admiration at the graceful sweeping symmetry of the staircase. 'That is a
wonderful design,' she commented. 'One day I
would like a staircase just like this. How wonderful to walk down it each day.'

'And it would be just as wonderful to watch you
doing so.' The words were out almost before
Peter realised, and his face reddened.

Lena saw the apologies springing to his lips and
preempted them. 'I am flattered that you think
so, Mr Hustwick,' she said quickly, to show she
took no offence, and then added, equally quickly,
'Your father is waiting.'

William and James had stopped in front of a
large four-panelled oak door, each panel carved
with oak leaves. When Lena and Peter joined
them William opened the door and led them into
a small vestibule from which another equally
ornate door was opened by a footman without
preamble. Lena judged that, wherever they were
going, Mr Hustwick was known there.

As the door opened a buzz of low conversation
reached them.

'Welcome to your fortune,' said William with
some satisfaction, as if he were guaranteeing
them immeasurable wealth. They stepped into a
room the like of which neither Lena nor James
had seen before. Several tables of differing sizes
were spread around it and occupied by people
while others stood around watching; some of
them Lena recognised as diners she had seen
earlier in the evening. From a bar discreetly situated at one end of the room, waiters circulated
serving all manner of drinks.

Seeing the surprised and curious expressions on his guests' faces, William gave them a moment to absorb what they were seeing and then said quietly to his son, 'You look after Miss Carnforth, I'll look after James.'

Peter nodded. Taking Lena gently by the elbow, he led her to two vacant chairs among several lining the walls.

'A gaming room,' he said quietly when they were seated. 'You can play any number of gambling games here.'

'I've heard of such places but never thought I would find myself in one. What I thought was exclusively for men, I see is not.' Lena had noted that there were almost as many females at the tables as there were men.

'And of all ages, from twenty upwards.'

'Twenty?'

'The owners set that age limit on who should be allowed into this room. Gaming houses have bad reputations for many reasons; some are suspected of cheating the gamblers, but that does not occur here. That is why it is so popular.'

Lena nodded. She was beginning to feel a buzz of excitement from the charged atmosphere generated by people who believed they could walk away with a fortune. 'It's exciting,' she commented, her eyes brightening, 'but I surmise you are not too pleased by your father bringing us here.'

Peter grimaced. 'Well, I didn't want to see you drawn into what could prove to be misfortune. But Father is Father. When I objected, he dismissed my scruples out of hand.'

'I'm glad he did,' replied Lena firmly. 'I see he has already got James seated at a table.' She started to rise from her seat. 'Come on, show me what to do.' Peter hesitated. 'You said my wish was your command?'

His lips twitched into a reluctant smile. 'You have a good memory.'

'For things that might be useful to me or pleasant in their associations.'

'I hope such things will always fill your mind, Miss Carnforth.'

'Miss Carnforth?' Lena's voice carried a note of irritation. 'We are here to enjoy ourselves, and I think we will do that better if we are less formal.'

He hesitated a fraction. 'As you wish.'

'My command.' Lena's eyes twinkled teasingly. 'Now, Peter, introduce me to gambling.'

'You need some tokens. Wait here.' He was back in a few moments and explained the value of the marked discs, then he took her on a slow tour of the tables giving her a brief explanation as they watched people playing faro, blackjack and grand hazard, finally finishing up at the roulette table watching James.

'He's about even at the moment,' William whispered. 'Are you going to play, Miss Carnforth?'

'Yes.' Lena's excitement and desire to play could not be denied.

James heard her and said, 'You can have my place. I want to try something else.' He waited for the last spin of the wheel and then stood up, regretting that he had not won that time.

Lena slipped into his place and her brother leaned forward to whisper instructions as to what to do. She quickly absorbed the simplicity of the game but was downcast that neither of her first two choices won, but then her third did and Lena felt a surge of excitement. Maybe she could do it again!

She placed her bet. The wheel spun. The ball bounced. The wheel slowed, slowed, slowed. Stopped. The ball carried by the momentum moved on, then seemed to hesitate ... go into the next hole or drop back? Lena stared wide-eyed. Her number! She willed the sphere to drop forward. Tension gripped her. The ball tumbled and settled.

'Mine!' She let out a cry filled with excitement. Her face was wreathed in a broad smile and there was laughter in her eyes as she looked round at Peter.

He laughed at her joy and she clapped her hands.

'Another!'

'Right. Place your bet.'

Lena hesitated thoughtfully for a brief moment and then risked all her winnings on number nine.

She tensed as the wheel slowed. It stopped. The ball settled.

'Mine again,' she cried, shaking with excitement. She looked up at Peter. 'This is wonderful!'

He laughed with her but put a restraining hand on her shoulder and warned, 'I think we had better move on while you are winning.'

'No! I'm feeling lucky,' she protested, in such a way that he knew it would be ill-mannered to refuse his guest.

She did, however, heed his advice not to bet her winnings each time. She soon learned the wisdom of that, but by the time Mr Hustwick and James came back to the table a crowd had gathered round. Word had spread that a lady at the roulette table was on a winning streak. Lena, absorbed as she was by the numbers, was oblivious to the onlookers. Peter realised this, he had seen a winning streak before, and signalled to his father and James not to break her concentration. Had she a way with numbers or was this beginner's luck? Whatever, he was pleased she was enjoying herself, while not in the least tempted to put his own money on the numbers she was choosing.

Another ten minutes went in Lena's favour but then she failed, twice in a row. It jolted her out of her trance-like state. She gasped when she saw so many people had been watching. 'I think I'll finish,' she told Peter.

'A wise decision.' he smiled and took charge. After a brief word with his father he left her chattering excitedly to James and William while he went to collect her winnings.

'I'm having a wonderful time,' Lena said joyously. 'Thank you for bringing us here.'

He beamed. 'My pleasure, Miss Carnforth. I'm so pleased you won. But ... a word of caution, my dear. Never think you can go on and do better. It is a wise person who knows when to stop. And never chase your losses. Retire gracefully and come back another time when your luck may have changed for the better.'

'I will bear that in mind, if ever I come back.'

'I hope you will, my dear. You have brightened our lives here. I think your brother and I will do more business in the future.'

'Where is James?'

'He has just stepped over to the table. I think he hopes for your luck.'

Lena smiled when she saw that James had indeed slipped away from them and taken a vacant seat at the roulette table.

Peter returned and with quiet ceremony presented her with her winnings. They watched James having moderate success for a little while, and then she and Peter wandered around the room observing other games. But Lena, remembering William Hustwick's advice, did not take part in any of them, merely storing in mind how they were played and secretly making a vow to return one day, before too long.

Chapter Nine

Lena settled back in the carriage with her brother, under the watchful eye of Peter.

'Have a safe journey,' he said. 'I look forward to seeing you both again in Whitby.' On the word 'both', his eyes lingered on Lena, implying that his forthcoming meeting with her was the more important.

Her enchanting smile in return left him in no doubt that she looked forward to seeing him again also.

'And to new business,' Peter added as his gaze returned to James. 'When we reached home last night, Father said he felt sure we could both profit from our collaboration.'

'I'm sure of it too,' returned James. 'Until we meet in Whitby, take care. And good wishes to your father.'

Peter nodded and stepped back. The coachman closed the door, took his seat, gathered the reins and then sent the horse forward.

'Goodbye!' Peter held his hat high.

Lena leaned from the coach for a last glimpse of the admiration she saw in Peter's eyes. Then she sank back in her seat with a contented sigh.

'You enjoyed your visit?' queried her brother as she settled herself more comfortably.

'Very much. And I'm so pleased to be out of those dowdy clothes.'

'Was that the highlight?' asked James, with fake disappointment, but Lena saw the teasing behind it.

'You know it wasn't,' she contradicted.

'Well, what was?' he pressed.

'So many new experiences in so short a time ... it's difficult to say, but coming to Hull made me realise that there are many more worlds besides those I know in Whitby. We've hardly been away from it after all.'

'Scotland, to Uncle Martin and Aunt Mary?' he reminded her.

'Oh, I know, but that was just like home. Coming here was entirely different. Living among strangers, seeing the way they live, gaining a new perspective on life.'

'And success on the gaming tables,' he chuckled.

'That as well,' laughed Lena, recalling the previous evening. 'But what about you, did you find it profitable?' She was eager for his answer, wondering if he would impart any more than he usually did when talking about the firm's commitments and prospects.

'I got a good price for hiring the *John Carn-forth*.'

'Father would be pleased. And the promise of more voyages?' she prompted.

'That is a possibility, if I fulfil this first assignment successfully and without delay.'

The use of 'I' irritated her. It was as if he was putting up a barrier, keeping her at bay where the business was concerned, allowing her only the barest knowledge of it. Lena wanted greater participation but knew she was unlikely to get it. As close as she and James were, she had seen a slight change in his attitude to her since the reading of the Will and knew he jealously guarded his position.

'I'm sure you'll do that successfully, then maybe Mr Hustwick will need to hire the ship again or even go into a more profitable business deal.'

'Maybe,' was all her brother said. She knew from his tone that she would get no further information, but felt sure in her mind that James and Mr Hustwick had discussed more than merely the hiring of the ship. If there had not been other deals in the offing, why cultivate the Hustwicks by inviting them to the launching of the *John Carnforth?*

'Lena!'

Recognising Olivia's voice as she alighted from the carriage outside the house in New Buildings, where sunshine seemed to bless the return of the Carnforths, Lena saw her friend hurrying to greet her.

'I was just on my way to the shops, but that can wait,' said Olivia. 'Welcome home, James.'

He read more than polite warmth in her kiss of greeting.

'Thank you, Olivia. It is good to be back.'

Lena held out her arms and hugged her friend, aware that Olivia had cast a curious glance over her clothes, her eyes neither disapproving nor approving.

'I could hardly wear mourning in Hull, it would have dampened the social aspect of James's visit,' said Lena by way of explanation as she took her friend's arm and turned to the gate. 'Besides, nobody in Hull would know, and what is the point in going back into them when it is so near the end of the approved period?'

'Quite right,' Olivia had to agree.

'Come and take a cup of tea with us – I'm dying for one – then I'll take a stroll with you. It will be good for me after sitting in that carriage.'

'Very well,' replied Olivia

'How is Alistair?' asked Lena.

'In good health I think. I hardly see him, he's so busy; Dr Jollif is doing less so Alistair looks for my help on occasion.'

Lena wondered if there was a hint to her behind

that observation, but she pushed the thought from her mind as she tidied herself in her room. By the time she came downstairs tea and scones had been brought to the drawing-room where Olivia and James sat deep in conversation, which ended abruptly when she appeared.

'James tells me you had a wonderful time in Hull, brief though it was,' commented Olivia as Lena took her seat beside her friend on the sofa and proceeded to pour the tea.

'It was very enjoyable. Such a change from the retreat from society I have had to follow this last year.'

'And you had a charming escort, I believe.'

Lena's mind was jolted. What exactly had James told Olivia? What had he read in the attention she had been given by Peter? 'Mr Hustwick was most considerate,' she replied, without committing herself to revealing anything. 'Thank goodness he was not involved in his father's negotiations with James or I don't know what I would have done on my own.'

'What of Hull?' asked Olivia, much to Lena's relief at the change of subject.

'An interesting place of many contrasts, though I don't suppose I saw the worst of them. It's a thriving port with lots of potential for anyone willing to take a chance, though.'

'And a good place to build a solid business, which is what the Hustwicks seem to have established,' added James.

'I didn't mean that,' replied Olivia a little irritably. 'What of its shops and public buildings?'

'They served their purpose, no better and no

worse than those of Whitby,' replied James with little enthusiasm.

'Oh, James, buildings aren't just brick and stone,' chided Olivia. 'They have character. They...'

'Well, if that's how you see them so be it,' he interrupted. 'Look, I have some things to see to and I'm sure you two can discuss the shops and fashions very well without me. Please excuse me.' He drained his cup and stood up. 'I will call on you tomorrow, if I may, Olivia.'

'You know you are welcome at any time.'

He bowed and started for the door.

'I look forward to launching day,' she called after him.

He stopped for a moment and told her, 'You'll meet the Hustwicks then. I have invited them to attend.'

He opened the door and was gone.

'He must have had a good reason to do that. How do you feel about it?' observed Olivia.

'James runs the business. I have nothing to say about what he does, or in this case who he invites to visit us. I suppose it was only proper to invite them as their cargo will be the first to be shipped in the *John Carnforth*.'

'I am so looking forward to it,' said Olivia, a touch of excitement in her voice.

They chatted for half an hour then she said, 'Are you sure you want to accompany me to the shops?'

'Of course,' Lena replied, rising to her feet. 'Have you anything special in mind?'

'Just looking, really, though Father promised

151

me a new dress.'

'Won't you have it made by Mrs Drew?'

'Most certainly, but I like to look around first, see what is on show and what I fancy.'

'No doubt you'll see something and then make suggestions about the style to Mrs Drew, as you always do,' said Lena, knowing her friend's passion for clothes and for keeping up with the latest style.

Later, when they parted in front of New Buildings, having spent a most enjoyable two hours together, Olivia said, 'I'll tell Alistair you are back.'

'Thank you,' was all that Lena said in reply, and as she walked into the house wondered if she had sounded less than enthusiastic.

Her mind was troubled as she changed her dress; Peter was drifting in and out of her thoughts as if trying to remind her of her visit to Hull and the new outlook it had brought to her life. It was as if he was saying, There is an exciting life beyond Whitby. And that, in its turn, made her think of the commercial possibilities in Hull and whether her dreams could better be fulfilled there.

Lena shook such speculation from her mind as she went downstairs. Whitby was her home, it was where she had been born and brought up. This house was filled with happy memories; she felt close to her parents in it. As she strolled into the drawing-room she seemed to hear them pleading, 'Stay with us.'

She picked up the novel she was reading, *The Woman in White* by Wilkie Collins, but could not concentrate; the words were only a blur in her mind so it came as a relief when there was a knock on the door. A maid came in and announced, 'Dr Nash, miss.'

Lena nodded. The maid stood to one side and Alistair hurried into the room. He came quickly to her, his hands outstretched, but waited until the door clicked shut before he spoke, his warmth leaving no doubt in her mind that he was delighted to see her again.

'It's good to have you back!' He took Lena's hands in his and, leaning forward, kissed her on the cheek. 'And to see you out of mourning.' He added this observation as he pulled a chair to face her and took hold of her hands again. Lena did not object, in fact, she enjoyed the sense of being wanted. He represented stability, was a good man, dependable and solid, one whose love for her she could not doubt. He was a person with whom she had grown up. She knew him as well as her own brother.

That night, as Lena prepared for bed, these thoughts about Alistair came back to her. He represented continuity and security. Marry him and her life would barely be altered. But she found she could not dismiss the possibilities of the wider world, symbolised by Hull and by Peter, and thoughts of them kept intruding on the memory of Alistair's warm welcome home to her.

What did she want from life? It seemed to Lena that the time was fast approaching when she must make a decision.

By Christmas she still had not done so. Besides, their visits to the Nashes and the coming of the

MacBrides occupied her mind, but the peaceful family holiday she had envisaged before going to Hull would not be the same because now Peter had entered her life, and try as she might to dismiss her thoughts of him, she was not very successful.

It became even more difficult when, during the week before Christmas, a letter arrived for her. She did not recognise the handwriting but her heart raced when, after opening it, she read the signature first – *Peter*.

She devoured the letter quickly, then, with its words still echoing in her mind, read it more slowly, savouring every expression. *'I think often of your visit. Something I will always treasure for it brought a new perspective to my life.'* This stirred Lena's memory and made her heart pound. Was she pleased that she had had this effect on him? *'I wish we had been able to meet again.'* Had she felt the same? *'But I have kept the thought in my mind that we will meet in March, and draw joy and hope from it.'* Hope? What did he hope? What lay behind that word? The letter went on to say that his father had been taken ill but the indisposition was short-lived, or at least Mr Hustwick made it appear so and still ignored the doctor's advice that he should drink and eat less. Peter also said business was steady and he hoped the *John Carnforth* would help to maintain the prosperity they were enjoying. He concluded, *'It remains for me to wish you a Christmas as happy as can be under the circumstances. Be sure that if my thoughts can ease the moments and shed a happier light on the time, then you have them. Yours respectfully, Peter.'*

Lena felt dampness in her eyes then and wiped it away, thankful that the letter had arrived after James had left to check on the shipbuilder's progress. She rose from her chair in the drawing-room and hurried upstairs. She sat in front of her dressing-table, read the letter again, and then placed it carefully under some fichus in one of the drawers.

'Mama, what are your plans for Christmas when we have James and Lena?'

Mrs Nash knew the reason behind Olivia's question.

'We must make it as enjoyable as possible without too many frivolities – piano playing only of a more serious nature and no dancing. And we'll play some of the more genteel games.'

'No Blind Man's Buff?' Olivia expressed disappointment at the probable absence of one of her favourite games.

'Certainly not,' replied her mother, her voice laced with shock at the thought of the hilarious capers the game engendered. 'Highly inappropriate at a time of recent mourning, especially for Lena and James. We'll have a Christmas tree and decorations, though, and we won't spare on the food.'

'Presents?' asked Olivia.

'Of course. As usual. They will help keep our minds from dwelling on thoughts of last year. And we could exchange Christmas cards. You had better put our proposals to Lena and James then they won't feel embarrassed if they overlook such things, expecting Christmas to be a sombre affair this year.'

Two days later Olivia talked to Lena, expressing her understanding of her mother's ruling but showing disappointment that some of the usual Christmas activities would be sacrificed.

'Have you seen Olivia or Alistair today?' Lena asked her brother when he came home early evening.

'No, neither of them.'

'I had a visit from Olivia. I'll tell you about it during our evening meal.'

When they were seated at the table she quickly explained what Olivia had told her. 'James, I don't want our situation to put a dampener on everyone's Christmas. I know we will miss Mother and Father terribly, but I don't believe they would want any of us to be miserable. I am sure they would tell us to continue with life as usual. I therefore propose to read the situation as it develops and act accordingly, but whatever I suggest, I would like you to back me.'

'Of course I will. What have you in mind?' There was a cautionary note in his voice, though.

Lena shrugged her shoulders. 'I don't know. As I say, it depends on the situation. All I want is for you to be in agreement.'

He nodded. 'Then I will.'

'And don't mention any of this conversation to Olivia or Alistair.'

'I won't.' James knew it was best to go along with his sister when she was hatching plots.

'Oh, and by the way, there will be the usual presents and exchange of Christmas cards.'

'Good. I may need your help in choosing something for Olivia. Of course we'll get something between us for Georgina, and we can't go wrong with some good cigars for Albert.'

'Olivia...' Lena spoke the name thoughtfully. 'I think I know the very thing. She admired a cape when I was out with her the other day. In fact, she tried it on and it fitted perfectly.'

'But she didn't buy it? Why not?'

'She's in the throes of choosing a dress which her father is buying for her. She said maybe she'd buy the cape later.'

'Will you purchase it for me soon?'

'I'll get it tomorrow.' Lena gave a little smile and said, 'I'm sure she'll go to look at it again. She'll get a shock when she sees it's gone.'

'And that will make the surprise even greater when she opens the parcel at Christmas. Splendid!' James chuckled at the thought of Olivia's expression when she saw the cape she thought she had missed by her own hesitation.

'I think a jet necklace and matching bangles for Aunt Georgina.'

'A good idea, Lena,' agreed James. 'Now, what about Alistair?'

'I'm going to get him a beautifully carved walking stick that I have seen. The design depicts a whale.'

'Splendid.'

'I also want to get him a pair of leather gloves. Can you help me with the size?'

'Of course! I think my size will be about right, maybe slightly less. Do you want me to try some on and buy what I think will suit?'

'Please.' Lena gave a little sigh of relief. 'That

settles everyone. And we'll give the staff a bonus as usual.'

'Well, not everyone. There's you.'

'No doubt you'll hatch that up with Olivia, just as I will with Alistair for you?' The twinkle in Lena's eyes showed she relished the prospect.

James was pleased to see his sister filled with the merriment of Christmas past, and hoped this same spirit would continue when the MacBrides came for New Year.

They were still sitting at the table when the maid came in to tell them that Mr Alistair Nash had called. 'I've shown him into the drawing-room, miss.'

'We'll be there in a moment,' said Lena, rising as she spoke.

After greetings were over, Alistair began, 'You know about the Christmas arrangements from Olivia, I understand. I felt I had to call to say how pleased I am that you will be with us.'

'It is most kind of your mother to ask us,' replied Lena.

'I know it will be a trying time for you both, but we'll do our best to make it as happy as possible.'

'And we will see that the events of a year ago don't cloud your festivities,' promised James.

'Just having you both there will disperse any clouds that might gather,' said Alistair.

James smiled. 'You mean, Lena's presence will do that for you.' Before Alistair could respond he added, 'I've some documents to read through. I'll leave you two, if I may?' He turned quickly for the door.

As it clicked shut Alistair took Lena's hand and

led her to the sofa. 'He's right. Seeing you will certainly brighten up my Christmas.'

'And you mine,' she replied as they sat down.

He smiled at her, a gentle, loving smile. It was as if he was searching for a further response that he hoped would be forthcoming from her. The words were on her lips, words she would have uttered without hesitation a few weeks ago, but were held back by the thought of that letter hidden beneath her fichus.

'I'm glad,' Alistair continued. 'You have always brightened my life, ever since we were children.'

'We did have some lovely Christmases. Remember when we...'

He put his fingers to her lips to stop her. 'Don't say any more – don't reminisce. Think of the time to come. Put sad reminders aside. And remember, if ever you need to share, memories good or bad, I am here.'

'You are so kind and thoughtful, Alistair. I am very grateful to you.'

'It has always been my pleasure and privilege.' He leaned forward and kissed her then.

Lena did not draw away but returned his kiss, yet even as their lips met she felt a shiver of distress run through her. That letter carefully preserved among her private possessions...

A week before Christmas Olivia paid her friend a visit. After greetings were made and local news and gossip exchanged, Lena was pouring some tea while Olivia expounded on the real reason for her visit. 'It's always a pleasure seeing you, my dear friend, but I have another reason for calling

159

on you today.'

Lena raised an eyebrow in query.

'The day after tomorrow I am helping Alistair distribute food and gifts to some of his more needy patients. He wondered if you would care to help too? He would have come to ask you himself but was called away to a woman in labour in Horizon Yard.'

Lena had never visited Horizon Yard which she knew to be a shocking misnomer. If ever there had been one, it was now closed in by hovels built to both sides of a rough narrow track that served as a footpath, climbing the cliff-side from the main thoroughfare of Church Street until it could go no further because of the exposed rock face. Here families lived – no, existed – in direst poverty: unskilled men with no work; women bowed down through constant childbirth and unable to properly feed their surviving brood. Yet not far away were streets of well-cared-for houses where skilled workers and tradesmen thrived, respected by all, and exchanged news of their employers living in the grand new villas being built across the river. Whenever she thought about it, which was rarely, Lena abhorred the contrast between some of the east side and the west, where thankfully she lived.

Yet now she was being asked to visit some of those poverty-stricken streets, for she knew only too well what Olivia meant by Alistair's 'more needy patients'. A shiver of apprehension ran down Lena's spine. But what else could she do but agree? To refuse point blank would hurt Alistair, as well as surprise and maybe even shock

Olivia whom she knew would not recoil from accompanying her brother to such places. Lena did not want to appear namby-pamby, but was this the sort of support he would always expect of her? Was this the function of a wife, in his eyes? She shuddered at the thought of what the future could hold for her, completely bypassing the adventure and excitement of the mercantile world pursued so vigorously from Whitby and from Hull.

'Well, Lena, will you?' Olivia's voice startled her. 'You were far away then.'

'Sorry. I was just thinking how Christmases differ according to circumstances.'

'So they do,' agreed Olivia. 'But Alistair sees how lucky we are generally and believes we should do what we can to help the less fortunate, particularly at this time.'

It was on Lena's tongue to say, 'Let them help themselves otherwise they'll always be expecting charity,' but she held the words back. It was no good provoking argument. It was the season of good-will towards all men.

'So will you help?' prompted Olivia again.

'Of course,' replied Lena, crossing her fingers behind her back.

'Then I'll call for you at nine the day after tomorrow. Be prepared for a long day. Alistair has said he will take us to the Angel for luncheon then we won't have to trek all the way back here.'

Lena nodded. 'That's very good of him.'

'It will save time, and that is important when it gets dark so early. And he doesn't want to spend another day at it.'

Then why start at all? Lena once again stifled the words but thought them with frustrated annoyance. 'I'll be ready,' she said with an agreeable smile that hid her real feelings.

Olivia was as good as her word; the grandfather clock in the hall was striking nine when she was admitted to the Carnforth residence. Knowing her strict time-keeping, Lena was ready.

'Good, I'm glad you've wrapped up well,' she commented when she saw Lena's brown redingote and small tight-fitting bonnet.

'I looked out to test the air before deciding what to wear. Nippy, but at least it's fine. It certainly wouldn't have helped if it had been raining or snowing.'

'God looks after those performing good works,' said Olivia.

Lena made no comment to this but started for the door. 'Are we meeting Alistair at the surgery?'

'No, at Mrs Moorsom's at the end of Henrietta Street. She offered to help and he suggested that if the gifts and food could be assembled at her house, it would be easier to distribute them from there as it is nearer the yards running off Church Street. It would have taken a lot of time if we had had to go back and forth to the surgery on the west side of the river.'

'Good,' approved Lena, but her mind most welcomed the fact that this would enable them to finish sooner.

Alistair was already at the house when they arrived, to find that he and Mr Moorsom had got some packages ready to be distributed. Mr and

Mrs Moorsom were to continue in the role of packers while the other three distributed the Christmas fare.

Alistair greeted Lena with a smile that said much more than his words of welcome. 'It is very good of you to help, Lena. It means so much to me to make Christmas a brighter time for those of my patients who otherwise face a bleak festive season. I'm sure you will find it very rewarding too.'

She made no comment but asked instead, 'Just helping your own patients ... won't it rouse jealousy in others?'

'I dare say it will, particularly if the doctors who look after them do nothing.'

'Won't those doctors then be antagonistic towards you, because you are doing this and they aren't? I would imagine that is not the way to remain popular in this town.'

'I don't seek to be popular with everyone. If I tread on some toes, then so be it. All I seek is to do some good for Whitby and the deserving cases under my own jurisdiction. But enough of this. Let's get started. Those boxes at the front of the cart contain toys for the children, the rest are Christmas hampers. We'll all stay together. We'll be in some rough parts of town but you'll be treated with respect if you are with me.'

Alistair proved to be correct from the start. Men touched their caps or foreheads to them but were openly curious about the two ladies who accompanied the doctor, though as the day wore on Lena sensed that some looked her up and down with more of a salacious gleam. Women with torn shawls around their shoulders and stains on their black dresses, though they had at least made some attempt to make their hair tidy and scrub colour into their cheeks, stood about in groups gossiping, but turned their gaze eagerly on the newcomers as they entered the confines of the yard.

Here and there Lena saw poor attempts to make these hovels more habitable, but there were others too where nothing had been done and filth lay all around. Lena almost retched when she entered the first such house; only by strength of will did she prevent herself from making a fool of herself, and as it was, was unable to hide her disgust. Other dwellings were more salubrious and there she could see a woman had struggled to make her home more habitable for an over-sized family. Children seemed to be everywhere; their excited shouts on seeing the toys were almost overpowering, especially when arguments arose over who should have what.

In spite of being affected by the general squalor Lena had to acknowledge their appreciation of the food and gifts the doctor had brought them, to brighten what would otherwise have been a bleak holiday.

'God bless yer, doctor.'

'Yer's too good.'

'Thank yer, good lady.'

'The kids will be happy.'

And with their thanks she saw tears dampen their eyes.

Sitting down to a fine spread for lunch at the Angel, Lena's eyes were newly opened to the

164

contrast she had just witnessed and she realised fully for the first time what Alistair was doing for these people. Olivia had willingly helped, and Lena was sure now that he would expect the same of her too.

Nevertheless, as she walked up the path to the elegant, comfortable, warm house where she had been brought up by loving parents, she knew she could not venture into those poverty-stricken streets and yards again. All she wanted now was to get out of these clothes. The redingote and dress she would burn; they had been fingered by too many dirty urchin hands, tugging at her for attention while she was distributing toys. She could never wear them again for they would always remind her of the filth and poverty she had seen. Besides they smelt of sweat, smoke, confined quarters and squalor; a smell that would cling to them forever. No doubt her petticoats and underclothes would have absorbed the odours too; well, they could all be burnt.

As soon as she was in the hall she called for a maid and ordered hot water to be brought that so she could bathe the dirt and smells away. It would not be so easy to erase them from her mind.

Chapter Ten

'Mrs Campion, be sure to see that the servants have as pleasant a Christmas as possible. Anyone who lives locally may go home if they wish, but see that they are back here the day after Boxing Day so as to prepare for the MacBrides' arrival,' Lena instructed her housekeeper as she pulled on her gloves, ready to go to the Nashes' on the afternoon of Christmas Eve.

'Certainly, miss,' Mrs Campion replied. 'There will only be Sarah and me staying.'

'Very well.'

'May I say, all the servants asked me to say how grateful they are for the wonderful Christmas meal you provided yesterday? Cook was especially appreciative of the fact that you brought in someone else to do the cooking, so she could enjoy it without all the preparation.'

'I am pleased everyone enjoyed it, and I know my brother will be too. And Happy Christmas to you, Mrs Campion.'

'You too, miss.'

As Lena walked to the Nashes' residence she realised that the time spent at the servants' party, though short, for she did not want to intrude or to embarrass them with her presence, had been good for her. It had enabled her to relax, forget the thoughts that troubled her and realise that even tragic anniversaries could be marked without any disrespect to the departed.

James had wanted to make a visit to the office so had arranged to see his sister at the Nashes'. She sensed from the sparkle in Olivia's bright eyes, as her friend hurried into the hall to meet her, that he was already there.

'Parcels for under the tree,' said Lena, placing the packages on a table at the foot of the stairs. 'I hope James hasn't forgotten the rest?'

'He hasn't!'

Lena slipped out of her coat, undid her bonnet and handed them, along with her gloves, to the maid who had admitted her to the house.

'Come on, we're all in the drawing-room,' said Olivia, slipping her arm through Lena's. 'We are going to have a splendid time.'

'We are,' agreed Lena, squeezing Olivia's arm as if to emphasise her observation and reassure her friend that nothing was going to spoil this festive season.

When they entered the drawing-room, the greetings from all the Nashes were warm, making Lena feel at home. Alistair was first to greet her.

'Welcome,' he said, admiration clear in his eyes as he raised her hand to his lips.

'Thank you,' replied Lena, returning his smile and inclining her head in acknowledgement. She was aware of Georgina Nash's eyes on her.

'James and I are most grateful to you for inviting us. We...'

'My dear, our families have been close for so long that you are one of us. You must make yourselves at home.' Georgina straightened her back and placed her hands firmly on her lap as if to

167

say, That is out of the way. 'Now, we are having a light luncheon, shortly, and will dine in splendour this evening. I have no doubt you young ones will entertain yourselves happily after that.'

After luncheon, when Georgina and Albert Nash seemed to be succumbing to the desire for a nap, the four young ones decided that a walk and some fresh air would sharpen their appetites for the evening meal. Although the wind had freshened it was not unpleasant, but they had wrapped up well.

'Where are we going?' asked Alistair as they stepped outside. 'West Cliff?'

'No,' replied Lena firmly. 'West Pier.'

'That'll catch the wind.'

'Do us good.'

'West Pier it is,' agreed James. Catching his sister's eye he winked and then, in order to show consideration, added, 'Acceptable to you, Olivia?'

'It will have to be if you are all going,' she replied with little enthusiasm. 'The sea will be running fast.'

She's trying to put us off, thought Lena, so said, 'Lovely!'

They came on to St Anne's Staith from where they could see the waters of the river rippled by the wind. They cut through Haggersgate on to Pier Lane where they felt the wind freshening, but it was not until they passed beyond the protection of the cliff and the Battery that they felt the full force of the wind and saw the waves piling behind each other in long lines stretching as far as Sandsend as they ran in towards the coast.

This was what Lena wanted. She enjoyed the sea in this mood: racing towards the piers, pounding the stonework, roaring in anger, and sending spray high where it was caught by the wind before it fell in a clinging mist. The crests of the waves, streaming in towards the shore like attacking cavalry, curled loftily before crashing down to run fast over the sand until they could run no more and swirled back towards the sea, seeking to recover before making another assault on the shoreline. The powerful motion of wind and sea filled Lena with excitement, which heightened with every step she took towards the sentinel lighthouse, built in the shape of a handsome Doric column at the end of the pier.

They were halfway to the lighthouse when they were buffeted by a sudden gust that sent Olivia staggering and grasping at James for support. Tense with fright, she cried out, 'I don't like it! Can we go back?'

'Come on, you'll be all right,' countered Lena.

'No!' Olivia grasped at her bonnet against the tug of the wind. 'James, take me back.'

He was on the point of trying to persuade her otherwise when he saw the stricken look on her face. 'All right, don't worry,' he said calmly and turned her round.

'I'm sorry, James, but I...' Her words faltered.

'Just walk calmly off the pier. Come on, hold on to me.' They moved away, Olivia gripping his arm tightly.

Alistair started to follow.

'You too, Alistair?'

Expecting them all to stay together, he was

169

startled by the challenging tone in Lena's voice. 'Well, naturally I'm concerned for Olivia. I think we should go with them.'

'What about me?'

'You want to go further?'

'To the end of the pier.'

'But it is blowing hard and the sea is...'

'The wind won't blow us away and the sea can't reach us. This pier's solid enough. We might get wet from the spray but we'll be safe enough. I'm going on. You go back if you don't like it.'

Alistair bit his lip in exasperation. He glanced in the direction of his sister then back at Lena. There was challenge in her eyes. 'All right. I can't say I like it, but I can't leave you on your own.'

She smiled. 'You'll like it. You'll see.' He made no comment as he fell into step beside her. 'Thank you, Alistair,' she said graciously.

Again he made no comment and she knew he was peeved by her stubbornness, but she had got what she wanted and that was enough for Lena. She slipped her arm through his and moved closer to him, a gesture calculated to wipe away any annoyance he might still harbour.

He glanced at her as they stepped out briskly towards the lighthouse, caught the laughter and joy in her eyes, and was happy that she was happy. His sister was forgotten; she was in James's capable hands and no harm would come to her. Although he couldn't enjoy it as Lena appeared to be doing, he had to admit the wind was exhilarating and there was something intoxicating about being on the pier alone, contesting the wild wind's desire to scour everything from its path.

Alistair stopped walking and Lena looked at him askance. He plucked his hat from his head. 'I'm tired of holding that on.' He threw it into the air. 'There, wind, you can have it!' he yelled, his eyes dancing with devilment.

Lena's laughter was torn away by the wind but it was still there in her eyes. She pulled at her bonnet ribbons. The wind took advantage and whisked it away. 'You can have that too!' she shouted. Holding on to each other, leaning against the wind, they watched it float the bonnet like a kite over the river where it relented and, in a final buffet, dropped it into the water. They laughed out loud together, then turned and headed for the end of the pier.

The sea pounded at the stonework below as if its fury would triumph over whatever man had raised in its path. The waves broke hard, were thrown into the air to crash down on the pier, swirled over it and ran down the channels to seek their rightful home. Wave followed wave with endless ferocity.

Alistair stopped and restrained Lena. 'Too dangerous to go on!' he shouted above the anger of the sea.

She frowned but knew he was right. Still she stood and watched, fascinated by the sea's power, ignoring the spray that was raining down all around them, soaking their clothes, sending water running in rivulets down their faces from sodden hair. She let her imagination take over – this was what it must be like on the deck of a ship, driving through a similar sea, except the deck would be unstable, unlike the solid stone of

171

the pier. How she wished she could experience it ... maybe, some day, on a ship of her own. The wind seemed to gather strength then and tear at her as if to say, Dare to venture into my kingdom and you'll see how destructive I can be. A defiant tremor ran through Lena.

Alistair felt that shudder but read it wrongly. He was thankful to be able to say, 'We had better go,' and started to turn her away.

For one moment she was tempted to protest but then he stopped and matched the wildness around them with a kiss that abandoned all decorum. It was fierce and demanding. She gasped as she held that kiss. This was so unlike Alistair, usually the epitome of good manners and respectability. What else lay hidden inside him? Had the violence of the elements sparked his most desires?

He broke away, his face clouded with confusion and apology. 'Lena, I shouldn't have done that...' Her mind was crying out, Why not? But the words would not come and he was faltering, 'Please forgive me. I don't know what came over me.'

'Alistair, don't apologise.'

'But there is a time and a place...'

'What was wrong with this time and place?'

'In public?'

'There is no one else here.'

'That's as may be but ... besides, strictly speaking, you are still in mourning.'

'I chose to come out of it, and will be officially next week.'

'I think...' But Alistair never finished. At that

moment a giant wave broke heavily against the pier, sending a wall of water high up in the air before it crashed down. It sent them staggering, grasping at each other tightly to keep their feet. 'We'd better get away from here!' Alistair grasped her hand and they ran towards safety.

Reaching the shelter of the cliffs they stopped and surveyed themselves – two people completely soaked by the sea, dripping water into pools at their feet. The exhilarating laughter that longed to break free from Lena was halted by Alistair's sombre expression. 'You're drenched! The sooner we get you out of those clothes, the better. We don't want you catching cold.' He hurried her off without waiting for her reply.

Her desire dampened, she sighed to herself – always the doctor! Would she ever again experience the passion she had witnessed from him on the pier?

Reaching the house, Alistair bustled her inside and called for the maids. Mr and Mrs Nash and Olivia came hurrying into the hall, followed by James. All four of them stopped, wide-eyed at the sight of the two people who stood there, looking as if they had narrowly escaped from drowning. Two maids, wondering what was happening, came rushing into the hall as well.

Georgina Nash took command immediately. 'Hot water for Miss Carnforth and Mr Nash,' she ordered. 'Olivia, go with Lena. Alistair, off with you!' All three of them started for the stairs. 'Leave your wet things outside your doors, they'll be collected in a few minutes and seen to,' she called after them. She turned to her husband and

173

nodded then. He knew exactly what that implied.

'James, come with me,' said Albert and headed for the dining-room where he made straight for the decanters and glasses set out on the sideboard. 'Take them both a glass of whisky,' he instructed as he poured.

Mrs Nash eyed the glasses when James came from the dining-room and hurried to the stairs.

'I don't know what Alistair must have been thinking, to go out on the pier in this wind and with the sea running so high,' commented Albert as he joined his wife.

'Don't be too ready to blame him,' murmured Georgina. 'From what Olivia managed to tell me when we were alone, it was Lena who insisted on going on. She can be headstrong at times. We'll say no more about it.'

They had re-entered the drawing-room as they were speaking and Georgina went straight to the bell-pull beside the fireplace while Albert stirred the fire and threw two more logs on to it. When a maid appeared, Georgina ordered tea and scones to be served as soon as all the young ones were down.

James returned after distributing the whisky. Alistair was the next to come into the drawing-room and was followed shortly afterwards by Olivia.

'Has Lena all that she requires?' asked Georgina.

'Yes, Mama. She won't be long.'

Ten minutes later Lena appeared, her face glowing after its buffeting by the wind. Noting she was the last to arrive, she apologised.

'Not at all, my dear,' said Georgina. 'You needed that warming bath.'

Before any more was said two maids arrived with the tea, and the foolhardiness of going out on the pier in such weather was not mentioned again.

As Georgina had promised earlier, they dined in splendour that evening and afterwards settled in the drawing-room. Georgina took out her embroidery, Albert his book: *Black Beauty* by Anna Sewell. Alistair challenged James to a game of chess, and Olivia and Lena contested their skills on the draughts board. It was a quiet, touching on sombre, evening compared to those enjoyed in the past. James could sense his sister's desire to liven it up but knew she would not go against his warning to do nothing to upset their hosts' plans … well, not this very first evening under the Nashes' roof.

On Christmas morning Lena woke feeling puzzled by a dream that involved two men who remained shadow-like presences. By the end of it she still did not know who she walked beside but felt alarmed by the upheaval that such a dream presaged. She was in low spirits as she dressed, but as she neared the bottom of the stairs she realised she must shake off this attitude or she would be questioned as to what troubled her. She paused at the dining-room door, took a deep breath and went in.

'Good morning, everyone,' she said brightly. 'I'm sorry I'm late.'

'My dear, you are not,' Albert Nash hastened to reassure her.

'We did not want to wake you unless it became necessary,' said Georgina. 'We still have plenty of time to get to the parish church for the morning service.'

So it proved. Lena was pleased to find conversation over breakfast light-hearted. As they climbed into the coach afterwards she felt the spirit of Christmas seep into her, and the feeling deepened as they were driven across the bridge and along Church Street to Green Lane where the coachman urged the horse to greater effort as it met the steepening gradient to the Abbey Plain. Leaving the coach between the ruined abbey and the church, Mr and Mrs Nash led the way inside to one of the box-pews.

The parson's words seemed to dismiss Lena's bad dream. Though she took in little of his sermon she relished singing the carols, recalling the peace and hopefulness of Christmases past.

After an enjoyable day marked by light-hearted laughter and a good rapport with their friends, an exceptionally pleasing Christmas meal and the exchange of presents which they had all taken care over choosing, Georgina suggested that their guest should play the piano.

'Some gentle pieces,' she stipulated as Lena took her place.

Lena ran her fingers over the keys, producing no music in particular as she got the feel of the instrument. Then she moved into Chopin. The notes were clear and bright under her touch. A respectful silence filled the room.

Alistair's eyes never left her, taking in every detail as if he wished to imprint it indelibly on his

176

mind, for fear of ever losing it. Though Lena would deny she was beautiful, to him her beauty filled the room. He knew that whenever he walked into it henceforth, she would be here for him and he would see her just as she was now, seated at the piano, her delicate fingers bringing joyous notes with every touch, features composed in concentration yet relaxed in the pleasure of making such beautiful sounds.

The last note faded. Lena stayed absolutely still, her fingers resting lightly on the keys.

For a moment there was a deep and complete silence as if everyone was absorbing what they had just heard and did not wish to mar its beauty. Then Georgina clapped her hands quietly, bound to show her appreciation. Her gesture broke the spell and everyone followed suit.

'Beautiful,' commented Georgina. 'Thank you.'

'I wish I could play like that,' said Olivia.

'You could if you practised as much as I suspect Lena has,' commented her father.

'Wonderful!' exclaimed Alistair.

Lena swung round on the piano stool. 'Thank you. I enjoyed playing for you again. It's a while since I have been able to.'

'Then play some more,' urged Alistair.

Lena glanced at her hostess.

'Please do,' Georgina approved.

She turned back to the piano and once again gentle music filled the room. It did so for another twenty minutes, then suddenly Lena changed the tempo, ran her fingers swiftly over the white notes and moved into *Good King Wenceslas*.

'Come on, everyone, just like Christmas past –

carols round the piano.'

There was no response for a moment. Then: 'Lena, do you think we should? It's not a year yet...'

'Of course we should, Aunt Georgina!' she replied brightly. 'Mama and Papa would want us to.'

'I think they would,' put in James quickly, in support of his sister. 'They loved carols round the piano and it will be a fitting way to commemorate them.'

Georgina shot a quick look at her husband who indicated his approval with a slight nod and said, 'I agree with James.'

Georgina made no further objection; even if in her heart of hearts she did not approve, she was not one to put a complete damper on the festivities. Her wishes had been observed yesterday and earlier today. If the others did not want this Christmas to be remembered as a miserable one, why should she? She rose from her chair, took Albert's hand, and in a matter of moments was singing along with everyone else.

Lena did not let up and went from one carol to another. She sensed regret in everyone when they realised she was nearing the end of her repertoire so without stopping went smoothly into a selection of music-hall songs. Georgina frowned but made no comment as everyone else was still singing energetically. Feeling her husband squeeze her hand she smiled at him and sang as enthusiastically as he.

The tone was set for the rest of the night. There was laughter in everyone's eyes as they finally said 'good night' at the bottom of the stairs.

'Thanks for backing me, James,' whispered Lena when she had his attention.

He smiled and winked, setting the seal on their little conspiracy.

'You were right, my dear,' said Georgina, a twinkle of appreciation in her eyes. 'I felt your mother and father near us, and they approved.'

Lena's eyes were damp as she kissed their good friend. 'Thank you.'

'We shall continue in that vein tomorrow, and we must see that your aunt and uncle and cousins pass an enjoyable stay. Oh, we won't forget what happened, but we must let them see that life must go on, even though we mourn.'

Chapter Eleven

'Pleased to be going home, Martin?' Mary asked her husband, watching him in the dressing-table mirror as she brushed her hair before going to bed.

He met her eyes and gave a small smile. 'Yes,' he replied quietly. 'Don't take that amiss; I like Whitby fine ... but not as much as Dundee.'

'Naturally. Our roots are there.'

He stopped undoing his cufflinks. With his gaze fixed lovingly on her, he slipped his arms over her shoulders and kissed her on the top of her head. 'I'm glad we came. I hope you are too?'

'I am. My mind will be at rest now, concerning

Lena and James.'

He gave a little nod of agreement. 'I am pleased they are coping so well. I know Mrs Nash's letters were reassuring, but what we have seen for ourselves more than confirms her views.'

'I was a little apprehensive when we first arrived, considering it was just a year on from the tragedy.' Mary's voice faltered slightly but she drew strength from the gentle pressure he put on her shoulders. 'But that disappeared when I realised how settled both the children seem in their new life.'

'And from what I gather, all is well between James and Olivia. I think we'll be coming back for a wedding before too long,' said Martin as he went to sit on a chair and remove his shoes.

'I gathered the same,' replied Mary, 'though no one has expressly said so. I think at the moment James is too engrossed in seeing his new ship built and put into service.'

'It will be a fine match. So will one between Pauline and Alistair,' added Martin firmly.

'You've heard something then?'

'No, but he's an excellent young man. He's fast becoming a good doctor and will make an equally good husband. It's bound to happen – they've known each other all their lives, just like James and Olivia.'

'Now don't you jump to conclusions,' warned his wife, swinging round on her stool.

'What? It's plain enough for all to see.'

'Oh, you men,' she replied with a touch of irritation. 'You see only what you want to see, and that is only the surface.'

'But...'

'I know nothing, no one has said anything, but I have felt sometimes that Lena is ill at ease.'

'Then ask her.'

'No! That's the very last thing to do. She is a capable young lady and will make up her own mind. We have no right to interfere.'

'I think we should query...'

'She will come to us if she wants our advice. She knows we will listen.' Mary eyed her husband with a stern expression. 'And you will do nothing. Heed my words, Martin MacBride. Leave well alone.'

He met her gaze and knew, without a doubt, he would not interfere.

'Both of you will be sure to come?' James's emphasis left no doubt in Martin's and Mary's minds that their nephew would be sorely disappointed if they were not at the launching of the *John Carnforth*.

'Nothing will keep us away,' replied Martin firmly.

'Of course we'll be there,' said Mary, hugging her nephew. 'Meanwhile, look after yourself and Lena.'

'I will. Have a safe journey.' He gave her a kiss, shook hands with his uncle, and turned to say goodbye to his cousins who had been fussing around Lena.

Her aunt held out her arms and Lena felt her warm and loving embrace.

'I look forward to seeing you again, Aunt,' she said sincerely.

181

'I'm sorry we can't stay longer but time will pass. Soon we'll be watching the *John Carnforth* take majestically to the water. No doubt you'll be conducting the launching ceremony?'

Lena gave a small shrug, 'I expect so, though James hasn't mentioned it yet.'

'It's early days for the finer details,' her aunt pointed out, and gave Lena another hug. 'I am pleased to see you so well. Keep it that way and look after yourself.'

'I will, Aunt.' Hearing footsteps, she glanced along the street. 'Here are the Nashes, coming to say farewell.'

There was gaiety in the greetings and wishes for a safe journey from Mr and Mrs Nash, Olivia and Alistair, and more excited exchanges as the coach rumbled away, taking the MacBrides on the first stage of their journey to Dundee.

'Should we walk on the cliff top?' Alistair suggested as the vehicle disappeared.

'You young ones go,' said his mother, 'I'll see to luncheon for you all in two hours.'

'We don't want to put you to any bother,' said Lena.

'It will be no bother, my dear. Cook is well prepared.'

Within twenty minutes, suitably dressed against the cold air, the four young people stopped on the cliff top to gaze out over a grey sea teased into whitecaps by the sharp wind.

Lena took a deep breath, revelling in the fresh feeling it brought. 'Wonderful!'

Alistair saw the distant look in her eyes, as if she

was trying to see beyond the horizon. He wondered what exactly she sought there.

Olivia shivered. 'It's cold. Let's keep moving,' she said, grasping James's arm and allowing him to fall into step beside her.

Lena stood still. Alistair remained silently beside her. This was not the time to break into her thoughts. She was so far away. A few moments passed before she took hold of his arm and turned to follow James and Olivia. Alistair, finding reassurance in her touch, resisted making any comment.

'Do you want to catch the others up?' asked Lena.

He eyed her with a wry smile. 'Do you think they would want us to?'

'I doubt it.' She had noted James and Olivia were hand-in-hand. Two people in love, certainly. She saw them take a path that led down to the strand of sand stretching away to Sandsend. 'Let's stay up here.'

'The bite in the wind not too much for you?' he asked considerately.

'No.' She drew in a deep breath. 'No, I love it.'

'I'm so glad everything went well over Christmas and the New Year. I was afraid the memories might be too much for you.'

'They were there, Alistair, but there was no point in dwelling on them.'

'That is a very brave attitude. I have seen other people torn apart under the loss of loved ones.' He stopped and turned her gently to him so that he could look into her eyes. 'Lena, please remember I am here if ever you need...'

'I know, Alistair, and am grateful for your consideration. You are a very dear friend.'

'I hope I am more than that?'

Lena's heart beat faster. Her thoughts raced. What else was he going to say? How would she respond if he proposed to her now?

He kissed her, his lips gentle on hers. She accepted them and enjoyed their touch. She felt his arms tighten around her and her own arms automatically slid up over his shoulders. She dwelt on that moment gratefully, savouring her own indecision. A gesture could send the result spinning one way; a single word could throw it in the opposite direction. His lips were warm on hers and she responded, but when he broke the silence to say, 'I love you,' Lena put a finger to his lips and said, 'No more, Alistair, not now.'

As those unwanted words struck at his hopes he expected her to turn away from him but she did not. Instead she kissed him again and he read that as a sign of encouragement. He withheld his own response but took her hand as they walked on.

Although her thoughts were racing Lena controlled them, knowing she must, at least until she was alone in her room. There, snug between white sheets, she allowed them full rein.

What if she had allowed Alistair to say what she believed he'd been about to? How would she have answered? Why did she stop him? And all the time she knew the single answer to all her questions: Peter. She tossed and turned, chiding herself over and over again for entertaining such a thought. What did she really know of him? Why

184

had he sparked such a feeling of restlessness in her? Was it merely his association with the sea, something she herself had enjoyed all her life? Was she seeing him as a way to fulfil her own thwarted ambitions and dreams? She fell asleep with no question fully answered but they were to haunt her over the next month, even when she was with Alistair. She knew the assurance he sought from her, but still did not feel ready to give it.

'Mr Alistair Nash to see you, miss.'

'Please show him in.'

Lena stood to greet Alistair when he entered the drawing-room.

He held out his hands to her and kissed her on the cheek. 'I can only stay a few minutes.'

She pulled an expression of displeasure. 'I hoped you were coming to ask me for a walk on this lovely February day.'

He gave a smile of regret. 'Sorry, but I've to see old Mrs Grimshaw in Ruswarp in half an hour. You could come with me? She's bed-bound and might like a bit of company. A new face might cheer her up.'

Lena's lips tightened and she gave a slight shake of her head as she recalled the one time she had deigned to accompany him to visit a bed-bound person – the smells had been overpowering and she had retched when she reached home. Never again, she had sworn to herself, even if she became a doctor's wife. 'Not today,' she said. 'I need some air. I'll take a walk on my own.'

Alistair shrugged his shoulders. 'I'm sorry, but as you wish.' His demeanour brightened. 'Now hopefully I'll divert you with the purpose of this visit instead.' He left a slight pause that was filled with intent.

Was this the moment when he...? No, it couldn't be. If it were, he would not be in such a rush to get away to see Mrs Grimshaw. Lena inclined her head, her eyes filled with curiosity. 'Well, what is it?'

'I've had an invitation from Mr and Mrs Charles Sugden of Weaver Hall, to a house party there on the last weekend of this month. Friday afternoon until after lunch on Sunday. They have asked me to bring a partner.'

'I don't know them,' replied Lena, seeking time to take in the implications of this invitation.

'He is from a wool manufacturing family in the West Riding. I was at school in York with him. We kept in touch only infrequently until last year when he inherited Weaver Hall from an uncle and moved there from the West Riding. We corresponded a little more after that. Apparently he has been having extensive alterations done; they are now completed and he wishes to baptise the hall with a few friends. About twelve, I believe.' His eyes were seeking Lena's reaction. When there was nothing immediate forthcoming, Alistair added quickly, 'He knows I'm not married and has set aside two rooms for me and my guest. So I'm asking you to accompany me?'

'It sounds interesting,' she replied. 'Of course I'll come.' It would certainly be a diversion, and perhaps in unfamiliar surroundings she would

186

see Alistair in a new light.

His face lit up with pleasure. 'Then I'm delighted. I shall inform Charles immediately.'

'You'll have to tell me a little more about them so I won't be totally ignorant when we meet.'

'Briefly, then, they have been married six months. His wife Marcia came from a wealthy carpet manufacturing family in the West Riding.'

'And he?'

'Plenty of money, even without the inheritance from his uncle. His father has built up a thriving wool business.'

'Is he not involved in that?'

'Oh, yes, and no doubt will go on benefiting from it, but Charles always had a hankering for the land. It will be interesting to hear of his plans now that he has inherited this estate.'

'Do you know who else has been invited?'

'No.'

'Then that will certainly make this weekend even more fascinating.'

The weather was milder and the snows of January had all but gone when Alistair drove Lena to Weaver Hall in the heart of the Wolds. He was solicitous for her comfort on the way and kept up a lively conversation about Whitby and his work there, so that it seemed to her he was trying to paint a picture of what life would be like for them both as man and wife, though she was aware that he was painting the glossy side only and ignoring what, to her, would be the more disagreeable aspects of being a doctor's wife.

The track dipped into a shallow valley and after

a mile Alistair turned the carriage between imposing gates that had been left open. He urged the horse up an incline, and when they topped the rise, Lena gasped.

'Beautiful!'

Alistair reined the horse to a stop. 'It is, isn't it?'

'You've been here before?' She knew the answer from the tone of his voice.

'I have, once.'

'You never told me.'

'I suspected from what Charles said that day there would be a small gathering to celebrate the completion of the renovations, and I wanted this view to surprise you.'

He held the horse steady while Lena drank in the prospect of a solid, foursquare stone house, its masonry glinting in the winter light. It had obviously been considerably embellished and improved recently: she could see extensions on the slight incline behind the main building. The track ahead gave way to a gravel carriage drive that swung in a wide loop in front of the house.

By the time Alistair was pulling their conveyance to a halt two groomsmen had appeared; one was immediately at the horse's head, holding it steady, while the other was lowering the step to help Lena to the ground. As Alistair stepped down after her a voice boomed from the stone veranda that ran the full width of the house.

'Welcome to Weaver Hall.'

Alistair looked up to see his friend standing at the top of four wide stone steps leading to the veranda, his arms held wide open in a gesture of welcome.

'Charles!'

Lena eyed their host as she held on to Alistair's arm for support.

'Come on, meet our host,' he said enthusiastically.

'Welcome to Weaver Hall, Miss Carnforth. Alistair told me a lot about you when he last visited. His words did not do you justice, even though he waxed eloquent, I assure you.' Charles Sugden bowed as he took her hand and raised it to his lips.

'Thank you, Mr Sugden.' Lena inclined her head. 'It is my pleasure to meet you, and may I thank you for your kind invitation. Your home enjoys an exquisite setting.'

'I'm glad you like it. Come and meet my wife.' He had heard her footsteps as she left the house and came towards them. 'Marcia, this is Miss Carnforth, Alistair's friend.'

Lena saw herself facing someone of about her own age but there, as far as physical attributes went, she felt the comparison ended, for she was dazzled by the beauty in this face of perfect symmetry. Marcia's skin was flawless. Thin eyebrows, gracefully arched, were complemented by long eyelashes as dark as the hair drawn neatly on to the top of her head. It took little imagination to picture it released from its pins and cascading beyond the nape of her neck like a delicate tumbling waterfall. It was Marcia's eyes that made the greatest impact, though. They sparkled like the diamonds in the leaf brooch pinned at the throat of her high collar. Lena saw they were full of vitality, as if this young woman would find joy in whatever attracted her attention.

'I am so delighted you could come. Welcome to our home.'

Lena was struck by the gentle warmth in her voice. The conventional welcome was expressed with such sincerity that even as they walked towards the front door, Lena knew the inside of the house would be warm and cosy, welcoming in its own way. This would be a home, not a show-piece, though she had no doubt that what she would see would be of the very best.

Servants had hurried from the house to take charge of their luggage. As they entered the house others appeared to take their outdoor clothes, while a footman came forward with a cup of steaming punch.

Lena realised not one order had been given yet everything had worked like clockwork. She knew this to be a well-run house. At that moment a straight-backed woman clad in a black dress crossed the hall towards them.

'Mrs Welburn, my dear and exceptional house-keeper! Mrs Welburn, this is Mr Nash and Miss Carnforth from Whitby.' Marcia turned to the new arrivals. 'Mrs Welburn will see to your needs. Anything you need or wish to know, ask her. She has allocated you a personal maid, Miss Carn-forth, and you a personal footman, Mr Nash.'

They both made their thanks. The housekeeper gave a polite smile and left Charles and Marcia to take their friends to the drawing-room.

'She is a gem,' said Marcia quietly to Lena as they entered the room. Lena knew that was true, but also reckoned that behind Mrs Welburn's efficiency lay Marcia's watchful eye and bene-volent authority.

The room she found herself in was larger than Lena had expected, with two fireplaces sending flames sparkling upwards and contributing the tantalising sound of crackling logs. The furniture was light and graceful, obviously made especially for this setting.

'This is delightful, Mrs Sugden,' said Lena, her expression filled with admiration as she looked round the room.

'I'm glad you like it, Miss Carnforth – oh, look, we cannot go on like this all this weekend. You are here to enjoy yourselves, and hopefully we will all be friends together.' She gestured impa-tiently with her arms. 'Mrs Sugden, Miss Carnforth – far too formal on such an occasion! Marcia, please. And do you prefer Pauline or Lena, Miss Carnforth?'

'Lena, please, everyone calls me that.'

'Good. That is settled then. I will tell everyone the same as they arrive.'

'How many guests are you expecting?'

'Originally there would have been twenty-four including ourselves, but two couples have had to cry off due to illness so there will now be twenty of us. Everyone except you and another couple is married. They should all be here for a light tea at five. You'll meet them then. Dinner will be at eight, and we'll gather here in the drawing-room half an hour before.'

'What would I do without such an organiser?' sighed Charles, gazing adoringly at his beautiful and accomplished wife.

191

When Lena was shown to her room she judged that no expense had been spared to make it comfortable and welcoming. A fire burned cheerfully in the grate and was reflected in the large mirror on the opposite side of the room. The chintz curtains were patterned with pink roses on a white background and complemented by the colours of the cushions in the easy chairs situated on either side of the fireplace. Feminine touches were everywhere and Lena knew immediately this room, with its single bed, had received Marcia's personal touch and thought when designated for a female guest. A dressing-table, frilled with chintz and lace, was positioned to catch the light from the large sash window. Her curiosity could not be stifled any longer so she went to the door next to a large mahogany wardrobe and opened it to find that she was seeing the latest innovation: indoor sanitation. Returning to the bedroom, she went to look out of the window.

Though the scene still held the sombre aspect of winter there was evidence in the small copse to the right that spring was not too far away. An extensive lawn, edged with now moribund flowerbeds, gave way to fields that gently climbed a hillside. Lena let her imagination run riot as she pictured the scene ablaze with colour throughout the ever-changing seasons. She experienced a sensation of space and freedom and realised it was similar to the sensation that had come over her when she stood on the banks of the Humber with Peter.

A knock on the door broke her reverie. She

turned and called, 'Come in.'

A girl of about sixteen appeared. 'Good day, miss,' she said brightly. 'I'm Marie, your personal maid. Is there anything I can do for you?'

'I'm pleased to meet you, Marie,' returned Lena, making her tone warm to put the maid at her ease. 'You may unpack my two valises,' she said, indicating them.

'Yes, miss.' Marie went about her task efficiently, hanging dresses with care and putting the rest of Lena's clothes neatly in the bow-fronted chest of drawers while she saw to her more personal belongings.

Without appearing too inquisitive, Lena learned that Marie had come to work at Weaver Hall when the Sugdens had inherited the estate and had been there throughout the period of renovation. She learned what the house had looked like formerly and how it had been altered, and realised from snippets that Marie let drop that she thought highly of her employers and could not imagine working anywhere else.

By the time tea was ready in the drawing-room, Lena felt fresher for her toilette after the journey as she viewed herself in the full-length mirror on the wardrobe door and considered which of her several brooches would be best suited to her blue-lavender day dress. She finally chose her favourite piece of jet, judging rightly that it would complement the narrow black trimmings on the jacket-style bodice, that emphasised her slender proportions.

She found several people already in the drawing-room but there was no sign of Alistair.

She knew Marcia had seen her, for she saw her make her excuses to the two people to whom she was talking and come over.

'I hope you found everything to your liking?'

'Indeed I did,' replied Lena. 'I will be most comfortable. And what a wonderful view you have given me.'

'And Marie?'

'She could not have looked after me any better.'

'Good, now come and meet some of my guests. The others are not down yet and Charles will be along shortly.'

Marcia escorted her around the room, making the introductions. Lena was warmly greeted in a friendly atmosphere that had been engendered by Marcia, who finally left her talking to Mr and Mrs Wallis from Bridlington and went to seek out her husband.

Lena's back was to the doorway so she was unaware of someone approaching until a request was voiced.

'Margaret, Kenneth, might I spirit Miss Carnforth away from you?'

Lena stiffened. That voice! Surely she was mistaken?

'Of course, Peter,' came the reply from Margaret who smiled at Lena. 'It has been very pleasant talking to you.'

Lena's mind was in such a whirl that she could do no more than incline her head in agreement. As the Wallises moved away she turned to see Peter Hustwick claiming her attention.

'Mr Hustwick! What are you doing here?' Even though she realised this was a silly question the words were out.

He grinned. 'The same as you, I expect, I'm a guest of Marcia and Charles.'

'But, Mr Hustwick...'

He raised his hand to stop her. 'If I am correct our hostess will already have insisted that you, along with the rest of us, be on first-name terms. So, Pauline, it should be Peter. I fear you are not here alone?' He cast his gaze around the room as if looking for a likely candidate to be Lena's escort.

'He hasn't come down yet,' she explained.

'The doctor, no doubt.'

'You have a good memory.'

'I have, and I still remember you said you would like to sail with me on the Humber. I will hold you to that.'

Lena's thoughts raced. He had remembered! Then he must have thought about her...

At that moment a young lady came to stand beside them and slid her arm through Peter's. She smiled at Lena. 'I have someone I want Peter to meet. Do you mind if I take him away from you?'

Lena was stunned but managed to make a courteous reply. 'Not at all.'

Peter made no introduction but bowed to Lena, his eyes teasing, as if he knew what thoughts were in her head.

As she watched them walk away, arm-in-arm, Lena found herself filled with jealousy. She tightened her lips and chastised herself for reacting like a young girl – and for wondering what rights that young woman exerted over Peter Hustwick.

Chapter Twelve

'You seem very thoughtful.'

Lena spun round, startled 'Oh, Alistair.'

'You looked far away.'

She gathered her thoughts quickly. 'I was admiring that dress,' she said, indicating the young woman on Peter's arm.

Alistair shot a quick glance in her direction. 'Not a patch on yours,' he commented. 'In fact, you are beyond anyone else in the room.'

Lena gave a small smile. 'That's sweet of you, but I'm sure you are mistaken.'

'Not in my eyes.'

'Have you met everyone?' she asked, directing the conversation away from where she thought it might be heading.

'No. I met two couples as I came downstairs.'

'Then let me introduce you to those I have already met.'

Conversation was flowing pleasantly as the guests got to know each other, and the atmosphere became even more relaxed when Marcia returned with Charles who apologised for not being there sooner because of a small crisis on the farm. When the gathering showed concern he quickly reassured everyone that there was no cause for unease as the problem had been solved.

A few minutes later it was announced that dinner was served and the guests followed their hosts to the dining-room where they quickly found their allotted places at table.

'So we are together again,' said Peter when Lena found herself beside him, looking for her place. She saw pleasure behind the teasing glance he shot at her. 'It seems fate is bent on drawing us close.' She made no reply as he held her chair out for her while she sat down. 'Where might the good doctor be?' He glanced along the table. 'Ah, near the end with Lady Devlin on one side and Jemima Fox-Patrington on the other.' He leaned towards her and lowered his voice. 'Fine name, isn't it? And there's money to go with it. She's an only child ... a good catch for someone.'

'And might your eyes be turning that way?' Lena retorted.

He chuckled. 'Not my choice.'

'Then who would be your choice?'

He pursed his lips in consideration as he let his gaze idle over the other female guests. 'Well, maybe you,' he said after due consideration.

'What would your companion say if she heard that?'

'I'll have to ask her.'

'Don't you dare,' snapped Lena indignantly. 'I want no trouble.'

'Trouble?' he asked in amusement. 'I can assure you, there will be no trouble. But rest assured – I promise I won't ask her unless you are present.'

That line of conversation was broken when the food began to be served and nearby guests could not be ignored. Brisk and merry talk flowed around the table. Guests settled, at ease with each other, as Marcia and Charles ably manoeuvred the conversation from opposite ends of the table.

When the chance came Lena posed the question that had occupied her mind since first seeing Peter. 'Are you friendly with the Sugdens and so merited an invitation?'

He gave a teasing smile. 'Should I keep you guessing or perhaps ask you the same question?'

Lena felt her anger rising at what she could take for criticism of her curiosity, but quelled her irritation and said haughtily, 'It's easy to answer. Alistair and Charles were at school together in York, kept in touch, and renewed a closer relationship when Charles and Marcia moved here.'

'I see, then you have a perfectly legitimate reason for being here.' Peter turned his attention to his beef as if he was going to say no more.

'And you?' she snapped indignantly, keeping her voice low so that her annoyance would not be obvious to others close by.

'Oh, me?' He feigned surprise, as if astonished she should want to know. 'I am here because our firm does a great deal of business with Charles, shipping the wool he produces abroad.'

'But I thought all the wool would have gone to his family's mill?'

'It does, but we transport all the Sugdens' wool there and thereby have exclusive right to ship the manufactured goods abroad.'

'That makes sense.'

'It might interest you to know I negotiated the terms, which proved highly satisfactory to both parties.'

'Not your father?'

'You seem surprised?'

'I thought he ran the business?'

'He does, but on this occasion he was not well and left the affair to me.'

'And have there been many more such triumphs?'

'No, though truly I'm not worried. Things are going along nicely.'

'But wouldn't you like to expand?'

Peter gave a shake of his head. 'I'm content with the way things are.'

She knew it was no good pressing the matter but locked the information away in her mind.

The gentleman on her right asked Lena a question about Whitby then and a brisk conversation developed between them. He showed some surprise that she knew so much about the mercantile side of the port. At the same time, Peter became involved in a three-way conversation with the lady on his left and a gentleman on the opposite side of the table, when that gentleman drew them into a conversation on the merits of Constable as a painter.

Lena caught snatches of their discussion and was surprised by Peter's knowledge of painting. It was something she would have to ask him about as she herself had a liking for the work of John Ward of Hull.

When the final course was finished, Marcia rose and was followed by the rest of the ladies to the drawing-room, leaving the men to their cigars and port.

The general talk was of the latest fashions and

the opinions expressed in several ladies' magazines. They were not publications to which Lena subscribed, though she did try to keep abreast of fashion trends to some degree. Now she realised that her knowledge should probably be extended, especially if she were to become a doctor's wife. She smiled to herself as she wondered what these ladies would have thought if they had seen her attire when she had roamed Whitby's quays and wharves. Gossip began to take over and when Hull was mentioned Lena strained her ears to catch any comments made about the Hustwick family.

'My dear Miss Carnforth, or should I follow our hostess's request for informality and say Pauline?' One young lady drew her attention. 'You were sitting next to the highly eligible Mr Hustwick, and I noticed that at times you were deep in conversation with him. How did you find him?'

'Polite and attentive,' replied Lena, without elaborating, and was relieved that the matter could be taken no further when the door opened and Charles led in the men to join the ladies.

Lena noticed Peter make straight for the young woman with whom he had arrived at Weaver Hall, whose name she had learned was Greta, though beyond that she knew no more about her. Laughter ran out from their exchanges. Lena's lips tightened in annoyance.

'I hope you are enjoying yourself.' Alistair's quiet voice broke into her thoughts.

She forced a smile. 'Oh, yes, indeed.'

'You looked somewhat preoccupied?'

'Just wondering how Mama and Papa would have viewed my coming here with you.'

'I'm sure they would have approved.'

'I believe you are right.'

Conversation flowed freely among the groups that had formed but host and hostess, without making it appear too obvious, made sure that their guests freely circulated so that a friendly atmosphere was encouraged generally. Wine was served and coffee and sweetmeats made available.

After an hour Marcia clapped her hands, bringing silence to the room. 'Eliza has agreed to play the piano for us.'

The murmur of approval coming from a number of guests told Lena some of them already knew of Eliza's talent. She found their opinion borne out when Eliza stroked the keys with a delicate touch, drawing out the most exquisite sounds as she played Chopin. She followed the piece with others by Mozart and Brahms. Whenever she finished a piece there were cries for more until finally Marcia intervened and called for a rest for her. She was loudly applauded and everyone wanted to make their own personal thanks until finally they settled down to conversation again.

'Wasn't that splendid?' Peter voiced his pleasure as he and Greta came to talk to Lena and Alistair.

'Indeed it was,' replied Alistair.

'Truly an accomplished performance,' said Greta. 'I wish I played as well.'

'You play the piano?' queried Lena.

'I do,' Greta confirmed, 'but not as well as

Eliza. I could never compare myself to her. Do you play, Lena?'

'Yes, I do, though I too could not compete with her. What about you, Peter?'

'No,' he replied with a shake of his head.

'It's never too late,' she pointed out.

'That's what I keep telling him,' said Greta.

'I have you to entertain me, my dear.'

Lena squirmed at the thought of these two enjoying a musical evening together.

Greta gave a small dismissive gesture. 'You make it sound as if I am a frequent visitor to Raby Hall.'

'You do not live nearby?' queried Lena.

Greta gave a little laugh. 'Goodness, me, no.'

At that moment Charles approached. 'I'm sorry to break in, but can I drag Alistair away? Jemima's not feeling too well. I wonder if you would have a word with her, Alistair?'

'Of course.'

'Marcia's taken her to the small drawing-room.'

'Can we be of any help?' Greta asked.

'No, no. She doesn't want any fuss, but I insisted she see Alistair.' The two men hurried away.

With a challenging smile Peter said, 'Maybe this is a good opportunity to put that question to the young lady who accompanied me here?'

Lena scowled but realised he had backed her into a corner from which she could not escape.

'A question for me?' asked Greta, mystified.

'Earlier, when we were dining, Lena asked me who I would choose from the ladies present this evening.' Lena blushed crimson. 'I said, "maybe you", meaning Lena herself. She asked what my companion would say to that, and I replied we would have to ask her but promised not to do so until we three were together. Well, here we are.'

Greta laughed. 'Peter, you are deliberately embarrassing Lena.' She leaned towards her. 'This man is a tease, take no notice of him.' She turned back to him. 'You know full well this has nothing to do with me.' She stopped in full flow. 'Oh, I see, you were making out that I was very close to you, someone special.' She turned back to Lena. 'We are close, I suppose, in the way of many cousins.'

'Cousins?' Lena queried with surprise.

'Yes,' confirmed Greta. 'Nothing more than that! He is very dear to me, though as free as the wind in matters of the heart.' She glanced across the room. 'Someone wants me,' she said, responding to a gesture. 'I will see you again later.'

Though angry at the trick Peter had played on her by his deception, Lena could not deny that her heart was racing and her thoughts soaring at this news, but he needed admonishing. 'That was an unkind trick you played on me, letting me think...' Seeing the laughter in his eyes she stopped, shrugged her shoulders and said, 'Well, I suppose you derived pleasure from it.'

'I did, and will do anew because now I have to make it up to you in some way. You must visit Hull again, then I can keep my promise to take you on the river.'

He did not receive her response because at that moment Marcia reappeared with Alistair and announced, 'Jemima will be all right. Alistair has diagnosed nothing serious. He has given her a sedative. A good night's sleep should do wonders.'

Murmurs of relief ran round the room. Sensing the atmosphere, which had dipped a little on Jemima's indisposition, lift again, Charles announced, 'Tomorrow we have planned a day out to Kirkham Abbey, weather permitting, and I believe the signs are good. Anyone who wants to ride there can take one of our horses; carriages will be provided for those who wish a more leisurely journey. Those who do not want to go are very welcome to stay here and enjoy our home. All I ask is that you let Marcia know your intentions before you go to bed this evening.'

Alistair crossed the room to Lena and Peter. Not wanting Peter to reveal that they already knew each other from her visit to Hull, she quickly stepped in to make a more comprehensive introduction. 'Alistair, it was Peter's father with whom James negotiated when I accompanied him to Hull. Peter kindly showed me the town and countryside.'

'It was a pleasure to find someone interested in Hull,' he put in, using a non-committal tone when he realised that she had not previously mentioned any details of her visit to Alistair.

'Then I must thank you for looking after Miss Carnforth in a strange town.'

'She was a charming companion, and brought a much-needed lightness of atmosphere to the moments when the four of us dined together. If Lena hadn't been there, my father would have talked nothing but business.' To move away from the subject Peter added, 'Will you both be going to Kirkham tomorrow?'

'I think I had better stay here because of my patient. I have recommended that she has a quiet day tomorrow,' said Alistair.

'Then I shall stay with you,' offered Lena.

'No, there is no need. You must go and enjoy yourself,' he urged.

'I'll be on my own.'

'You can accompany me and my cousin,' put in Peter quickly.

'There you are, my dear, you can't refuse,' said Alistair, putting weight behind Peter's offer.

Lena hesitated. She wanted to agree but did not want to make it look too obvious. The chance to spend more time with Peter, even with his cousin around, was tempting. She wanted to know more about him, and in her mind was already busy making comparisons between him and Alistair. 'Very well,' she agreed, not at all reluctantly.

'Excellent,' said Peter. 'You can rest assured that Miss Carnforth will be well looked after and returned safely to you.' He turned to Lena. 'Do you ride or will we take a carriage?'

'I'm afraid I do not ride,' she said, a touch of regret in her voice.

'Then it will be a carriage. I will tell Marcia of our intention.' He made his excuses and left them to seek out Greta first.

When he was able to get her on her own, he informed her of the arrangements.

'Oh, dear.' She pouted. 'I had so looked forward to riding. Charles tells me he has some fine horses in his stable.'

'Please, on this occasion, accompany Lena and me in the carriage.'

'Ah!' The light of knowing curiosity came to her eyes. 'Do I detect a growing interest in Miss Lena Carnforth?'

Peter smiled. 'Who knows?'

'I suspect I am right, but what about the good doctor? Do her feelings lie in that direction?'

'I feel I have the advantage – she has inherited an interest in mercantile matters from her father.'

Greta raised an eyebrow. 'Ah, the plot thickens.' She gave a sly smile. 'Do you really want me as chaperone?'

'I think it would look better, but chaperones can sometimes slip away.'

Her eyes twinkled. 'No doubt. And for my very dear cousin, I expect it will happen.'

When everyone was gathered at breakfast, Charles announced there were seven people for carriages, four for one and three for the other; six people, including himself and Marcia, would ride, and the rest would stay at Weaver Hall.

Twenty minutes later Peter was shepherding Greta and Lena into their coach. All around was excitement as others mounted their horses and those staying behind waved them off, wishing them a good day. Alistair remained with the party at the Hall.

'Follow me!' called Charles, and set a steady pace in consideration for the coaches.

After a mile he turned off the main track and took one that ran round the edge of a large field towards a group of buildings including two small cottages. As they neared them, two men dressed as grooms emerged, one from a cottage, the other from a nearby building that bore all the hall-marks of a stable.

'Good day, sir,' they called as Charles halted the party and swung down from his horse.

'And to you, Bob, Jack.' He called to the others. 'Would you all like to dismount? There's something I'd like to show you in which I think you will be interested.'

Two boys had run from the stable. They and the groomsmen quickly had the horses tethered to a rail provided for the purpose and then followed the group Charles was leading towards the stable.

'All this has been recently renovated,' commented Peter as he cast his eyes over the buildings. His observation was borne out by conditions inside, which showed a strict observance of neatness and cleanliness. The visitors' remarks of surprise and approval grew in volume when they saw stalls stretching the full length of the building. It was obvious that these animals were special. Those who knew horses realised they were looking at thoroughbreds. Questions began to flow towards Charles, who smiled and held up his hands for quiet. He held out his hand to Marcia, indicating that he wanted her beside him. She slipped her hand into his.

'This is our new venture ... well, I know my wife would want me to use the word "our" but it is really her suggestion. I am sure it will prove a wise one and also be profitable. We have sought expert opinion and gained the advice of several well-known figures in the racing world about our stock.'

'I knew you were both keen riders but I did not

know you had an interest in the racing world,' someone said

'We hadn't. This is something completely new for us.'

'It looks as if you are going into it in a big way,' came another observation.

'We don't believe in half-measures,' Charles confirmed. 'The full hog for us – but within our means, of course! Apart from racing some of these horses, we hope to run a stud. It all stems from the downturn in the corn market because of cheap imports from America. We won't be hit as hard as some; we aren't dependent on corn, though we will continue to grow some. As you know, we have flocks of sheep and some cattle but we wanted something to replace the corn. Marcia came up with the idea of thoroughbred racehorses. So that is what we have done.'

'You'll be sure to give us the nod when you have a likely winner?' someone called, a suggestion that brought jovial murmurs of agreement from the rest of the party.

'Maybe you'll have a chance later this year. We have our minds set on a runner at Beverley.'

'Which one?'

'Don't really know yet. Look around and take your pick.'

As people spread out along the row of stalls, admiring the animals, Greta found one particular horse captured her attention. Peter led Lena on as he asked, 'Do you follow racing?'

'No.'

'Then that is something else we'll have to put right.'

As they walked though the stable, Lena's thoughts were awhirl. What was Peter offering – racing, sailing, more than that? And then there was Alistair, dear Alistair, a lifelong friend who would bring her stability and standing in the community, respect and every comfort. She could never imagine him sailing or attending a race meeting, though, and he certainly was no passport into the mercantile world.

'You're deep in thought,' Peter whispered close to her ear.

Lena started. She had not realised how abstracted she had become. 'I was thinking about what you just said.'

'Favourably, I hope?'

She shrugged her shoulders. 'You are too far away to put it right.'

He pursed his lips. 'Maybe ... you'll have to let me think about it. In the meantime lesson one begins.' He led her to the next stall and displayed his knowledge of what to look for in a racehorse that might make it a potential winner. Lena found herself rapidly becoming fascinated.

'I did not know you were such an expert. You must have been around horses a lot.'

He smiled. 'Not at all! Though I had a number of friends who were. They attended races regularly at Beverley and York and I generally went along. I learned a lot from them.'

'Everyone!' Charles's voice resounded above the chatter. 'We'll leave in five minutes.'

The chattering continued as they went back to their horses and carriages. Thanks were passed to the grooms and stable boys, and congratulations

209

and best wishes for the new enterprise were showered on Marcia and Charles.

'That was most interesting,' mused Greta as she settled down and the carriage got under way. 'You know, Peter, there's nothing to hold me in Northampton. I think I might consider moving back to Hull.'

'That would be splendid. It would be good to have you near again. We had some grand times together.' He glanced at Lena. 'Greta is an only child. When her parents moved to Northampton and were seriously injured in an accident, she felt obliged to leave Hull to look after them. Their injuries did not take their final toll until two years later. Now Greta has been left on her own. Think seriously about a move, Greta.'

'I believe I already have.'

Lena felt a pang of jealousy and tried to quell it with the thought that Greta had intimated she and Peter were nothing more than close cousins. He was romantically free. Nevertheless alarm bells rang in her mind. It was not too unusual for cousins to marry!

Chapter Thirteen

'There's someone I want to have a word with,' said Greta as they came out of the inn opposite the ruins of Kirkham Priory. 'I'll see you at the carriage when it's time to leave.'

Peter took his chance. 'Care to walk by the

water?' he asked Lena.

'That would be pleasant,' she replied.

They strolled towards the water and then along the bank of the river flowing gently through the pleasant Yorkshire countryside, each waiting for the other to speak but feeling content just to be together.

'It would be companionable for you to have Greta near, if she is serious about moving,' Lena broke the silence.

'It would. I detect from her remark that she has almost made up her mind and whenever she does, she acts quickly so it wouldn't surprise me if a move takes place soon. I look forward to that. It could give you the perfect opportunity to visit Hull.'

Lena looked askance at him. 'How? What do you mean?'

'It would look better if an invitation to visit came from Greta rather than me; you would not be staying under a gentleman's roof.'

Lena gave a small smile at the intrigue he was proposing; it sent a certain thrill through her. 'She could invite you to attend Beverley races or some other function, for example,' Peter continued.

'You seem to have given this some thought?'

'No. It has just burst upon me. In affairs of the heart, where you are concerned, I don't believe in missing an opportunity.'

'You flatter me, Peter, but don't get too many ideas...' She laid a hand on his arm.

He stopped and turned to look at her. Their eyes met with an expression that said everything without their needing to utter a word. He drew her to him then and their lips met, gently at first then more firmly in an expression of their deep feeling.

All of a sudden, Lena felt conscience-stricken. Since leaving Weaver Hall she had never given Alistair a thought. And now, here she was, in another man's arms. She drew back from Peter, a startled expression in her eyes.

'What is it?' he asked in concern as he tried to hold on to her, but as she pushed him away his voice turned sharp. 'Does the good doctor, the hero of the hour, come between us?' he asked.

Her eyes flared angrily at his tone. She swung on her heel and hurried away.

Bewildered, he took a step after her then stopped himself. To pursue her now might do more harm than good. He watched her go, filled with dismay. What wouldn't he give to turn back the clock to the moment before his unwise words? Dejected, he strolled on, wondering how he could put things right with Lena.

But the opportunity did not arise as other guests engaged them in conversations until their carriage arrived. However hard they tried to act normally, the stilted words they exchanged once sitting inside it were not lost on Greta. A wise head on young shoulders, she realised her scheme to let them be alone had not answered its purpose so, to try to lighten the atmosphere, she talked almost non-stop until they arrived back at Weaver Hall.

Those who had stayed behind came out to meet them when they saw the carriages and riders approaching.

Alistair was quickly beside Lena, eager to know if she had enjoyed herself. 'A splendid day,' she replied, putting all the enthusiasm she could into her voice and embracing him more ardently than she might otherwise have done in public, aware that her every action was closely observed by Peter.

'I'm so glad,' returned Alistair. He held out his hand to Peter. 'Thank you for looking after her,' he said with an appreciative handshake. 'And thanks to you too.' He bowed his head to Greta.

'It was our pleasure,' said Peter. Turning to Lena he said, 'Thank you for your pleasant company.' She saw the sorrow and apology in his eyes and inclined her head in acknowledgement, slipping her arm through Alistair's.

Greta tapped on her cousin's door and stepped inside the room as soon as he opened it. 'Now what went wrong at Kirkham?' she demanded. 'The chaperone left you on your own but it was readily apparent that something had gone amiss.'

'Was it that obvious?' he asked plaintively.

'To me it was,' she said impatiently. 'Others, engrossed in their own affairs, probably didn't notice anything. Tell me what happened?'

'So, nothing momentous,' she commented when he had finished. 'But if you are serious about Lena then you had better put things right with her – and quick. There is a very presentable doctor lurking out there who has the crucial advantage over you: he lives in Whitby.'

'What do I do?'

'Apologise. Tell her you did not mean any discourtesy. Tell her how you feel about her and that you never meant to hurt her feelings. I've only known her for the few hours we have been here but I think I am a shrewd judge of my sex and I believe Lena thinks highly of you. Whether it goes beyond that I can't tell, but I think she is straightforward and respects people who are straightforward with her. Don't make any excuses; she'll see through them. If I'm not mistaken, she'll admire your honesty. From there on I cannot tell you what to do. Only you can decide. The party breaks up tomorrow, remember, you haven't much time.'

She started for the door but stopped with her hand on the knob to glance back at him. 'By the way, I came to a decision after you went for your walk. I'm definitely coming back to Hull. That might be of advantage to you.' She did not expand on her meaning. She did not need to.

'I had already thought of that when you said you might return.'

But Peter was unable to secure a private conversation with Lena that evening or the next day. It was with regret and sadness in his heart that he watched her drive away with Alistair on Sunday before he and Greta mounted their horses to ride back to Hull. The next time he would see Lena would be at the launching of the *John Carnforth* – and who knew what might happen before then?

'You're quiet, Lena, is there something wrong?'

She started; Alistair's expression of concern broke into her confused thoughts. 'Sorry, I was far away, thinking of the pleasant time we have had at Weaver Hall.'

He glanced at her and smiled. 'I'm so glad you enjoyed it. I have no doubt we'll be asked again, and we'll have to invite Marcia and Charles to Whitby.'

His use of 'we' jolted her. Was he taking for granted that they had a future together? She found herself bothered by this supposition. At one time, not so long ago, she would have welcomed such a hint in his words. But since then she had met Peter, and now she recalled with regret the look of sadness in his eyes as her carriage had driven away. She wanted to turn back and ask his forgiveness for her overreaction, but that could not be done. Her next chance would be the launching ceremony.

She tried to talk nonchalantly about what had happened at Weaver Hall and other subjects closer to Alistair's heart.

On reaching New Buildings, he was quickly to the ground to help her from the carriage.

'Hello, you two.' Looking round they saw Olivia hurrying towards them. 'Have you had a splendid time?' she asked, her eyes full of excited enquiry.

'Wonderful,' replied Alistair.

'And memorable,' added Lena, feigning equal enthusiasm.

'Where are you off to?' Alistair asked his sister.

'Window shopping, hoping to find a dress or an idea for one to be made for the ceremony.'

'Oh, my, I'll have to give that some thought too,' said Lena.

'I'll forego my shopping to hear all about

Weaver Hall and then we can both go dress hunting tomorrow,' said Olivia, in such a spirited way that Lena could hardly refuse.

'Very well,' she agreed. 'Come in, we can chat over a cup of tea after I have freshened up. Are you coming, Alistair?'

He gave a small laugh. 'What! And listen to you two, chattering sixty to the dozen? I'd be better off at home. I'll see you later.' He climbed on to the chaise and drove it away.

Lena and Olivia hurried into the house where, after contacting Mrs Campion to let her know she was back and ordering tea for two, Lena quickly tidied herself and then rejoined Olivia in the drawing-room.

She soon led Lena into telling her all about Weaver Hall. She hung on every word of description about the house and surrounding countryside, and was even more attentive when it came to the guests and the fashions that had predominated throughout the visit.

When Lena had told her all, with the exception of the new contact with Peter Hustwick, she asked, 'Has anything happened in Whitby?'

Olivia pursed her lips thoughtfully for a moment then shook her head. 'Nothing out of the ordinary.'

'What about the *John Carnforth?*'

'On schedule, as far as I know! I see so little of James. He's very busy, anxious that she will be ready on time.'

'And will she?'

'James talks little about the ship when I do see him, but I'm sure she will be.'

216

'Good. I would hate anything to go wrong at this stage.'

'So would I. He's put so much into this, and is determined to make a success of it.'

'And with the first commercial venture for the *John Carnforth* already lined up, the vessel must be ready on time.'

'That will be a momentous experience for you – launching a ship named after your father?'

'I haven't been asked to perform the ceremony.'

'You haven't?' Olivia did not disguise her surprise and when Lena shook her head, added, 'Well, I expect you soon will be. And tomorrow we'll have to see you get an extra-special dress for it.'

When James came home he showed interest in Lena's visit to Weaver Hall during their evening meal and was especially pleased to know that Peter Hustwick had been there. He saw any continued contact with the Hull firm as valuable.

'I have Ralph coming in an hour,' he told her. 'There are some details regarding the ceremony that I want to go over with him. We'll use my study so need not disturb you, unless you care to join us for a glass of Madeira afterwards.'

'That would be pleasant,' she agreed.

'It will take us about an hour.'

'Join me in the drawing-room when you are finished.' Maybe her brother would ask her to perform the launching ceremony then?

But Lena was disappointed. They talked little about the business and she went to bed wondering why he had not yet broached the subject?

217

As arranged, Peter arrived in Whitby two days before the ceremony. After finding his way to the Angel and claiming the accommodation that James had booked for him, he enquired the way to Carnforth's office. He was impressed by what he saw of Whitby as he made his way over the bridge and crossed to the east side. A busy atmosphere emanated from the port, but he could see its differences from Hull. Whereas his home town took advantage of its situation, with the River Hull joining the Humber in flat terrain that encouraged expansion, Whitby was enclosed by high cliffs to either side of the river. But with much activity around the ships at the quays, he realised this port still retained its importance, and from the sounds coming from the shipyards it still did good business building stout ships.

Entering the building, he was greeted by Ben who escorted him to James's office. As soon as Peter was announced, James was out of his seat and greeting him with a warm handshake.

'Delighted to see you. I trust you have had a pleasant journey?'

'It went very well, and I thank you for booking me such a splendid room at the Angel.'

'Do sit down. A glass of Madeira?'

'That sounds an excellent idea. Thank you.' Peter laid his hat and walking stick on an adjacent chair and sat down in the place indicated by James.

'Your father?' he asked as he poured two glasses. 'Have you left him at the Angel?'

'He is not with me. Sadly he is not well and thus unable to travel.'

'Nothing serious, I hope?' enquired James in concern as he handed a glass to his guest and resumed his own seat.

'No, no,' Peter replied, giving a little shake of his head. 'Father will overindulge and you know the result. I keep telling him he over imbibes but he takes no notice. It's one of his pleasures.'

'I'm sorry he isn't here but it is good to have you. It would not have been quite the same if there had been no Hustwick present when *John Carnforth* takes to the water for the first time.'

'It is a privilege for me.'

'Good.' James raised his glass. 'Here's to our continued co-operation.'

'I hope so.'

'Now, you are dining with us at home this evening. As you don't know Whitby, I think it might be wise if I walk with you from the Angel and show you the best way.'

'Splendid. But can you spare the time?'

'Oh, yes! Everything is in hand and Ralph is competent enough to see to anything that arises now. I'll introduce you on the way out. Besides, it will give me the opportunity to collect some papers from home for him. I forgot them earlier today. I was going to have to go back for them so I'll kill two birds with one stone, so to speak.'

They finished their wine and he took Peter to the next room along the corridor.

'Ralph Bell, my manager and trusted friend,' James announced, 'Knows more about this firm than I.'

'James belittles his knowledge,' said Ralph. 'He has a very shrewd brain for business.'

'But you can often see further beneath the surface than I.'

'It sounds as if you make a good team, one of whom competitors would do well to be wary,' observed Peter. 'I hope we never become rivals.'

'I'm sure we won't,' said James.

'We had a good teacher in James's father,' Ralph explained. 'He employed me as a youngster and I will ever be grateful to him for that. James and I more or less served under him together. He taught us all we know.'

'Ralph, I'm going to show Peter the way from the Angel to New Buildings. I'll return with those papers I forgot earlier,' said James, starting for the door.

'Very well,' said Ralph, and wished Peter a pleasant stay in Whitby.

'Ralph seems a very likeable person and I would surmise you are very fortunate in having him working for you,' observed Peter as they walked towards the bridge.

'Indeed I am. I make it worth his while to stay with me too.'

'A wise move.'

'If ever I expand, I will give him more responsibility and he knows that.'

As they made their way to New Buildings James pointed out landmarks and praised Whitby's many amenities. 'But,' he finished as they turned into New Buildings, 'I realise there is greater potential in Hull, with its ease of access and facilities for expansion.'

'True,' agreed Peter, 'but there is something to be said for compactness, especially for anyone who is content with the way his firm is situated and has no further wish to expand.'

It was a debatable point and James did not want to reveal anything remotely connected to his own ambitions. So he was glad that at this point he was able to say, 'Here we are.' He stopped at a gate giving access to a path that divided into two, with each side running alongside the garden to steps at either end of a stone veranda. He led the way through the front door to an imposing hall.

James crossed to a door on the right. Peter laid his hat on a small table, leaned his stick against it and waited. He felt his heart quicken when he heard James say, 'I've brought someone to see you.' He stood aside then, a signal for Peter to enter the room before him.

'Miss Carnforth, what a delight to see you.' The sincerity in Peter's voice was not lost on her.

'And you,' Lena replied automatically as he came forward to take her proffered hand. He took it and raised it to his lips but kept his eyes intent on hers, trying to read her true reaction.

Lena had imagined this meeting many times since learning that James had invited Peter to dine with them this evening, but she had not anticipated it would occur before his arrival for the meal. Now, when she asked if they would both take tea, she found the scenario taking an unexpected turn when Peter accepted but her brother said, 'I can't stay, Lena, I have some papers to take back to Ralph.' He was heading for the door as he said, 'You'll be able to find your own way, Peter?'

'Of course! You have been an attentive guide.'

'Good. See you this evening.'

As the door clicked shut Lena and Peter spoke as one.

'Mr Hustwick...'

'Miss Carnforth...'

He was the quicker to recover. 'I have been troubled ever since leaving Weaver Hall. I apologise most sincerely for what I said to you, and the way I said it. I hope in your heart you will see a way to forgive me? I meant no harm by it; I am sorry to say it reflected jealousy, for which I am extremely embarrassed. I beg...'

Lena held up her hand to stop him. 'Say no more, Mr Hustwick. I should apologise to you for reacting so suddenly and not taking care to consider your words fully. As soon as I had reconsidered them, I was urged to ask forgiveness but sadly the opportunity never arose. I thought maybe it never would but now it has.'

'Miss Carnforth,' he said, moving quickly as she left a momentary pause, 'I am thankful we have been given this chance to be alone and make our peace. Please let us say no more about the matter. It is a thing of the past and should be erased from our memories. Say you can do that and let us begin again?'

'That is my wish too.'

'Then I am content.'

'Very good, Mr Hustwick. Let me ring for tea.' Lena rose to her feet.

He stopped her. 'At Weaver Hall, formality was

cast aside. May we continue in that vein?'

'Of course, Peter. It will recall pleasant times.' With her heart beating a little faster, Lena went to the bell-pull.

He watched her with admiring eyes, hoping there would be only the three of them at dinner this evening. He definitely did not want the doctor's company. As she turned back to resume her seat, his cousin's words were ringing in Peter's ears.

Within a few minutes tea was being served and their conversation drifted idly over a variety of topics until he said, 'Lena, I meant what I said about taking you on the river and also to the races. It would be an honour to do so.'

'I thank you for your most generous offer but a chaperone...'

'My cousin Greta. She is moving to Hull and has offered you accommodation whenever you choose to come.'

Lena allowed an amused smile to appear. 'And then she'll absent herself conveniently, as she did at Weaver Hall?'

Peter felt his face redden. 'You noticed?'

'Well, it seemed a little obvious, though I welcomed it.'

'You did?'

She nodded and looked down a moment. 'I wanted to get to know you better.'

'And you did, but only the worst side of me.'

She raised her hand. 'We are not to speak of that. I did see much to admire in you.'

'And I in you. Lena, I cannot hold back any longer. Your image has haunted me every day since I last saw you.' Her ears were ringing, her heart pounding. A cautionary voice told her to stop this, but a more adventurous one urged her not to. 'I cannot go on like this, Lena, I cannot be tormented any longer. Please be my wife? Please marry me?'

Pleasure swept through her but her ears had not yet fully grasped what was happening. Oh, she had considered the possibility, but had dismissed it as unlikely. Now here it was, confronting her. A decision was being thrust upon her. But there was Alistair to consider. He had always been the most likely choice. She needed to escape. Time to think.

'Peter, I'm flattered, but this is most unexpected. I do need time.'

The desire to press her for a decision was strong. There was the doctor ... but to err now could easily ruin his chances. One wrong word from him and his whole world could collapse.

Peter reached forward. He took her hands, brought her to her feet and looked deep into her eyes as his arms slipped round her waist. His lips came down to hers and she did not resist. She could feel love and passion in his kiss. 'I love you, Lena,' he whispered as their lips parted. 'I respect your wish for time and will wait in hope.'

As Peter left the house his heart was singing. There was a chance for him! Lena had not said no. She had not pulled away from his embrace either and her kiss had been filled with promise.

Chapter Fourteen

If she'd thought the atmosphere during the evening meal would be tense Lena was mistaken. From the moment Peter arrived and was shown into the drawing-room, where she and James awaited him, she sensed his desire not to allow what had happened between them to intrude on their reunion.

Peter was guarded when he first entered the room, not knowing if his proposal had been discussed with James. When he became aware it had not, and realised that no one else would be dining with them, he was relieved. He would be alone with the two people he wanted to get to know better.

When he left the house later for his room at the Angel, he felt highly delighted with the way things had gone. Apart from a sumptuous meal, he had had the pleasure of being with Lena, getting to know her interests and her outlook on life. He'd seen her keen awareness of the commercial side of Whitby and been charmed by it. Behind her gentle demeanour, he saw a considerate loving person with a particular devotion to her brother whom he was surprised to learn was in reality her step-brother.

When Lena went to bed she had much to think about, linking the man she had got to know better this evening with the man who had proposed to her and whom she silently thanked for his discretion in not raising the matter again. He occupied her thoughts as she dressed the following morning, but she had other things to think about as the day progressed for this was the day when Aunt Mary, Uncle Martin and her three cousins would be arriving from Dundee. It was the second time she would face having so many people to stay in the house and she was thankful for Mrs Campion's competence now and during the celebrations after the ceremony.

James had sent a carriage to collect the Mac-Brides at York station and as the time approached for their arrival in Whitby an excited atmosphere started to fill the house. Though it would mean extra work, the staff had looked forward to this occasion, signalling a return to the heady days of frequent entertaining by Mr and Mrs Carnforth.

'They are here!' Lena called, all decorum thrust aside in her excitement as she rushed into the hall from the drawing-room where she had been keeping watch.

Maids came hurrying into the hall followed by Mrs Campion at a more sedate pace, alert to the actions of her staff.

James came bounding down the stairs and was close behind his sister who was first to the door. She flung it open, paused on the veranda and waved to the new arrivals who were dismounting from the carriage. James took Lena's hand and they went quickly down the steps to welcome their relatives.

Happy conversation filled the air as greetings, hugs and kisses were exchanged amidst queries about health, the journey and friends. Chatter continued until they were in the house when maids took charge of outdoor clothes and escorted the MacBrides to the rooms allocated to them before tea was served in the drawing-room.

Lena nodded to Mrs Campion who was supervising all the activity.

'Please send someone to the Nashes' and invite them to take tea with us in a few minutes. I'm sure they would like to greet the arrivals.'

'Very good, miss.'

A quarter of an hour later, in the drawing-room, the buzz of conversation rose and fell as tea cups and plates clinked, and compliments about the delicious scones and cakes were bestowed. All the young ladies queried what was to be worn by the others the next day, but found that each of them wanted their choice to remain a surprise. When the menfolk tried to extract information about who was going to launch the ship, James's reply was mysterious. He would not confirm what they had all imagined would be his answer. On the periphery of those questions, while talking to her cousins, Lena wondered why he still had not primed her about the ceremony so that she could get used to the idea. With this thought in mind she had wandered to a corner of the room where she stood alone, looking around her at everyone so happy together on this occasion. If she accepted Peter, she would miss all this: the visits of her relations, the air of nearness of the Nashes, the comfort and permanence this house exuded.

'You are far away.'

She started. Only then was she aware that Alistair stood before her.

And Alistair! The thought of how she would miss him if...

'Day dreaming,' she replied lamely.

'Care to share them? If I return to the fray I might get caught by your uncle again, though Avril did rescue me for a few minutes.'

Lena laughed. 'I saw he had cornered you. Medical stuff, no doubt. Was it really that bad?'

'No! I didn't mean it that way,' he hastened to reassure her, his face serious.

She laughed even more. 'I know you didn't, Alistair. Don't look so concerned. I also know my uncle.'

He relaxed and smiled. 'He's always interesting when he does get talking about health matters – well, to me he is – but I wanted to escape and come and talk to you.'

'He means well. And can be fascinating on other subjects, but in you he has someone who shares his first love, medicine.'

'I know.'

'You'll have to be the one to change the subject. Don't let him monopolise the talk with medical topics.'

'I won't, but I don't like to hurt his feelings.'

'He's a tough old bird.'

'You have him summed up.'

Lena smiled and wondered if she had Alistair summed up also. Would he become a medical bore too, one who had to be constantly steered away from talking medicine, as she was advising him now? Could she be sure he would embrace other conversations, about topics close to her heart? She knew her aunt sometimes escaped to tea parties with the good ladies of Dundee and into the work of charitable organisations. Was that her probable fate too if she married Alistair? Lena glanced round the room again. Would this, family and close friends, be sufficient to compensate her for the loss of the excitement she had experienced in her father's world?

Maybe her answer lay in James's secrecy about the launching ceremony. Might it be his way of inviting her to take a greater role within the company from which she felt shut out?

Tomorrow she would know.

In another part of Whitby someone else was thinking about tomorrow.

Peter walked the streets, spent time absorbing the bustle on the quays, watched construction work on a new vessel at one of the shipbuilding sites, talked to a rope maker. Then he went strolling on the West Cliff above the strand of sand that stretched away to Sandsend, climbing the hundred and ninety-nine steps to the old church and ruined abbey. He took luncheon in the Angel and was back there for his evening meal. He took his time over all this. Even when he was concentrating on the new sights and sounds, though, Lena commanded his thoughts. He would not allow himself to visit her home again, he'd decided. That would be impolite; he had not been invited and knew her relations from Dundee were arriving. He could not intrude. He would have to wait until tomorrow to see her.

Would she have an answer for him then? Could he expect one amidst all the excitement of the launching and the celebrations that were to follow?

The day after that he would be leaving for Hull. He wondered if he would be leaving in ecstasy or with hopes dashed into misery? It was a long day and an endless night.

Anxious eyes searched the morning sky for tell-tale clues about the weather. People turned away from their windows satisfied that they were able to foretell a good day.

No one was happier about this than James. Everything was in place; his meticulous concern for every detail should ensure a perfect ceremony and celebration afterwards.

Awake early, unable to sleep any longer, he rose and dressed in the clothes he had purchased especially for this important day. When he viewed himself in the full-length mirror he was satisfied that he cut a dashing figure.

As early as he was, he was surprised to find Lena about to start breakfast.

'Couldn't you sleep any longer either?'

She gave a wan smile. 'No. I had a lot on my mind.'

'Want to share those thoughts?'

'No. I wouldn't want to spoil your day.'

He raised a querying eyebrow but knew from her expression that he would get no more from her – not now.

'This is going to be a great day,' he said and added with more enthusiasm, 'an important day for Carnforth's.'

She half expected him to go on but he didn't.

'You have more plans?' she probed.

'Ah, still so curious? I have. But they must wait for after the launching.'

She was longing to ask what he meant by that, and if the plans concerned her, but knew she had to bite her tongue.

James changed the subject by saying, 'Excuse me, I'll be back in a moment.'

He rose from his chair and hurried from the room. When he came back he said, 'Stand up a minute.'

She looked askance at him but did as he'd bidden her.

'Now I can see the full elegance of your dress. You look wonderful and have chosen your apparel with great care and thought.'

'You have too, James. Your tailor has done a wonderful job.'

'No better than your dressmaker.' She was pleased by his admiration, especially when he added, 'Mother and Father would have been proud of you.'

'And of you.'

'I have a little present for you, in remembrance of today.' He held out a small red box.

'James!' She took it from him. 'Thank you.' She opened the box tentatively and stared wide-eyed at the contents. A replica of a sailing vessel, exquisitely worked in silver, was mounted on a piece of jet and presented as a brooch. It rested on a bed of red velvet that showed it off to perfection. 'Oh, James, it is wonderful! A treasure.' Her

231

eyes were damp as she looked at him lovingly. 'What can I say but a sincere and heartfelt thank you?' She stepped forward and kissed him on the cheek. Her mind was racing. Was this a prelude to something else he was to ask her?

Instead he said, 'Enjoy today. We'd better have breakfast. The others will be coming down soon. I don't want to be delayed ... things to see to. I'll say good morning and then be off. You will come with them?'

'Of course.'

'There are seats for all of you as well as the dignitaries of the town and special guests. Ralph will be there to direct everyone. There's a special area for our employees too. Oh, and ... well, there's no need for me to go through it all now. You'll see when you get there. And I've asked Ralph to be especially attentive to the family and close friends.'

'James, don't fuss. I know everything will already have been taken care of by you and I'm sure nothing will go wrong.'

No more was said as their uncle and aunt and cousins all appeared and, after admiring James's gift to Lena, they were soon partaking of breakfast while enthusing about the day ahead. After a few minutes James took his leave.

'Everybody ready?' called Lena to gather everyone in the hall. They came from the drawing-room and down the stairs, their excitement charging the atmosphere with anticipation.

She had a final word with Mrs Campion. 'The staff know where they are to go?'

'Yes, miss, and after the outdoor ceremonies will all be back in time for the party here.'

'Good. Tell them to enjoy the day.' When she turned back, a quick glance told her everyone was assembled and waiting for her to take the lead. Once in the street the Nashes, who had been on the lookout for them, joined them.

Olivia exchanged a quick hug with Lena and slipped away to join Fiona and Avril MacBride, allowing her brother to pair up with Lena.

'You are looking very elegant and beautiful,' he said with open admiration.

'You are looking very smart yourself,' Lena returned.

'Excited?' he asked.

'It is an important day for Carnforth's. This is the first ship to be added by my brother to the fleet. It should open new horizons for us. James has done well in just over a year.'

'He has indeed. And I have news too.'

Lena's heart skipped a beat. What was he going to say? Suggest? Offer?

'Dr Jollif has offered me a full partnership in his practice.'

'That is wonderful, Alistair. I am so pleased for you.'

'It means my future lies here in Whitby.'

Her mind started racing. Was she going to be forced into a decision sooner than she'd expected? If this launching opened up new possibilities for her ... if James...

Her thoughts were interrupted when her cousin Robbie fell into step beside them and said, 'Cousin Pauline, may I ask you a question?'

233

'Of course, Robbie. What is it?'

He looked slightly embarrassed and from the glance he shot Alistair, the doctor knew he would rather put his question to his cousin alone.

'I see Avril has drifted away from the others and is on her own, I'll go to her,' Alistair said tactfully.

Lena nodded and, as he moved away, turned to her cousin. 'Well, what do you want to know, Robbie?'

He swallowed hard as if plucking up courage. 'You know Dundee is an important port? Well, it has got into my blood. I want to gain experience of the mercantile world. I've seen how James has managed and what he has done. Do you think he would give me a job down here, so I could learn more about it?'

'I am very surprised, Robbie,' said Lena, not disguising her astonishment. 'I thought you would follow in your father's footsteps.'

'So did he. He expressed opposition at first but quickly realised he was wrong to take that attitude. If my heart wasn't in it, I would not make a good doctor. I am fortunate in having under-standing parents who realise that I am more likely to succeed in what I really want to do.'

'So they know and approve?'

'Yes.'

'And they know you are thinking of asking James?'

'Yes, but I thought if you had a word with him first, you might soften him up for me.'

Lena laughed. 'You think I'm that influential?'

'Oh, yes! You know a lot about what goes on in that world. Look how your father involved you, and I am sure James relies on your judgement.'

She held back from telling him the true situation and said instead, 'I'll have a word with him, but I may not get the opportunity to do so until later today or even tomorrow.'

Robbie's face lit up with a broad smile as if in these few moments his future had been assured.

Lena's thoughts were turning over and over. Here was a young man eager to join the world she loved, a world from which she was feeling shut out. But might something happen today to make that change for the better?

When they reached the shipyard on the west bank of the river, upstream from the bridge, they stopped to gaze in admiration at the new vessel resting on its launching cradle. Though Lena had seen it grow from individual timbers, she was still in awe of its beautiful lines and stout appearance. Oblivious to all the activity in the vicinity of the yard and of the people around her, she let her eyes run over its every line and allowed them to rest high amongst the rigging. Her imagination took her aboard the ship as, with white sails filled by the wind, she skimmed through the sea, sending foam streaming behind her. The horizon lay ahead and beyond it ... who knew?

'Good morning, Miss Carnforth.' She started, brought back to reality by Ralph's voice.

'Oh! Ralph, I was miles away.'

'You certainly were, miss. On board the *John Carnforth?*' He already knew the answer.

'Father would have been proud of her.'

'Indeed he would. Now, miss, if your party would follow me?'

235

Lena called to them and they followed Ralph to seats at the foot of a platform that had been erected close to the bow of the ship.

'James?' she asked of Ralph, as her party started to seat themselves.

'He won't require a seat; he'll be up there,' he replied, indicating the platform.

She nodded and said she wanted her uncle and aunt to sit on one side of her and Olivia on the other. Alistair looked askance at this, but getting no response from Lena he took a seat next to his sister. As he sat down Avril came to sit beside him.

Some of the seats were already occupied by several of the town's dignitaries who rose and came to exchange a quick word with Lena.

'James has put a lot of thought into this arrangement,' observed Olivia.

Apart from the area in which they were sitting there was a space roped off for all who had worked on the ship or been involved in supplying it, for the employees of Carnforth's and for those engaged in domestic work at the house in New Buildings. All of these people were separated from the public area where many others from the town were gathering to watch the launch and wish the *John Carnforth* well when she was baptised. The tempting smell of roasting oxen drifted on the sea air from two sites: one for the guests, the other for the general public.

Eyeing it all, Lena remarked, 'He certainly has and he never breathed a word about what he was planning.' There was a little touch of criticism in her voice but it was lost on Olivia who was enthralled by the atmosphere of gaiety.

'I've been admiring your brooch. I noticed it when we came out of the house but didn't get a chance...'

'James gave it to me at breakfast,' broke in Lena, 'a memento of a very special occasion.'

Olivia hid her jealousy; James had not given her a present by which to remember today.

The seats were filling up. Work along the quays had stopped; other shipyards were silent; shops were closed. Everyone was anxious to see a new ship take to its rightful place and join the fleet of Whitby vessels.

Lena looked round, searching the faces of people being directed to seats by Ralph who had also enlisted the help of Ben and Jude. Where was he? Then she wondered why she was feeling so concerned. She glanced past Olivia and saw Alistair deep in conversation with Avril. She frowned, then just as quickly chided herself for the thought that had crept into her head. She gave herself a little shake, stiffened her resolve and fell into polite conversation with her uncle and aunt. But her eyes still moved restlessly over the new arrivals.

Her uncle pulled a watch from his waistcoat pocket, flicked it open, noted the time and, as he returned it to his pocket, said, 'Only a few minutes to go.'

Lena made no reply. Where was Peter? Had further news of his father's illness taken him back to Hull? Or had something she'd said on the day of his arrival sent him away? Why did she feel so anxious? Why would it be a relief if she saw him?

She swept her gaze over Alistair and Avril again. They were enjoying laughing together.

Then her confused thoughts were stilled. He was here, standing before them, his smile just for her. Peter.

'Miss Carnforth. A delight to see you again.' He swept his hat from his head and pressed her hand to his lips as he bowed.

Out of the corner of her eye she saw her uncle's gaze settle on the young man. 'I'm so pleased you are here, Mr Hustwick. Please meet my uncle and aunt from Dundee.' The introduction quickly over, Lena added, 'And my dear friend Miss Nash who lives a few streets away. Of course, you already know Alistair from our time at Weaver Hall.'

Peter bowed to Olivia, shook hands with Alistair, and had to leave any further introductions until later, forced to take his seat as James was mounting the steps to the platform.

Lena just had time to whisper an explanation to her uncle whom she knew was dying of curiosity. 'He's the son of the owner of a firm of merchants in Hull. They have hired the *John Carnforth* for her maiden voyage.' Martin gave a little nod, satisfied with the explanation of how his niece knew this young man.

James reached centre platform with the bow of the ship towering behind him. The buzz of excitement began to wane and then was silenced completely by the roll of a drum from the band that had gathered to one side of the platform. A hush hung in the air.

'Ladies and gentlemen, I welcome you all here

today to witness what is an important day for Carnforth's – the launching of the *John Carnforth*, named after my father, the founder of the firm. Through his enterprise and foresight it has grown to what it is today. I hope this ship will help us build on the foundation he laid down. I know you don't want long speeches, and I want you all to enjoy the celebrations and eat and drink your fill, but first I ask you to leave those things from your mind while our good Reverend blesses the new vessel.'

At those words, Ralph, who was sitting at one end of a row, got to his feet and escorted the clergyman on to the platform. As he took his position Ralph hastened to his seat again.

'This new vessel results from the hard labours of many and now carries the hopes of more, for her future can determine the future of many of you here. Ultimately that depends on those who sail in her, so may they handle her well and may she sail the oceans proudly and safely – a consummate example of Whitby's ability to build stout ships. May God bestow on us all His blessing, especially those whose lives will depend upon this ship.' He drew a small bottle of Holy Water from his pocket. 'May He bless this craft and keep her safe on the far-flung oceans of the world,' he added, splashing the water on the bow of the ship.

As he walked back to the steps Ralph sprang to his feet to meet him and escort him to his seat. A buzz started again amongst the crowd.

Lena watched her brother with eager anticipation. The time was here; the moment she so

239

desired. In commemoration of their father, a signal that she could be an active part of the firm.

James gave a signal. The drum rolled again and silence fell across the assembly.

'The launching of the *John Carnforth*,'he called in a strong voice. 'It is my pleasure to ask Miss Olivia Nash to perform the ceremony!'

There were some gasps of surprise but those of Lena and Olivia were completely different. Lena was shattered. So the brooch was a sop! Olivia was breathless, shaking, and with her heart racing for joy because James had chosen her. This was better than a brooch! She sat dumbfounded until she became aware of Ralph standing in front of her.

'Miss Nash, may I escort you on to the platorm?'

She was too moved to speak but rose to her feet, glad of the support of his proffered arm. She was unaware of anyone or anything else as she walked towards the steps. It was only as she mounted them that she heard the applause and saw a smiling James holding out his hand to her at the top of the steps.

'What do I do?' she asked in alarm.

'Come with me.' He led her to a small table beside the towering bow. 'I have written down something for you to say, and then you smash this bottle of whisky on the bow.'

'Oh, but...' Her voice trailed away in confusion.

'You'll manage. Speak out – or shout if you'd rather. Take the bottle.' She picked it up while he took the paper and moved her so she was in a position to hit the bow with the bottle. He sensed the air of expectancy hanging over the hushed crowd. 'Now,' he whispered.

She swallowed hard, licked her lips and unknowingly shouted as she read the boldly executed words: 'I name this ship the *John Carnforth*. May God bless her and all who sail in her.'

'Smash it!'

The word from James galvanised her. She swung the bottle. It broke, sending whisky running down the bow and splashing into the air. Automatically she ducked to avoid it then, as she felt James's grip on her hand, she straightened up and joyful laughter burst from her lips.

'There, that wasn't so bad, was it?' He didn't expect an answer. The joy on her face told it all.

'It's moving,' she gasped.

The keelblocks and other supports had been removed earlier and at the moment of the launch the restraining triggers had been removed. Now everyone watched anxiously as the *John Carnforth* slid down the slipway. The band struck up with 'A Life on the Ocean Wave' and great cheers rang out when the vessel touched the water and settled comfortably into her new and rightful home.

James's face was alight with joy. He saw the excitement in Olivia's eyes too. They became aware that their arms were around each other's waist. He pulled her closer and above the cacophony of sound shouted, 'Marry me? Olivia, marry me!'

For one moment she stared, unable to believe her ears. This was not the way she had dreamed his proposal would be, but what did that matter? This was more exciting!

241

'Yes! Yes! Yes!' And laughter pealed from her lips.

He silenced it with a long and passionate kiss, oblivious to any attention they might be receiving – he knew everyone was caught up in the excitement of the immediate aftermath of the launching.

But one person watched. Lena, shocked by his choice of Olivia to launch the ship, felt even more shut out from the life she had hoped would be hers. Her eyes burned with hatred, a feeling she had never expected to feel towards the two people on the platform. The hope that had died in her heart was replaced by a desire for revenge on them.

In those moments her decision was made.

Chapter Fifteen

Amid all the exhilaration around her Lena watched James and Olivia come quickly down the steps and sensed something different about them. The laughter on their faces was intensified by the sharp light of joy in their eyes.

'James has just proposed,' Olivia announced, 'and I've said yes.' She turned to her father. 'Thank you for approving when he asked you yesterday.'

'I was pleased to do so,' said Albert. 'May you both be very happy.'

'We will be,' she said and revelled in the congratulations showered on them.

Lena stiffened; though this union had always been expected, coming as it did at this time it seemed to be closing the door against her hopes even more. But she should keep herself under control. There was the rest of the day to get through and then the celebrations at home, celebrations that would be even more poignant now. She would not be able to put the decision she had made into operation until tomorrow, but her resolve to do so was even stronger now.

'James, Olivia, I'm so happy for you.' Lena took their hands. 'I know you will have a wonderful life together.'

'Thank you,' said Olivia, her eyes damp with a happiness now sealed by the approval of her long-time friend. 'It will be marvellous to have you as my sister-in-law. It will be a natural extension to a friendship I have treasured so long.'

'As have I,' replied Lena. The pleasure she displayed was genuine enough. Olivia would make the perfect wife for James; content to let him provide while she enhanced their station in the community through her looks and charm, which she would skilfully display in social gatherings, both private and public.

'James, Dr MacBride is waving at us,' said Olivia. 'I think he wants us to meet someone he is talking to.'

'Oh, yes! You go to them, Olivia, I'll be with you in a moment. I want a quick word with Lena.'

Olivia left them. When James faced his sister his expression was contrite and serious. 'Lena, I hope you weren't offended that I didn't ask you to perform the launching ceremony? I thought asking Olivia would make the day extra-special, by linking the new ship and our engagement. That is why I did not mention it beforehand. I wanted it to be a complete surprise to her.'

Lena knew James. In his own euphoric state of mind, he would not notice that her smile was cold as she said, 'Think nothing of it. Oh, I would have liked to have performed the ceremony, but I can see it made sense to combine it with your proposal. Of course I understand.'

He kissed her on the cheek. 'Thank you. What have I done to deserve such a wonderful sister?' Then he glanced in the direction of his uncle. 'Oh, I must go.' He stopped and turned back. 'It would give me great pleasure to see you engaged to Alistair. We four must always remain close.' He hurried away then towards the group awaiting him.

Lena remained where she was. Her eyes narrowed as she watched her brother. How much credence should she put in his last remark? After all, she already knew that James valued his own feelings above anybody else's.

'Walk with me?'

She was startled to hear the words spoken close to her ear. 'Alistair! I didn't notice you.'

'You were miles away. Where were you?'

She gave a wan smile at that. 'Only I need know.'

Alistair thought he sensed a rebuke in her tone but ignored it. He took hold of her arm and said, 'Let's take a closer look at the ship.' He shifted his grip to her hand and started towards it.

Lena felt ill at ease with what she assumed was going to happen. She looked back as if seeking help in her dilemma. From whom? Who could help her? Where was Peter? But he could not interfere. She would have to deal with this herself. Then she saw him talking to Avril. Their eyes met. His jealous glance towards Alistair also pleaded for an answer to his proposal. Her gaze took in Avril then and Lena received a jolt. Her cousin was staring at Alistair with an expression that was very revealing. Avril had known Alistair a long time but Lena had never suspected that her cousin had any other feelings towards him than friendship. It seemed she had been wrong about that.

Unsuspecting, Alistair led her on. Finding a quieter place he stopped.

Lena felt ill at ease. 'I didn't know you were interested in...'

He placed a finger on her lips to stop her. 'It was an excuse to get you away from everyone.' His eyes had taken on an intensity that struck at her heart. 'Lena, let's make this a double celebration. Marry me!'

The words thundered in her mind, words that at one time she would have been overjoyed to hear but had anticipated more doubtfully since Peter had entered her life. She had hoped Alistair would not propose before she could implement the decision she had made when Olivia climbed the steps to launch the *John Carnforth*. It would have been easier for her not to face this moment that had been thrust upon her now.

'Alistair.' Lena's voice was scarcely above a whisper. She hesitated, her eyes damp.

'Say yes,' he prompted.

'I can't, not at the moment.' She gave a little shake of her head as if to dismiss the question. 'So much has happened, I need time...'

He looked astonished that her answer had not been an instantaneous yes. 'But I thought you and I always had an understanding?'

'Please, Alistair, don't press me now.'

'But...'

'Please.' Lena turned and walked away.

Astounded and puzzled, he watched her go. What had upset her? What held her back? He knew it had been a trying time for her since her parents were killed, but he thought she'd got over it and was now coping well. Maybe today had brought back too many memories? He should have waited; had misjudged his moment. Annoyed with himself, he strolled back in the direction of the crowds. He would have to face Lena again at tonight's party; he would make sure he did not mishandle *that* meeting.

Not fully aware of where he had walked, he was suddenly conscious of someone standing in his way. 'Oh, Avril.'

'You were looking so thoughtful. A penny for them, Alistair?'

He smiled. 'They would not be worth that to you.'

She gave a little shrug of her shoulders and said, 'Ah, well, they can remain yours. Come and have something to eat?'

'That's not a bad idea,' he agreed, grateful for a

distraction from thoughts of Lena.

As she picked her way through the crowds Lena searched for Peter but saw no sign of him. She became even more exasperated as the day wore on and he was still nowhere to be seen. Her emotions became even more strained when she kept seeing Alistair and Avril who were, to her mind, enjoying each other's company. People wanted to chat with her. Though she tried to respond, she did not sparkle as she usually did. The attempt to do so began to tell on her and she realised she would not be able to face the evening ahead if she did not escape for a while. She sought out James and told him she was going home in order to see that everything was ready for the evening party.

'But Mrs Campion will be seeing to that,' he protested. 'Stay.'

'I'd rather make sure. After all, it is now an extra-special occasion,' she pointed out.

'You are thoughtful. Thanks, Lena.'

She shrugged her shoulders dismissively, thinking, More than you are to me. But she bit her tongue and only said, 'Be happy, James.'

'I will. Let me get someone to see you home, I can't leave now.'

'I know. I'll be quite safe.'

'Let me ask Ralph.' He glanced in his manager's direction.

'No need. He's talking to some of the town officials, no doubt putting in a good word for the firm.'

'Let me find Alistair then.'

'No, no.' Lena realised she'd been a little quick

with her refusal. 'He's talking to Avril.' She glanced in their direction. 'Don't disturb them.' Then she added in a jocular tone, 'It's not as if I don't know my way.'

As she left the shipyard and celebrations behind a familiar voice brought Lena to a halt. 'Leaving already?' At the same moment someone stepped out of the shadows ahead.

'Peter!'

He inclined his head. 'Miss Carnforth. Or will it be Mrs Nash?'

She stiffened. 'You ask a strange question.'

'I saw you today with Alistair.'

'And thought you could predict the outcome?'

'I...'

'You should never presume to do that where I am concerned.'

'Then tell me why was there anger and hurt in your eyes when Miss Nash climbed on to the platform to launch the ship? I take it you had assumed it would be you who performed the ceremony?'

She nodded, relieved to find that one person at least understood her feelings.

'You are leaving the celebrations early?'

'Things to see to for this evening.'

'May I walk you home?'

'You may.'

'My arm, Miss Carnforth.'

As she took it their eyes met and she saw hope rekindled in his. 'Thank you, Mr Hustwick. How formal we are of a sudden.' Then she astonished him by saying, 'I think we can drop this formality. I have my answer to the question you put to me

248

two days ago.'

Peter stopped walking and turned her to him quickly so that he could look straight into her eyes and discover what she truly meant. 'You'll marry me then?' His eyes were blazing with hope.

'Yes, I'll marry you, Peter. I'll marry you!'

There was no resisting that promise. He swept Lena into his arms and kissed her.

'Come on, let's tell everyone now.' Holding her hand, he started to return to the shipyard but she held him back.

'No, Peter! We must do this my way. When do you leave for Hull?'

'I'd intended going tomorrow, but will delay my departure as long as you wish.'

'Tomorrow will be ideal. I'll be ready then.'

'You'll come with me?' He was astounded by the speed of events.

'Yes.'

'But...'

Lena started walking and he matched his pace to hers as she explained what she wanted. 'No one must know about this; there must be not one hint. I require no one's blessing on my marriage.'

'But as you have no father, shouldn't I seek permission from your brother?'

'No!' she replied emphatically. 'It is my own decision, requiring no one's approval. I am of age, after all.'

'Whatever you say.'

Though he knew that her relatives and close friends would be shocked by such an abrupt departure, Peter was too intent on securing Lena for his wife to worry unduly about their reaction.

They would come round from their disappointment, in time.

'We must act as if this conversation has not taken place,' she warned him, 'so be careful this evening. Tell no one. I will be at the Angel at eight tomorrow morning. I think the others will be late to rise after the celebrations. I'm thankful you drove yourself here and have a conveyance ready. Be ready for me. We will be well on our way before anyone knows I have gone.'

'You think your family might try to stop us?'

'If we have left I think not, but if they got wind of this before our departure then there would be those who would try persuasion.'

'You seem to have given this matter much thought?'

'No. I merely have a mind that can deal rapidly with the detail once I have decided upon a course. Besides, how could I have settled on this? I was not certain myself of my answer to your proposal until a short time ago.'

'You have made me very happy, Lena. I will do everything in my power to make you happy too.'

'You will, Peter, I know you will.'

When he left her at the gate of the house in New Buildings she hurried to her room. She had much to do before morning but sat for a few moments, enjoying her exhilaration at the step she had taken, one she knew would bring a great change to her life. She was determined there would be no looking back now; she would reach out and grasp a bright, beckoning future in a world she had thought would be hers by right but which had been snatched away from her by a few

250

words in her father's Will. Now that wouldn't matter any more. The future was hers for the taking.

Chapter Sixteen

Peter's steps were light as he started back to the Angel. He had won the girl he had set his mind on during their first meeting in Hull. When he had proposed and Lena had asked for time, he had thought that Alistair, her family and her love of Whitby would dictate her answer and send him back to Hull broken-hearted. But now there was only joy ahead of him. As he grew accustomed to his change in fortune he began to wonder what had made Lena decide in his favour. Was it something to do with what had happened at the ceremony? And why didn't she want to announce their forthcoming marriage to her family? He gave a little shrug of his shoulders and dismissed these questions. What did they matter after all? Lena had said yes and that was all that concerned him.

When he arrived at the house in New Buildings that evening it was ablaze with light, and the atmosphere inside was one of light-hearted enjoyment laced with celebration, as befitted a gathering of family members and a few close friends. As he was introduced around, Peter felt privileged to have been included among this circle, and, although he was introduced merely as the gentleman whose firm had hired the *John Carnforth* for her maiden voyage, he wondered if there were in fact other reasons why he had been included. If the invitation had originated with Lena, why did she want to keep their relationship a secret? Why was she prepared to leave Whitby without making any formal announcement? If James was the instigator on the other hand, was he seeking to consolidate their business relationship or had he some other motive?

'You are looking rather too serious,' said Lena quietly as she came up beside him, signalling a maid to bring him some wine.

Peter took a sip before he replied. 'It is a serious step we are taking tomorrow morning. I still feel we should tell your brother of our feelings for each other. Why do we have to sneak off behind his back?'

She frowned. 'We do it my way or not at all! Any other course would spell disaster for us, and ruin the day for James and Olivia.'

'I thought it would make for a double celebration?'

'No, for disaster.'

'Because of Alistair?'

'That's who everyone expects me to marry.'

'But you don't want to?'

'Expectations aren't always fulfilled.' There was an urgent expression in Lena's eyes as she met his gaze. She had seen Alistair approaching them. 'If you love me, do it my way,' she said quickly.

He was with them before Peter could reply. 'I must take Lena away, people are asking me if she will play the piano.'

252

Peter bowed his agreement.

He stood beside the door to listen, his thoughts dwelling on tomorrow, and as his gaze settled on Alistair and he saw the adoration with which he looked at Lena, Peter knew he was taking her away from a man who loved her.

Lena breathed a sigh of relief when she finally reached her bedroom that night and closed the door. The party had gone on until after midnight and she needed to be up early. She retrieved two valises from her closet where she had placed them on her return from the shipyard. She quickly threw some clothes into them; for the rest she would have to go shopping in Hull. She was pleased she need not be dependent on Peter for her needs. She was after all entitled to her income from her father's Will; nothing could change that. Valises packed, she sat down to pen two letters.

Dear James,

When you read this I shall be on my way to start a new life with Peter whom I love and will marry. Such a course will also permit me to lead a life which was once dear to me in Whitby, but from which I have felt more and more excluded, by Father's Will, and by your subsequent actions. You consulted me not at all about the business; informed me of very little. The life I was left with here was not to my liking; the one I shall share with Peter will be.

Do not come to Hull to try to persuade me otherwise. Any such effort will be to no avail. I am determined to follow the path I have chosen.

Wish me well, dear brother, as I wish you all the best in your life with Olivia and in the progress of the firm Father placed solely in your hands.

Your affectionate sister,
Lena

She read it over and, satisfied, folded and sealed it. Next she wrote:

Dear Alistair,

When you read this I will be gone. I know this will hurt you and for that I am truly sorry. Maybe I am a coward not to tell you to your face that I am in love with Peter and am going to find a new life with him in Hull. If I had faced you with this, though, I know you would have tried to persuade me otherwise, and others would have done so too. None of that would have done any good. My mind is made up.

We have been close all our lives and I will always cherish our friendship and all we have shared. You are very, very dear to me but I don't believe I could have helped you as a doctor's wife should, and in the way you want. You deserve someone who can and I don't think you have far to look to find a replacement for me, if you would only see.

Please forgive me for the hurt I have caused you.

I will pray for your understanding and future happiness.

Yours affectionately,
Lena

Sleep did not come easily and when Lena woke she did so in a panic – she was late. She flung back the bedclothes and slid out of bed. It was only then that she realised it was barely light and she had not after all overslept. Nevertheless she hurried with her preparations to be away before anyone else was up.

Finally, she took one last look around her room. Sadness threatened to descend, but she shook it away, picked up her luggage and quietly crept down the stairs. She placed her valises near the front door, went to the dining-room and left the letter for James on the table there. After putting on her cloak and bonnet, she left the house.

She walked briskly to Alistair's home, pushed the letter for him through the letterbox, and resisted any recollections of happier times spent here. At the end of New Buildings she stopped and looked back. A life lived, the past gone. Mother and Father ... what would they have thought? But had they lived, had that bridge not fallen, what might her present life have been? She shivered. The reaction convinced her she had chosen the right course.

Reaching the Angel, she saw a carriage drawn up outside attended by a stable boy. Inside the inn, she found Peter awaiting her.

'Lena!' He was by her side at once, his face alight with pleasure.

The landlord signalled to a boy who had been standing by. He came forward, took Lena's luggage and hurried from the inn.

'Mine's already stowed,' Peter informed her, 'so

we can be on our way.' He turned to the inn-keeper. 'Thank you, landlord.'

'Thank you, sir. Have a safe journey.'

Peter took Lena's arm and led her outside to the carriage. He checked the luggage was safely stored, tipped the two boys and climbed in beside her.

'Are you comfortable?'

She nodded. The moment was upon her; she felt her whole world was turning topsy-turvy and the pressure in her chest became almost over-whelming. She gripped her hands tightly together, trying to draw strength from somewhere.

Peter glanced at her, and when he saw her strained features, fear gripped him. 'Are you sure about this?' he asked with tender concern.

Lena turned her eyes to him, locked her gaze on his and filled her voice with resolution as she said, 'I'm sure!'

The MacBrides were already sitting at the dining table when James came in for his breakfast.

'Good morning, James.' Martin MacBride's breezy greeting resounded round the dining-room.

'Good morning, all,' he said brightly as he went to the sideboard to get a plate.

'We've beaten Lena,' said his aunt. 'Still, extra sleep will do her good after yesterday's excite-ment.'

'A splendid day, yesterday, splendid,' his uncle went on.

'It was indeed,' James replied, helping himself to some porridge. He went to his place, saw the letter and recognised his sister's writing. Why had she written to him? Mystified, he broke the seal and unfolded the paper. He read the words quickly and then, having taken in the gist of the message, read it again in utter disbelief.

'James! What is the matter?' his aunt asked in alarm when she saw his face drain of colour.

'Lena has left for Hull with Peter Hustwick. They intend to marry.' His hoarse voice was filled with incredulity.

A stunned silence descended on the room.

'What?' The first word exploded from Doctor MacBride. 'We must bring her back.' He started to rise but was stopped by his wife. 'Martin, we don't know how long she's been gone, nor which way they will go.'

'James, you must have some idea?' urged his uncle.

'They could have taken any of several routes.'

'We must be off to Hull at once then and bring her back,' blustered the doctor.

'Martin, calm yourself,' warned Mary.

'But we must do something,' he urged.

'Rushing off in a rage won't do any good. We know they are going to Hull; it's not as if they are trying to hide. James must know how to contact Peter and therefore how he can find Lena.'

Martin's lips tightened with frustration. He wanted action now, but he knew his wife was right. 'I thought she and Alistair...'

'We all did,' said James.

'The way's clear for you,' whispered Fiona surreptitiously to her sister.

Avril flushed as, under the table, she dug her

sister in the thigh.

'Forcing her back against her will won't achieve anything,' Mary pointed out. 'Reasoning with her might, but I doubt it. If Lena has made up her mind, I don't think you will budge her.'

'I believe you are right, Aunt,' agreed James. 'I think I may be to blame to some degree for Lena making this decision, though no one can anticipate the dictates of the heart.'

'How is that?' his uncle demanded. Without waiting for an answer he added, 'Lena made the decision, not you. You cannot blame yourself for this. And we must do something – make the girl see reason, realise the mistake she is making.'

James gave a shrug of his shoulders. 'We shall see,' he said quietly.

At that moment all further discussion was interrupted by a loud knocking on the front door.

The Nashes were seated around the breakfast table; only Alistair was in introspective mood although outwardly he hid this from the others. His thoughts were fixed on Lena's attitude to his proposal. Why had she wanted more time? Why couldn't she have said yes there and then, and made the day one of double celebration? What exactly had held her back? These thoughts had troubled him all night, especially as he believed she had avoided being alone with him during last night's party.

His thoughts and the gaiety around the table were interrupted by a knock on the door, followed by the appearance of a maid carrying a letter.

258

'I found this at the front door, sir,' she said, approaching Alistair.

'Thank you,' he said, taking the paper. A glance at the inscription told him it was from Lena. But why had she written? Why not call and see him if she wanted to apologise – or to give him her answer? He broke the seal and sent his gaze eagerly over the words, hoping to find the ones he wanted.

'No!' The half-whispered word drew every-body's attention. 'Oh, no!'

'What is it?' asked Georgina tentatively.

He did not speak but pushed the letter to her. She picked it up and read it, her expression becoming more incredulous with every second. Her bewilderment was so intense she could not speak. Albert picked up the paper, and by the time he'd finished reading his face was wreathed in disbelief. Olivia stared from one to the other of her parents and then at her brother.

'What is it?'

'Lena has left for Hull with Peter Hustwick, intending to marry him.'

'I don't believe it!'

'It is there in black and white.' He indicated the letter and she read it quickly.

'But you were...'

Alistair pushed his chair back and got to his feet, interrupting her. 'I want to hear if James knew about this.' The anger in his voice did not bode well for his friend if he found the answer to be yes.

As he headed for the door Olivia jumped to her feet.

'Stay here,' warned her mother.

'I want to know if James knew too,' she said, and was gone before more could be said.

'Mr James?' Alistair asked when the Carnforths' maid opened the front door.

'The dining-room, sir,' she replied, and was almost swept aside as he and Olivia stormed past her.

'Did you know about this?' demanded Alistair as he flung his letter down in front of James.

'I got one too,' he replied, holding up the paper.

Alistair's anger subsided and Olivia felt relief sweep over her. If James had known of Lena's betrayal...

'What are we going to do?' Alistair asked.

Dr MacBride was about to voice his own strong opinion but caught his wife's eye. In her expression and almost imperceptible shake of the head he read disapproval of any intervention on his part.

'You know Lena almost as well as I do. You know she can be headstrong, but no doubt you'll want to try to persuade her to come back?' James asked his friend.

'I do, even though in her letter she says she is not cut out to be a doctor's wife.'

'And she tells me how disappointed she is at being excluded by father's Will from taking any prominent role in the firm,' said James. 'I think she has seen in Peter Hustwick her chance to enter the mercantile world again.'

'But that's no place for a lady,' stormed Martin.

'Lena won't see it that way,' replied James. 'Whether she is truly in love with Peter, infatuated by him, or is merely using him to attain the life she wants, I do not know. Whatever the answer, I don't think we will be able to persuade her to return, but we must try. If you are in agreement, we will leave for Hull tomorrow morning.'

Though he would have preferred to leave immediately, Alistair agreed; he knew his friend was right. He would have to inform Dr Jollif of his intended absence and ask him to take over his partner's scheduled visits.

'I think we should go now and hire two horses from the Angel,' James suggested.

Arrangements were made so that they could be in the saddle by eight the following morning.

Chapter Seventeen

By the time they reached the outskirts of Hull in the late-afternoon, Lena was convinced she was stepping back into her rightful place – the world of ships, trading and far horizons. This was what she had expected and should have had in Whitby. As much as she loved her father and was grateful for the introduction he had given her to that world, could she ever forgive him for passing the running of the business solely to James who, after all, was only his stepson? And though her love for James was strong, could she ever excuse him for carrying out to the letter their father's last unfair decision? She had soon realised that James loved to be in charge and revelled in his power. Well, she would see if he could cope with her rivalry in business, whether he could hang on to something she regarded as rightfully hers.

Even as she was visualising a bright future for herself she was reminded of the present necessity when Peter said, 'We'll go straight to my cousin's,' and added with a chuckle, 'she will be surprised.'

'As no doubt will many people today,' said Lena.

'I was surprised there was no pursuit,' commented Peter.

'What? An irate James and Alistair, dragging me off the carriage and forcing me back to Whitby?' Lena laughed as she pictured the scene. 'No need, Peter, they knew where I was bound.'

'You wrote that in your letters?'

'I saw no reason to lie.'

'Then we can soon expect a visit?'

'Certainly.'

'You aren't having any doubts about what you have done, I trust?'

Lena's comforting smile was accompanied by a shake of her head. 'None, Peter, don't ever think that.'

'My cousin purchased a house in Anlaby Road, a new area being developed to accommodate Hull's merchants, ship-owners, traders and so on. It is a fine house and came up for sale at just the right moment for Greta, who always moves swiftly once she has made up her mind.'

When he'd halted the horse Peter was quickly out of his seat to help Lena to the ground. He

262

escorted her along the short curving path to a small portico where three steps led up to the front door. Two Tuscan columns supported a simple architrave, frieze and decorated cornice. Apart from providing a covered porch, the whole design lent elegance to the front entrance of an otherwise plain brick villa.

Peter gave a sharp tug on the metal bell-pull and a few moments later the front door swung open.

'Mr Hustwick,' said a girl of about fifteen, neatly dressed in a maid's black uniform.

'Is Miss Clancy at home?'

'She is, sir,' the girl replied, knowing she had no need to enquire if her mistress was receiving visitors when it was Mr Peter Hustwick who was calling. 'I'll tell her you are here.'

The girl stood to one side to allow them to enter, bobbing a quick curtsey to Lena. The maid hurried to the drawing-room and in a matter of moments Greta came out into the hall, her arms outstretched in greeting. Her broad smile took on a slight air of surprise when she saw Lena, but that did not mar the warmth of her welcome. After her talk with Peter at Weaver Hall, Greta's sharp mind was already pinpointing the probable reason for Lena's presence. She hugged her cousin. 'I'm delighted to see you.' Then she turned to Lena. 'Welcome to my home, Miss Carnforth.'

'Thank you,' replied Lena, accepting Greta's embrace, then added quickly, to establish the closer friendship she was hoping for, 'It was Lena at Weaver Hall.'

Greta seized on this offer gladly. 'And so it shall be at Clancy House.'

'That makes it sound as though you are really settled in,' said Peter, remembering the house had had no name as yet when he'd left for Whitby.

'I truly am. I'm very glad I decided to come back to Hull.'

'So am I, because I want to ask you a great favour.'

'Ah, so that is the only reason you are glad to see me here.' Greta feigned hurt but there was a teasing twinkle in her eyes.

'No, not at all,' Peter rushed to defend himself.

'Should I believe him, Lena?' Greta laughed.

She pursed her lips thoughtfully. 'Mmm, maybe you should. I certainly hope you will.'

'That sounds as if you both have something to ask me, so come into the drawing-room.' Greta gestured to the maid who had been hovering to one side of the hall. Seeing the signal, the girl hurried away to bring tea for three.

As they proceeded to the drawing-room, Lena and Peter shed their outdoor clothes which Greta laid in a closet near the front door.

'Now,' she said as they settled. 'What is it you want of me?'

Peter licked his lips nervously. 'Can Lena stay here with you?'

'What do I detect behind that request?'

'I did what you told me to when we were at Weaver Hall.'

Greta smiled and raised her eyebrows.

Lena looked askance at Peter, 'What was that?'

'I sought my cousin's advice about my feelings for you.'

'And I told him he should not hesitate to disclose to you how he felt about you.'

'The chance never arose at Weaver Hall,' added Peter, 'So I had to wait until we came face to face in Whitby.'

'And I presume you put the question then?' asked Greta.

'Yes.'

'I also presume, because you are here, that things did not go smoothly in Whitby?'

The tea arrived, halting the explanation momentarily, then between them Lena and Peter explained what had happened.

Greta listened intently but did not immediately speak when they had finished. She remained deep in thought for a few moments. 'I have made my assessment of the situation,' she said finally. 'You have not known each other very long so I must ask you – do you both truly love each other?' Then, before they could answer, she laughed. 'Listen to me! You'd think I was your mother, and here am I, younger by two years than you, Peter.' She raised her hand. 'There's no need to answer my question. I am sure I know the answer. I think I knew it at Weaver Hall and that is why I gave Peter such advice. I thought otherwise Alistair might win you, Lena.'

'He might have done if I hadn't come to Hull with my brother when Mr Hustwick and Peter were negotiating the hire of the *John Carnforth*.'

'That was my lucky day,' he said.

'And mine,' said Lena. She turned to Greta.

'You'll help us then?'

'Of course! You can stay here as long as you like ... well, I don't suppose you'll want to stay after the wedding!' She smiled at them. 'Now, what about your father, Peter?'

'We'll go and see him next. He'll be at our town house, I expect.'

'He is.'

'You know he didn't come to Whitby? He had been overindulging and said he couldn't face the journey.'

Greta gave a small smile that was more like a grimace and Peter realised she had news of William. 'I thought it was more than that so I called in the doctor the day you left. He verified that your father is far from well. I got a nurse in for him...'

Alarm gripped Peter. He jumped to his feet. 'I must go to him at once. You should have told me as soon we arrived.'

'It was hardly necessary and I saw you had other important things on your mind. But go now, and take Lena with you. The news will do my uncle good. He has talked a great deal of the young lady who came to Hull with James Carnforth.'

When they returned they were able to tell Greta that Peter's father had become positively jaunty on seeing them, though they were still concerned for his health.

'It pleased him to know I will be staying in the town house for the time being,' said Peter, 'and that you were going to look after Lena.'

'I thought you might be staying close,' said Greta, 'so I have arranged for you to dine with us this evening. It will help Lena settle in and give you a chance to plan for tomorrow when we receive visitors from Whitby, as I am sure we will after what you told me. They'll soon trace you here.'

When Peter arrived at Clancy House the following morning he sensed a nervous atmosphere on entering the dining-room where Lena and Greta were having breakfast. At the look that Greta flashed at him, he knew he would have to tread carefully. As he pulled out a chair to sit next to Lena he noted that her breakfast had hardly been touched.

'Peter, what are we going to do?' she asked, her tone edgy. Several times during the night she had woken, assailed by doubts. Each time she had quelled her anxieties, but by morning they had left their mark and were now filling her mind again. Her strength seemed to be deserting her.

'We face what is coming, together,' said Peter firmly. 'No doubt we will soon have visitors. I think they will come to my office first because that is really the only place they can start to try and trace you.'

'Where would you like the meeting to take place, Lena? In Peter's office or here?' asked Greta.

'Here,' she replied, and added, 'If that is all right with you?'

'Of course!'

'Thank you.'

267

'I'll go to the office now, see if there is anything I should attend to due to Father's illness, and leave word where I can be found,' said Peter.

'Come back soon,' Lena pleaded.

'I will.'

During the afternoon an uneasy atmosphere settled over the house in Anlaby Road. It was disturbed by a loud knocking on the front door which, although expected, still startled the three occupants of the drawing-room.

They glanced at each other, did not move but tensed as they listened to the maid crossing the hall. A few moments later there was a knock on the door and she entered to inform them, 'Two gentlemen are asking to see you, miss.'

'Show them in, Tess,' ordered Greta.

A few moments later James entered the room followed by Alistair. Peter was instantly on his feet.

James's eyes fixed on Lena without any warmth. He came straight to the point. 'We've come to take you home.'

The challenge in his tone riled her so that her reply was charged with new resolve. 'I'm not coming!'

'What? I don't know what has happened to you – your letters did not make sense.'

'They make a lot of sense, if you read them carefully.'

'You can't mean what you wrote,' put in Alistair.

'I did.'

His eyes filled with disbelief. 'But you and I...'

'At one time, maybe,' Lena interrupted. 'No longer.'

'All because of this blackguard?' he snapped, inclining his head in the direction of Peter.

'I love him,' Lena said quietly, but with an emphasis that was meant to leave no doubt in their minds.

Alistair looked disgusted. 'How can you?'

'Easily.'

'You hardly know him.'

'Enough!'

'Only since the day I brought you to Hull,' James pointed out. 'How I wish I hadn't.'

'And I'm very glad you did.'

'Rubbish! Get your things; you're coming home.'

'I'm not.'

James's eyes were dark with fury. Anger mounting, he asked her, 'Do you realise what you are doing? The scandal you are precipitating? You'll be ostracised in Whitby. Will never be able to go back there. Your family and friends are outraged at your lack of propriety and callous disregard for them.'

Lena's chest tightened. 'Indeed?' she said with disdain. 'Then I shall have to live with that.'

'Yes,' put in Alistair forcefully, 'but is it what you really want?' He softened his tone as he added, 'Lena, please come home. Stay with me.'

She shook her head. 'I'm sorry, Alistair, truly I am.'

James snorted with contempt.

Alistair addressed Peter. 'Do you want Lena to live as an outcast?' he said in desperation.

'She won't be, not in Hull,' he retorted. 'We shall marry as soon as may be, and meanwhile she is living here with my cousin Greta. There is nothing to outrage public opinion in that.'

Alistair turned back to Lena. 'What have I done? Let me put it right.'

'You can't because you aren't to blame. Things were always too easy between us. Everyone took our marriage as inevitable, but when Peter entered my life I saw that everyone was wrong. I realised there was another world out there.'

'But why didn't you say so?' demanded James fiercely.

'Because I knew what opposition there would be, and not only from you two. I can imagine how Uncle Martin has reacted for instance, because he would dearly have loved me to marry a doctor! But my choice of husband is my decision, no one else's. Alistair, I respect your calling and your devotion to it, but being a doctor's wife was never for me. I knew a great deal of pressure would be brought to bear on me to do what everyone would regard as right. So I took the only course of action I could – I left without saying a word, to secure the life I want for myself with Peter.'

Before anyone else could speak Greta intervened. This encounter had to end. 'And that, gentlemen, is the final word. Lena has made her decision clear and I think it should be respected.'

James's lips tightened. What right had this woman to dictate to him? As Peter's cousin she would obviously be sympathetic to his cause. Heated words sprang to his lips but he held them back. He would not sully his reputation as a gentleman by getting into low altercation.

He addressed his sister. 'I am sorry if the terms of Father's Will have led to this. I could do nothing but follow them.'

'Couldn't you?' she said quietly. 'Or wouldn't?'

His eyes narrowed at the inference that he'd wanted total control of the firm. 'Think what you will. After what you have done, I would alter, if I could, the provisions granting you an income from the firm. Sadly I can't, though I'm sorry for that. I will pay you a fair rent for the house as you needn't think you will ever be able to live in Whitby again, not after this.' He turned to Peter. 'Be wary of her. She has only one objective in mind: by marrying you, she believes she will get to control your business.'

'Enough of your insinuations!' Peter's voice was like a knife. 'I must ask you to leave – now!'

Feeling ran high; anger boiled over. Alistair lashed out and caught Peter high on his right cheek sending him staggering. He would have fallen to the ground but for Greta who managed to support him. She grabbed his arm, preventing any retaliation.

'Don't sink that low,' she whispered, close to his ear.

'I'll leave now, *with* Lena.' Alistair grabbed her arm and glowered at her. 'We'll not bother with your things!' He started for the door but she resisted fiercely.

'I'm not coming,' she stormed, eyes wide with fury. 'Get it into your head: *I'm not coming!*'

'You heard her!' shouted Peter, still struggling

to free himself from his cousin.

Alistair stiffened.

James stepped over to him and gripped his arm. 'Leave it, Alistair, we'll do no good here.' A gaze devoid of sympathy was directed at his sister. 'Have it as you will. You have besmirched the name of Carnforth. Never set foot in Whitby again. Do so and you'll pay the price.' He started for the door.

Alistair stared at Lena, one last look of contempt. There was no need for further words.

Halfway across the room James stopped. He ignored his sister but let his eyes bore into Peter's. 'The contract for hiring the *John Carnforth* on her maiden voyage is signed and sealed and will have to be honoured, but you will never hire a ship of mine again.'

'We won't need to. We'll find them elsewhere,' came Lena's sharp retort.

'*We?*' sneered James. 'I didn't know you had any say in Hustwick's?' He eyed Peter again. 'As I said, be very wary of her.' He swung on his heel and was gone.

After their unwelcome visitors had departed Peter came to her and took her by the shoulders. He looked deep into Lena's eyes. 'I love you, Pauline Carnforth, and all I want is your happiness. So I will ask you one more time – are you sure about what you are doing? James and Alistair are probably right in what they said – you will be ostracised in Whitby, and scandal will taint your name.'

'Hush, Peter. I am here in Hull, not Whitby, and I am with you.'

272

'Music to my ears,' he whispered as he embraced her.

Eventually Lena gently pulled herself from his arms, holding his hand while she reached out to take Greta's as well. 'Thank you,' she said.

Greta smiled at them both, and Lena began to hope that one day she could replace the friendship she had lost with James and Olivia.

The trials of the day receded with the passing hours, and when Peter said goodnight to return to his father's house Lena was beginning to feel more settled, a feeling that deepened when she and Greta sat together in the drawing-room. The staff had been introduced to her, she had been shown round the house and told by Greta to regard it as her home for as long as she liked.

'I am more than grateful for what you are doing,' said Lena.

'Peter is very dear to me. I want him to be happy. He has no one else but me, and I have no one else but him. We were close before I went away.'

'I gathered as much at Weaver Hall.'

'I am pleased to be near him again and to see him so happy. Keep him that way, won't you?'

'And his father, how do you get on with him?'

'You met him when you were in Hull. What did you make of him?'

'Bluff but likeable, probably a fool to himself since his wife died.'

'I do understand what you are insinuating and must say you are probably right. But his wife's death hit him hard and overindulgence in all things was his escape from misery.'

'But he had his business to occupy his mind.'

'Right, and it did so. But you can't work for twenty-four hours a day. There had to be an outlet.'

'One thing I detected on my first brief visit was that although Peter is involved in the business, he has little responsibility or say in it.'

'That is true. He was involved from an early age but has got into the habit of letting things be as long as they keep him comfortable. Not a bad policy, I suppose, if you are content, which he seems to be.'

Lena took these words to bed with her and, as she lay down, speculated on the future of Hustwick's of Hull.

The question of that future was brought vividly back to mind when she was woken by a loud hammering on her door early the next morning and Greta burst in, still in her nightdress and robe.

'Sorry, Lena, but Peter's father has collapsed and is asking for you.'

She sat up in bed. 'Me?' She was rising to dress before Greta had left.

A distant clock struck six.

Ten minutes later the two young women were leaving the house. Neither of them spoke as Greta led the way, both reserving their breath to walk as fast as they could.

Reaching the Hustwicks' house they were ushered quickly upstairs where a solemn-faced Peter, hearing them coming, met them on the landing. He answered their unspoken query. 'Two doctors are with him. It's his heart. They don't hold out much hope. I heard him cry out and found him collapsed on the floor. He's asking for you, Lena.' Then he ushered them both into the room. They glanced at the doctors as they went closer to the bedside but neither man spoke.

'Uncle William,' said Greta quietly as she laid her hand on his and looked down into a pale face that used to be so florid.

He opened his eyes and gave a brief smile. 'Thank you for coming,' he said with difficulty. 'Is the other young lady with you?'

'I am here,' said Lena, stepping forward and taking his other hand.

He gave a little nod. 'I remember you from earlier.'

'And I you, sir.'

He moved a finger as if to quieten her. He had to speak. 'The doctors give me no hope but I was determined to see you again. Peter tells me he is going to marry you. I am pleased ... you have my blessing.'

'Thank you.' Instinctively Lena bent forward and kissed him on the forehead.

'Peter has told me all that happened yesterday.' William winced with pain then took a determined grip on himself. 'I am glad you stood up to those who would have dissuaded you. You have spunk, young lady, and I admire that in people. See that you always have it.' A startled grimace crossed his face then; he stiffened and sank back on the pillows.

The doctors stepped forward quickly; Lena and Greta moved out of the way. A moment passed before the doctors straightened up and looked at

275

Peter. One of them shook his head slowly and the other confirmed his meaning with a solemn expression.

Peter stepped over to the bed and looked down at his father, making a silent goodbye. Then he turned to Greta and Lena who, with tears in their eyes, came into his arms.

Lena's mind was still on his father's last words. Spunk? Unknowingly William Hustwick had stifled all initiative in his son and it could prove hard for Peter to resurrect it. But, she thought, I have enough for both of us.

Chapter Eighteen

When James and Alistair reached Whitby the next day, having stayed overnight in Beverley, they found the Nashes with the MacBrides, as if needing each other's support to face the news. Their hopes were dashed when they saw the sombre faces of the two men.

'There was nothing we could do,' James concluded. 'Lena would not budge even though we pointed out she would be tainted by scandal.'

'What's wrong with her?' cried Olivia. 'This is not the Lena I grew up with and loved.' Her lips tightened and a catch came into her voice as she added, 'I never want to see her again. She's hurt too many people and thought only of herself.' Tears streamed down her face as she finished speaking.

Her mother put a comforting arm round her.

'What is to be done?' asked Albert.

'There's little we can do,' his son told him.

'I suggest we don't make any hasty decisions now,' put in Mary MacBride, which brought a nod of agreement from her husband. 'Think things over, sleep on them and see what our attitudes are tomorrow.'

They agreed, but when the Nashes joined James and the MacBrides the following morning no one had any constructive suggestion to make.

'I've thought long and hard during the night and, as I see it, only Lena can change this situation, and I think that highly unlikely,' said Alistair.

'Alistair is right,' James agreed. 'I don't think we can do any more. We have our lives to live. I know there will be a big gap in them without Lena but she has brought shame on this family by her hasty action and is not worthy of our future consideration. I've already told her that if she refuses to break this engagement she will never be welcome back in Whitby. I would therefore be obliged if no one in this room attempts to communicate with her.'

His request hit his uncle and aunt hard because of the liking they had for their niece, but, after her behaviour they could understand his attitude.

Albert and Georgina glanced at their son, who remained stony-faced, but his little nod at James's words confirmed what he had told them last night in the privacy of their own home. Then, they had expressed their horror and surprise at what Lena had done. They had always thought, like most people, that the two children who had grown up together would one day marry; now all they could do was to support their son and daughter through their disillusion and disappointment.

A loud knocking at the front door interrupted James. The urgency it conveyed set them looking askance at each other. A few moments later a maid appeared to say, 'Mr Ralph Bell would like to see Mr Carnforth on a matter of importance.'

James hurried from the room. 'What is it, Ralph?'

'A ship from Hull has just docked. It has brought news the captain heard just before she left. Mr William Hustwick died yesterday.'

'What?' James's face registered disbelief. 'There was no indication that he was in danger when I was in Hull, though it's true he did not attend the ceremony here. Are you sure the source is reliable?'

'Yes,' replied Ralph. 'I've had personal dealings with Captain Hanson. He would check any facts before he passed them on.'

James nodded. 'Thanks for letting me know.' He started to turn away then stopped. 'Will you keep your eye on things? I may not be in the office for a day or so.'

'Of course,' Ralph replied, but could not hide the curiosity he felt.

'Look, I may as well tell you myself rather than let you hear it from someone else. It will soon be all over town and rumours don't always represent the true facts. Miss Pauline has left Whitby with Peter Hustwick.'

For a moment Ralph could not believe what he was hearing, but coming from Miss Carnforth's brother it must be true.

'Not to return?'

'Never. She won't be welcome here.'

'But I thought she and...'

'So did we all,' cut in James. 'My sister has chosen another path, without anyone's approval.'

'I'm sorry.' Ralph saw no reason to prolong the conversation so asked, 'Does this alter anything about the *John Carnforth*?'

'No. We have a contract for her maiden voyage which we will fulfil, but I have told Peter Hustwick in no uncertain terms that after that we will never hire a ship to Hustwick's again. As planned, you and I will sail on her to Hull, see her set out on her maiden voyage.'

'If it will be painful for you to be there, I could go alone.'

James gave a little shake of his head. 'I will be there.'

Ralph left and James returned to the drawing-room. 'A ship just in from Hull has brought the news that Mr William Hustwick died yesterday of a heart attack.'

Everyone was incredulous but it was Olivia who broke the hush. 'I hope you won't be going to the funeral, James.' There was a vicious undertone to her words and her eyes held his.

'Of course I won't,' he replied firmly, leaving no doubt in anyone's mind that his decision had already been made.

'But I will be sailing on the *John Carnforth* to hand her over for her maiden voyage. It will only be a business visit. Afterwards Hull will never see me again.'

Olivia gave a small nod of approval.

'Then things seem to be settled,' observed Dr MacBride. 'We can do no more. I really should get back to Dundee so we will leave the day after tomorrow. Mary and I and our family thank you for your hospitality and extend ours to you. You will receive a warm welcome any time you wish to come north. And, of course,' he chuckled, 'we expect to be invited to the wedding.'

'We couldn't possibly have that without the MacBrides,' said Olivia, with a smile James was glad to see return.

Further down the Yorkshire coast another wedding was being discussed, but overshadowed by a recent death.

'The funeral arrangements are all made for the day after tomorrow,' Peter informed Lena and Greta when he arrived at Clancy House. 'Eleven o'clock, Holy Trinity Church, and afterwards at our town house. Will you act as hostess for me, Greta?'

'Of course I will,' she replied quickly. 'I'll go round there now and brief your staff. Will they be staying on or will you be closing the household?'

'I will keep them in my employment until I decide what to do, after I've discussed the matter with Lena.'

'I'll leave you to it then,' said Greta, heading for the door.

When it closed Peter gave his fiancée an apologetic look. 'This is not turning out as I had planned. I'd intended we should marry soon, to still the idle tongues, but I'll have to observe a period of mourning.'

'I know, Peter. I experienced it myself not so long ago. A year for me. How I chafed at it!'

'You have no need to wear mourning clothes now as you had no direct connection with my father. It is not so bad for me, I will at least be at work and mixing with people, but I will observe mourning for six months. We shall plan our wedding for soon afterwards. Does that sound reasonable to you?'

'Of course. Whatever you wish.'

'I have had a word with Greta and she is quite amenable to your staying with her meanwhile. In fact, I think she is pleased of the company.'

'That's wonderful, Peter. I'm so glad. It settles my mind about the immediate future.'

'Then why don't we think about my two houses now? As you know I live mostly at Raby and...'

'Please don't sell it on my account,' she broke in quickly. 'I fell in love with it when you first showed me round.'

Peter smiled. 'That pleases me. Now what about the town house?'

'I don't know it. My only visit to it was the other day.'

'If it has bad memories for you, then I'll sell.'

'On the contrary, although the circumstances of my visit were sad, there was also comfort in the knowledge that your father asked to see me and seemed to approve of our connection.'

'He did,' agreed Peter, recollecting the circumstances.

'Then why sell the house? It is convenient for you for work.'

'True. It could be useful. I'm going to have to apply myself much more to the business now. More than Father ever allowed.'

'I'm sure you will manage.'

He pulled a face. 'I'm not so sure, but the way things are, the business just about runs itself. As long as it continues to do so, we will have nothing to worry about.'

Lena held back from criticising this attitude; it was not the time to try to exert any pressure on him. Instead she said, 'My father schooled me in the ways of mercantile trading so I have some knowledge that might be useful. If I can be of help...' She left the suggestion hanging in the air.

Holy Trinity Church was packed for the funeral of William Hustwick, such was his standing among Hull's shipping and trading fraternities. Greta, being known from her earlier days in Hull, accompanied Peter, but Lena took her place among the general mourners, the three of them having decided this was the best course at the moment. Taking her place alongside Peter could have led to speculation and rumour, which they thought best avoided.

Peter spent the following fortnight dealing with his father's estate and residences and getting to know what needed most urgent attention as far as the business was concerned. At Greta's insistence he came to her house for a meal each evening. It not only ensured he saw Lena but enabled him to relax in feminine company.

One evening three weeks later, as he arrived, Greta showed concern for him.

'Peter, I think you should get away from that office for a while. You are looking very pale.'

'There's so much to see to. I had never before realised how much Father had kept from me.'

'Leave it for a couple of days and go to Raby. You love it there, it will help you forget work for a little while.' Sensing his hesitation, she added, 'Knowing your father as I did, I doubt he would expect you to lead a sombre existence on his account.'

Peter nodded thoughtfully, but before he could mention what was in his mind Lena came into the room. He immediately brightened and Greta, seeing this, was glad for him.

'How has your day been?' his fiancée asked.

'Middling.' Without expanding on his reply, he added, 'I'm considering taking a couple of days off. We could go to Raby and I'd take you on the river as I once promised?' The suggestion hung for a moment then he added quickly, 'And Greta will come as chaperone so the staff can't start spreading rumours.'

'That would be wonderful.' Lena smiled.

'A splendid idea,' agreed Greta.

'Then I'll send word to Mrs Nevill to expect us.'

Two days later, with valises packed into the carriage, Peter picked up the reins and drove the two young ladies out of Hull. The brilliant sunshine lightened their mood and soon laughter filled the air.

The rumble of carriage wheels brought Tom

hurrying from the stable block to take charge of the horse and carriage at the front of the house.

When Lena stepped from the carriage she paused and let her eyes run over the house and on towards the river. A feeling of well-being and contentment filled her. She smiled warmly at Peter as she took hold of his arm and hugged it to her. 'Thank you for bringing me here,' she whispered.

'You like Raby then?'

She gave a little shake of her head. 'No, I love it.'

'Then this is where we shall live.'

'Those six months can't pass quickly enough for me!'

'Let's go in.'

They followed Greta who had already gone into the house where Mrs Nevill was waiting to welcome them.

Peter's friend, Graham Shackleton, with whom he shared the boat, arrived the following morning and the four of them spent an enjoyable afternoon on the river. Lena felt even more at home as a result, for, although this coble was a far cry from the merchant ships she had been used to seeing in Whitby, it at least brought her closer to the life she craved.

The following week a terse letter from James arrived at Peter's office, informing him that the *John Carnforth* would sail into Hull on the following Wednesday under the command of Captain Elijah Webb and a crew who were familiar with the timber run to the Baltic port of Riga. Peter could have chosen to appoint a new crew from Hull, but in the circumstances did not insist.

When Peter brought this news to Lena she felt a strange sensation in the pit of her stomach. Although she had known all along that the arrival of the *John Carnforth* would reawaken memories of her old life, she still experienced unease at the announcement.

'Do you want to see her arrive?' asked Peter.

'Does James say he is coming?' she queried tentatively.

'No.' Peter's answer had a deciding effect on her. A potentially unpleasant confrontation had been avoided. Lena's apprehension disappeared.

'Then of course I'll come! She is named after my father. I will certainly welcome her here.'

At about the same time, in Whitby, James was informing Olivia and Alistair that he and Ralph would shortly be sailing for Hull on the *John Carnforth*.

'Do you expect to see Lena?' Olivia asked coldly.

'I don't intend to,' he replied. 'This is purely business, with an eye to the future. I want to see how the ship handles.'

Olivia nodded with satisfaction. 'If by any chance you do see her and exchange words, you can tell her how utterly disgusted I am and that I want nothing more to do with her. Our friendship is dead.'

'Olivia!' cried Alistair, shaken by his sister's venom, though he too knew he would have adopted the same attitude if challenged.

'Don't you soften,' she snapped. Only now, confronted by this possible contact with Lena, was the width of the gulf between them apparent. Since Lena's sneaked departure Olivia had had turbulent thoughts about their relationship. So close for so long, almost closer than sisters, the bond between them had appeared unassailable – but it had been shattered by what she saw as Lena's betrayal of their intimacy and disloyalty to Alistair. There could be no forgiveness for that.

Olivia watched the *John Carnforth* slip between the two piers and meet the first swell of the sea. She was filled with pride; there was an air about this ship, the first built entirely under James's orders. She seemed to promise good things for the business. The *John Carnforth*, along with the three ships already in service, would help fulfil James's dreams and point the way to the purchase of further vessels and a prosperous future. She knew James wished for this and, although she herself had little interest in the mercantile world, she would naturally give him her moral support and encouragement. He and Ralph were standing at the ship's rail, arms waving in a vigorous farewell. She waved back.

Alistair, standing beside her, watched with an air of indifference. He had little interest in the sea and ships, in spite of his boyhood when his father had tried to direct him that way. He wondered now if his antipathy towards a mercantile life had lost him Lena? Then gave a little shrug of his shoulders. What if it had? Oh, yes, he regretted that she would not be his wife, but wasn't it better this rift had occurred now rather than later? She would be hard to forget, but the first step had been taken when he had confronted her in Hull. As he saw it now, that wound could never be healed. But what if life in Hull with Peter Hustwick was not the idyll she sought...? He shook such ideas from his mind. He must get on with his own life; pursue his ambition to be a good and caring doctor.

He felt a touch on his arm.

'You were far away, Alistair.'

He gave a small smile. 'So I was.' He offered his sister no more and she did not press him.

'Let's go,' Olivia said, taking his arm after one last glance at the ship with its sails spread to catch the wind. 'Safe voyage,' she whispered.

The *John Carnforth* made good time, running with a favourable wind and good sea. As she sailed into the Humber, Captain Webb came to join James and Ralph who were enjoying the views along the river. 'She's a sturdy ship, sir, and handles well.'

'I thought so too, but I'm glad to hear a seaman of your calibre praise her.'

'Can't do anything else, sir. She's a wonder.'

'A good first voyage to the Baltic and she's yours to command.'

Captain Webb could not hide his surprise but it was soon replaced by one of appreciation. 'Sir, I thank you for your confidence. You know little about me as yet.'

'More than you think, Captain. We checked your record sailing out of the Tyne, and Ralph and I have seen how you have been handling the crew – firm but fair. Their respect is not always easily won, especially when a captain is not from their home port, but you've won theirs.'

'Thank you again, sir.'

'There she is, Peter!' cried Lena excitedly. 'Isn't she beautiful?'

He smiled at her enthusiasm and obvious love for this vessel, a love that in fact extended to anything sailing the seas. 'Almost as beautiful as you,' he whispered, close to her ear.

Lena smiled at him. 'Father would have been so proud of her.' She concentrated on taking in every detail as she watched the *John Carnforth* draw nearer and nearer.

'He's there!' Her voice was low but its sharpness jolted Peter.

'What?'

'James ... by the rail ... he and Ralph.' Her face tightened. 'Why did he have to come? There was no need, was there?'

'Not so far as I was concerned. Maybe he's come to offer an olive branch?'

'Not very likely.' She sighed.

'Give him a chance if he does.' Peter took her hand and started along the quay. Lena would have pulled away and left, but, guessing she might do this, he gripped her hand tighter.

The vessel was brought skilfully to the quayside. Immediately the gangway was run out, James strode purposefully down it.

Peter held out his hand in greeting but James refused it.

'I trust you had a good voyage?' Peter said courteously.

'We did,' was the terse reply. 'Everything is in order as per our contract. The ship is now in the hands of Captain Webb. Negotiate any instructions regarding the voyage with him.' He showed no sign of acknowledging his sister.

'Sir,' said Peter sharply and with some contempt, 'do you blatantly ignore a lady?'

'Who?' rapped James.

'Me!' Lena challenged him. She was glad of Peter's reproof to him but would do her own talking.

'Oh, you,' said her brother with derision.

'Yes, me! Come now, brother, can we not be civil at least. Tell me, how is Olivia?'

'Olivia? You feel concern for her then?'

'Yes, I do. She was my dearest friend.'

'Ah, you use the right word – was. She gave me a message in case I saw you.'

'And you weren't going to give it me?

'Oh, yes, I was, because you deserve to hear it. She wants nothing more to do with you, ever.' He smirked to see her pained expression then.

Even though it was what she might have expected, Lena had retained the smallest of hope of a reconciliation with Olivia at least, but now her hopes were dashed. It was a grievous blow and left her in the mood for retaliation.

'As I told you before,' James announced haughtily, 'keep away from Whitby, and don't ever come near my firm – there'll be no more dealings between Hustwick's and Carnforth's.'

'*Your* firm?' Lena's voice rose. 'You're no true

289

Carnforth, and never can be. But one day the firm you usurped will come back to its rightful owner – the last true-blooded Carnforth!'

Chapter Nineteen

Three weeks later, on the day of the *John Carnforth*'s expected return to Whitby, her mission for Hustwick's completed, Jude had been posted on the cliff as a lookout. After making a positive identification of the ship, bearing in towards Whitby, he raced though the streets to the office. His sudden appearance brought everyone to their feet. The clerks hesitated, but as James and Ralph rushed out they called to the men to leave their work if they wished. They needed no second bidding and hurried to the quay where they knew the ship would dock.

But James and Ralph could not wait that long. They dodged their way quickly between the folk on Church Street and, panting hard, climbed the one hundred and ninety-nine steps to the cliff top. They hurried through the churchyard without giving the ancient building beside it a second glance. Even the magnificence of the ruined abbey was lost on them today. Gulping in air, they stood on the edge of the cliff.

'She's a grand sight,' gasped Ralph.

'Aye, she is that,' panted James.

Neither of them spoke again as they recovered from their exertions but both thought them well worthwhile so as to get this view of the *John Carnforth*.

They watched the vessel manoeuvre towards the narrow gap between the piers, admiring the way the sailors responded to Captain Webb's orders. For a breathless moment it seemed she would collide with the West Pier, but then she was through the gap and leaving the fast-running sea for the calm of the river.

'Come on,' called James.

They headed back the way they had come and were at the quay as the ship was skilfully brought through the swing bridge. News of the sighting of the *John Carnforth* had swept through Whitby and already there was a considerable gathering on the quayside: wives to greet husbands, mothers to welcome sons, girls to meet sweethearts, others to find one – if only for the day – old sailors reviving memories of their time on similar ships, and sightseers proud of Whitby's maritime heritage. James and Ralph made their way to the spot where they judged the gangway would be run out. As soon as it was they were on board, greeting Captain Webb.

'Welcome home!' said James. 'How did she handle?'

'Never had better, sir.'

James's face lit up with delight, and when he turned to Ralph he saw his manager too had a huge grin on his face.

'Sir, I took the liberty while in Hull of taking on board a cargo of a hundred cases of Spanish wine, so the return voyage here would bring some profit.'

'Good man!' cried James. 'A case for each of us and two bottles for every crew member. This is a memorable occasion. See to it, Captain. And, as I promised you earlier, command of the *John Carnforth* is yours, if you want it?'

'You don't have to ask me again, sir.' Captain Webb's chest swelled with pride and satisfaction. 'I have the paperwork connected with the voyage here.' He held out a folder.

'Thank you, I'll take that,' said Ralph. He glanced at James. 'I'll return to the office and deal with it.' Turning back to Captain Webb, he said, 'If you come there when you are ready, we can have a preliminary discussion about your next voyage and then tomorrow we'll talk further with Mr Carnforth. In the meantime, sign the crew off for a week.'

Ralph took his leave. When he was out of ear-shot James said, 'Did you see anything of Mr Hustwick when you were in Hull?'

'Oh, yes, sir. He was there when we arrived and delighted with the cargo, though I thought him not too sure of its storage and onward sale. He appeared to be uncertain where the sale documents were – if, indeed a sale had been arranged.'

James nodded thoughtfully. 'I know his father was the king-pin. It seems he must have kept much to himself.'

'That could be the way of it. I spoke with several captains while we were there and most of them were wondering how Hustwick's would fare now. All were of the opinion that the father ran the firm and kept his son in the dark. Maybe a case of easier to do it yourself.'

James chose not to return to the office immediately; instead he crossed the bridge and strolled along Pier Road towards the West Pier. There he hoped the fresh wind would clear his mind so he could weigh up Captain Webb's observations and decide on his next course of action. But for now his impending wedding would take up much of his time.

Three days later he and Olivia settled down to compile a list of people to be invited. When that was done it would be passed to her mother and father for their considerations and additions.

'Well, that seems to be that,' said James with some satisfaction as he leaned back in his chair, his eyes fixed on the sheaf of paper lying on the table in front of them, but Olivia detected a note of hesitation in his voice.

'Something the matter?' she asked.

'No,' he replied, but she knew that was untrue.

'Yes, there is,' she said firmly. 'If you have something to say, say it.' She studied him carefully.

His eyes met hers but still he hesitated.

'It's Lena, isn't it?' she said quietly.

He bit his lip. 'Yes.'

'You want to invite her?'

'She *is* my sister.'

'Half-sister, I'll remind you,' said Olivia tersely. Her voice hardened. 'How can you even consider it after what she did to Alistair? The scandal!'

'But...'

'There are no buts!' she rapped. 'If you go any

further with such foolishness we might as well tear up the wedding invitations now.'

The determination in her eyes and voice startled him. This was an Olivia he had not witnessed before but he found it did not detract from his love for her. Instead he felt admiration and knew, then and there, that Lena would never be part of his life again.

Two months later when Peter came to Greta's for his evening meal as usual, he handed a copy of the *Yorkshire Post* to Lena. 'There is something on page three you might like to read.'

She looked at him askance as she took the paper and then found the page.

'"Notable Whitby Merchant and Ship Owner Marries",' she read.

'So they've done it,' she whispered, and quickly scanned the report. She laid the paper down without saying another word.

'They didn't even offer an olive branch by inviting you,' said Peter regretfully.

'I hoped for it, but didn't expect them to,' she responded, then added slowly, 'not after what I said to James at our last parting.'

Remembering that, Peter felt uneasy for a moment but said nothing about it to his fiancée.

'I'm sorry James made no attempt at a reconciliation with Lena by inviting her to the wedding,' commented Dr MacBride to his wife as they prepared to leave Whitby for home. 'Maybe I should have tried to intervene.'

'There's nothing you could have done. It is

their affair. They are both old enough to know what they are doing,' his wife replied.

'I know, but I feel a certain responsibility after the loss of their parents.'

'Well, if it eases your mind, think instead of some good coming from this rift,' Mary pointed out.

'Some good?' Martin looked puzzled.

Mary gave a little chuckle. 'You men don't see what is happening under your noses. Avril and Alistair.'

'Our Avril?'

'Yes, our Avril. She made a lovely bridesmaid and he was most attentive to her.'

'Well, it was his duty as best man to see to all the bridesmaids' comfort.'

'True, but he was extra-attentive to Avril.'

'Well, we shall see. I wonder if Lena and Peter...' He left the question hanging wistfully in the air.

Mary came to him then and slid her arms around him. 'Martin, don't worry about her. If I judge Lena correctly, she'll look after herself. Think about your own daughter.'

'You look worried, Peter,' said Lena when he arrived at the house on Anlaby Road one evening.

He sighed and threw himself into a chair. 'I don't seem able to get on top of things at work. Why did Father want to do everything himself?'

'Maybe it was his way of trying to deal with the tragedy of losing a wife – throwing himself into his business affairs.'

'Perhaps.'

'And maybe he had the mistaken idea that he shouldn't burden you with too much.'

'I wish he had, it would have made things far easier now. I think I'll have to get someone in, appoint an experienced manager, to sort things out.'

'Let me help,' Lena offered swiftly.

'You?'

'Yes. Why not? My father gave me a good grounding.'

'But...' He hesitated.

'You are going to say that I am a woman? What does that matter? Women are starting to be accepted in many roles from which they were once excluded, so why shouldn't I help you?'

'The other merchants in Hull will frown upon a woman entering their domain.'

'Then cock a snook at them! Employ me and together we'll show them they ignore us at their peril.' Lena's voice had become charged with excitement.

'I believe you really mean this.'

'Of course I do!'

He stared at her for a moment, seeing once more the vibrant young woman who had defied convention to run away with him. She deserved this chance to show her brother he shouldn't have shut her out of Carnforth's. Peter had always felt her father had erred in making his Will the way he had.

He pushed himself from his chair and held out his hands to her. Lena took them in hers and he pulled her to her feet and clasped her to him. 'We'll start together tomorrow.'

Her eyes brightened. 'We will?'

'Yes.'

The kiss she gave him was full of promise. 'Thank you, Peter.'

'I love you, Lena Carnforth.'

'And I you.'

When she lay down in bed that night Lena hugged herself for joy. She had taken the first step on the road she wanted to travel but knew she would have to tread carefully from now on. Peter was no simpleton. His ambition had merely been thwarted by his father. She would see about changing his attitude, but she knew she must go about it gradually.

The following morning, Greta was surprised when Lena announced Peter would be calling to take her to the office.

'He thinks the experience I gained with my father might help unravel some of the problems left by his father's death.'

'Yes, there were times when he kept Peter in the dark. It has been a worry for him so I hope you can be of assistance. Be wary of his rivals, though. Most of them view a woman's role as running the home, seeing to her husband's needs and those of her family.'

'Well, Lena Carnforth may just make them think twice about that.'

Hustwick's office occupied two floors of a building close to the docks. While they approached it Lena had taken in the atmosphere of the area and immediately felt elated. There was a vitality about it: carts clattered on the cobbles, orders were shouted, jocular exchanges made, disputes noisily conducted. The setting to all this thrilled her. She could see vessels at quays, masts soaring heavenwards; warehouse doors standing open, ready to receive or dispatch. Lena's steps quickened. It was so good to be in her old world again.

Two rooms on the ground floor were unoccupied. When Lena queried this, Peter informed her that his father had dispensed with the firm's two clerks, preferring to do the record-keeping himself.

'He took on too much. The burden of it, together with his mode of living, took its toll. No wonder he chose not to expand the business, he would never have managed more on his own. And because he wanted to do it all, he saw no reason to involve you. Well, that will have to change,' she announced.

Peter nodded. The authoritative note in Lena's voice pleased him; it meant there was someone else to share the responsibility. 'Let me show you upstairs.'

There were two more rooms overlooking the docks, each furnished with large oak desks and the appropriate chairs, two armchairs, a small side table and cabinet. Paintings depicting the great whaling days of Hull hung on the walls.

Lena nodded with satisfaction. 'Ideal,' she commented. 'It is a question of what you want to do, Peter. I can see great opportunities here but it is up to you how far you wish to go.' She knew exactly how far she would like to go but she was wary of pressing her opinion too hard; she must make it appear that all the decisions were his.

'I do see that things will need sorting out. To be put on a solid manageable footing that we can cope with.'

Lena was pleased to hear him say 'we'. 'Right, I suggest you have one of these offices.'

'And you the other,' he put in quickly.

'If that is what you want?' She was inwardly delighted at his offer. 'Now, I think you had better engage two clerks – those who were employed here before, if possible. They will know what is required of them. One room downstairs is already equipped for clerical work. The other, I think, should be used by the manager whom you will appoint. You will need to leave someone in authority when you are not here, so choose carefully. Of course, these appointments, which I do think are necessary, will depend on the financial situation.'

'Then you'd better see the ledgers. We'll have to go downstairs.' Peter led the way down to the clerks' office and unlocked a cupboard from which he took two big leatherbound ledgers.

Lena perused the pages quickly, concentrating primarily on the entries for the last six months. Her father had schooled her well in ledger-work and she soon discerned that the firm was in a healthy position financially, something she would be able to verify later with the bank; the leading one in Hull, Peter told her.

'Everything appears to be sound, but I am surprised there is no entry for the sale of the timber the *John Carnforth* returned from the Baltic. I understood from your father's dealings with my brother that he had a customer for it.'

'I was under that impression, too, but can't find any paperwork relating to it.'

'And no one has come forward enquiring about it?'

'No.'

'So that timber is still in storage somewhere in the docks?'

'Yes.'

'Your warehouse?'

'No, we have no warehouse of our own.'

'So you are paying for storage?'

'Yes.'

Lena was appalled. Goods that should have made money were costing them instead. 'The first thing you must do is sell that timber. Go out and find a buyer, the sooner the better. Today if you can.' Then she added to ease any notion that she was dictating to him, 'You've had a trying time, Peter. It has not been easy for you to assimilate some aspects of running this firm after your father kept you in the dark so long. It was natural to think he had a customer for the timber but since no one has come forward to claim it by now, I think you had better sell.'

'It will be my priority.'

'Good. Now can we check with your bank that my assessment of the financial situation is correct?'

They left the building and Lena was soon assured that her interpretation was correct.

As they left the bank she said, 'Sell that timber and you will be in a very healthy position financially.' She wanted to add, It could open up all sorts of other possibilities, but she kept quiet –

time enough for that later.

Within the week, the two clerks, Jos and Dan, who had been dismissed by Peter's father, were persuaded to return. A competent manager, Alan Frampton, was lured from another firm by the offer of higher wages, and the timber was sold at a handsome profit. Gleaning information casually from Frampton, during the coming weeks, Lena passed it on to Peter in such a way that he took action without any prompting from her.

A month later when Lena came into the office she found Peter in a state of euphoria. 'Did you see a gentleman leaving?'

'A tall man, well dressed, hat at a jaunty angle, looking pleased with himself?'

'That would be him. Chris Strutman. He called on me representing his father's merchant's business on Teesside. He was looking to buy local commodities, eggs, butter, and so on, and link them into any coming into Hull from abroad, such as tea, coffee and other foodstuffs. When I raised the question of transport and hiring a ship, he said he would deal with that and arrange for the vessel to be here a fortnight today. So I have instructed Alan to begin assembling the commodities at the best prices.'

'And we add a percentage on to that as our profit?'

'Exactly.'

'Good. And this could lead to further orders from him, I take it?'

'I hinted at that, and he said it was more than likely if we made good with this one.'

Lena looked thoughtful. 'You know, Peter, it

would be better if we had our own ship to bring in commodities from abroad. There would be fewer handling costs. All we'd need do would be to load the local goods on board when our ship docked here and then it could be back on its way to the Tees.'

'I can see that, but we haven't our own ship and do you really think we should take the risk? We are making a steady income now, why risk upsetting that?'

'Because I think, until your mother died, your father intended to expand the firm. He would be pleased to know you were taking up his mantle, trying to accomplish all that he intended. It would be a fitting memorial to him if you did this.'

'It would, wouldn't it?' Peter still hesitated, though. 'There will be a lot to see to. You know what it is like, having seen your father and brother commission ships. I would need you to help.'

'And I'm willing to do all I can. It will greatly strengthen our position in Hull and along the Yorkshire coast.' Lena kept her innermost thoughts to herself. She blessed the day that Chris Strutman had walked into their lives and given Peter the final push to act on what she had always planned to do. Soon Hustwick's would be a force to be reckoned with – as would she. James Carnforth, this day I become a keener rival and thorn in your side, she vowed.

Her joy was unbounded when Peter came to Clancy House later that day. He made it in his way to have a word with Greta before seeing Lena, with the result that Greta excused herself after the meal on pretext of wanting a word with her housekeeper.

Peter escorted Lena to the drawing-room and as soon as the door clicked shut behind them he wasted no time.

'Let's get married, let's not wait any longer.'

She thrilled at the light in his eyes but had to say, 'Your mourning is barely over.'

'Never mind that! If anyone is critical, we'll take no notice. Say yes, Lena?'

'Yes!'

He pulled her to him and kissed her soundly.

When their lips parted he said, 'That eases my mind,' with some relief.

'What do you mean?'

'I always feared that, until we married, you might change your mind. And apart from wanting you as my wife, I have realised, since you came to Hull, how much I need you beside me to run my firm ... no, *our* firm.'

Lena rejoiced that everything she had hoped had come to pass. 'I love you, Peter Hustwick,' she told him then.

Arrangements went ahead immediately. They knew that under the circumstances they could not plan a big wedding and so decided invitations would be kept to a few of Peter's close friends, with Greta as bridesmaid. After they'd decided this, Lena gave a little smile. 'And I'm going to invite James and the others.'

Peter looked surprised. 'But you can't expect any of them to come, surely?'

She laughed. 'Of course not! I know they wouldn't entertain the idea, but it will be a suitable gesture of defiance for the way they reacted to you.'

'Just leave it,' he protested.

'No!' The strength of her reaction showed her determination and warned him to not to pursue the matter.

'Thank you, Sarah.' James took the letter that had just been delivered while he and Olivia were having breakfast. He recognised the writing but made no comment for the moment. He opened the paper and scanned it quickly. 'Insolent hussy!' he hissed then, startling Olivia who looked up sharply at him.

'What is it?' she asked in alarm.

He did not answer but slid the letter across the table to her.

As she read it, her lips tightened in a grim line. 'You're surely not thinking of going?'

'What, when Lena caused such a public scandal and hurt us all so deeply? Never! I won't even answer this.'

A few doors away, Alistair stiffened in his chair. 'The gall of her!'

'What is it?' his father asked.

Alistair gave him the letter. Albert read it and grunted in disgust, passing it to his wife. 'How dare she?'

Georgina looked up from it. 'Burn it, Alistair. And with it any thoughts you once had about Lena Carnforth.'

'Do you think we should go, Mary?' asked

Martin MacBride.

'It is putting us in an awkward position... I think this is Lena's way of criticising us all for the attitude we took. If she has sent invitations to Whitby people, I don't think any of them will go. How can they, after what happened?'

'I know, but I always had a soft spot for her. Maybe she is looking for forgiveness?'

Mary shook her head slowly. 'I don't think so. But we shall be able to clarify matters next week.'

'How?' He looked mystified.

'Oh, Martin! Have you forgotten, that Alistair is coming for a few days?'

Martin made a gesture of annoyance with himself. 'Of course. He's coming with Dr Jollif's approval. Wants to learn about my new measures to counter outbreaks of measles.'

'He's also having a holiday staying a whole week... So don't take up all his time with medical matters!' instructed his wife.

'Avril, will you take one of the traps to meet Alistair at the station?' said her father at breakfast. 'I need Angus to drive me today.'

'Very well, Papa.' Avril secretly felt a sensation of delight run through her. She would have Alistair to herself, for a short while at least. When she first learned he wanted to come for a week she had started planning how she might be able to get some time alone with him but had soon decided it was no use doing that, she would just have to seize any opportunity that arose. Now it had.

She secured the horse and trap in the station

concourse and strolled on to the platform. She was thankful it was a fine warm day, for she knew stations could be draughty places. Time seemed to stand still, in contrast to her own impatient pacing. Would Alistair have changed since she had seen him at James's wedding? Then he had been very attentive towards her, but had he only been following his duties as best man? How she looked forward to being with him again!

A distant whistle and then the rumble of iron on iron sent her heart racing, bringing with it an unforeseen nervousness. The train clattered to a halt amidst steam and smoke. Doors swung open; people descended on to the platform and set off for the exit, some hurrying, some in less haste, eyes peeled for those who were to meet them. As the passengers swerved around her she strained to catch sight of Alistair. She could not see him. Had he missed the train? Had he...? The flow of passengers thinned. Alistair? Then relief swept over her. He was here!

'Hello, Alistair, welcome to Dundee!'

'Avril! This is a pleasant surprise. I had expected to take a cab.'

'As if we could allow our guest to do that!'

They fell into step.

'How is everyone?' he asked.

'All well,' she replied, 'and looking forward to having you with us. What about you? How are you?'

'In good health,' he answered.

This really was not the answer she wanted but she could hardly ask if he had got over Lena.

They chatted amicably during the drive home.

Before reaching the house, Avril told him, 'I know you are here about some medical matters you wish to discuss with my father but don't let him monopolise all your time with them. As I think you know, he'll go on and on.'

Alistair smiled. 'Indeed. I assure you I won't let him start too many medical hares.' His expression turned serious then. 'I do want a little time to refresh my mind, after all that has happened.'

She was turning into the drive. Once clear of the gates she kept the horse to a walking pace and looked at Alistair with an understanding expression. 'If there is anything I can do to help...' She left the inference unspoken but the light pressure she gave his arm conveyed it for her.

'Thank you,' he said, with a shy smile.

The MacBrides came out in force to meet him: the doctor, his wife, Fiona and Robbie. They greeted him as one of the family. Servants were attentive in taking his hat and coat and valise.

'I'll show you your room,' said Mary. 'You can join us later in the drawing-room for coffee.'

'Thank you.'

'And treat this as your home, my boy,' Martin put in.

'Thank you again, sir. You are all most kind.'

As Mary escorted Alistair upstairs, Fiona saw her elder sister stand and watch them go. She sidled up to Avril. 'Well?'

'Well what?' she snapped, annoyed that she had been caught staring after Alistair.

'How did you get on? Father gave you a good opportunity, sending you to meet Alistair like that. He is rather handsome, isn't he?'

'And a gentleman,' replied Avril, as if that would stop her sister.

'Is he over Lena?'

'How do I know? I couldn't ask him, could I?'

'No doubt you'll find out before he goes home. I do hope so ... then maybe you'll stop mooning over him.'

'I don't moon over him!'

'Yes, you do,' Fiona grinned and skipped out of the way of Avril's playful slap.

They were finishing their coffee when Dr Mac-Bride said, 'Alistair you are here with some questions from Dr Jollif. I suggest we go to my study now and get them out of the way so that you can concentrate on what we might term your holiday.'

'That's very thoughtful of you, sir. It would be good to have them dealt with as soon as possible.'

'Then let us make a start.' Martin got to his feet. Alistair emptied his cup, placed it on the table and followed the doctor from the room. He glanced at Avril and the look she gave him exhorted him to remember what she had said.

'Take a seat, my boy.'

'Thank you, sir.'

They fell to discussing the medical situation in Whitby, and Dr Jollif's desire for information on handling outbreaks of measles.

An hour later the doctor said, 'I will have some case notes copied out for you.'

'That is very good of you. Dr Jollif will be most grateful.'

'It is my pleasure to help, and I am flattered

308

that he should value my opinion. If there is anything else, please ask before you go home. Now, let us relax over a wee dram.' As he was speaking Martin rose from his chair and went to a decanter and glasses on a side table.

With both glasses charged, he raised his. 'To an enjoyable holiday.'

Alistair acknowledged this.

'And how is life in Whitby?'

'Good.'

'James and Olivia?'

'Couldn't be better.'

'I'm pleased to hear it.'

Alistair could sense that the doctor was trying to lead into something and could guess what it was. 'Sir, I believe you are wondering if we have received an invitation to a wedding recently?'

'Then she sent you one?' Doctor MacBride frowned. He had hoped to hear of James and Olivia's reaction.

'She did. I suppose you got one too? After all, you are a close relation.'

'The whole family were invited but we are minded to refuse. We cannot condone the scandal Lena caused by running away with Peter Hustwick.

'Now, if I may give you a bit of advice, as difficult as it may seem at times, you must occupy your mind with other things, work and pleasure. What has happened is behind you. I'm sure you will find someone more worthy of you.'

And that someone is within the walls of this house if his wife had her way, which she usually did.

Three days later, with Alistair feeling comfortably at home in the MacBride household, he was sitting in the drawing-room with Avril, discussing the works of Wilkie Collins, when they heard the sound of the bell ringing. It was immediately followed by a loud knocking on the front door. Startled, Avril jumped from her chair and headed for the hall. Alistair was swiftly on his feet to follow.

The maid was already at the door when Avril entered the hall.

'Dr MacBride please – quickly.' The words came from a distressed female.

'He's not in,' started the maid, then faltered when she became aware of Avril's presence.

'All right, I'll see to this,' she said, taking charge immediately.

Relieved, the maid bobbed a quick curtsey and hurried away.

'What is it?' asked Avril, eyeing the dishevelled caller who had obviously rushed to their house without taking time to consider her appearance. A dark coat hung loosely on her shoulders and the belt around her plain brown dress had come loose. A shawl had dropped to her shoulders, allowing her hair to stream free from the ribbons that had held it. Her face was drawn by anxiety and her eyes were rimmed red with tears.

'Please fetch Dr MacBride for me.'

Avril reached out to help the woman inside. 'He is out visiting patients.'

The woman looked despairing. 'Oh, what can I do?' she cried.

'Come, sit here and tell me what the matter is.' Avril guided the woman to a chair by the door.

'Giles had been repairing some guttering on our house. He came into the kitchen, and next thing I knew he was on the floor,' explained the woman, between gasps and sobs. 'Oh, please, do something!'

'I'll come. I'm a nurse.' As she got to her feet Avril glanced at Alistair. He immediately read her query and nodded. 'This is Dr Nash, visiting us from Whitby. He'll come as well.'

The woman raised tear-filled eyes to him. 'Oh, will you, please?'

'I will.'

The woman, who introduced herself as Peggy, directed them to her home at the end of a row of terraced houses in a respectable area of Dundee. They saw a group of women standing near the front door.

'Neighbours,' Peggy explained. 'I expect Maggie's inside with Giles. She said she would look to him while I came for the doctor.'

When Avril brought the trap to a halt, Alistair was quickly to the ground, calling to two boys to look to the horse. He helped Avril and Peggy from the trap and they hurried into the house.

'Has he moved?' Alistair asked her neighbour.

'No, not even opened his eyes. I laid a blanket over him.' She looked at Peggy. 'I got it from your bed.'

Peggy nodded and looked anxiously at Avril and Alistair who were on their knees beside the man.

Within the hour they had him comfortably in

311

bed and had helped him regain consciousness. Peggy's relief when she saw him open his eyes was more than evident. When she finally saw Avril and Alistair out of the house, in the knowledge that Dr MacBride would visit as soon as he returned, she was profuse with her thanks.

'Mind you do as Dr Nash has instructed until Dr MacBride gets here,' instructed Avril as she climbed into the trap and took up the reins.

'You handled things back there remarkably well,' commented Alistair. 'You instructed them with authority, but also with reassurance and gentleness. People like that when they are in trouble and don't know what to do.'

'It is kind of you to say so, but I have had some training as a nurse and Father being a doctor, well, naturally some of his knowledge and experience rub off.'

'But the gentleness and tenderness are all yours.'

'You're very kind.'

'No. I merely speak the truth and am steeped in admiration for you.'

Avril blushed. Her heart was racing. Did he admire her in the way she hoped or was his admiration only for the way she had handled the situation today? Was he beginning to realise there were other people who could come into his life and enrich it? If only he would forget Lena!

Chapter Twenty

Lena and Peter were quietly married in Holy Trinity Church. Greta was the bridesmaid, a close friend of Peter's was best man, and six of his other friends, including Charles and Marcia Sugden of Weaver Hall, also attended. The reception afterwards was a quiet affair, though most enjoyable. Afterwards, Lena and Peter left to spend the night at Raby Hall before going on the next day to spend their honeymoon in what was designated a cottage on the Weaver Estate, though in fact it was an old hunting lodge updated luxuriously by the Sugdens, who had also appointed two of their staff to see to the young couple's comfort.

They enjoyed an idyllic time together, though by the end of the fortnight they had chosen to be away Lena wanted to be back in the hustle and bustle of the business world. Now she was Mrs Hustwick her chances of widening her influence would be greater, and she was going to make the most of those chances, working towards her ultimate aim.

Two months later, when Peter drove into Hull from Raby, he dropped Lena off at Greta's. At their last meeting they had promised themselves a morning's shopping followed by lunch at Greta's, so it was mid-afternoon when Lena arrived at the office to find a buzz about the place.

'What is it? What's been going on?' she asked.

Peter had jumped from his chair when she entered his room. He grabbed her round the waist and twirled her. The excited laughter on his lips made her laugh too.

'I've had a visit from Mr Strutman. He was highly satisfied with the cargo we assembled for him and has decided we can do the same next month, and the first week of every month thereafter until further notice! He also indicated that if we can arrange it he would like us to handle a consignment of cloth which he has bought in Halifax. He wants us to bring it from there to Hull, transport it to Middlesbrough where a quarter of it will be offloaded, and the rest will go on to Riga. The ship can be filled to capacity on the return voyage to Teesside with timber.'

'He wants us to do all that?'

'Yes.'

'Wonderful! How exciting!' cried Lena with enthusiasm.

'You were right about having our own ship. I've contacted the Welburn brothers who will be here shortly to discuss the type of vessel we want.'

'You've moved quickly!' As Lena hugged him she realised this brought her one more step closer to her goal.

By the end of the day a ship had been ordered to their specifications. It would not be ready for this particular voyage, but in view of Strutman's promise of further trade the Welburn brothers promised it would be built with all speed.

The *Lena*, so named on Peter's insistence, was launched with great ceremony. Once again she had sent invitations to James, Olivia, Alistair and the MacBrides, knowing full well the impact it would have on them in different ways, but the one reaction she would dearly have loved to see was James's. She reckoned he would be disturbed by what she had achieved and link it with the promise she had made him after the launching of the *John Carnforth*.

'Captain Washbrook?' Lena enquired of a sailor who was attending some ropes near the gangway of the *Maid Marian*, newly arrived on its weekly visit from Whitby.

He straightened from his task and touched his forehead. 'I'll fetch him, ma'am.'

A few minutes later the captain appeared.

'Good day, ma'am.'

Lena smiled. 'I can see from your eyes that you recognise me?'

'Aye, I do that, ma'am. I still remember the lass that used to visit Whitby's quays with her father and run off to explore whenever his attention was diverted to shipping matters.'

She laughed at the picture of her he'd conjured up. 'I wonder if I could ask a favour of you, Captain?'

'If I can fulfil it, ma'am, I will.'

'Bring me a copy of the *Whitby Gazette* every week?'

'No trouble at all, ma'am.'

The captain was as good as his word and it was from this newspaper that she learned of the birth of a son, John, to Olivia and James, named after his grandfather.

'He'll be heir to a thriving business,' commented Peter when she told him.

Lena made no comment. 'If there is a business left for him,' she thought to herself.

She also found the *Whitby Gazette* useful for keeping an eye on trading out of the port, especially anything related to Carnforth's which was always prominent in the trading news. She was annoyed she had not thought of this source of information before, but had been kept fully occupied with Hustwick's business while all the time allowing Peter to think he was making the decisions.

'I'm sorry you did not come with me this morning,' he said on Lena's arrival at the office one day two weeks later.

'So am I,' she said, returning his kiss. 'I always like to share the ride from Raby with you, but there were some domestic matters I had to see to.' She eyed him curiously. 'I know you, Peter Hustwick. There is something you are dying to tell me.'

'Indeed. Sit down.'

She took the chair he indicated on the opposite side of the desk.

'I've had a visitor, a Mr Glenville from York.'

'Should I know him?'

'No. This is the first time I have met him. He came with a proposition.'

'More trade for us?' put in Lena eagerly.

Peter gave a little smile. 'No. He came here with an offer to buy our business.'

'What?' Lena's voice was charged with surprise and shock. Had she taught Peter too much? Had he taken it upon himself to decide to sell? After all, the business was in his name and as the owner he had the legal right. She felt her heart thumping.

'He has made us an outstanding offer. It took all my self-possession to say I would think about it. I wanted to see what you thought.' But Peter gave her no time to comment and went on to detail the offer with such enthusiasm that she knew what he was going to propose.

'Let's sell. We'll never get an offer like this again. We'll have no financial worries and will have all the time in the world to ourselves. Just think what we could do.'

Lena's mind was spinning. She would have to handle this carefully. She was intent on man-oeuvring the firm into a position of strength so that she could proceed to the next stage of her plan. 'Peter, I don't know how you could seriously consider selling the firm your father founded and built up.'

'From that point of view, I have no sentiment about it. I respect my father and what he did, but after Mother's death he shut me out. Certainly he did not encourage me to take a deep interest in the firm. It is you who have really developed that.'

'Well, don't let that interest wane! We can achieve so much more, become pre-eminent in Hull's trading circles. Other traders are taking notice of us and more work is coming our way every day. It hasn't all been easy, as you know.

Some merchants and ship-owners are still opposed to me, and because of that shut us out of their social gatherings, but...'

'All that would soon cease if we sold,' Peter broke in.

'I'm not in the least disturbed by their attitude.'

'But I don't like to see my wife shunned in certain quarters.'

'If I don't mind, why should you? Those people will all come round in time. We are accepted by so many more now. Don't sell, Peter, please. This firm has a great future and is gaining more and more respect. Instead of selling, I think we should build another ship.'

'Another ship?' It was Peter's turn to look surprised. He had not expected this proposal at such a time. 'It will be costly and I don't like getting in too deep with the banks.'

'I'll put in the money my father left me plus my regular allowance and rent from Carnforth's.' Lena gave a little smile. 'It must rile James to know he must pay me every month. Just think how he would feel if he knew it was going to fund another ship to rival his!'

'No, Lena, I can't take your money,' protested Peter.

'You won't be taking it. I will be giving it willingly so that you can expand and take advantage of the new trade that is coming your way. Regard it as an investment in you by me.' Lena was careful to keep her proposition angled as if it centred purely round Peter.

'But if anything were to go wrong with the trading undertaken by the *Lena* we could find our-

318

selves in trouble. Perhaps, if she has a successful year, we could look at the situation again then.'

The last sentence sounded promising. Lena judged she had steered him far enough away from Mr Glenville's offer so decided not to press him further now. The subject of building another ship could be approached at a more suitable time. 'All right,' she agreed. 'And we forget this offer?'

'If that is what you want?'

She nodded.

'Then it's one concession for another.' Lena smiled. 'We make a good team.'

A smart middle-aged man left the train at Whitby, carrying one small valise. He strode purposefully to the Angel, booked a room for the night and, after refreshing himself from his journey, crossed the bridge and entered the offices of Carnforth's. He was known to the clerks from several previous visits and so was shown quickly to James's room.

'Mr Glenville.' James came from behind his desk to shake hands with the new arrival. 'I hope you bring news of a successful conclusion to our deliberations?'

'I'm afraid I don't, Mr Carnforth.'

James's hopeful expression faded. 'I thought it was irresistible.'

'So did I,' Glenville agreed as he sat down in a chair proffered by James. 'I saw Mr Hustwick during the morning. He seemed enthusiastic at the time and openly showed me the latest figures to see if they were appropriate to my offer.'

'And were they?'

'Oh, yes, even better than we thought they might be. You would certainly have secured an asset to your present firm. Hustwick's are forming a very solid foundation and are definitely on the up. It would not surprise me if they looked to expand, though I did detect a cautious streak in Mr Hustwick.'

'Do you think it was that caution which held him off from selling?'

'No. He was very enthusiastic initially, I thought I had hooked the fish for you, but then he asked for time to consider my proposition. That I considered only natural, as I had arrived unheralded with your offer. Something must have happened between my first visit and the second, to obtain his decision.'

James's lips tightened in exasperation. 'You saw no one else?'

'No.'

'Did he talk of anyone he might have consulted?'

'No. He gave the impression the decision was all his own, though I was not altogether convinced of that. I'm sure he consulted someone.'

James nodded. He judged that someone to be Lena. Mr Glenville had failed but at least from this information, and James's own knowledge of Peter and Lena, he felt sure that his sister now influenced the running of her husband's firm. Maybe she even controlled it. Recalling her threat the last time they'd met, he cursed his luck at being unable to thwart her this time. Another opportunity would arise, no doubt, and with Mr Glenville keeping a close watch on developments in Hull, James would seize his chance when it did.

Lena liked the days when she knew Captain Washbrook would be sailing into Hull bringing the *Whitby Gazette* for it enabled her to walk the quays and feel the call of the sea – it was there among the sails, the rigging, and every vessel she could see. It set her mind racing and always recalled for her the vow that some day she would walk the decks of a ship as it ploughed its way through the sea. Today was no exception.

The *Maid Marian* was just tying up when she reached the quay. Seeing her coming, Captain Washbrook handed over the finalities of docking to his First Mate and went to his cabin. When he re-emerged on deck the gangway was being run out and he was quickly on to the quay to greet Lena with a salute.

'Good morning, ma'am.' He held out the newspaper to her.

She smiled graciously as she took it. 'Good morning to you, Captain. I trust you had a good voyage?'

'Indeed we did, ma'am.'

'And how was Whitby when you left it?'

'As usual, ma'am.'

'You have nothing in particular to report?'

'Trade is good. Several firms are looking to the Mediterranean.'

'Any I'd know?

'Well, rumour is buzzing around that Mr Carnforth is not interested, but I think that is merely his bluff and he'll probably move before anyone else.'

'Any particular commodity?'

'Not sure, ma'am. Could be anything: spices, fruit, wine, olive oil, lace, pottery.'

'They all sound so exotic,' sighed Lena. 'Thank you for this, Captain.' She held up the newspaper.

'My pleasure, ma'am.' He saluted and went back on board.

Lena hadn't far to go to the office but made it a leisurely stroll, taking in the atmosphere of a busy port. At length she returned to her room, sat down at her desk, unfolded the paper and spread it out. She began to scan the words but lingered over those that especially caught her notice. She turned the page and as it settled a small headline towards the bottom attracted her attention: 'Carnforth Turns His Eye on Hull'. She read on. 'It is rumoured, and I understand it *is* only a rumour, that James Carnforth has tried to buy a Hull firm with similar trading facilities to his own. When this correspondent tried on several occasions to make an appointment with Mr Carnforth it was said he was unavailable. Make of that what you will.'

Lena stared at the words for a moment and with a racing mind read them again. They gave no information, not even a hint, of the name of the firm in which James was interested. But it struck her as strange that this report should appear so soon after Mr Glenville's visit to Peter.

She went quickly into her husband's office. 'Look at this.' She put down the newspaper, folded at the report she had just read.

He read it then looked up at her. 'So?'

'I think it is referring to Mr Glenville's visit.'

'You think your brother was behind it? That it was really he who was trying to buy us?'

'Yes. You raised no questions about Mr Glenville's principal?'

'I saw no reason to. His credentials were impeccable. He did not say he was acting on another's behalf...'

'Of course not. James would have seen to that.'

'Why should he want to buy us?'

'To get at me. To eliminate the threat I made him.'

'You mean, he took that seriously?'

'He knows me, and so he knows I meant it.'

'And I nearly played right into his hands.' Peter looked distraught. 'I'm so sorry, Lena.'

She responded quickly, 'I'm not blaming you, Peter. A very tempting offer was put in front of you and you would have been quite within your rights to accept. It is your business after all.'

'Thank goodness I told Glenville I would think it over.' He paused thoughtfully. 'We'll put this right straight away.' He jumped from his chair and grabbed her hand. 'Come on.'

Lena could do nothing else but follow him. 'Where are we going?'

'My solicitor. I want him to draw up Articles of Association stating that we own this firm equally, then neither of us can act on any major transaction without the approval of the other.'

Lena stopped him. 'Are you sure?'

'Never more so. Come on!'

As they hurried to the lawyer's office Lena felt

a glow of satisfaction at what had come about from Mr Glenville's unexpected visit. How very angry it would make her brother should he learn how his plan had misfired. As he would one day, when she returned to her rightful place in Whitby.

Chapter Twenty-One

Lena revelled in her sense of new power but curbed her desire to move things on quickly. She and Peter built their trading business, together and individually, but Lena still had her mind set on a major development. She kept her eyes open for another opportunity to suggest it. It came after the *Lena* had had a particularly harrowing trip and had sustained some damage that necessitated a fortnight's inactivity while she was made seaworthy again. They had found some difficulty in hiring a ship to replace her for the period of repair.

'Peter,' said Lena, hurrying into his office, 'I've managed to hire a ship in Grimsby. An agent has just come in with a possibility. The ship will be in Hull tomorrow. She's not an ideal vessel but will be able to take all our local produce to Teesside.'

'Capital!' As well as looking pleased, Peter was also relieved. 'Thank goodness we'll not have the cargo left on our hands.'

'Peter,' Lena's expression was serious as she sat down opposite her husband, 'we could have avoided this trouble if we'd had another vessel. As I said before, I'd contribute my money towards its cost.'

Looking thoughtful, he tapped his pencil on the desk a moment then rang for Frampton to join them.

'Alan, bring me our latest balance and the costings from when we built the *Lena*.'

'Certainly, sir.' When the manager returned a few minutes later he laid the papers in front of Peter and said, 'I have also brought the expected revenue figure for the cargo that is awaiting disposal.'

'Excellent,' said Lena. 'There will be a ship in from Grimsby tomorrow to collect that particular cargo so the figures are relevant to our considerations.'

Peter was already looking at the accounts and continued to do so after Alan Frampton had left the room. Lena said nothing to interrupt him. Finally he looked up and silently pushed the papers across. She pulled them nearer and studied the figures. After her thorough perusal she looked up and saw that Peter was watching her intently.

A little trickle of alarm passed through him. He had detected a light in his wife's eyes he had never seen there before. For one moment he saw ambition touched with ruthlessness. But even as he looked at her it vanished and he wondered if he had been mistaken. He was left staring into familiar, dear eyes filled with life and hope.

'These figures look sound to me, but they would not have been if we had been left with that cargo,' Lena prompted him.

'Exactly my assessment! If we take the cost of the *Lena* for a guide, though I think a new ship will cost more, I believe we can manage. I don't like taking your money but it would help finance a new ship...'

Lena's eyes lit up. 'Then we can go ahead?'

'Why not? As you pointed out, it makes sense.'

Lena sprang from her chair and rushed to him. 'I love you, Peter Hustwick,' she cried as she flung her arms round his neck and dropped on to his knee. Her kiss held much promise and he responded eagerly.

Returning to her office, she sank into her chair feeling delighted with herself. The storm that had damaged the *Lena* had played into her hands and she had grasped the opportunity. Another ship for Hustwick's would warn her brother that the firm was stronger than ever. It represented a rival to his own rather than an opportunity for more subterfuge on his part. Lena hugged herself and vowed to see the new ship was built with all haste. It marked another step nearer to her ultimate ambition.

The ship was half-built and, much to Lena's satisfaction, ahead of schedule, when one day Peter burst into her office.

'Lena, I have mentioned it before but it seems you have taken no notice...'

'What's the matter? Calm down. It can't be that bad.' She put on an air of innocence, though she was almost certain what was coming.

'There are more complaints about you interfering in the building of the ship.'

'I'm *not* interfering.'

'But I'm told you visit the yard most days.'

'Don't believe all you hear.'

'I have it from more than one source ... the latest the owner, Mr Starbeck himself. His manager and foreman have both complained to him about your visits. They say the men are uneasy that a woman is always spying on them.'

She tutted with annoyance. 'Spying? I'm not spying on them.'

'That's how they see it when the foreman urges them on soon after you have left.'

Lena scowled. 'And hasn't it paid off? The ship's ahead of schedule.'

'True, but I hope it is not at the cost of slipshod work.'

She bristled. 'If there is any of that, don't blame me, blame the men. And if there is, Mr Starbeck will feel my tongue.'

'Please, Lena, just stop going there. Let them do their work without any interference.'

'I've told you, I'm not interfering,' she snapped. 'I just want to get on with things. Get this firm into a position where it will really mean something, along this coast and beyond.'

Peter was disturbed by the wildness that had come into her eyes and voice. He recalled the ruthless streak he had seen in her the day he'd approved the construction of another ship, and remembered her brother's warning, too.

'I regret that I approved the building of this ship. It has brought out an unpleasant side of you that I did not know existed.'

'What on earth are you talking about?' Lena glared at him.

'It seems to have put you on edge. It appears as if, for you, the whole world revolves around this ship. You've just said what you desire, and that road could lead to ruin! We were comfortably off, running a good business...'

'Have you no ambition?' she challenged him harshly.

'Yes – to keep things as they were. But too late now. I fear we may be on the wrong road. It might have been better had I sold out to your brother...'

Lena's face darkened with anger. 'Don't you ever think that! And don't you dare reverse our agreement and go behind my back to sell to that no-good brother of mine.'

'No-good brother? There was a time when you didn't think so.'

'Maybe, but look what he did to me.'

'He didn't let you launch a ship? How trivial can you get?'

'He shut me out of the business.'

'I thought your father did that with his Will?'

'James could have let me in, in spite of what Father did, but he chose not to.'

'Ah, so that's what this is all about – revenge? You've just mentioned your ambitions to make this firm the most powerful along the Yorkshire coast ... and that means outsmarting your own brother.' Peter's eyes narrowed. 'I'm beginning to think you're using me and my firm towards achieving that revenge. Be very careful how you tread, my dear.'

'Is that a threat?'

'Read it how you like.'

He swung towards the door but Lena was quickly beside him, grabbing his arm to pull him round. 'Peter, I'm sorry. You're right – I've let things get on top of me. I'm so anxious for this to be a success for you. Please don't let us fall out.' Lena's eyes were pleading for forgiveness.

He felt his anger die as she looked up at him, and then he was lost. His arms came round her waist. He pulled her tightly to him and met her lips with a fierce kiss. As it ended he said hoarsely, 'No more quarrelling. But, please, keep away from that shipyard.'

She nodded. 'I promise.' She kissed him again. 'Sealed with a kiss.'

He smiled. 'Let's go home, there are better things to do there.'

Lena went willingly. But the thought never left her head that she had let things slip and now Peter was aware of her true ambition. She would have to play it down, tread warily as he had warned her.

During the next three months she did so and life resumed its old pattern, as if nothing eventful had happened between them. On his visits to the shipyard Peter found the men more settled thanks to Lena's continued absence from the site, except when she occasionally accompanied him at his invitation. She concentrated instead on building up goodwill with suppliers of goods she knew would bring Hustwick's decent profits when their new ship was ready.

Olivia and her mother were in the nursery where little John was having his afternoon nap when they heard a loud knocking at the front door. They exchanged glances and received their answer when, a few moments later, a maid rushed in.

'Ma'am, ma'am, come quickly!'

Her concern alarmed Olivia. 'What is it, Anne?' she cried as she started for the door which the maid held open for her.

'Mr Carnforth!'

Anxiety flooded Olivia. 'What's wrong?'

Reaching the top of the stairs from which she could look down into the hall, she saw four men standing beside her husband whom they had laid on the floor. Fear almost suffocated her. 'James!' she cried as she rushed down the stairs with the maid close behind her. Mrs Nash, concern lining her face, waited at the nursery door.

'What happened?' Olivia asked, casting her glance around the four men, who were strangers to her.

'Mr Carnforth was knocked down by a runaway horse and trap,' one of them explained.

Olivia was on her knees now beside her unconscious husband, feeling some relief in the fact that he was breathing at least. 'Anne, quickly, find my brother!' The maid rushed from the house. Olivia looked at the men. 'Can you bring him upstairs?'

They lifted him gently and proceeded up the stairs with care. On the landing, Olivia led the way to a room where they laid James on the bed.

'Thank you,' she gasped.

Mrs Nash, who was still on the landing, also thanked them and, with a quick glance at baby John that told her he was asleep, hurried to her daughter's side.

Olivia was loosening her husband's dirt-stained jacket and then his cravat.

'Do no more, wait for Alistair,' her mother advised.

As much as she felt she should be doing something, Olivia knew her mother was right. For endless anxious minutes they prayed James would regain consciousness, but he did not.

They heard the front door bang followed by footsteps hurrying up the stairs. Olivia was instantly at the bedroom door. 'In here,' she cried, seeing her brother.

'What happened?' he asked.

'Knocked down by a runaway horse and trap. He must have been coming home, though why, at this time of day?'

Alistair was already at the bedside, making a quick observation. He began unfastening James's clothes so he could make a closer examination.

Olivia and her mother stood by, anxiety mounting with every passing second. Finally Alistair straightened up and looked at them with a serious expression. 'I cannot disguise the gravity of his injuries. He has a broken leg and arm, but what concerns me most are the broken ribs and the possible internal damage from these. I would judge that he has taken a severe blow from a galloping horse and one of the trap's wheels then caught him as he fell. It's hard to tell at the moment all the damage that may have done. Can you send your maid to find Dr Jollif? I'd like a second opinion.'

Mrs Nash left the room to send Anne on another errand.

'Olivia, help me get him out of these clothes and make him more comfortable so that I can attend to his broken limbs.'

Dr Jollif's arrival was a relief to Alistair. He gently persuaded Olivia to leave them so they could make a more thorough examination. The men went about this quickly but with care. Both were alarmed when James still showed no sign of regaining consciousness.

Dr Jollif was sombre-faced as he looked across the bed at Alistair. 'It is difficult to assess the extent of the internal damage. I'm afraid we can do little more at the moment but wait for him to tell us exactly where the pain is so we can treat him accordingly.'

'But you do think he will come round?' Alistair's doubt was evident in the way he voiced the question.

Dr Jollif read that doubt, which he shared but had not so far voiced. Now he did. 'I don't think it very likely. Those blows on the head, which may have been caused by horse or trap or even the ground, are more severe than I first thought. The internal aspects, as you know, are difficult to assess and the patient may well have suffered internal bleeding as well as all the blood he has lost externally.' He paused then added solemnly, 'I'm afraid I don't hold out much hope. I'm sorry, my boy. But there is always a chance. Care and attention can do wonders.'

'I'd better get Olivia.' Alistair started for the door.

Dr Jollif bent over the prone figure again. 'Wait!'

The sharp command stopped Alistair in his tracks and brought him swiftly back to the bedside.

Dr Jollif had his stethoscope to James's chest. The tension in the room was palpable.

'The heartbeat is a little stronger.'

'There's a chance then?' cried Alistair hopefully.

'There's always a chance, my boy. It is only in the last resort that a doctor gives up. This young man will need a lot of care and attention.'

'Olivia and her mother will see to that.'

'I think a proper nurse is needed, someone who knows exactly what to do. Olivia can help but she has not the knowledge to do all that may be necessary.'

Alistair nodded. 'I'll bring her in.'

A few minutes later he returned with his sister. Dr Jollif explained the situation to her. 'I'm afraid I cannot recommend anyone in this area. Nurse Simpson is fully occupied. I'll contact a doctor friend of mine in York, but...'

'Wait,' Olivia interrupted. She glanced at her brother. 'Do you think Avril would come?'

'Dr MacBride's daughter about whom you have spoken?' queried Dr Jollif.

'Yes,' replied Alistair. 'I think she would be most suitable.'

'Then write to MacBride immediately.'

Alistair did so and three days later was in York

to meet Avril.

'Thank you for coming so promptly,' he said after the initial greeting was over; it had been too formal for Avril's liking, but maybe his mind was preoccupied with his patient.

'It was no more than I should do,' she replied as they hurried from the station to find the carriage he had driven to the station from Whitby. 'How is James?' she asked, bearing in mind the information that had been revealed in the letter to her father.

'No change. He's still in a coma. At least, he was when I left yesterday. I stayed the night in York so I would be here when your train arrived. Do you feel up to the drive to Whitby after your journey?'

'Of course! The sooner I am there, the more I will feel I am doing something to help.'

Once he had told her all about James, the diagnosis, and Dr Jollif's conclusion, Avril put the question to him, 'Do you agree with this?'

'Oh, yes, it was my conclusion too.' The firmness and certainty of his reply told her he was not slavishly copying his more experienced mentor but had formed his own opinion. Avril was pleased but kept that observation to herself.

Once the medical aspects were out of the way she directed their conversation to news of her family and more light-hearted topics, for she recognised Alistair was under severe strain. If only she could be the one to stay at his side, to offer him comfort and support. In the meantime, she would do all she could for his brother-in-law.

Avril quickly settled into the routine of the

Carnforths' house. She took charge of the sick room quietly and without intrusion, sensing Olivia was more than pleased to have someone there who was trained in nursing the sick and incapacitated. Though Avril made no comment, after four days she shared the two doctors' outlook on James's likely prognosis.

A week passed during which Alistair visited the patient twice every day. On the eighth day he arrived mid-morning. When he came into the sick room he asked, 'Any change?'

Avril shook her head. 'None. He seems peaceful. The internal injuries you and Dr Jollif thought he might have sustained have not so far manifested themselves, and in that at least I think he has been very lucky. But I am not so hopeful concerning his head injuries.'

'They can create unusual or unforseen repercussions in the rest of the body. We don't as yet know enough about the brain, I'm afraid, but head injuries are the hardest to treat.'

'We can only keep on as we are, and trust in God.'

'I think for an hour or so we must break the pattern.'

She looked sharply at him. 'Is there something I am not doing right?'

'Oh, my dear Avril, you are doing everything right. We are so lucky to have you. No, it is you for whom I am concerned. Apart from snatching some sleep, you are constantly in the sick room. You need to get out, have some fresh air.'

'I don't...'

'You are going to protest, and I am going to

stop you. It is a beautiful day. Get your coat. You and I will take a walk on the West Pier. The sea air will do you good. I mentioned this to Olivia when I arrived and she is in full agreement. She will come and sit with James. Come on.' Alistair held out his hand and when she took it, pulled her to her feet.

When they reached the West Pier and felt the salt-laden breeze, Avril snatched her bonnet from her head and let the wind blow through her hair as she shook it free and turned her face to the sun. She breathed in deeply several times, and then her shoulders relaxed. 'Oh that is so good,' she said, half to herself, but he caught the words.

Alistair smiled. 'I'm so glad. Let's walk to the lighthouse.'

'I'd love to.'

They fell into unhurried step, speaking little but enjoying being away from the confines of the sick room. When they reached the lighthouse they stood still while Avril admired the view, with the white-flecked sea running fast into the shore or crashing against the towering cliffs beyond.

'That's a wonderful sight,' she said, then glancing at him, asked, 'You like being in Whitby, Alistair?'

'It has always been my home.'

'And you still regard it as such, in spite of bad memories?'

'Those belong the past. The happier ones to come I will treasure.'

'Did you never consider the sea, in view of your father's successful business?'

'Never.'

'What made you want to become a doctor?'

'I think it was visiting Dundee and seeing what your father was doing there to help people try to better their living conditions. I vowed that one day I would do the same in Whitby.'

'Are you having any success?'

'I like to think so, even if only in a small way.'

'I'm sure you'll succeed.'

'But there is so much that still needs doing ... no, enough of me! You have a gift for being able to help people in their illnesses, and I do appreciate your being here to help with James. I know Olivia does too. Whatever happens, we always will be grateful to you. And I am especially grateful that today you have taken my mind off more sombre things.'

'And I am glad to have shared these moments with you.'

Later, alone in her bedroom, Avril thought of those words, those moments, and wished they had been more intimate. But Alistair did not appear to want to take a step closer. Did he still yearn for Lena? Maybe her own constant quiet presence would... But how long would that go on? How long would it take James to recover or would he... Avril shuddered; she should not even entertain such a thought. Whatever happened between them, some day she would have to return to Dundee.

Two weeks later James's condition suddenly worsened.

The reluctant way Dr Jollif straightened up from the bed told Alistair what he didn't want to hear. Colour drained from his face as he watched his partner shake his head slowly and silently mouth the words, 'I'm sorry.'

Alistair, his thoughts in confusion, walked slowly from the room. His steps were heavy as he took each stair, crossed the hall and entered the drawing-room.

'No!' The word was torn out of Olivia. 'No! No!'

The day was sunny with only a few wisps of cloud drifting lazily across a blue sky, a perfect day for Lena to enjoy her walk around the docks to meet the *Maid Marian*, due in from Whitby. It was an expedition that always set her pulses racing and never more so than today.

Their new ship would soon be launched, and only yesterday she had pleased Peter with her suggestion that they name her the *William Hustwick*.

'Father would have been delighted. In the short time he knew you, I know he came to like you. It would have delighted him that you commemorated him this way.' Peter had taken his wife into his arms to express his love for her.

Yes, life is good, Lena thought now.

'Good day, Captain Washbrook,' she greeted the Whitby man pleasantly.

'Good day to you, ma'am.' He saluted her but she saw that his usual smile was absent. He handed the newspaper over. 'I'm afraid I have some bad news for you, ma'am. Mr James Carnforth died last Wednesday.'

Lena was stunned. For a moment she did not seem to comprehend the news. James, dead? But he was still so young.

'I'm so sorry.'

'What happened?' she asked hoarsely.

'He was knocked down by a runaway horse and trap some weeks ago.'

'Weeks ago? I was never informed! Nor of his death, a week ago tomorrow.'

The captain knew of the scandal that had rocked Whitby society and caused the rift between brother and sister, but was not prepared to comment. 'For some reason the family wanted to keep it quiet. Apparently his injuries were serious but were not made known at the time nor in the succeeding weeks. I heard they resulted in a coma from which he never regained consciousness. I'm sorry to be the bearer of bad news, ma'am.'

She nodded. 'Thank you, Captain Washbrook, I am grateful to you. Do you know when the funeral is?'

'The day after tomorrow, ma'am.'

She nodded and appeared to sway. He was by her side in a flash, seeing she had lost colour. 'Ma'am, are you all right?'

Lena stiffened and pulled herself together. 'Yes, thank you.'

'Would you like me to escort you home?'

She shook her head. 'No. I'll be all right.' She started off slowly but with a more assured step.

He watched her for a few moments and then started up the gangway. From the deck he looked in her direction. She was walking a little more quickly now. Captain Washbrook turned to his crew and began to supervise the unloading of his cargo.

Lena's thoughts were in a daze as she tried to take in the news. Why hadn't anyone informed her that her brother had been badly hurt? Even as she posed the question she realised the answer and it made her feel even more of an outsider, not wanted anywhere near the circle in which she had once moved. The business? What would happen to it now? Olivia couldn't run it; Alistair had no interest in it, selling it must be the only solution for them ... and that would mean it would be lost to the only true Carnforth! Lena couldn't let that happen; she couldn't allow the family business to fall into the hands of strangers. She was determined that one day it would be hers, and had been building up Hustwick's to a position from which she could challenge James and oust him from control of Carnforth's. Now the chance to acquire it had come, in a way she had never visualised. She must seize it. But Hustwick's capital had been stretched by acquiring the new ship. She knew Peter would not condone the idea of borrowing to buy Carnforth's, a major decision on which, by the terms of the Articles of Association they had signed, they both must agree.

Thank goodness Captain Washbrook had arrived in Hull when he had, otherwise she would have heard the news too late for her to reach Whitby for the funeral. After that, Lena reckoned Olivia would dispose of her business asset. Lena *must* be there.

Chapter Twenty-Two

Reaching the offices, she went to find Peter. He realised from his wife's pale and worried face that something was wrong and was instantly out from behind his desk and beside her as she sat down wearily.

'What's the matter?' he asked her.

'Captain Washbrook has just told me that James died last week.'

'What?' Peter felt a shiver of disbelief run through him, but he knew there was no reason to doubt the veracity of what she'd said. He sank to his knees and took her hands in his, wondering how she would be affected by this news. 'What was wrong?'

Lena quickly told him what she knew. 'I must go to the funeral,' she added.

'Hasn't it taken place yet?'

'No. Captain Washbrook told me it's the day after tomorrow.'

'That's a long while after...'

'They'll be following the old conventions. The timing has worked well for me, at least. I'll be able to go.'

Peter was momentarily confused. James was her stepbrother; he and others close to him had slighted her. Why should Lena walk into a situation where she might be shunned or ostracised further? 'Do you think it wise to go?' he asked.

'Why not?' Lena replied with a touch of defiance. 'James and I shared much of our lives. And, apart from that, I think I should be there, for Mother's and Father's sakes.'

'Then I'll come with you.'

She pressed his hand and, with a wan smile, said, 'I think that would be most unwise. You look after things here, but hire me a coach and coachman to drive me to Whitby. It will be the quickest and easiest way. I'll stay at the Angel. Expect me back when you see me. Who knows what will happen when I'm there?'

Arriving in Whitby next day, she took a room at the Angel and asked the landlord to arrange accommodation for her coachman. Recognising her, and approving of the black dress with its close-fitting bodice and jet ornamentation, he told his wife to show the lady to the best accommodation in the inn. Lena wore a simple bonnet but one item of her three-part luggage was a hatbox, which the landlord's wife judged would contain a smarter veiled hat for the funeral.

She was right; Lena was wearing it at eleven o'clock the next morning when she left the Angel, having decided that she would join the family mourners at the house in New Buildings before the service and interment in the churchyard high on the East Cliff. That was to take place at twelve o'clock. The coachman had been told to hire a trap to take her to the house that had once been her home, and to wait there until she wanted to go to the church.

Lena stepped from the trap and paused to view the front of the house that still belonged to her.

Memories of a happy childhood spent there flooded back, bringing a lump to her throat. She tightened her lips and drew her shoulders back. She did not know what reception she would receive but was determined to show no weakness. No one would know she was outside – the curtains and blinds were all drawn. She walked resolutely along the path and up the steps to the front door, where she tugged the iron bell-pull firmly.

A few moments later the door opened and a maid, dressed in sombre black, without any relief, gasped, 'Miss Carnforth!'

'Mrs Hustwick, Sarah,' Lena corrected with a friendly half-smile as she swept past. 'Are they in the drawing-room?' she queried over her shoulder.

'Er ... er ... yes, miss ... er ... ma'am.' Sarah scuttled in front of her. 'Should I announce you?'

'No need, I'll announce myself.'

The maid bobbed a quick curtsey, and, now fully in control of her surprise, hurried away to impart the latest news to her fellow servants.

Lena did not hesitate; she flung open the door and swept in. She was immediately hit by the gloom, not only from the oil lamps that made a feeble attempt to emulate daylight but also in the atmosphere. People spoke in hushed voices as if afraid they might desecrate the sombre occasion.

'Hello, everyone,' she said, keeping her voice level and non-committal. Her eyes surveyed the room. Olivia, holding a handkerchief to her mouth, was sitting in the most comfortable armchair, her solemn-faced mother and father sitting to either side of her on straight-backed oak chairs. Alistair stood with Avril who dabbed her eyes with a delicate lace handkerchief. Dr and Mrs MacBride were sitting on the sofa, and standing behind them were Fiona and Robbie, trying to look more than serious while inwardly wishing they were safe at home in Scotland. Lena did not expect or wait for acknowledgement but went straight over to Olivia, carving her way to her former friend's side.

'Olivia, I only heard the news two days ago. Naturally I'm devastated.' She bent down to kiss her on the cheek, felt Olivia recoil and saw her narrow astonished eyes fill with coldness. As Lena straightened she was aware of all other eyes on her before Alistair openly reacted.

He stepped towards her. 'How dare you?' The words were meant to cow her. He had not reckoned on Lena's strength of will.

'I have every right to be here.' She defied his implication and added, 'I see you informed my uncle and aunt? Quite right too. But you lacked the decency to inform me.'

'Decency? You think you deserve that?'

Lena gave a little shrug of her shoulders. 'Depends how you view it. You obviously thought not, but I know James would have wanted me here.'

'You assume too much.' The words came coldly from Olivia. 'You don't realise, nor ever will, the hurt you caused him. I saw more closely than anyone what your actions did to him. Before most people he coped admirably, but there was an inner wound that never healed. You are not

344

welcome here.'

Her father, sensing how much worse this exchange could get, intervened then. He had risen from his chair. 'It is almost time we left for the church. I would ask you all to allow Lena to attend the funeral. After all, she spent many happy years here with James, and they were a support to each other during their tragic loss.' He fixed his gaze on Lena. 'There is sadness enough here today. We want no more. I respectfully ask you not to return here after the funeral.'

This was not what she wanted; there were other things to be settled. But she could do nothing else but agree.

The church on the wind-swept cliff was packed as the people of Whitby paid their last respects to the leading member of a well-respected mercantile firm that had brought money and employment to this Yorkshire port. There were more people outside to witness the interment, conducted in a dignified fashion to match the short but poignant eulogy in the church. It brought so many memories flooding back for Lena. At one stage her conscience was pricked by the momentous decision she had made on the day of the launching of her brother's new ship. But she quickly assured herself she had made a wise decision and set her course accordingly. She must see things through. Carnforth's was in danger of being lost. She could not let that happen!

Lena moved away from the graveside before the rest of the mourners. As she walked to her carriage she felt many eyes fixed on her and saw heads draw close to whisper about her, as they had done when she first entered the church. She directed the coachman to the Angel where she was to stay until the following day when she would return to Hull as planned. But before that she had a call to make.

Lena breakfasted early and was driven to the family house in New Buildings where she judged that everyone would be gathered again, to ease the loneliness for Olivia. Her judgement proved to be correct. When the maid opened the door she was able to answer Lena's question, 'They are all in the dining-room, ma'am.'

Lena pushed the door open slowly and took in the low buzz of conversation as she stepped into the room. No one noticed her until the door clicked shut behind her, then conversation stopped abruptly and all eyes were on her.

Albert Nash jumped to his feet. 'I thought I told you...' he started angrily.

'You did, but I need to speak to Olivia.'

'I certainly don't want to speak to you,' came the sharp retort.

'It will be to your advantage.'

'Nothing you could ever say would be to my advantage! You destroyed our friendship, destroyed all that James felt for you, and almost broke my brother's heart. You have already said quite enough!'

Lena retained an appearance of calm, though her heart was pounding in her chest.

'What I have to say now will I hope, go some

way to repairing the estrangement between us. All I ask is that you listen to me, just for a short while.'

For a moment Olivia did not speak. Valuing her brother's opinion, as always, she glanced at Alistair and saw his almost imperceptible nod.

'Very well, we shall indulge you.'

'I'd like to talk to you in private.'

Olivia frowned. What was Lena up to? Surely she wasn't going to play on a friendship that once had been deep and sincere? Best not to give her the opportunity. She shook her head as she said. 'No, I'll only speak to you if Alistair is present as my witness.'

Lena knew it would be unwise to agree immediately or with any enthusiasm, but in fact Olivia's demand suited her admirably. Far better to have a witness! 'I agree,' she said after a pause.

'Let us use the drawing-room then.' Olivia rose from her chair and headed for the door. 'Come, Alistair,' she called to him over her shoulder.

As Lena followed her from the room she realised that marriage had strengthened her former friend's character. Olivia the widowed mother was not the malleable girl of yesterday. She was now a formidable woman.

Alistair closed the door of the drawing-room. Olivia took a stance in the middle of the floor and faced Lena, halting her in her steps with, 'I don't think there is any need for us to sit. This won't take long.' Her dismissive tone was not lost on Lena.

'You are right, it won't.' She fixed her gaze firmly on her sister-in-law. 'You will no doubt be

347

in a quandary about the future of the firm my father and James built up. You have no interest in affairs mercantile and nor has Alistair. The only thing that may have crossed your mind is to sell to your father, but with no family member interested in following in his footsteps, I don't think he will want to expand his present operation. Therefore I am offering to buy the firm from you.'

Lena's mind was racing. She had spoken quickly, wanting to pre-empt any possible interruption. Now the enormity of what she had just done hit her, but she kept any visible reaction from showing. At that moment she did not even know where the purchase price would come from, but 'Sufficient unto the day'... She devoutly hoped she would have an ally once she told Peter what she had done and convinced him that the combined businesses would make them unbeatable in the North East. Her motivation, of course, was altogether simpler. She believed Carnforth's should belong to its rightful heir.

No one spoke for a moment. Olivia and Alistair just stared at her aghast. Lena started again: 'I'll get my lawyers to examine your accounts, make an assessment of the firm's market worth. If you get your lawyers to work with them, we should be able to reach a speedy conclusion.' She felt she had gained ground, but she had interpreted their silence wrongly.

Olivia and Alistair exchanged knowing glances and then Alistair started to laugh. 'You thought you could push your way in here and buy Olivia out? So *that's* why you came to the funeral! Not out of any respect for James, you came to seize an opportunity to further your own ends.'

'I did not!' Lena replied indignantly, annoyed that her purpose was so transparent.

'Don't make matters worse by lying,' Olivia spat contemptuously. 'I cannot believe the change in you, Lena – a change very much for the worse. Ambition is everything to you. Is that why you rejected Alistair and chose Peter Hustwick?'

'Your father cut you out, James kept you out ... so you saw Peter as your means of creating a rival firm with which to challenge James,' Alistair put in astutely.

'What does any of that matter now?' cried Lena passionately. 'Neither of you can run the firm, and even if you could it's not rightfully yours. A Carnforth should have it, and I'm the only true Carnforth left. I don't want it to fall into the hands of strangers, whereas I...'

'I? That's all you think about ... yourself,' Alistair blazed. 'Let me tell you, the firm has not come to a standstill because of James's death. It will continue to thrive. With Olivia's approval, I immediately gave Ralph Bell full authority to run Carnforth's. Your father himself saw great potential in him as a boy. He became close to James, as you know, and worked closely with him. He was only too delighted to carry on managing it for Olivia, fulfilling James's plans for the future and expanding upon them. We will have a solid thriving firm for Olivia's son to inherit one day.'

Lena saw her plans crumbling around her. She had been outwitted by Olivia and Alistair, and she didn't like it.

'You have no say in this,' put in Olivia coldly. 'It will be my son's inheritance and you can do nothing about that.'

Seething with frustration, Lena said, 'We shall see! James was never a true Carnforth. He only bore the name through *my* father's good grace. And if he wasn't a true Carnforth, then neither is your son who carries no Carnforth blood. But I do, and don't you forget it! One day the family firm will be mine.'

She left them then, straight-backed and resolute. She would not cry, not in front of these former friends who were now her enemies.

The journey back to Hull was torment for Lena. Moments of high resolve and determination were replaced by despair and dejection, but gradually she calmed herself and concentrated on the task ahead. She was angry with herself for ever thinking that obtaining the family firm would be easy and not foreseeing the change in Olivia and Alistair. But, no matter for that. They had never been her equal in business, and never would be. She would prevail.

She drove straight to Raby and was surprised to see Peter hurrying out to greet her.

'This is unexpected,' she said as they embraced. 'I thought you'd be at the office.'

'I thought you would be coming home today and anticipated you would come straight here,' he said as they strolled into the house together. 'I missed you, Lena.'

She smiled at him sweetly. 'And I you.'

'Did things pass off without undue hostility?'

'I shocked them when I walked in shortly before they were to leave for church. They would have run me out there and then, but Albert Nash prevailed. The others remained antagonistic, except for Uncle Martin and Aunt Mary who managed to have a quick word with me as we left the service.' They had entered the hall by now and she added, 'Come, I'll tell you all about it as I change.' She headed for the stairs and Peter followed.

As the door closed behind him she said in a tone full of suggestion, 'Lock it and unbutton me.'

He said nothing but his fingers deftly released the buttons down the back of her dress before returning to slip it from her shoulders. Lena let it slip to the floor and stepped out of it before turning to him and saying with a longing that was reflected in her eyes, 'Love me.'

Later, as she lay in his arms, she felt all the frustration and disappointment she had experienced in Whitby had been purged, and the determination forged on the ride home had been tempered by what she had just shared with Peter.

He ran his fingers gently across her stomach. 'You ought to go away more often,' he said with clear implication.

Lena chuckled. 'I don't think that will be necessary, do you?' She slid her arms around him and kissed him passionately.

'Who's running Carnforth's now?' he asked casually as they both dressed.

'Olivia has appointed Ralph Bell as manager,

351

with discretion to run the firm as he sees fit. It was all done very quickly after James died, on Alistair's advice. I think they hoped to discourage speculative offers.'

He sensed the annoyance beneath her words. 'And you don't like that?'

Lena was annoyed that she had allowed her feelings to show. 'No, I don't. The firm should be in the hands of a true Carnforth and...'

'...you are the only one?' he finished for her.

'Exactly!'

'Well, you are going to have to get used to it, my love. There's nothing we can do about it.'

Lena said nothing. Her mind was made up about her best course of action. But better to wait for now, tread carefully until Peter could be made to see the wisdom of her plan.

The day before the MacBrides were due to leave Whitby for Dundee, Olivia asked Avril to walk a while with her.

'I wanted to have a word with you alone,' she explained as they headed for the top of the West Cliff.

'This sounds serious,' said Avril when Olivia paused as if searching for the right words to go on.

She gave a half smile. 'It is, and I have deliberated long and hard on how best to ask you.'

'Come straight out with it then,' Avril suggested.

'It requires my asking a great favour of you.'

'Ask away. I'll do my best to oblige.'

'It will involve your mother and father.'

Avril eyed her with curiosity. 'Ask,' she prompted.

Olivia left a slight pause and then the words poured out of her. 'I have so appreciated your coming here to look after James. I don't know how I would have managed without you. I have got used again to having a close female friend – like Lena used to be. I am dreading your departure Avril. You'll leave an immense gap in my life with no special friend to fill it.'

'Olivia, don't think like that. I realise the void that must have been left in your life when you lost Lena's friendship after all those years. But rest assured, I now regard you as a special friend.'

'You do?'

'Probably more than you know.'

Olivia brightened. 'That makes it much easier for me to ask ... could you possibly consider coming to live with me and helping with John? Not as a nurse or governess but purely as a friend – a dear, dear friend?'

'That requires no deliberation. The answer, as far as I am concerned, is yes.'

'Oh, Avril, are you sure?'

'Yes. But I will have to see what Mother and Father have to say.'

'Of course. I live in hope.'

Avril felt the same, though she did not voice it. This would present her with every possibility of seeing more of Alistair, and who knew what that might lead to?

When the women returned home they sought out Dr and Mrs MacBride and put the suggestion to them. After considering it carefully they gave their permission, with the doctor adding, 'I am sure Dr Jollif and Alistair can make use of your nursing talents from time to time, Avril. Don't neglect them.'

'I won't, Father,' she reassured him. And, as eager as she was to inform Alistair that she was staying, she fought to curb the desire. After all, as yet he appeared to be offering her no more than friendship.

She did not see Alistair until the following morning when her family were about to get in the carriage for the journey to York. He came rushing up to make his farewells and received a surprise when he saw Avril was not attired for travelling.

'What about you?' he asked.

'Avril is staying,' put in Olivia, laughing at the expression on her brother's face, and went on to explain.

'That's wonderful,' he said, turning back to Avril. Her heart soared. But then her reaction was tempered when he went on, 'It will be comforting to know Olivia has such a good friend with her.'

'I'm only too glad to be of help,' Avril replied demurely.

'You'll be more than that.'

She certainly hoped so. It was her entire object in staying.

A week after Lena's return to Hull, when Captain Washbrook came down the gangway on to the quay to deliver her copy of the *Whitby Gazette* as usual, she said, 'Captain, can you spare a few minutes to stroll along the quay with me?'

'Very well, ma'am. My First Mate is able to see to the unloading. Your wish is my command,' he said with a slight inclination of his head.

'I hope that will always be so.'

A strange comment, he thought. What did she mean by it? He knew Mrs Hustwick worked alongside her husband in a local firm. They had recently added another ship to the one they already owned. Maybe there would be more; maybe a captaincy for him in a firm bigger than the one he worked for out of Whitby. He wouldn't mind moving to Hull if it meant promotion; a bigger ship and more distant horizons.

'The *Whitby Gazette* is most useful to me, Captain. I wonder, would you be willing to extend other services also?'

This was not quite what he had hoped for, but who knew what it might lead to in the future? 'If I can, ma'am.'

'I'm sure you can.'

'I await what you have to say with interest, ma'am.'

'Before I explain, let me stipulate that, no one, and I mean *no one*, must know of your connection to me. You're a young man, Captain. To have reached the position you already have shows aptitude and determination. No doubt your ambition extends further than your present position. Who knows what prospects may arise in the future?'

'True, ma'am, true. Particularly if my service to you proves valuable.'

Lena smiled. 'I think you and I understand

each other. Then you are interested in what I have to say?'

'Very. Might I add, even if nothing comes of it, my lips will remain sealed on whatever you are about to propose.'

'Good. You are most understanding. Now, what I want from you is information.'

'Information?'

'Not just now but every time you dock in Hull, I want you to keep me up to date on what is happening in Whitby: what is being traded by which firm, what expeditions are being mounted, what deals are being made. You are in a position to glean what is been rumoured along the quays, what is being talked about in the ale-houses, the inns and dining-rooms where captains and merchants gather. Information of that sort could be very useful to a firm trading out of Hull.'

'So that you, ma'am, can pre-empt any of the projects you see as of likely benefit to Hustwick's?'

'Exactly. And why not, if I have prior information?'

He gave a little chuckle. 'Why not?' His smile broadened when their eyes met.

'I see you like my proposition,' Lena said.

'Aye, but I like my future prospects better.'

'Then keep them always in mind. And in the meantime you will find me generous. One last warning: the arrangement is void if word gets out about our joint undertaking.'

'Understood, ma'am.'

'Good day, ma'am,' Captain Washbrook greeted

Lena brightly as he handed her the newspaper as usual after docking in Hull two weeks later.

She eyed him with curiosity. 'I think you have something to tell me.'

He smiled. 'Is it that obvious?'

'To me. If you have, you have exceeded my expectations. It is only a fortnight since I put my proposition to you, and a week ago you were a little despondent that you had nothing to tell me. So what is it that has brightened your eye? I hope it brightens mine.'

'An agent for a Spanish wine business has been visiting ship-owners in Whitby, sounding them out about shipping from Spain.'

'With any success?'

'As far as I could gather no particular firm has been engaged as yet because he wanted to visit other ports. I understand he is coming to Hull tomorrow.'

'How fortuitous that you arrived today.'

'Maybe. I always say that in your world, ma'am, you need a little bit of luck on occasion.'

'How true, Captain. Do you know any more about this gentleman?'

'I made it in my way to get a sighting of him by visiting the Angel when I heard he would be dining there with Ralph Bell.'

'Carnforth's,' hissed Lena. 'But he can't have concluded a deal with them if he is coming here tomorrow. What does he look like?'

'Small, rather weighty round the middle, fussy, dark, small moustache, well-dressed. He's English, name of Adam Carter-Brown. I also found out he would be staying at the Cross Keys

357

in the Market Place here.'

'I know it. Good work, Captain. You have exceeded all expectations. Now I can meet him there, and hopefully charm him into giving us the contract.'

'I am sure you will meet with no resistance, ma'am.'

'You are too kind. And thank you again. This is proving to be a good partnership already. You have done well.'

As she left the quay for the office Lena was in a buoyant mood. Developments had started sooner than expected; she must seize her chance. She considered the best tactics and in doing so realised she could not side-step Peter. He needed to know about the possibility of their entering the wine trade; it was hardly something she could keep to herself.

Accordingly she went straight to her husband's room. 'Tomorrow evening we are going to dine with Adam Carter-Brown at the Cross Keys.'

'Who's he?' asked a mystified Peter.

'By the end of the evening, I hope we will have a contract to ship wine from Spain for him.'

'What's this all about, Lena?'

She explained what Adam Carter-Brown was doing in Hull. She made no mention of his visit to Whitby nor of how she came to have news of his visit, making it appear it was through a conversation she had overheard in the draper's shop. 'One of the ladies was a Mrs Hopwell who let slip something about a contract her husband was hoping to win for a shipping firm in Newcastle.' An explanation that Peter did not question. 'This is a prime opportunity for us, Peter. With this foreknowledge we can get our proposal in first, charm him, and sign a deal before anyone else can.'

'Don't get carried away,' said her husband cautiously. 'The terms will have to be favourable. And, remember, the *Lena* will not be available, she's under contract to Chris Strutman. But we could probably have the *William Hustwick* free, depending when this man wants the first shipment made.'

'Then you are agreed, we should pursue it?' Peter looked thoughtful. 'The decision is yours,' added Lena, wanting it to appear that he was making the decision but prepared to argue if he decided against it.

He looked up from the pencil he was fiddling with and met her gaze. 'Of course we'll pursue it. We'd be foolish to miss the chance of widening our operations.'

'Good.' Lena's mind was racing but she kept her excitement firmly under control. Peter had just unwittingly agreed to go into direct competition with Carnforth's! 'I think you should arrange a dinner for three at the Cross Keys tomorrow. Leave a message for Mr Carter-Brown that he is invited to dine with us, and say we will meet him there at six-thirty.'

'I'll do it right away.' Lena followed him out but, after wishing him luck, went into her own room, feeling highly delighted with the way things had turned out.

Lena and Peter arrived at the inn a quarter of an

hour before the appointed time and a boy was sent to inform Mr Carter-Brown of their arrival. Minutes later he appeared and Lena immediately realised that Captain Washbrook's description of him was accurate except that he had not mentioned the man's eyes. Although they were friendly, she knew they would be capable of shrewd assessment and behind them lay a razor-sharp brain, able to make swift judgements and decisions. She and Peter would have to be on their mettle tonight.

With introductions over, Peter summoned the wine he had commanded the day before. It was expensive, but for a possible client in the wine trade no ordinary vintage would do.

Carter-Brown took a sip, savoured it and said, 'Mr Hustwick, you have made an excellent choice.'

'I am pleased to hear you say so, sir. Though I readily admit I am an amateur of wine – unlike yourself.'

'Indeed. I have to take a professional interest when I am buying for several English companies who all vary in their requirements, according to the market they are supplying. May I add how much I appreciate your invitation to me this evening? Generally I dine alone or in male company so it is a great pleasure to have such a charming and beautiful lady present.'

'You flatter me, Mr Carter-Brown,' put in Lena demurely.

'My name is a little ponderous in informal exchanges, so please, let us use Christian names. It leads to a more convivial atmosphere.'

360

Lena and Peter were only too ready to agree. They both felt the evening was starting well.

'Good,' said Adam. 'Now I'll make my last request. If you are agreeable, perhaps we should not talk business while we eat? I enjoy my food and don't like it spoiled by the intrusion of the mundane necessities of life. This evening, with such delightful company,' he glanced at Lena, 'why should we allow them to intrude?'

The enjoyable meal, fortified with appropriate wines, passed off pleasantly, with the conversation ranging over a wide array of topics that Lena realised Adam had introduced in order to assess these people who were busily courting his trade.

'That was a splendid meal,' he commented, leaning back in his chair pleasantly satisfied. 'I thank you both for your hospitality and most agreeable conversation. Now, should we find a quiet corner and get down to the real purpose of this evening?'

When they were seated comfortably Adam opened the discussion. 'I must say at the outset that I was intrigued to receive your invitation because I have never been to Hull before and as far as I know no one here knew of my visit. So I wondered how you came to contact me?' He looked from one to the other of them for the reply.

'My wife will have to answer that,' said Peter.

Lena glanced coyly at Adam. 'If you were in my shoes, would you reveal the source of such information?'

He smiled. 'Ah, you catch me out. I admire your

361

discretion as well as your loyalty to your source.'

She inclined her head graciously.

'But I will be frank with you on one matter. Arriving in Hull when I did gave me the opportunity to check on your firm's reputation.' He smiled. 'Like you, I will not willingly reveal my source. I was surprised to learn however, that Mrs Hustwick ... sorry, Lena ... is actively involved in the business. That is most unusual.' He looked hard at Lena.

'Yes, it is, but Peter realised I could be an asset to him, having learned a great deal from my father,' she explained, and added quickly to divert Adam from enquiring more about that, 'who sadly was killed in the Tay Bridge disaster.'

'My condolences,' Adam said quietly.

Lena went on to express her opinion about female involvement in the world of commerce, and how one day it would be quite the norm. 'I believe I have much to contribute to the growth of our firm, and Peter is of the same opinion.'

'From what I have seen, and heard so far this evening, I'm sure you are both right. Now let us get down to more detail. As I mentioned, I buy for several English companies principally from one big Spanish firm. I arrange the deals and transport and endeavour to find new markets in England. I found that there was an opening to be exploited in the North particularly on the eastern side of the country. The first necessity was to find someone to ship the wine to one of the north-east ports. I have been to Newcastle and Whitby, now I am here in Hull. So far I have two firms in mind.'

Lena took advantage of his pause. 'Might I ask who those firms are?'

Adam gave a little laugh. 'You would not expect me to tell you, nor to reveal their offers, surely?'

She met the implied rebuke with a disarming smile.

He went on to detail the cargo he wanted shipping and asked, 'If you received the commission, would you be able to arrange onward transport to the English companies in the North East?'

'Sounds like a big shipment,' said Peter when Adam had finished speaking.

'It is,' he agreed. 'Could you manage it?'

'I estimate it will require two ships.'

'You have two, and of the right capacity,' said Adam, 'I learned that from my enquiries.'

'We have,' agreed Peter, 'but one is engaged more or less permanently in shipping goods to the growing market in Middlesbrough.'

'A lucrative business on the back of the iron trade, no doubt.'

Recognising his uncertainty about giving them the contract with only one ship available, Lena intervened quickly. 'If we get the contract we will hire a second ship.' She saw unease in Peter's eyes but chose to ignore it.

'You can do that?' asked Adam.

'Yes,' replied Lena firmly, and with obvious assurance.

'All right. Then we'll get down to details and you can quote me a price.'

An hour later, with all aspects of the proposed shipment thrashed out, Adam said, 'Do you want to see me tomorrow with your figure or would you like a few minutes on your own now?'

'Now,' said Lena quickly, sensing her husband's hesitation.

'Very well,' said Adam, rising from his chair. 'Twenty minutes?'

'Twenty minutes,' Lena confirmed. 'What are we going to quote?' she asked, urgency in her tone as Adam walked away and left them to confer.

'I don't think we can proceed,' replied Peter.

'We must!'

'But we haven't secured a second ship.'

'As I said, we hire one.'

'Where?'

'We'll find one.'

'We have no idea of the likely cost.'

'We'll guess.'

'We might be a long way out, and that could prove to be a disaster.'

'We've got to take a chance and estimate now! I don't think we'll be far out.'

'Then we have to find a new captain and crew...'

'That shouldn't be any trouble.'

'They'd have to be vetted and found reliable. We've got a comfortable business as it is, why take on more?'

'Oh, Peter, haven't you any ambition?'

'Yes, to keep things as they are.'

'But we've a great opportunity here. I think we have created a favourable impression on Adam – we shouldn't miss our chance. I want to take it.' Her eyes bright with enthusiasm, she trained them tantalisingly on Peter. 'No, I want *us* to take it.'

He hesitated but could not resist the promise she was exuding. 'All right, we'll quote, but it's going to be a shot in the dark.'

They quickly discussed figures, made their calculations, and by the time Adam returned had settled on a quotation.

He sat down and looked at them expectantly, seeming thoughtful when Peter put the total to him. 'You are sure that is your final figure?'

'Certain,' replied Peter.

Adam glanced at Lena for confirmation and received it when she nodded.

'You are sure you'll have two vessels ready by the date I mentioned?'

'Yes,' replied Lena, not wanting her husband to show any uncertainty.

Adam made no comment but sat deep in contemplation. Peter was still mulling over what they had done, troubled that they might be risking the entire business.

Lena was alive with hope; she badly wanted this commission because she had a feeling that one of the quotations in Adam's possession was from Ralph Bell, hoping to further the fortunes of Carnforth's. She wanted the contract so as to best him.

Adam looked from one to the other of them and said, 'The contract is yours.'

Relief swamped Lena. She felt the tension drain from her. Peter was touched more by apprehension. Had they done the right thing?

Chapter Twenty-Three

Three days later Alistair made time to call in at Carnforth's office on the east side. He was making it a habit to do so once a week in order to keep an eye on his sister's interests. His father could have done so but had deemed it best that Alistair take on the responsibility. 'Ralph Bell might see a visit from me as an attempt to glean information to further my own business. He knows you have little interest in trading matters and would be lost in the technicalities, but you should be able to keep a general eye on things for your sister.'

So it was that on this pleasant morning Alistair crossed the bridge, combining his visit to the office with one to see a patient. He knocked on Ralph's door and frowned when he received a gruff, 'Come in.' The frown deepened when he saw Ralph's usually placid expression seemed dark with annoyance.

'Something hasn't pleased you,' commented Alistair.

Ralph did not speak but thrust a letter at him. Alistair took it and read:

Dear Mr Bell,
Further to our discussion re the proposed shipment of wine from Spain, I beg to inform you that your tender has been unsuccessful. Yours

was a very tempting bid but could not match that of Hustwick's of Hull.

Yours sincerely,
A Carter-Brown, Esq.

Adam had written a similar letter to the firm he had consulted in Newcastle, seeing no reason to hold back the name of the successful firm. It would be out soon enough once they set up operations.

Alistair's lips tightened in exasperation as the word 'Hustwick's' burned into his mind. 'Do you think they knew of our bid?' he asked, recalling the day Ralph had first mentioned the possibility of gaining some lucrative wine shipping.

'I don't see how. There is no way they could know the figure I gave Carter-Brown, and he would not tell them because if it ever got out that he had done so, his reputation would be shattered and his lucrative employment in jeopardy. I think it's just bad luck for us that their bid was lower.'

'But they may have learned that we met Carter-Brown, and bid low in the hope of beating us.' Was this an attempt by Lena to undermine the business? 'Take care, Ralph.'

'You think Mrs...'

'It doesn't matter what I think,' Alistair interrupted. 'I believe you have put two and two together and made four about what has happened between our families, and your assumptions are probably right. I know how highly you thought of James and his father, and no doubt still do, so all I'll say is, be aware there is someone not too far away who would like to see a reversal in the fortunes of this firm and seize their chance of taking it over.'

'You need have no worries. This firm's survival means a great deal to me. I owe my good fortune to Mr Carnforth and James. I will endeavour to see their business thrives and that no one can succeed in undermining it.'

'Thank you for your loyalty,' said Alistair. 'Now let us put this setback behind us. But be aware all the time of our watchful rival in Hull.'

Lena and Peter studied the instructions received from Carter-Brown regarding the dates the consignment of wine would be available in the Spanish port and when he expected it to be in Hull for disposal in the North East of England.

'The ships have to leave here next week.' Peter pointed to the date stipulated in the document with a trace of concern in his voice. 'The *William Hustwick* will be ready, but we need that second ship.'

'Then go out and find her,' came Lena's retort. She was irritated by the tight schedule detailed on the instructions, and the reminder of the penalty clause written into the contract they had signed when Carter-Brown was in Hull. She had expected longer to get the operation underway.

Annoyed by her terse reply, which had sounded like an employer's rather than a pleasant suggestion between man and wife, Peter rose from his chair. He said nothing, though. It was no use adding to an already worrying situation.

He did not see Lena again until he returned to

368

their town house in the early-evening.

'Well?' she asked, turning from the window when he came into the drawing-room 'What took you so long?'

'There isn't a ship available in Hull when we want it,' he said, crossing the room to her.

'What?' she exclaimed in disbelief and turned her head away when he bent to kiss her, so that his lips only grazed her cheek. 'What on earth have you been doing all day?'

'I have scoured Hull, but no one can help until a week after the contract date.'

Lena's lips tightened in exasperation. 'Then we'll have to look beyond Hull.' Her voice was sharp. This was a problem she had not anticipated.

'You should never have said we could hire a second ship without investigating first,' complained Peter.

'And lose the contract?'

'Better that than fail to fulfil it.'

'Fail? Don't be defeatist!' she snapped.

'Well, where are we going to find a ship?'

'Outside Hull, as I've said.'

'Whitby then?'

'What? And reveal our dilemma to Ralph Bell? Not likely! Get yourself off to Grimsby tomorrow.'

Lena spent a restless night, which did nothing to lighten her mood the next morning when she remarked to Peter, on seeing him leave, 'And don't come back without a ship.'

Two days later he arrived home to be greeted by his wife's expectant enquiries.

'I have a ship of sorts,' he confirmed.

Before he could explain that further, Lena snapped, 'Of sorts? What do you mean?'

'She's the right size. Her condition leaves much to be desired, but she'll survive unless she meets any violent seas.'

'What? And if she does, we're likely to lose the whole cargo?'

'That can happen with any ship.'

'But from what you say, it is more likely with this one?'

Peter shrugged his shoulders and retaliated, 'It was the best I could do. I had to take her crew besides.'

'The cost?'

When he told her Lena raised her eyes heavenwards. 'Exorbitant! You agreed to that?'

'She was the only available vessel. And you yourself told me not to come back without one.'

'I suppose that's it then. We'll make a profit, but nowhere near what we should have done. Let's hope all goes well and this leads to future orders from Carter-Brown.'

'We'd have been far better staying as we were. The business was sound, trading was good without being exacting, and we would have been saved all this anxiety.'

'And forego the chance to put this firm on top, not only in Hull but along the Yorkshire coast?'

Peter's mouth set in a grim line. 'And where exactly will that get us? All it brings is worry upon worry.'

'Don't you want to make more of yourself? Don't you want to have real standing and respect in this town?'

'People already respect the Hustwicks. They won't if we fail!'

'Then fail we shall not. We'll show other merchants here and elsewhere that the Hustwicks are a force to be reckoned with.'

'Elsewhere?' He picked up on the fact that this was not her first reference to looking beyond Hull. 'What have you in mind?' There was a suspicious look in his eyes as he fixed them on Lena. He recalled her homecoming from James's funeral and her reference then to Carnforth's being rightfully hers. 'You have your eyes set on the firm your father created, I take it.' It was more a statement of fact than a question.

'And why not? It is rightfully mine, and if I can get it I will.'

Peter stiffened at the venom in his wife's voice. He grasped her shoulders and stared hard into her eyes. 'Lena, you could destroy us all with this. Stop – now.'

'Never!' She shook herself free from his grip and walked briskly from the room.

Peter gazed after the woman he loved until the door closed behind her. Then he sank into a chair with his head in his hands. He did not want to lose Lena but what could he do to prevent her from continuing down the dangerous road she travelled? He had taken her into the firm because of the ability and knowledge nurtured in her by her father. He wished his own father had treated him the same way. He had recognised that his wife would be an asset to him in running the firm. To remove her from her position of authority would not only be unthinkable, it would be fraught with legal difficulties because of the way the Articles of Association had been drawn up. It had been agreed that major decisions would need their joint approval, but he now knew that Lena would be capable of stepping around that if it suited her. All he could hope to do was try to rein her in; temper, as best he could, her unquenchable ambition and desire for revenge.

When word reached the office that the ship from Grimsby, the *Seagull*, had docked Lena and Peter hurried to the quay.

'Due to sail for Spain tomorrow and he arrives today? He'll get my tongue around him,' grumbled Lena, her face dark with anger. 'He little knows the anxiety he has caused us this last week.' On seeing the vessel, she pulled up short. 'Oh my God, what have we here?' She could not believe a ship could look so worn out, as if it was reluctant even to go to sea. She wondered when it had last seen a lick of paint or even when the decks had last been washed down. Some of the timbers were broken, and at one point two sailors were making a desultory attempt to repair part of the rail. The rest were lounging around the deck as if they had reached their destination and wished to go no further.

'You engaged this lot?' snapped Lena.

'I had no choice, remember?' countered Peter.

'Right, where's the captain?' Lena started towards the gangway. Reaching it, she called to the man leaning against the rail, near the top of the gangway, 'Where's the skipper?'

The man straightened up and was about to reply when he saw Peter. 'Ah, Mr Hustwick, sir.' He touched his forehead in half-hearted acknowledgement of the man who had engaged him in Grimsby.

Lena looked at her husband in surprise. *'He's the captain?'*

Peter did not reply but called out, 'Captain Goss, good day to you.'

Lena stared open-mouthed at the man before her. A less likely captain she had never seen. His clothes were dirty, he was unshaven, and despite the cap he wore as the mark of authority, he did not look like a man liable to inspire loyalty or obedience in any self-respecting sailor she had ever encountered.

'You are late, Captain,' she called, without any attempt to disguise her displeasure.

'Ma'am, who might you be?' he replied lazily.

Peter spoke up quickly. 'Captain Goss, this is my wife who is my equal partner in the firm.'

The captain touched the battered peak of his cap again. 'Ma'am.' Then he looked back at Peter. 'You said nothing about working for a female, Mr Hustwick?'

'Do I detect hostility in your tone?' demanded Lena.

'Read it how you will. I don't know how my crew might react to this.'

'Then you'd better see they react the right way.' Lena put on a warning tone. 'And might I remind you that you are under contract? My husband signed you on in Grimsby. Break that

373

contract and there'll be no wages for anyone.' She saw the man bristle for a moment but he said nothing and she knew she had scored a victory. 'If anyone ought to break that contract, here and now, it should be me because of the rotten hulk you have brought me. I expected better.'

'You get what you see, ma'am, and will have to accept it and like it if you want your cargo bringing from Spain.' He gave a little smile. 'I don't think you have time to find yourself another ship.'

'You're right, captain, I haven't. But I will remind you again that I hold the purse strings, and unless that cargo reaches Hull on time and entire, with not one bottle broken or opened, you will have pay deducted in proportion.'

Captain Goss eyed her for a moment then said, 'It seems we understand each other, ma'am.'

'I'm glad to hear it, Captain. You sail on tomorrow morning's tide in the company of the *William Hustwick* – Captain Checkton, master.'

'Aye, aye, ma'am.' He saluted her and turned away, heading for his crew.

Lena watched him for a moment. 'He'll be back with the cargo on time,' she said to Peter, then added with a little laugh, 'The *Seagull?* I suppose she was so named because once upon a time, with her sails filled, she could fly. Let's pray she still can.'

News that the *Seagull* was back in the Humber astounded Lena and Peter. Both ships were due back from Spain today but they had expected the *William Hustwick* to be first.

374

They went to see Goss's ship dock.

As soon as the gangway was run out Captain Goss was on the quay. 'Ma'am, sir.' He made a mocking little bow as he added, 'Your wine is served.'

'Well done, Captain, you have made good time,' commented Peter.

'The *William Hustwick?*' Lena queried.

The captain smiled and waved his hand in the general direction of the sea. 'Somewhere out there, ma'am.' A twinkle came into his eyes. 'You expected her to be home first, no doubt?'

'Maybe she left after you?'

'No, ma'am. Four hours ahead.'

'But...'

He laughed. 'You thought this old tub couldn't fly? She ain't named the *Seagull* for nothing. Glides over the sea as if she has taken wings.'

'Unloading has all been arranged,' put in Peter. 'Stevedores and their foremen are arriving now.' He nodded in the direction of a group of tough-looking men approaching the ship.

Captain Goss followed his gaze. 'Look a likely lot. I'd best be off.'

'Come to the office tomorrow morning...' started Lena.

'I think the crew might like some cash in their pockets tonight,' interrupted her husband.

'Aye, they would that,' agreed the captain, and started to walk away.

'Captain Goss, call at our office first thing tomorrow morning,' Lena called after him.

He raised a hand in acknowledgement.

'You see to the advance on their wages, Peter. If

the *William Hustwick* docks before you are back at the office, I will meet you there.'

He agreed with her suggestion and left for the bank.

Lena noticed the *Maid Marian* at her berth then.

'Captain Washbrook?' she enquired of one of the crew.

'I'll fetch him, ma'am.'

A few moments later she was receiving the *Whitby Gazette* and enquiring if her source had any information for her.

'It seems Ralph Bell was very upset about the contract to ship a particular consignment of wine from Spain.' Lena felt a surge of pleasure at that. So she had guessed right about the identity of the Whitby firm Mr Carter-Brown had mentioned, and had stolen the contract from under Carnforth's noses. 'It left a couple of ships idle.'

And that would undermine their profits, she thought with satisfaction.

'From what I hear,' Washbrook went on, 'Bell is hoping to recoup that loss by trading more timber from the Baltic.'

Lena nodded. 'That could be useful. Thanks, Captain.'

She headed for the office, deep in deliberation, and was still so inclined when she sat down without any thought for the papers that were awaiting attention on her desk; she had much more interesting and far-reaching things to consider.

Peter had just arrived at the office when news of the sighting of the *William Hustwick* reached them.

'A good voyage, Captain?' queried Peter, when he and Lena met the ship.

'Excellent, sir. But I am surprised to see the *Seagull* already here. We left before her.'

'Four hours, Captain Goss said.'

'Four hours?' The man looked astonished but agreed it must be right by the remark, 'It will be entered in his log.'

He quickly let the matter drop. 'The vintner's were very efficient in Spain, and, if I may say so, I believe a lucrative trade could be established there.'

'Very interesting,' commented Lena thoughtfully. 'Thanks for the information, Captain.'

As they walked back to the office Peter remarked, 'Two very contrasting masters and two very different ships.'

'Yes. And both performed superbly,' she said. 'An excellent result! I hope Carter-Brown is satisfied.'

'There's no reason why he shouldn't be. It could mean more orders from him, and that will make our own business more solid.'

But Lena detected a cautionary note in his remark and the way it was delivered. It was as if he was saying, Don't get ideas about building on this; rest on your achievement. She smiled to herself and linked arms with her husband. He needed softening up. 'We've cause to celebrate. Let's do it at Raby Hall?' Her sensual tone tempted him and told him they would not be returning to town that evening.

The following morning, as he turned to get out of bed, Peter rolled back and kissed his wife hard on the lips before murmuring, 'You were won-derful last night.'

Her arms encircled his neck and held him tight so that she could look deep into his eyes. 'There will be other nights,' she promised. Peter smiled, kissed her again, and said, 'We'll have to go, Captain Goss will be waiting.'

She was tempted to say, Let him wait, but did not want to get on the wrong side of a captain who could be important to them in the future.

They had a quick breakfast and drove fast into Hull where Lena was relieved to see Captain Goss just entering the office as they neared it. He was making enquiries of the clerks when they walked in.

'Good timing, Captain,' commented Peter. 'We'll go up to my room. Our manager had instructions to pick up the rest of the necessary funds from the bank this morning. He should not be long.'

'Your ship returned unscathed?' Lena asked casually.

'She did, ma'am. I know she looks a bit scruffy but she's a real gem. Dare say she'd be better if she was done up a bit. I always mean to have it done but...'

'You are the sole owner?'

'Yes, ma'am.'

'And no one else has a vested interest in her?'

'No, ma'am.'

Peter looked askance at his wife. What was she up to? He gleaned nothing from her, though. Lena ignored the query in his eyes.

'You would not consider selling her?'

'No, Ma'am, never.'

Thank goodness for that, thought Peter, but he still felt uneasy somehow.

'Then would you consider hiring yourself to us on a permanent basis?'

Captain Goss's eyes narrowed as he met Lena's intent gaze. 'Depends on the terms, what was required, and whether it would be worthwhile for me and the crew. I would not hire unless their jobs were guaranteed.'

'Highly commendable, Captain.'

Peter's heart and mind were racing. He wanted to intervene, wanted to halt what he could only see as her extension of the business which might put it into an unstable position. Lena's own capital was already eaten up. But he did not want to provoke a confrontation with her in front of Captain Goss. A glance at his wife told him she knew this and was prepared to take advantage of the situation.

'I am going to put a proposition to you, Captain. I would like you to think it over care-fully, but if it tempts you there is no reason why we couldn't conclude arrangements quickly. In fact, the quicker the better! Well, here it is. You hire the *Seagull* to us on a permanent basis; because it will be permanent rather than a single engagement, the remuneration will be slightly lower. You will be her master and will engage the crew. You will sail as directed by us.

'I am prepared to have the ship repaired where absolutely necessary – you will draw up a list of what you think is required but it must be within reason. Don't think you can get away with padding the shipwright's bill – my husband and I know ships. However, there is one alteration to her I will want; the bow must be strengthened in case she meets ice when she sails to the Baltic to engage in the timber trade – a sensible precaution if she sails late in the season. How does that sound to you, Captain?'

'Intriguing, ma'am! Tempting because it means ongoing work, possibly the whole year through.' He hesitated for a moment. 'Does this mean you will want the ship based in Hull permanently?'

'Because of certain cargoes, she will be here a lot of the time, but as trade comes in, and we can look ahead, there is no reason why you cannot operate out of Grimsby. Then your crew will not miss out on home life when that is possible.'

'When do you want my answer?'

'As I said, as soon as possible.'

'I'll have a word with my crew when I go to pay them the rest of their wages then return with my answer. Although I think I know what it will be.'

'Good, then let us go and see if our manager has returned from the bank.'

Alan Frampton was waiting for them in his office. 'I collected the sum you required in cash, and have all the necessary documents ready for Captain Goss to sign.'

'Well done,' commented Lena. She turned to the captain, avoiding her husband's eye as she did so. 'Everything satisfactory for you, Captain?'

'Ma'am, there is no need for me to count the money. I am sure the amount will be what we agreed.' He took the pen offered to him by Frampton and signed the four documents with a flourish.

Almost before he had finished, Frampton was dusting them with fine dry sand and then examining them to see the ink was dry. He folded two sheets and handed them to the captain. 'Your copies.'

Captain Goss smiled. 'Thanks.' He swept Peter and Lena with his gaze, letting it settle finally on Lena. 'It has been a pleasure dealing with you, and your offer for the future is very tempting. I'll away and consult my crew.' He touched his cap and strode from the office.

Before anyone could speak Lena was out of the door and heading up the stairs. Peter was quickly after her, and by the time they'd reached the next floor she could feel his displeasure.

She started to head for her room but Peter's terse tone stopped her. 'My room!'

From the time she had started to put her proposition to Captain Goss she'd known this confrontation was inevitable. There was no point in trying to avoid it. She followed Peter into his room and closed the door behind her.

As it clicked shut he swung round to face her. 'What have you done? You know full well we cannot possibly go ahead with this scheme to hire Captain Goss, his crew and the *Seagull*. To offer to repair his vessel and suggest fortifying the bow ... what's got into you? You know we can't afford any of it.' His eyes darkened with every word he spoke.

'Can't? There's no such word in my voca-bulary.'

'Don't talk so foolishly.'

'I'm *not* talking foolishly. This last transaction

381

went well except that we did not make as much profit as we expected, and what was that due to? The terms *you* gave Captain Goss.'

'And if I hadn't, we would not have got the second ship we needed for Spain and so would have lost the contract. And then it might have been taken by Carnforth's,' he spat the words viciously, 'and *that* would have hurt *you!*'

'Yes, it would. And so it is not going to happen in any future transactions.'

'You are letting this need to best your family firm turn into an obsession. If you don't watch out, it could lead to disaster.'

'I'll see that it doesn't.'

'You can't guarantee that. Pull back, Lena, before it's too late. When Captain Goss returns, rescind your offer.'

'No!'

'Well, I will.'

'Don't you dare!'

'Let me remind you that on all major decisions we have to act as one. If either of us is against it, a project is null and void. And I regard engaging the *Seagull* as a major decision. I know I hired her once, but only when I was desperate. Now, heed me, Lena, I'll not have my father's firm destroyed.'

'For goodness' sake, Peter, I'm not going to destroy it – I'm going to make it the biggest firm along the Yorkshire coast. People will look up to you. Look to you for a lead.' She was careful to make the future appear rosy for him but, seeing he was not to be drawn into her web, added, 'Might I remind you that I put money into this firm too!'

'That's all been swallowed, and what you have in mind carries risks I am not prepared to take.'

'Well, you had better be prepared to do so. If you don't, we'll get nowhere.'

'But I am satisfied to remain as we are.'

She spun away in disgust. 'I thought I had married a man, not a…'

He reached out, grabbed her arm and pulled her back, preventing the words she was about to speak. His expression was cold. 'Don't you dare use a derogatory tone to me.'

Lena held his gaze for a moment then softened so that he would release his grip. With a swaying motion she inched closer to him and relaxed into his arms which reluctantly came up to support her. She looked into his eyes. 'Don't let us quarrel, Peter. There is too much at stake for us to be in conflict with each other. Believe me, I don't want to jeopardise what your father built up and you have so skilfully maintained. I only want to make sure that the firm will never be put in danger, especially from outside sources. What I have suggested to Captain Goss was only to strengthen our ability to withstand any possible setbacks.' She left the slightest of pauses to emphasise how reasonable her response was. 'Let me see this through? I promise you won't regret it.'

He held her gaze and the doubt he felt drained away. How could he resist his own beloved wife and the enticement she conveyed in the way she held herself so close to him?

A sharp knock on the door made them draw apart.

'Come in!' Peter called.

Alan Frampton looked in. 'Captain Goss is here.'

'Show him in.'

The manager pushed the door wider and stepped to one side to allow the captain to enter. Frampton pulled the door shut and returned to his office.

'That did not take you long, Captain,' said Peter, eyeing him quizzically.

'I didn't think it would. An offer of full continuous employment was too tempting for my crew, especially when they heard that the *Seagull* would be repaired. They are a rough lot but feel a special affection for that ship.'

'That's wonderful, Captain,' put in Lena quickly, afraid that Peter might still say no, although the softening she had just detected in him seemed to approve her plan.

'Captain Goss,' said Peter firmly. 'This is an important venture upon which we are staking a great deal. This third ship is vital to its success. We expect you to play your part. If you are successful, you and your crew will do well by it. I suggest that you return tomorrow to sign the necessary documents of engagement and to discuss the immediate course which Mrs Hustwick has in mind.'

'Very good, sir, ma'am.'

As the door shut behind him Lena flung herself into Peter's arms. Her eyes were bright; her smile rapturous. 'Oh, Peter, thank you! You will never regret it, I promise you.'

Chapter Twenty-Four

'Dr Jollif and I are so grateful for the help you have been able to give us,' said Alistair as he and Avril hurried along Church Street. 'And I know old Mrs Smurthwaite will appreciate your visits. It has been hard on her since her daughter died; her neighbours are good but they are elderly too and she likes younger company.'

'You know I'll do what I can,' replied Avril, pleased to be of help and to use her nursing knowledge. 'I am very glad things have worked out so well with Olivia, but I would like to see her participating in society more often.'

They had reached the turning to the bridge where Alistair stopped. 'While I am here, I'd like to visit Ralph at the office. Do you mind?'

'Of course not. I'll be all right.'

'I'll see you later then.'

Avril started towards the bridge and he stood and watched her for a few moments. It might have been Lena if... He tightened his lips and continued on his way, annoyed that she still had the power to shape and shadow his thoughts.

'Good morning, Ralph,' he called cheerfully on entering the office.

'Good day to you, Alistair. Hard morning?' he asked as his visitor flopped into a chair.

'No, not really, just some distracting thoughts.'

'We can always be hard on ourselves.'

'True,' agreed Alistair. 'What news have you? I see the *John Carnforth* is back.'

'Came in on the evening tide. Full cargo from France. We're unloading now. Three days and she'll be off to Portugal.'

'So things are going smoothly and we have made up for losing the Carter-Brown contract?'

'Mostly, but that could have been ongoing regular work whereas we have had to compete for other contracts.'

'But you are managing to keep trade flowing?'

'Oh, yes, but as I say, it would be easier with regular work. However, I hope to put that right to some extent later this year by sealing a lucrative deal for regular shipments of timber from the Baltic.'

'Good. I look forward to hearing more. Any news from Hull?' Alistair knew that Ralph kept an eye on the situation there since Hustwick's, or more precisely Lena, had outsmarted them.

'I hear that the ship they hired from Grimsby for the Spanish trade is being repaired by them and being hired permanently to increase their fleet. That is going to cost them a lot. I would dearly love to know what they have in mind.'

Alistair nodded thoughtfully. 'Beware of them.'

'I will.'

Lena lay quietly in Peter's arms, enjoying the sensation as he ran his fingers over her skin. She felt a deep contentment, not only from his loving but because she had won him over to her way of thinking about the repair and hiring of the *Seagull*. The ship was on its second voyage since the work had been completed and Captain Goss had proved his worth. She looked forward to using the information Captain Washbrook brought weekly from Whitby about Carnforth's even if it could not be verified – she believed there was no smoke without fire and presumed there must be something in the rumours. She knew that soon she would turn her attention from Spain to timber shipments from the Baltic.

Peter stirred. 'Lena, I think we should have a son.'

His words, quiet but firm, startled her.

'We should have an heir for the business.'

She twisted round in his arms so she could prop herself on her elbows and look down at him. 'We shall, Peter,' she replied quietly. 'But not yet. I'm not ready to have a child.'

'Why not? It would give us every reason to make sure the firm is set on a solid foundation, with no undue risk-taking. You know I'm uneasy. We are stretching ourselves too much at present.'

'Things are working out. You've got to admit that hiring Captain Goss and the *Seagull* proved to be a good move?'

He nodded. 'So far.'

'And will continue to be so. What we are doing now will make for that solid foundation you want. We'll achieve it by next year. Then we can throw precautions aside and you can have the son you want.'

'Promise me?'

She nodded. 'Promise.'

'And no more schemes to expand?'

'Agreed.' But Lena had crossed her fingers. She

crossed them again when she answered his next question.

'And no more thoughts of trying to win back Carnforth's?'

Her lips tightened for a brief moment but she said, 'None.'

From the way he pulled her to him she knew he was satisfied with her assurances. She uncrossed her fingers; the vows she made then were only to herself. Peter had agreed to dispatch the *William Hustwick* and the *Seagull* to the Mediterranean to bring back exotic fruits, spices and silks; what he did not know was that on information received from Captain Washbrook, Lena had seen to it that Hustwick's ships would be back in port first, leaving Carnforth's to arrive home to a flooded market and depressed prices. Hustwick's would make a good profit; Carnforth's less of one – maybe even a loss.

'What news, Captain Washbrook?' Lena asked as she took the newspaper from him.

'I haven't gleaned very much since my last visit, only a rumour, and I must say it doesn't sound likely to me.'

'Any little item of gossip might be of use,' she urged him. 'Tell me.'

'There's a story going around that Ralph Bell is thinking about having a steam ship built.'

'Steam!'

'It's the way we'll all go, ma'am, sooner or later.'

'I have no doubt, but I think it's far too early for a firm like Carnforth's or ourselves – too costly as yet. But prices will come down as the bigger shipping firms turn more and more to steam. That will be time for us to invest.'

'I agree with you, ma'am. I hear that if Mr Bell takes this step, he will wait until after next year by which time he hopes profits from the Baltic timber trade will be big enough to finance Carnforth's move into steam.'

Lena had much to think about over the next few days as she awaited the return of the *William Hustwick* from London and the *Seagull* from France. She formulated a plan for the next six months, terminating at the onset of winter in the Baltic, but acted on it only when Peter was in Beverley on business connected with Raby Hall.

She wrote a letter to Chris Strutman, dissolving their trading arrangement, and took it to the captain of the *Lena*, with instructions to deliver it personally and return with an answer.

Two days later, knowing the *Lena* was due in from Middlesbrough, she asked Peter to accompany her to the quay. When she did not offer any explanation he naturally enquired what lay behind the request, but all he got was, 'You will see when Captain Poulson arrives.'

When the captain saw them on the quay he was quickly down the gangway to hand a sealed letter to Lena.

'Thank you, Captain,' she said, and stopped him as he turned away. 'Did Mr Strutman reveal anything about our correspondence to you?'

'No, ma'am.'

'Then I think you had better wait for it will no

doubt concern you. Mr Hustwick does not know I wrote to Mr Strutman so has no idea what this sheet of paper might contain.'

Both men looked askance but could do nothing but wait until she'd read the letter. It was short and brought a smile to Lena's face. She looked at them triumphantly. 'The letter you took to Mr Strutman for me, Captain, terminated our trading arrangements.'

Astonishment crossed the faces of the two men. 'Why?' demanded Peter.

'I have greater things in mind for Captain Poulson and the *Lena*.'

'But she's earning us a steady income,' Peter protested.

Lena ignored that remark and turned to the captain instead. 'Captain Poulson, I want you to be ready to sail to the Baltic with the *William Hustwick* and the *Seagull* as soon as they return from their present voyages; they should be here the day after tomorrow. You can assure your crew that all jobs will be secure so long as they fulfil the new commission. You will be shipping timber from there until the winter freeze up and will have full authority, as will Captain Checkton and Captain Goss, to buy timber on our behalf. The crews will get a share of the profits so it is up to you to buy good timber at a good price and get in as many voyages as possible. The more the better, for everyone.'

'Yes, ma'am. I am sure all be willing to serve, though the Baltic can be a bit daunting when winter nears. The start of the freeze can be unpredictable.'

'I am sure you can cope with anything, Captain.'

'I can, ma'am.' He glanced at Peter. 'Sir.'

Peter nodded and waited until he was out of earshot before turning on Lena. 'What's this all about? You never mentioned terminating the Strutman deal or any idea about the timber trade. You've made a major decision again without consulting me!'

She did not rise to his criticism but linked arms with him affectionately. 'Don't look so angry. It's all for the best.'

'Best? What is so good about this hare-brained plan?'

'We're building a solid foundation for the son we will have.'

If Lena thought her mention of a son and heir for him at this moment would soften Peter's attitude, she was wrong.

'You are concentrating all our vessels on one commodity – and prices could fall.'

'Timber is always needed,' she retorted sharply.

'Yes, but the market may not always be buoyant. We'll be competing against other timber importers instead of having changing markets for goods of a very diverse nature. With timber only we'll be dangerously exposed...'

'Oh, Peter, why do you always look on the dark side of things?'

'I don't. Only when you do something risky like this! You should have consulted me first.'

'And you would have said no.'

'What if I had? We would still be profiting from Strutman's orders and from commodities that...'

He stopped and looked angrily at her. 'I think you have something else in mind, something you are keeping from me?'

She hugged his arm. 'Oh, Peter, I'm not. I only did it because it will benefit the firm. Make it more prosperous for our son.'

'I trust you are right.'

Lena did not comment but thought to herself, I hope I am.

Two days later, when the *William Hustwick* and the *Seagull* arrived in Hull, Lena slipped from the office without telling Peter and was at the quays to meet them. Seeing her, Captain Checkton and Captain Goss were quickly ashore, enthusiastically reporting back on successful voyages.

After hearing them out, Lena offered her praise of them. 'You have done very well. Now I have a new assignment for you. I want you to clear your cargoes quickly and be ready to sail the day after tomorrow with the *Lena.*' She inclined her head in the direction of the third ship, idling at her berth.

'For Teesside?' Both captains, expecting some respite before sailing for the Mediterranean again, expressed surprise.

'No, I have taken her off that run. I want all three ships to sail for the Baltic, for the timber trade.'

'Ma'am, my crew, and I believe Captain Goss's too, are expecting some leave...'

'Mine certainly are,' said Captain Goss, adding his weight to Captain Checkton's objection. 'They've not been home for six months because of the quick turn-arounds we have been doing.'

'And I'm afraid those will continue until the winter makes Baltic voyages impossible. Between now and then I want as much quality timber shipped into Hull as possible.' Before either man could speak she went on quickly to outline the tempting terms for the crews, as she had already done for the men of the *Lena*. When she had finished she did not see the expected enthusiasm in the two seamen's faces, however.

'This won't be popular with the crews,' Captain Goss pointed out.

'Popular or not, that is what they have to do or risk being out of a job,' came the sharp retort. 'And might I remind you that the terms I have outlined will bring them all extra money if you two buy well and achieve quick voyages.' She did not give them chance to make any further objections, adding quickly, 'That is all, gentlemen. Take it or leave it. I expect to see your ships ready in two days' time.' She turned sharply and strode away.

The captains eyed her for a moment before Captain Checkton spoke. 'She has got us. My men want regular money for their families and it won't be easy to find other employment. And her terms are good – very tempting in fact. Might be different for you, you're on hired terms?'

Captain Goss pulled a face. 'It's not as easy as that. As you say, money is money, and her terms for the Baltic voyages are good. But I am also bound by the terms of the hiring contract. I am hired until the end of the year; if I break our agreement it before that, I have to repay the money she spent on repairing my ship. If I don't, or can't, she has the power to confiscate it.'

'Good grief, she has you over a barrel! Why did you sign on such terms?'

'I saw it as a way of getting the *Seagull* repaired and at that time my crew were wanting steady employment which was hard to come by with the tub in that state.' He gave a shrug of his shoulders. 'So, looks like it's the Baltic for us.'

Both captains had a hard time with their respective crews but, faced with the prospect of losing their steady berth, they finally settled down. Two days later, on a day when the breeze swelled the sails, the *Lena, William Hustwick* and the *Seagull* slipped away from the quayside for the open sea.

'I have some disturbing news, Mr Bell,' said a grim-faced Captain Webb when the *John Carnforth* docked in Whitby. 'The Hull firm Hustwick's already had three ships trading for timber in Riga when we arrived, and I was told this was their third visit recently. As a result they have got their hands on much of the best quality timber, with agreements to take even more until winter freezes the Baltic.'

This was something Ralph had not wanted to hear. He had pinned his trading hopes on timber from the Baltic and believed few others knew of his intentions. Though it was difficult to keep plans watertight in a port, he had tried – and failed. Someone had obviously talked. It would be impossible to find out who, though. He would have to accept the setback and plan around it. But it made him curious about Hustwick's trading in Riga with a full complement of ships. He recalled Alistair's warning and wondered if this was another spoiling tactic by Mrs Hustwick.

'What timber did you bring?' Ralph asked.

'A full cargo but not of the best quality. If you have any customers wanting that, they will have to go to Hustwick's of Hull.'

'I have such customers, and it would stick in my throat to have to direct anyone there.'

'You want me to keep sailing to the Baltic as intended?'

'You'll have to. I have other orders to fulfil in which top quality is not essential, though of course the better quality would have brought a far greater profit. I am fortunate in having you, Captain Webb. You have previous experience of the Baltic and the vagaries of its climate. I want you to keep a close watch on that. Use your past experience and that of the locals to safeguard the ship at all costs. See to the cargo now, and come to my office tomorrow.'

'Very good, sir.' As he watched Ralph stride down the gangway and hurry along the quay, Captain Webb wondered what he had in mind for he felt sure the manager was hatching a plan.

Three days later, with water streaming from his Inverness coat and dripping from the matching woollen cap, Alistair rushed into Carnforth's offices. Hearing the commotion, Ben left his ledger and peered out of the door to see pools of water forming around the doctor's feet as he shrugged himself out of his coat.

'Mr Nash! Let me take that and your cap. I'll

hang them on the coat rack.'

'Thanks, Ben,' he said, handing the garments over. 'It's most unpleasant out there.'

'It is, sir. The old stagers predicted it a couple of days ago.'

Alistair nodded. 'So I heard. These old sailors are better than barometers. Is Mr Bell in his office?'

'He is indeed, sir. Would you like me to announce you?'

'No need,' replied Alistair, with a dismissive shake of his hand.

'Very good, sir.' The clerk disappeared into his office.

Alistair brushed some of the rain from the bottom of his trousers, and entered the room.

Ralph rose and extended his hand, which Alistair shook warmly. 'Haven't seen you for over a fortnight,' said the manager.

'No. I've been busy. There's been an outbreak of measles among the local children.'

'I hope you are able to contain it?'

'I think Dr Jollif and I have it under control, but we are keeping a watchful eye,' said Alistair as he sat down on the opposite side of the desk from Ralph. 'I have just come from Mr and Mrs Verity's. Their youngest is showing symptoms. I'm hopeful my early treatment might prevent it from being a bad attack.'

'Indeed, I hope so.'

Alistair grimaced. 'But I didn't come here to talk medical matters.'

Ralph smiled. 'I don't suppose you did.' He held up his hands as if to stop Alistair saying more. 'I take it my clerks are taking care of your wet clothes? Now let me give you a drop of whisky to drive the damp away.' He rose from his chair as he was speaking and went to the mahogany press, opening it to reveal a bottle and glasses.

'Thank you,' said Alistair, picking up his glass and savouring his first sip of the malt. 'As I said, I have just come from the Veritys'. Mr Verity had a word with me as I was leaving. He knows I really have very little to do with the firm but was alarmed that you had had to direct an order for good quality Scandinavian timber, required for his building trade, to another merchant.'

Ralph tightened his lips. 'I'm sorry to say that is so.' He went on to explain how the situation had arisen.

Alistair nodded his understanding but posed the question, 'What can we do about it?'

'The immediate answer is, nothing. When Captain Webb brought the news to me that Hustwick's were operating in Riga with their full complement of ships, I suspected they had somehow heard of my intention of sending a ship into the Baltic for timber and so pre-empted me with their bigger fleet, to corner the market.'

'This is not the first time they have moved in on one of your enterprises. While those never truly failed, they did not make the profits they would have done if Hustwick's had not moved first.'

'I agree, and it will be the same with this particular venture. But I am working on a plan to counteract what Hustwick's are doing.'

Alistair raised an eyebrow in query.

'I really don't want to say any more at this

stage,' said Ralph, then added quickly, 'Not that you will reveal anything, I know, but I want to be especially cautious about this. I have things to work out. You can't keep the movement of ships a secret for too long so timing will be of the utmost importance here. I don't want any early speculation to reach Hustwick's ears.'

'I understand perfectly well, and you do right to keep your cards close.'

'John has woken from his nap with a heavy cold,' commented Olivia in concern when she came into the drawing-room, carrying the young boy.

Avril put down the book she was reading and was quickly on her feet. 'Let me take him.' She reached out then hesitated. 'Olivia, have you had measles?'

'No, why?' Reading the inference behind Avril's query, alarm tinged her voice. 'You think he has caught it?'

'I can't be certain, but I don't like that redness and watering of his eyes, particularly as it's combined with an exceptionally runny nose. I think you had better let me take him back to bed. You should not have contact with him now.'

Olivia reluctantly handed her son over. She wanted to hold on, comfort her snuffling child with a soft embrace.

Avril murmured to him as she headed for the door. Olivia, her brow furrowed with worry, followed them upstairs. As Avril laid him gently back in his bed, she said over her shoulder, 'I think you had better leave the room.'

'But, I...'

398

'I know what you are going to say, but it is for the best, I promise you. We don't want you catching measles. It seems to be worse for adults.'

'Will John be all right?' his mother queried anxiously as Avril ushered her from the room.

'With care and attention, there is no reason why he won't be. Let us hope it is not a serious case. From what I have seen in Dundee, it doesn't look to be at the moment.'

'What can I do?' Olivia asked, glancing back at her child from the doorway.

'I'll see to things here. You slip home, tell your mother and father, and ask them to send Alistair here as soon as they see him.'

Olivia nodded and turned towards the stairs.

'And don't worry,' Avril called after her.

When Alistair arrived he confirmed that John had measles and commended Avril on the precautions she had taken and the way she had treated the patient. While he approved of her banning Olivia from the sick room, he asked uneasily, 'Have you had measles, Avril?'

'Yes, when I was two. I've also had experience of treating the illness with my father so I'll do all I can for John.'

His relief was palpable. 'We are lucky to have you here. But I don't want you overtiring yourself.'

'Can we get any help for Avril?' queried Olivia.

'With the outbreak of the disease in Whitby, I have no one to ask.'

'I'll be all right,' stressed Avril.

'Mother could relieve you now and again,'

suggested Alistair.

'That would be a help. I will call on her only if necessary, but her support of Olivia would be invaluable.'

'I'll tell her,' said Alistair, and went on to give his instructions. 'Olivia, you must not enter that room; you can view John only from the doorway. If measles runs its course, he'll develop a nasty-looking rash – not a pretty sight, but don't be alarmed, that is entirely normal. He'll also have a high temperature, which will make him restless.

'Avril, you need to control the fever, protect his eyes, give him plenty to drink and make sure he rests in bed. But I'm sure you know all this. If there are no complications with care and attention there shouldn't be ... he will be recovering well in about ten days.'

Alistair straightened up from the bed as John came out of a deep sleep and grinned at his uncle. 'There, that's what I like to see. You gave us all a shock but you are all right now. Another day or so and you'll be running about as if nothing had happened.'

'Can I take him down to his mama?' asked Avril, giving John a reassuring smile.

'Of course.'

She picked up the boy carefully, keeping him well wrapped up in a blanket. She hugged him as she went to the door, which Alistair opened, and walked to the top of the stairs. As he watched, he was struck by the Madonna-like pose. The faces of the woman and the child glowed with peace and contentment. Avril looked beautiful – how had he missed that before? Why hadn't he seen it? Had Lena got in the way? Why had he not rejected all thoughts of her and replaced her in his affections with the young woman who stood just a few yards away?

He stepped towards her. Avril turned her head and smiled at him, a smile that not only expressed her joy at John's recovery but also met on level terms the loving light she saw in his uncle's eyes. Avril's heart leaped. Alistair put out one arm to support her. 'Let's go down,' he said, but there was more than mere words to reassure her. It was the way he spoke to her, and his touch. Their eyes met and the message that passed between them was joyous and unmistakable.

Chapter Twenty-Five

As the year wore on Lena was delighted whenever merchants from Whitby came to them for quality timber from Riga, for it meant she had scored another victory over Carnforth's undermining their income and stability as well as weakening the trust merchants set in them.

The pleasure he saw in her on these occasions made Peter realise the real cause of her insistence on sending their three ships to the Baltic, and the reason why she was ordering the captains to make quick turn-arounds without any thought for respite for the crews.

They had just watched the three ships sail

again. As they turned away from the quay he said, 'You are driving them too hard, Lena. You'll have to let up soon or there will be trouble.'

She gave a mocking laugh. 'You think so? Money talks, and that's keeping them happy. Always will.'

'They'll only take so much. I'm told there are murmurings.'

'Let them murmur – they daren't take any action.'

'Who knows? Men have their breaking point. You are driving them excessively hard in your attempt to bring Carnforth's to the point of ruin so that then you can make them an offer they won't be able to resist. It will be that or face ruin.' His voice charged with warning, Peter added, 'Remember, it needs both our signatures to agree such a purchase.'

She stopped walking, grabbed his arm and pulled him round to face her. He looked into eyes that were burning with fury. 'Don't you ever *dare* to oppose me on this.' Lena's voice was cold. 'Yes, one day I will have the firm that should be in the hands of a true Carnforth. And then I can pass it down, along with this one, to *our son.*'

If she thought the mention of an heir would soften Peter's attitude, she was mistaken. He reached out and, taking her shoulders in a firm grip, stared into her eyes with a resolve she had never seen before. 'James has gone. Don't destroy yourself or us in your pursuit of revenge. You can't...'

'There's no such word as *can't!*' she raged. 'Certainly not where a Carnforth is concerned – and I am the only true Carnforth. I will have what is mine by right!' She stormed away from him.

Sorrow was filling Peter's heart as he stared after her. He was losing the girl he loved to an obsession that ran so deep he did not know how or if he could fight it.

Ralph Bell leaned back in his chair and stared at the wall. He saw nothing; his mind was full of an idea that he had been formulating for a little while. With the last sailings for the Baltic approaching, the time was coming when he would have to try to implement it or forget it. But no one could accurately predict when the Baltic would become impassable ... Over the previous two months he had become increasingly irritated by being constantly outdone by Hustwick's. Though he would never be able to prove it, he was sure they had mounted a campaign to bring Carnforth's to its knees. To do that they needed inside information. Had they obtained it with someone's deliberate intervention or merely interpreted rumour and gossip to their best advantage? He looked again at the notes he had made about sailings from Whitby to Hull and one stood out because it was regular – the *Maid Marian*, with Captain Washbrook in charge. He knew Washbrook as a competent and honourable man but he was also a gossip; his knowledge of activities in Whitby, even innocently aired, could have been picked up and acted upon by the Hustwicks. Ralph had no desire to tackle Washbrook direct and undermine his reputation, but maybe he could use him without the man knowing. The last piece of his plan was falling into place.

Two weeks later, with the arrival of the *John Carnforth* from Riga, Captain Webb reported to Ralph Bell. 'The locals believe we may not get another visit before the port is frozen in.'

'From your own knowledge, do you think this is a fair assessment?'

'I do.'

'I thought the time was drawing near.' Ralph looked thoughtful, as if weighing up the action he should take. 'Contact Captain Merryweather and Captain Turner for me and tell them I would like to see all three of you here in two hours' time.'

When they had assembled, Ralph made his orders clear. 'I want your ships ready to sail the day after tomorrow.'

Surprised, the three captains reminded him of the news from Riga.

'I still want you to sail, but your destination must be known only to you. Word of it must not leak out. As far as your crews and the rest of Whitby are concerned, you are sailing to Riga. In fact, I want you to deviate from your course and put in at Lerwick. Remain there two days before returning to Whitby.' He saw questions coming from the captains and held up his hands to stop them. 'There is no need for you to know my reason for this, just carry out my orders, the most important of which is that you don't breathe one word of them to anyone.'

The captains acknowledged his instructions and left his office.

Ralph left half an hour later, knowing Captain Washbrook was due to sail on his weekly run to

404

Hull that evening and would no doubt follow his habit of relaxing in the Angel before heading for the *Maid Marian*. His surmise proved correct and, after collecting a tankard of ale, he found a chair within earshot of the captain. Ralph drank steadily and signalled to the landlord to bring him another.

'You're looking very thoughtful, Mr Bell,' said the florid-faced landlord as he placed the tankard in front of Ralph.

He gave a thin smile. 'It isn't always easy, sending men to sea wondering if you have made the right decision.'

'I'm sure you won't have blundered.'

Ralph grimaced. 'I'm not. The day after tomorrow I'm sending three ships on the evening tide to Riga, hoping to get some of the best timber to fulfil our orders before winter makes the voyage impossible. It's tricky, judging it just right, and I certainly don't want those ships iced in...'

'Ma'am, I have news for you.' Lena read eagerness in Captain Washbrook's delivery as the morning light began to flood the sky in spite of the glowering clouds above. 'Mr Bell is sending his three ships to Riga for quality timber, sailing tomorrow on the evening tide.'

Lena hid her excitement. This was first-class information but she needed to react with caution. 'You seem certain. You are sure this isn't idle rumour?'

'No, ma'am! I overheard Mr Bell myself, telling the landlord of the Angel. He wants to complete the voyage before winter sets in there.'

Lena nodded and pursed her lips thoughtfully. 'Good. And my thanks, Captain Washbrook.' She took her copy of the *Whitby Gazette* from him and walked away. Her three ships were at their quays, having arrived back yesterday from the Baltic. Anger gripped her when she saw that some timber remained unloaded. According to her orders it should have been completed yesterday. Backs would have to bend today. If her ships were to outrun Carnforth's vessels and pick up the cargo Ralph Bell had in mind, they needed to leave immediately. She quickened her step and headed for the quay where her ships were tied up.

The captains were soon coming down the gangways, but before they reached Lena she saw Peter coming on to the quay. She cursed to herself; she would rather he had not been present.

'I was surprised to find you gone,' said Peter to his wife when he reached her. She was thankful he went on without waiting for an explanation, eyeing the three captains coming towards them. 'What's this – an early-morning conference?' He sounded wary.

Lena did not answer but acknowledged the captains' greetings and then said sharply, 'Why wasn't the unloading completed yesterday?'

'I told them it could be left until today,' put in Peter quickly. 'The crews had had a tough return voyage. I thought they deserved...'

'I want those ships to sail for Riga today.'

The captains looked astounded and all of them started to protest.

'I'll not countenance any objections,' Lena said

406

emphatically. 'You have to sail today, so see to it. Hire stevedores to finish the unloading, get your victuals on board. Winter in the Baltic can't be far off and I want another cargo of timber before that.'

'Ma'am, there's a chance that winter will come early there,' said Captain Poulson.

'And if it does, we either won't get into port or there's a chance we'll be iced in,' said Captain Checkton, adding his weight to Captain Poulson's observation.

'And there's also a chance that none of it will happen,' came Lena's sharp retort.

'But is it worth the risk?' asked Peter quietly, close to her ear.

She ignored him.

'My men aren't going to like it,' objected Captain Goss.

'They don't have to like it,' she snapped.

'They'll like it even less if this weather deteriorates.' He raised his eyes to the quickly darkening sky.

'Are they such weak-kneed ninnies?' She saw anger rising in the three seafarers and moved quickly to quell it. 'If you don't sail, you get no pay for the voyage you have just completed.'

'You can't do that, ma'am,' they protested.

'I can. I hold the purse strings. You'll get that pay when you have completed this coming voyage. Your men won't need the money until they get back.'

'Supposing they refuse?' asked Captain Goss.

'They'd be treated as mutineers, and you with them. Now, gentlemen, let's have no more nonsense.' Lena's voice hardened. 'You sail or you suffer the consequences. Now, move! I want those ships away.'

Muttering among themselves, but knowing she held the upper hand, they went back aboard.

Peter waited until they were out of earshot before turning on Lena. The glare he gave her froze her heart. 'I kept from contradicting you in front of them but you are wrong, Lena. Those men are weary after the way you have been working them lately, with barely enough time ashore between voyages, and now this! An immediate turn-around without any respite, and withholding their pay until after this voyage? You are tempting trouble.'

'I am their employer, I don't have to be considerate.'

'*We* employ them, not just you, and they deserve...'

'Peter, *stop!*' she broke in. 'If I hadn't taken such decisions on important matters we would not be where we are today. Don't you ever forget that.'

His lips tightened. 'And yet you still aren't satisfied. You'd risk all to get this one shipment of timber. If those ships are iced in we'll not be able to fulfil our trading with Spain, Portugal and the Mediterranean this year. Think what a loss *that* would be.'

'It won't happen! They'll be into Riga and out again before the ice. I'll not let Carnforth's get that timber...' The words were out before Lena realised it. How she wished she could unsay them!

Peter glared furiously at her. 'So that's it? Carnforth's! As I thought, you're obsessed with getting...'

'And I will get it!' Her eyes were wild with desire for revenge.

'Not through this voyage. I'll stop it!' Peter started towards the ships.

'And then you will never have a son!' Lena's threat sent a shiver down his spine and stopped him in his tracks.

He turned and their eyes met, hers triumphant, his bereft. Lena gave her husband a supercilious smile and walked away.

Rain began to fall from the dark, threatening sky.

Captain Goss, shoulders hunched against the wind and rain, strode along the quay to the *William Hustwick*. He was quickly at the Captain's cabin.

'Are we sailing?'

'I agree the weather's not good, but I think it has eased a little. If we are worried about conditions in the Baltic, I think we sail now. And if the situation there looks to be against us, even slightly, we turn straight back. Mrs Hustwick can't stand against that.' Captain Checkton pushed himself from his chair. 'Let's see what Captain Poulson thinks.'

'We've got to be of one mind on this,' pointed out Captain Goss as they came out on deck.

They were halfway down the gangway when they heard the clatter of hooves and saw a carriage approaching.

'This will be her,' muttered Captain Goss. 'Not

trusting us to sail without her cracking the whip.'

They waited on the quay as Lena drew the carriage to a halt. 'I thought you'd be underway,' she shouted. 'You are not afraid of a bit of wind and rain, are you?' She fought to prevent her horse from being spooked by the gusty wind.

The two men, tight-lipped, looked at each other and knew that neither of them would stand being labelled a coward.

'No, ma'am,' called Captain Checkton. 'We were just going to make last-minute arrangements with Captain Poulson.'

'No need, I'll see that he's ready. Get underway!' Lena flicked the reins and sent the horse towards the *William Hustwick*.

The two captains looked at each other, shrugged their shoulders, and returned to their ships.

Lena felt exultant when, through the falling rain, she watched the three vessels set sail. They would beat Carnforth's fleet to the Baltic and snatch another shipment of timber from under their noses, and then she would acquire even more of the orders the Whitby firm could not honour. Peter would have to admit that she was right and, considering her promise to bear him a son, would have to agree to put in a bid when Carnforth's inevitable collapse occurred.

Unloading the remaining timber before preparing to sail had meant the three ships leaving the Humber late in the afternoon. If the captains had had their way they would have waited until the following day but, with Mrs Hustwick's

410

threats hanging over them, they dare not hold back.

Sailing again did not sit easy with the crews. Lena had forced this last turn-around to be sharper than most and had not taken into consideration the weather portents which, with sailors' knowledge, they eyed with suspicion as their ships left the wind-lashed Humber and met the crash of a fast-running sea. The gathering darkness had been brought early by the heavy clouds overhead, that lashed men and ships with driving rain.

Bows dipped, scooped up water, and sent it streaming along the desk. The captains kept a watchful eye on conditions and their crews, cajoling them to be vigilant about their work lest one moment of slackness jeopardise the safety of all on board, but they knew all the care in the world could be undone by a ferocious storm. Many a hardened sailor glanced at the brooding clouds and offered up a prayer for a safe passage.

The ships ploughed on but, in the gathering darkness, with rain forming an impenetrable curtain, it was inevitable they would lose sight of each other. When that happened great vigilance would be required. Who knew whether they would move further apart or closer together, with the subsequent risk of collision?

As darkness shrouded the *Seagull*, Captain Goss raised his eyes to the heavens and cursed. 'Damn that woman! I'd give my wage to have her here on this deck now.' The ship lurched as another wave battered her. He staggered, only just managing to keep his feet, and braced

411

himself for the next impact. He half expected a shout of 'Man overboard' to come, but it didn't and he was thankful. The weather was atrocious, the high sea running viciously, but if it got no worse they could win through.

It seemed as if his hopes were being fulfilled; in fact, he thought he sensed an easing in the storm, but from long experience knew those hopes could soon be dashed and turned into a nightmare.

Standing close to the helmsman, he tensed, every nerve in his body crying out that what he had just sensed was wrong. A change in wind direction! It was coming from the north-east and it was strengthening. Orders flew thick and fast but the majority were torn away by the wind. Confusion reigned on deck and with it helplessness which turned to horror at the sight of dark, towering waves flecked with wind-driven white, bearing down on them.

Men grabbed anything they could hold on to. The first wave struck then, sending the *Seagull* lurching and listing alarmingly to port. Miraculously she righted herself, only to find she was being swept along at the sea's will.

Battle as he might to bring order and maintain a situation in which the ship could withstand all the storm could throw at her, Captain Goss realised he was losing out to the ferocious conditions. Two sharp timber-rending bangs pierced the howling of the wind; Goss knew his masts were gone, which was confirmed when one crashed on to the deck, the other into the heaving water. They were now at the mercy of the sea.

How long they were driven at its will his numbed mind could not tell him, but eventually one horror was replaced by another when looming shapes, darker than the night, came into view. Before a warning could be raised there was the tearing sound of timber being ripped away from the vessel's side. The *Seagull* lurched on, as if intent on driving into the wall of rock that towered above only yards ahead. Just as suddenly she stopped, with the sea pounding over her, before grounding herself on the rocks at the foot of the treacherous cliffs.

Captain Goss knew he was powerless now; the crew accepted it would be every man for himself, but each would help a mate if he could. A giant wave swept over the ship. Goss heard cries of horror all around him, but could see no one. Screams rent the night only to be stifled by the wind and the greedy sea, eager for more victims. Goss grabbed a rail, steadied himself and hunched his body against the next wave with the tell-tale white flecks signalling its ferocity. He held on and was left with water streaming from him, but he had survived. He knew he must try to find safety ashore or else be battered to pieces like his ship before the unrelenting sea. As he straightened he glanced seawards to try to estimate when the next wave would strike, then stiffened with horror.

Two black shapes, held high on a wave, were thrown together in a rending collision, tossed this way and that by the sea's will and then sucked down into the maelstrom.

Captain Goss felt sick with dismay and helplessness. The men he knew and had talked to earlier in Hull were all gone. He let the next wave break over him then slid over the side. He found purchase between some rocks and, with difficulty, scrambled clear of the sea that would draw him back to join his drowned crew.

Captain Goss stirred. There were voices talking far away, a note of urgency in them. They became more distinct and seemed to be directed at him. His eyes flickered open but he shut them again quickly. Too bright! Daylight? Someone was touching him.

'Can you hear me?'

He opened his eyes again. Squinting up, he became aware of a circle of people surrounding him. A bearded face leaned towards his.

'Can you hear me?' the man said again.

Captain Goss nodded, and saw the relief on the face above reflected in the others around him. He struggled to sit up and felt strong arms help him.

'Do you want to stand?'

He hesitated, opened his eyes wider, then nodded and was immediately assisted to his feet. He swayed a little, and was thankful for the support.

Everyone was curious to know more about him but, having been forewarned by the bearded man, did not crowd him.

Goss glanced around. They were standing beneath cliffs, which, to the right, sloped away to more gentle terrain and cottages clinging to a lower incline. 'Where am I?' the captain asked

'Ravenscar cliffs. That's Robin Hood's Bay.'

He nodded. He knew of the fishing village and the bay, which was a notorious graveyard for storm-bound ships driven ashore.

'I'm Captain Goss of the *Seagull* out of Hull. Are there any other survivors?'

Heads were shaken and the bearded man said, 'None. We found no one else. Two other ships foundered as well. We found timbers from their bows, the *William Hustwick* and the *Lena*.'

'We all left Hull together, bound for the Baltic.' Goss glanced round at their doleful faces, panic in his eyes. 'I must report the news!'

'You need medical attention first,' the bearded man pointed out.

'I'll survive. What I need is help getting to Hull. If there is no other means of getting there, I'll take a horse.'

'But...'

'I ride. I worked on a farm before going to sea.'

'I'll let you have a horse,' someone offered.

'Thank you, Mr...' Captain Goss started to move towards the speaker.

'Wilf Gregson,' the man introduced himself. 'Come with us.' He indicated the woman next to him. 'My wife, Mildred.'

'You can have a bite to eat while he gets the horse ready.'

'I'm obliged, ma'am.' Goss glanced round the crowd. 'Thank you all for your concern. If there are any questions, the three ships belonged to the firm of Hustwick's in Hull.' On legs that seemed hardly to belong to him, he stumbled after his Good Samaritans.

Half an hour later he was riding fast for Hull,

the thrumming of the hooves matched by the name repeated again and again in his tortured mind. Lena Hustwick … Lena Hustwick … this was all her fault and she must pay.

The news of the shipwrecks spread quickly to nearby Whitby. Ralph Bell received the news in his office and was saddened and horrified to hear of this loss of life for which, in some part, he realised he was responsible. But Lena Hustwick had fallen for his bluff when she need not have done. Greed had been her downfall. Ultimately the blame was hers. Meanwhile he had Carnforth's vessels to direct. They need not sail. Well, not to the north, that could wait until after the winter. Now they could head for southern markets left open by Hustwick's losses. He would inform the captains of the change in their sailing plans.

Captain Goss had recognised a strong animal as soon as he saw the mare and did not spare her on his ride to Hull. She responded well as if knowing the urgency of her mission. The white-flecked, steaming horse, ridden fast, attracted attention when he reached Hull, and people quickly recognised the Grimsby captain or else heard his shouts of: 'All Hustwick's ships lost!' The news spread through the streets like wildfire; soon knots of people were gathering, and comments and opinion ran rife. Lena's insistence that the ships sail in bad conditions had not gone unnoticed by the townsfolk.

Peter, making his way to the office, gasped

416

when he heard some news being shouted from person to person. *Three* ships lost? It couldn't be true. Yet he sensed the information must be right; there was no reason for anyone to set such a rumour abroad, and last night the weather had been cruel. Voices ran like a river through the streets and the name of Hustwick was spoken everywhere with loathing and condemnation.

Peter kept his head down, hoping people would be too busy talking to each other to notice him. He gathered from the storm of abuse hurled at his wife that her insistence on the ships' sailing was widely known and she personally was being blamed for what had happened. There was every indication the townsfolk were forming into a mob and he feared their anger would prevail if the situation got out of control. Although he had not condoned his wife's order, and knew there was every justification for people's hostility towards her, he could not let Lena face them alone. He must go to her.

Captain Goss realised he had set the fire and vowed he would be at the office before it gathered heat. He pulled up outside the building and was out of the saddle almost before the horse had stopped. He flung the reins to an urchin looking to earn a copper or two. 'Look after her,' he called to the boy, who caught the reins. Before he could say anything, Goss was into the building.

He did not wait to be announced but ran straight up the stairs where, without ceremony, he flung open the door to Lena's room and stormed in.

'You cruel, murdering bitch!'

A shocked Lena jumped to her feet. 'Captain Goss! What....?'

He cut her short viciously. 'Your three ships are lost, and I am the only survivor. You wouldn't be told, would you? You greedy, stupid, good-for-nothing she-wolf! All those good men gone because of *your* stupidity; you who wouldn't listen. All those ruined lives! Widows and orphans face a bleak future ... because of you!'

The hatred blazing in his eyes sent a shudder through Lena. The horror of this news stunned her. Her face drained of colour, she sank down on her chair. It was finished for her then. She foresaw nothing but contempt and hatred wherever she went in Hull. Everyone here would hold her responsible for the deaths and the dire consequences they brought in their wake. She saw that a reputation for risking the lives of others would never leave her. Her world lay in ruins, and with it her ambitions.

Hustwick's, with which she had been determined to wreak her vengeance and seize control of Carnforth's, was finished. She had lost Peter's inheritance and had nothing of her own to fall back on save for the six-monthly credit stipulated by her father and rent from the house. There would be virtually nothing left. How could she face Peter?

Even as these and other questions raged through her mind, she was aware of Captain Goss continuing his tirade against her. Accusation and condemnation assailed her. She clasped her hands over her ears, trying to shut out the damning words, but failed.

The door burst open then and Peter burst in. He had heard the last expletives shouted at his wife by Captain Goss. His stride did not falter as he swung his fist at the captain, catching him square on the jaw. Leaving the man unconscious on the floor, Peter grabbed Lena's arm.

She recoiled from the condemnation and disgust in his eyes, too. For one moment she saw that he was on the point of leaving her alone, to face the consequences of those ill-judged, selfish orders which had sent so many men to their deaths. But then his look changed to one of pity.

'Come on, before things get too ugly out there,' he urged, bustling her out of the door. On the landing, she stood frozen in indecision, terror stark in her face. Outside she could hear the jeering and catcalls of the families of the lost men and their sympathisers, gathered outside the building. They were demanding retribution for her insistence on forcing the ships to sail.

She stared at Peter, unable to speak. 'Come on, it will be all right.' He did his best to sound reassuring as he propelled her to the bottom of the stairs, where she resisted again. 'We've got to get out of here before that mob turns ugly. Is the trap out the back?' he called to Frampton who had been drawn into the corridor downstairs by all the commotion.

'Yes, sir.'

Peter hustled his wife outside. As soon as she was in the trap, he was beside her, urging the horse on its way.

The trap swayed with their gathering speed and

Lena held on tight as Peter urged the animal away from the building before their escape was discovered.

He came out on to one of the main thorough-fares. When he judged they had put sufficient distance between them and the office, he slowed the horse, not wanting to attract attention. They kept up a reasonable pace until he pulled the animal to a halt outside Greta's house.

Greta jumped to her feet, alarm in to her face when she saw the agitated state of her cousin and his wife. 'What's the matter?' she asked.

'We need to stay the night,' said Peter. 'I'll explain after I've seen to the horse and trap.'

The urgency of his tone was not lost on her. 'I'll get Gideon to see to that.' She was already at the bell-pull, signalling for her groom to be called.

As soon as the door closed behind him, Greta said, 'You both look as if you could do with a drink.' She poured two glasses of wine and encouraged them to take a sip. 'Can you tell me what happened?' she enquired.

Lena's glance told Peter to make the explana-tion, and she knew from the look he gave her in return that he would hold nothing back. It seemed as if the whole world had turned against her. But what else could she expect? She started to shake.

Greta noted it. She picked up her shawl, which she had laid on a chair earlier, and draped it round Lena's shoulders. 'Now tell me,' she said, looking to Peter for an explanation.

'We have lost three ships,' he began, and even

Greta's astonished 'What?' did not stop him then. Words poured out of him like a tide: inexorable, overwhelming, their meaning stark and inescapable. 'So, you see, with a crowd howling for Lena's blood, we could not go to either of the houses. They would be sure to think of looking there. I hoped you might help.'

'You don't think they will look for you here?'

'Few people know of our relationship, and those who do will not be among the baying mob.'

'Of course you can stay here, but what do you propose to do next?' she said.

Grim-faced, Peter shook his head. 'Right now, I don't know. By morning I hope to have a solution. Otherwise...' He gave a little shrug of his shoulders.

'Anything I can do, you know you only have to ask,' said his cousin. She glanced at Lena who, numbed by the dreadful turn of events, sat in silence, shoulders hunched as if to ward off a blow.

Greta got to her feet and went to the bell-pull. 'The beds are always ready, you can stay as long as you like. Come, Lena. A bath for you and then a rest, I think. We'll talk more tonight.'

Lena got meekly to her feet as if all free will had been drained from her. Peter felt a brief pang of sympathy for her. This pale-faced, shivering creature was not the woman he had married. She was a stranger to him now and he was not sure if that would ever change.

It was an uneasy meal that evening, with no one wishing to broach the subject of the future; Lena fearing what Peter's decision might be, Greta not wanting to interfere, and Peter undecided where his future lay, but knowing a decision had to be made, for both their sakes.

Unease hung between them as he and Lena made their way upstairs. Once the bedroom door clicked shut they were cocooned in a world that seemed to have no connection with what lay beyond, but one word out of place now could shatter that illusion and plunge them into a course from which there would be no return.

The word that broke the spell and brought past and future clashing together was spoken by Lena. 'Sorry.' It did not seek forgiveness nor seek to give an excuse.

'Sorry!' Peter's eyes were blazing. 'How deep-felt can such a word be in these circumstances? You have destroyed lives. You have destroyed me. Our future is ruined. *Why* did you have to send those ships out when all those with more experience were against it? You could see the weather was deteriorating...'

The words stung Lena and sparked retaliation in her. 'I couldn't foresee it would worsen!'

'You were determined to take no notice of wiser counsel, just to satisfy a whim.'

'I sent them out to make money for us.'

He laughed derisively. 'Don't try to justify your actions! They were driven by only one thing – your obsessive desire to have your revenge on a dead brother.'

'Step-brother!' she screamed. 'A Carnforth in name only! That firm should have been mine!'

'And your obsession has brought us to ruin. Don't think I haven't been aware of what you were trying to do.'

'And you were too weak to stop me!'

Peter grabbed her by the shoulders. 'Never that. But I made a mistake. I thought running the firm alongside me would be sufficient for you. I allowed you more power, thinking that would satisfy you, but you could not content yourself even with that. You sent those ships to their doom. I bitterly regret my part in it all. I should have done more to stop you, but I was afraid that if I did it would destroy the love we had. Now...' He let his voice trail away.

She grabbed his arms and, wild-eyed, met his condemning gaze. 'Peter, I'm sorry ... so terribly sorry. I thought I was securing a future for us all. You, me ... our son.'

'We had more than enough already,' he said coldly.

'I know that now and regret what I did. What can I do to make amends?'

'Do?' he spat.

Lena realised she was fighting for her future. 'I love you, Peter. Please ... don't desert me.' Tears started rolling down her cheeks.

He pushed her roughly from him. She collapsed on the bed, sobbing, as he strode out of the room.

In her bedroom, Greta heard his footsteps cross the landing and go downstairs. She listened intently but only heard the drawing-room door open and close. She would have gone to him but knew she had no right to interfere. They would have to resolve matters for themselves, and let tomorrow bring what it would.

Chapter Twenty-Six

When Greta came down early the next morning, she found Peter standing staring out of the drawing-room window. She noted that his greatcoat and hat were laid on a nearby chair.

'I heard you come down. Have you been here all night?' she asked.

'Yes.' Seeing concern in her expression, he added quickly, 'I've been well attended, and it gave me time to think. I'm glad you are down before Lena. I want to be away before she is up.'

Greta frowned. 'Things are that bad between you then?'

'I will not deny it.'

'What are you going to do?'

'I don't wish to disclose that because I may not be able to put into practice what I have in mind. But I would like you to do something for me.'

'I will do whatever I can, you know that.' Greta could not hide her affection for him or her desire to help.

'Take care of Lena until I get back. I think it best you both leave Hull without anyone knowing where you have gone, not even the servants here. Lena's life could still be in danger from some hot-head. What I suggest is that you go to Weaver Hall. I have written a letter,' he indicated a folded paper on the small table next to the window, 'to Charles and Marcia, asking them if you and Lena can stay there until I come to fetch you. I can't say how long I'll be, but don't expect it to be inside a week. Explain to them only as much as you think necessary.' He turned to pick up his coat but Greta stopped him.

She grasped his arms and looked intently into his eyes. 'I will do all I can for you and will anxiously await your return. Take good care, wherever you are going, and may whatever you do turn out to be the right decision.' She kissed him on the cheek.

Peter smiled, hugged her to him for a moment and was gone.

In the half-state between being awake and still asleep, Lena slid her hand across the bed. The expected contact did not come, bringing the realisation that she was alone. She was jolted awake and for a moment lay there, unaware of where she was. Then recollections of yesterday pierced her like shards of glass.

Peter! Where was he? She needed him; she craved his reassurance. She flung the bedclothes back, swung out of bed and rushed from the room. The house was silent. Panic gripped her, sent her hurrying down the stairs to fling open the door to the dining-room where she felt a measure of relief to find Greta seated at the table.

'Peter? Where is he?' cried Lena, her voice pleading for an answer.

Greta was rapidly on her feet, coming forward to place her hand on Lena's arm in reassurance. 'He has things to attend to. He will return.'

'Where is he? Where?' cried Lena. 'I need him

here.' Her face was twisted in distress.

'I don't know where he had to go but he did leave instructions with me,' said Greta, gently leading her to a chair. 'Sit down and let me explain.'

Bewildered, she automatically did as she was told and stared at Greta.

'Peter thinks it would not be safe for you to stay in Hull. He has asked me to take you to his friends at Weaver Hall, where he wants you to remain until he comes to find you. He has written a letter asking them to accommodate us both.'

'But didn't he say where he was going?'

Greta shook her head. 'He would not tell me. Said only that he might be away more than a week.'

'Oh, Greta, I can't bear it! I need him here, I need his forgiveness.'

'We can do nothing but place our trust in him now.' Not wanting this exchange to be prolonged, Greta said firmly, 'We must be away as soon as possible. The carriage will be ready in an hour. You get dressed and have some breakfast.'

Lena wanted to protest but knew she had no choice but to do as she was asked. The only mild objection she made was to say, 'I'll need some clothes.'

'I've thought of that and packed some of mine for you. We cannot possibly think of going to either of your houses, in case they are being watched.' Seeing the anguish on Lena's face, she quickly added. 'I believe the hostility will die down eventually. But until then we must do as

Peter wants. Please hurry.'

In spite of her disturbed thoughts, Lena found a measure of comfort when Weaver Hall came into sight. Its solid mass set amidst tranquil country-side, far from the upheaval of Hull, represented stability and peace to her. How she wished that Peter was beside her now and they were coming on a social call, to enjoy time spent with friends. Tears came with the realisation of all that had been lost through her own fault.

'What have I done?' she cried, turning a pleading face to Greta.

She placed a comforting hand on Lena's arm. 'Don't pillory yourself,' she said soothingly. 'Try to be strong. I'm sure Peter will arrive at a solution. Wipe your eyes and be patient.'

The inference that they should appear as normal as possible to meet the Sugdens was not lost on Lena. She wiped her eyes, smoothed her dress and stiffened her shoulders.

Greta brought the carriage to a halt outside the front entrance of the Hall. In a matter of moments the door was opened by a footman.

'Are Mr and Mrs Sugden at home?' she en-quired pleasantly. Her mind raced as it dawned on her that neither she nor Peter had considered the possibility that they would not be in residence. So it was with great relief that she heard the footman saying, 'They are indeed, ma'am. Please step inside and I will see if they are receiving visitors.' His enquiring look brought the answer, 'Mrs Hustwick and Miss Clancy.'

'Ma'am.' He bowed then hurried across the

hall, opened a door and stepped inside.

A few moments later Charles and Marcia came hurrying out. Their greetings were effusive.

'Peter not with you?' Charles asked.

'No, I'm afraid not, but he asked me to give you this letter,' said Greta.

Charles took it but did not open it until he and Marcia had seen the newcomers comfortably seated in the drawing-room. Then he stood with his back to the fireplace and opened the letter. He read it quickly and handed it to his wife who took it with a questioning look at him, wondering why he had made no comment. As soon as she read it she knew that his silence sought her agreement. Their exchange of glances showed the close understanding between them.

'Of course you may stay for as long as it takes Peter to sort matters out. He does not say what these matters are, and we do not seek to know. You are welcome here without further explanation.'

'Neither of us knows where Peter has gone nor how long he will be, but I think you should hear something of what has happened.' Lena glanced at Greta and saw her nod of approval.

She was pleased that Lena had taken this course as it would make for an easier relationship throughout their stay. She decided she would not interfere in the telling of the story but allow Lena, as the chief perpetrator, to explain as far as she saw fit.

Charles and Marcia listened without interruption.

Lena left out some of the details but the

Sugdens soon had a good impression of the recent disasters and understood how Lena's unreasonable ambition had led to the present situation. She leaned back in her chair when she finished speaking and experienced a moment of relief.

There was a short silence as if Charles and Marcia were weighing up what their attitude should be. When Charles finally spoke he did so for them both. 'I am pleased you thought it right to confide in us. Your trust will make for a pleasanter stay, no matter how long it lasts. You can rest assured, your story will not go beyond these four walls.'

'Now, I think we had better get you settled in,' Marcia took over.

She led Lena and Greta upstairs and showed them the rooms they would occupy. While they were doing that two servants arrived with the luggage from the carriage.

'I see you have only a little,' Marcia observed when only one valise was brought to Lena's room.

'Peter thought it unwise to return to either of our houses and took me straight to Greta's, so all I have is what she has kindly lent me.' She made a gesture, indicating the clothes she stood up in.

Marcia nodded. 'We must put that right tomorrow. A woman in the village makes my everyday dresses. She is very good but I have never employed her on anything more elaborate – I go to York or sometimes London for those.'

'I am sure whatever she produces will suit me until Peter returns and deems it wise for us to go home, but ... I have no money.'

Marcia dismissed the objection with a wave of her hand. 'Charles will pay and Peter can settle with him.'

'This is beyond kind,' said Lena, a catch in her throat and tears brimming in her eyes. 'You are too generous. I don't deserve such sympathy.'

'We have all made mistakes in our lives. There was no malice in yours. You weren't to know those poor men would meet a storm of such ferocity. We are both only too pleased to help. Besides, what are friends for if you can't turn to them in an hour of need?'

Lena stepped forward and impulsively gave her a hug.

'How can I ever thank you?' When Marcia responded with an embrace Lena felt safe. Now she longed only for equal forgiveness from her husband, then the future could take care of itself.

Peter turned up the collar of his coat, pulled the brim of his hat down and kept his head low as he walked at a quick pace through the side-streets of Hull. Coming within sight of the office he slowed his steps. Hostility emanated from the crowd assembled round the front door. Two men, urged on by the rest, hammered on it with clenched fists. Peter knew that if he was seen there would be little hope of his escaping unscathed. He slipped down an alley and quickly made his way to the back of the premises. He tried the door and was thankful to find it locked. His staff had either not come to work today or had locked themselves in. He hoped it was the latter because he needed to see them. He took his keys from his pocket and let himself in.

Alarmed by the noise in the passage, Alan, Jos and Dan came out of their rooms, ready to confront intruders, but breathed easily when they saw Peter.

'Mr Hustwick!' Alan gasped.

'All of you, upstairs, quick!' Peter was on the stairs even as he issued the order.

Entering his office, he swung round to greet the others with, 'Has it been worse than this?'

'Bad after you left yesterday. Did you encounter any trouble, sir?'

'No. I got Mrs Hustwick away safely.'

'Good. What do you want us to do now?'

'As you have no doubt guessed, the loss of the three ships means the firm is virtually finished. Besides, I don't think Mrs Hustwick or I will be tolerated in Hull any longer. I have some plans in mind but don't want to reveal them now in case they don't materialise But I wish to assure you, I will do all I can to see you three are not left without work.'

Their murmurs of thanks momentarily interrupted him.

'I will be out of Hull today but here is what I want you to do. Get word to everyone who lost someone in the wrecks to attend a meeting – ask permission to use or hire the recreation room in the Sailors' Home at eleven o'clock in three days' time. Get word to Captain Goss to attend, together with a list of the relatives of his crew.'

'Can we tell them why?'

The banging on the door increased then and

431

the shouts outside grew louder. Jos and Dan flinched at the noise.

Peter ignored it and carried on. 'You can't tell them anything because I don't know if my plan is achievable yet. Just tell them I will be there – that should bring them, if only to bay for my blood. It is sure to be a hostile meeting so I would like you three to act as my bodyguard, and bring another three men with you if you can.'

'We will,' said Alan, an announcement that brought agreement from Jos and Dan.

'Good. I'll meet you here at ten-thirty in three days' time. I'll go now. Give me half an hour then you can make an announcement to the crowd outside.'

Three days later, when Peter approached the office, he was gratified to find that there were no loiterers to be seen. He took this as a sign that Alan had successfully carried out his instructions. The first evidence of that was when he went inside and was instantly introduced to the three burly men his manager had brought in for reinforcements.

'Just stay close to me and don't take any action unless the situation gets really ugly. No doubt there'll be plenty of abuse and criticism thrown my way when we arrive, but I hope what I have to say will quell any outright violence. You are not there to antagonise the crowd. Understood?'

They all accepted Peter's instructions.

'Right. Let's go.'

The protective wall of six formed a circle round him and matched his quick determined stride that only slowed when the Sailors' Home came in sight and they saw black-clad people streaming towards the building. They were close to it when someone spotted Peter.

'There he is!' a shout went up. Immediately Peter's name was bandied from tongue to tongue, and soon foul abuse was directed not only at him but at Lena. Entry into the building was impossible. Peter found their way blocked.

'Let us through,' he called.

Hostility hung in the air.

'Allow Mr Hustwick to get in,' shouted Alan.

That brought a further tirade from the crowd.

Alan was not to be deterred. 'If you want to hear what Mr Hustwick has to say, let him through. He cannot address you out here. There are people already inside and what he has to say needs to be heard by everyone.' He paused and, detecting something of a response, pressed on. 'Please make way there. Let Mr Hustwick say what he has to say – it is only right for him to do so, and you should respect his desire to speak to you all.'

There were some calls of support for what he had said. Gradually people stood back to allow Peter and his bodyguard through.

Those inside the building had no idea what had happened outside and as soon as Peter appeared in the hall he was howled at, spat upon and threatened with the worst possible fates. People were jumping to their feet. Men, shaking their fists, eyes blazing with hatred and anger, would have torn him apart if it had not been for the presence of his bodyguard. Women with babes in

433

their arms and young children clinging to their skirts did not hold back on the abuse they hurled at Peter's wife, even though she was not there. Others made no effort to subdue the tears that ran down their careworn faces, reflecting the devastation that had shattered their lives. This sight, more than anything else, tore at Peter's heart.

When he climbed on to the platform, rotten vegetables and small bags of flour were thrown, but he stood his ground.

Alan came forward and thundered over the catcalls, 'Let Mr Hustwick say what he has to say! The people outside agreed to let him in because he couldn't address them and leave you out. He wants *everyone* to hear his news.'

The people who were still filtering in from outside added their voices to Alan's and gradually the noise abated somewhat, though there were still those who wanted to broadcast their opinion of the Hustwicks.

Peter held up his arms. 'Hear me out! Please!'

'Why should we?'

'Murderer – you and your bitch wife!'

'Let me speak,' yelled Peter.

But the abuse rose again and came thick and fast. He realised that some hot-heads were bent on causing a riot and was about to send his men to sort them out when Captain Goss jumped on to the platform. For one moment Peter thought the captain was going to attack him and was aware that two of his bodyguard had started to make a protective move, but Captain Goss turned to face the packed hall.

'I say we let Mr Hustwick speak!' he yelled, and repeated this when the crowd responded to his appearance. Silence gradually descended. He turned to Peter. 'Say what you have to say,' he ordered curtly.

Peter moved to the front of the platform. He waited until a dropped pin could have been heard. He sensed an air of curious expectancy among the crowd and decided there and then that his best ploy was not to make excuses but to hit them hard with what he had to say. 'I am going to pay compensation to all those who lost someone on my three vessels!'

This completely unexpected announcement brought general incredulity. The silence deepened.

'I sincerely regret what happened. I cannot bring back your loved ones and friends, but I will ease your circumstances; I have arranged it with my bank. My manager, Alan Frampton, will see you are all paid. He has a list of the crew members of the *William Hustwick* and the *Lena* and will require a responsible member of each family to report to him at Hustwick's office in two days from now. He will issue notes to your entitlement which you will present at my bank.' He turned to Captain Goss. 'Captain, will you present him with a list of your crew also? And see me when this meeting is over?'

'Aye, aye, sir.'

Murmuring broke out around the hall. Now, instead of vilifying him, they were praising Peter. People crowded on to the platform, wanting to shake hands with him or offer him thanks.

When this eventually died down, Captain Goss approached him. 'You wanted a word, sir?'

'Yes, Captain. First, I wish to thank you for your intervention. Things were beginning to look ugly there.'

'A few loud mouths, sir. But I should apologise to you and your wife for what I said to her.'

'Understandable at the time, Captain.'

'I should have curbed my tongue.'

'I'll give her your apologies. Now there's one more thing, Captain. You will be reimbursed for the loss of your ship.'

Captain Goss stared at him in disbelief. 'But...'

'No buts, Captain. I have made my decision. My manager will arrange that with the bank after I have cleared up several other matters. It may take a week or so.'

'Sir, I'll build another and sail for you again!'

Peter gave him a wan smile. 'That won't be possible, Captain. I shan't be here.'

'But your firm can rise again from this tragedy.'

Peter shook his head. 'I don't think so. Too much damage has been done, not only the loss of my ships but in the trade we had built up; that will be gone now and with it all confidence in us, not only among the firms and traders with whom we worked but also the residents of Hull. No, I'll not stay.'

Captain Goss held out his hand. 'Then wherever you go, and whatever you do, may God be with you.'

The days passed pleasantly enough in the company of the Sugdens and Greta, but were not without their anxieties for Lena when still Peter did not appear at Weaver Hall. Her companions did all they could to ease her troubled mind but their concern deepened when, after ten days, Lena voiced the worry that was beginning to haunt her. 'I don't think Peter is going to return. He probably never intended to.'

'You mustn't say that!' Greta sharply told her.

'Nor even think it,' added Marcia.

'But what else can I think?' wailed Lena, her face creased with anxiety. 'He should have been back by now.'

'Lena,' said Greta sternly, 'we do not know where Peter was going nor what he intended to do there. You must have faith in him. He will be back, I'm sure of it.'

'But what if something has happened to him? If he went to Hull, he'd be in danger. The mob there was in an ugly mood.'

'He wouldn't put himself needlessly at risk,' said Marcia. 'Whatever he was planning must be taking longer than expected, that's all.'

'Be patient,' advised Greta.

The next two days were not easy for Lena but she kept her unease hidden. The result was that enormous relief swept over her when Peter, accompanied by Charles, finally strode into the drawing-room of Weaver Hall.

'Peter!' Lena leaped from her chair and flung herself at him. He just had time to open his arms to her. 'Oh, Peter, Peter! Where have you been?'

He hugged her but she did not find the comfort she had once felt in his embrace. 'All in good time. I've a lot to tell you.' He eased her away from him.

Marcia looked askance at her husband.

'Saw him riding up the carriage way,' Charles explained. 'You'd have thought the devil was after him.'

'We've been so worried,' put in Greta, 'and are so glad to have you safely back, Peter.'

'I'm pleased to be here.'

'Where have you been?' Lena repeated.

He gave a wan smile. 'I'd like to get out of these clothes, if I may? I've had a long ride.'

'Of course,' said Charles. 'I'll take you to your room.'

'I'll come with you,' offered Lena.

'No,' replied her husband. 'What I have to say, I want to say to you all.'

Disappointment flooded through her. Seeing it, Marcia said the first thing that came into her head. 'By the time you've changed, Peter, tea will be waiting for you.' Her remark seemed to take the sting out of the situation and put their eagerness to hear what he had to say in perspective.

'Thank you,' he said, and hurried to the door with Charles.

'He didn't want to be with me,' cried Lena, tears of hurt and desperation filling her eyes as she turned to Greta.

'You're reading him wrong,' she said, springing to her cousin's defence. 'He said he has had a long ride; he just didn't want to get into an explanation of what he has been doing until he felt more refreshed.'

'I believe he's decided he's had enough of me.'

'Don't talk like that,' snapped Greta.

'But I destroyed his firm. Peter's lost everything, and I am the cause. He can't possibly want me any longer.'

'If that had been the case, he wouldn't have asked me to bring you here and instructed us to await his return.'

Lena gave a slight shrug of her shoulders as if she wanted to believe Greta but couldn't bring herself to do so. She paced the room, ignoring Greta's instructions to sit down and relax. She gave way a little when Marcia returned but could not contain herself until Charles arrived with Peter a few minutes later. Lena looked expectantly at her husband but he raised a hand to stem any questions. At that point tea appeared. As soon as it was served and the maids had gone, Lena could hold back no longer. Her eyes fixed hard on him, revealing her keen disappointment that he had not come to sit beside her.

'Peter, what have you to tell us?' she demanded.

He met her gaze without revealing anything. 'There is much to tell and it concerns all of you. Since I left here, I have made several visits to Hull.'

'Hull? But wasn't that dangerous?' she asked.

'It was. Families don't take kindly to losing loved ones, especially under such circumstances.'

Lena knew he was directing criticism at her but made no retaliation, as she might once have done.

Peter noted this muted reaction to the words he had deliberately used, and was glad.

'I was careful. I went to people I could trust. After two visits to Hull, I went to London also.'

439

'London? What has London to do with it?' asked Lena, mystified.

'All in good time.' Peter left a little pause for dramatic effect then announced, 'I have sold everything.'

A momentary silence came over the room and then it was filled with gasps of disbelief and words of enquiry.

Lena stared at him wide-eyed. 'Why?'

'I realised that after what had happened, people in Hull would not want to work for me, and with three ships lost I was in a precarious position. I decided it was best to raise what I could for the assets I had.'

A chill was enveloping Lena's heart and mind at his use of the words 'me' and 'I'. He was excluding her. Her future looked bleak.

'I found a buyer for what was left of the business. I also sold the town house and all its contents. Raby, too, I'm afraid.'

'No!' Lena cried, knowing with this announcement that she would never again visit the place she had come to love.

'I found I could no longer call it home after what had happened,' he said quietly.

'Oh, Peter, what have I done?' The words caught in her throat and tears started to flow down Lena's cheeks.

Marcia, deeming that the time had come when Peter and his wife should be alone, cast a glance at Charles and Greta. They took her meaning and all three of them slipped quietly from the room without either Peter or Lena seeming to notice.

'You ruined everything through your stubbornness and stupid obsession with Carnforth's.'

'But, Peter, I...'

'Don't try to make excuses of any kind. Just hear me out.'

Tears still running down her cheeks, Lena gave a little nod.

'When I knew I could assemble all the money from the sales, I got Alan Frampton and Jos and Dan to summon to a meeting the immediate relatives of the men who were lost. I got Alan to arrange for Captain Goss to be there. Alan, Jos and Dan, along with some of their friends, acted as my bodyguard. And it was a good job they did! I tell you, there was uproar when I appeared, but things calmed down when I was able to tell people I was paying them compensation for their loss. Captain Goss will see that the people of Grimsby are duly paid, and I told him he too would be recompensed for the loss of the *Seagull*.'

'So you have nothing left?' asked Lena, her voice scarcely above a whisper but full of remorse, accepting her own responsibility for this state of affairs.

'I kept sufficient for the purpose I had in mind.'

'And what might that be?' Lena lifted her gaze to meet his, feeling a glimmer of hope.

'That can wait a little longer. First I must tell you how I raised much of the money I handed out in compensation ... not that it could ever be sufficient recompense for the lives you destroyed.' He hesitated as if considering the best way to tell her, but in reality he was letting her own thoughts torment her a little longer. He fixed his eyes on her then and she could not turn away. 'Your brother once had designs on buying Hustwick's, remember? Sadly, he did not live to see Carnforth's as its owner!'

Speechless, Lena still could not tear her eyes away from his. Then she understood. 'You sold the business to them?' she whispered.

'I did,' he said in a tone that left no room for doubt in her mind.

She stiffened slightly. 'I thought we had an agreement that we should both act upon major decisions?' As small as they were, there were hints of defiance and hostility in her tone now.

'You dare to bring that up, after the way you flouted that same agreement!' Peter's disgust was unmistakable.

The challenge that had flared in his wife was gone almost immediately, but he had sensed it and surprisingly, he gave a slight smile. 'Ah, I see there is still a little spunk left in you. That is good for what is to come.'

'And what is that? It can be no worse than letting Carnforth's win.'

'I'm going to Australia!'

Lena stared. She couldn't be hearing right. 'Australia?'

He nodded. 'I am going to ask Greta to come too. She has no ties, no relations, and will otherwise be left on her own.'

Lena felt cast aside. Memories of the past flooded in and the enormity of what she had brought on herself was overpowering. She couldn't fight back. Helpless and defeated, she gazed at him with tear-filled eyes. 'What am I to do?' she sobbed.

'Lena, you'll do what you want to do ... you always have. But I'm going!' The utter certainty in Peter's eyes shook her to the core.

As dismayed as she felt, cold and unloved, Lena found a spark of her old strength. She pushed herself quickly to her feet and started for the door. 'Go then, and take Greta with you!' she flung over her shoulder. 'I'll manage, even if I have to crawl in the gutter and beg from the people I've wronged!'

'Stay with me.' His words, quietly spoken, stopped her in her tracks.

She turned round slowly. 'What did you say?'

'Stay with me.'

She held his gaze. In those three words, she heard forgiveness.

'I still love you. Come with me, Lena. There is sufficient capital to start out there again, but only on one condition: I run the firm. You merely help, just as Greta will.'

'I promise,' she said. The tears welled over then. 'I don't deserve you, Peter.'

He held out his arms to her. As she felt them embrace her, Lena resolved that their new life in Australia would never again test their love for each other.

Epilogue

Lena stood at the window of their house on a Sydney hillside, with magnificent views across the sparkling waters of Port Jackson. She smiled inwardly. It beat the view even from Raby Hall. And Whitby? Well, that would always hold a special place in her heart, in spite of the trauma of her final days there.

She looked down into the well-kept garden in front of the house and saw Peter stand still and gaze up at the window. He waved and she raised her right arm in reply, then held up one-year-old William. Laughter lit up Peter's face then and he waved again before blowing them both a kiss goodbye.

A few moments later he was lost from their sight, on his way to the office of Hustwick–Merchant for another day of hard work towards making their firm into one of consequence in Sydney's thriving port.

Lena was happy for him. She hugged William to her, enjoyed his smile, kissed his forehead. Then she whispered in a wistful tone, 'You'll have a thriving business to inherit here, but one day I will tell you of your ancestry ... of the Carnforth blood that flows in your veins only, and of the firm far away in Whitby that is rightfully yours.'

The publishers hope that this book has given you enjoyable reading. Large Print Books are especially designed to be as easy to see and hold as possible. If you wish a complete list of our books please ask at your local library or write directly to:

Magna Large Print Books
Magna House, Long Preston,
Skipton, North Yorkshire.
BD23 4ND

This Large Print Book for the partially sighted, who cannot read normal print, is published under the auspices of

THE ULVERSCROFT FOUNDATION